DUNGEON LIFE

BOOK 4

DUNGEON LIFE

BOOK 4

Khenal

Podium

To Aranya, who was more confident in the story than I was, and who encouraged me to start posting it in the first place.

Cover design by Istvan Straban

ISBN: 978-1-0394-5400-2

Published in 2025 by Podium Publishing
www.podiumentertainment.com

Podium

DUNGEON LIFE

BOOK 4

Chapter 1

In the elven capital city of Horlon, there are many who directly serve the crown. Those who do are often recognized as the pinnacle of their particular class; whether it's the crown chef or the crown sculler, it's a title with honor. Of course, sometimes the honor paid is mere lip service, and sometimes the position would demand honors even without the association with the crown.

Such as with the crown inspector.

Most often, the position is filled by a retired Dungeoneer's Guild member; one who has experience with dungeons. While the guild is still the maximum authority on dungeons, it behooves a government to have an expert on its own payroll. Olander Wideblade is the current crown inspector, and he likes to think he does well enough at his job. From the nervous looks he tends to garner when he goes about his duties, he gathers everyone else would agree.

Usually, he will simply run independent inspections of the dungeons local to the capital, like the Royal Cemetery. It's a strange dungeon, and a quick delve. The Capital Sewers is a much less pleasant delve, despite how jovial its Voice is. A sewer can only do so much to make a delve pleasant.

Occasionally, though, he is tasked to investigate other dungeons around the nation. He's even been requested to go on diplomatic inspections in Holdhome and the Beastkin Principalities, to offer a second opinion on odd situations. But now, he must investigate an odd situation in his homeland.

He wears his full regalia as he strides the streets, his armor bright and unblemished, his glaive on his back, its signature wide blade sticking over his shoulder. The royal insignia stands proudly on his chest and the base of the blade, a final warning to the foolish that Olander is not someone to mess with.

Despite his fearsome equipment, his elven face holds a friendly smile. He's looking forward to this investigation, and having the king himself backing it only makes him more eager to get to it.

None bar his path as he enters the Dungeoneer's Guildhouse, though the receptionist troll looks like he may need a change of pants after this.

"Oh! Uh . . . W-Welcome, Crown Inspector! H-How can I help you?"

Olander decides to skip the small talk and tries to have mercy on the troll by making their interaction brief. "Would you please let the archives know I'm coming? I need to investigate a new dungeon from the north."

"Yes, sir! Uh, do you need a . . . guide?" he asks, realizing too late the elf before him must know the route. Olander has mercy and just smiles a little more as he shakes his head.

"No, but thank you."

"Uh, v-very good, sir. I'll let them know you're coming." The troll trails off a bit, still fighting his embarrassment, but starts scribbling a note to the archives. The elf nods and makes his exit, making a mental note to compliment the troll's professionalism. He's had receptionists literally faint at the sight of him. A few verbal stumbles are nothing.

It doesn't take him long to get to the archives, where a stern matron of an elf greets him with a focused stare. Even with his training, he has to fight flinching under that look. Soon, it softens, and she speaks.

"You're here about Fourdock," she states, not questions, and Olander nods.

"Yes, ma'am. The dungeon, obviously, not the town."

She smirks at him and motions for him to follow her through a door and past a legion of scribes plying their trade. "Obviously. You are also out of the loop. The dungeon has a name: Thedeim."

That earns a raised eyebrow from the crown inspector. "A name? Already? Who gave it to it?"

The chief archivist smirks as she opens the door to her office. "It did. It named itself, approximately three months after discovery."

Olander stops and stares at her as she enters her office before hurriedly following and closing the door behind him. "Naming itself at only three months old? That's impossible."

"Isn't it wonderful?" she replies, her excitement fully at odds with his growing dread and confusion.

"Wonderful? Since when do you think lying on your official forms is wonderful?"

"Because it's not a lie! I did not say it was three months old, nor did the report. The report said approximately three months since *discovery*. Inspector Tarl is one of the few whom I think could succeed you, once your tenure as crown inspector is finished. He just needs some more levels, possibly some more varied delving experience. His choice of wording was no accident."

Olander frowns at that, his mind turning over what she's saying about the dungeon's age. "Since discovery . . . You think it's been there for a while? If this Tarl is so skilled, how did he miss it?"

"As I see it, there are two options. The first will be the official opinion of the guild, because it is the most likely: Thedeim was Cloistered. Inspector Tarl failed to notice it earlier because of several mitigating circumstances, including but not limited to the loss of his mentor to a toybox turning extremely belligerent, and an active murderous dungeon nearby. Dungeon Thedeim likely stayed unnoticed by the inspector and the other two dungeons for a decade or more, probably helped by its Fate affinity."

The crown inspector's frown turns thoughtful at the news. That kind of confluence of coincidences is exactly the sort of thing Fate dungeons get mixed up in. But he knows the archivist isn't finished.

"And the second option, which I assume is your own opinion?"

She laughs at that. "I don't think I'd even go that far, but it is an intriguing possibility. It's outlandish, but nothing in the reports contradicts the conclusion, and much of it arguably supports the idea." She pauses, hoping to goad Olander into asking, but he declines to give her the satisfaction. It also helps he knows she won't be able to resist spilling the idea quickly.

"I think it's Lost."

Olander's eyebrows shoot up in alarm before quickly furrowing in confusion. "Lost? How? It's in the middle of a town!"

"Which is what makes it so intriguing! It would have had to travel to get there, but Dungeon Menagerie of the Principalities has shown that traveling dungeons are theoretically possible!"

He finds it difficult to not let his imagination run away with that idea, especially with how excited she looks, but he manages to try to be the voice of reason. "What makes you think it's Lost instead of Cloistered?"

The archivist deflates a bit. "There's . . . little direct evidence, but its growth rate—and scion growth rate, especially—indicate more than just the unorthodox methods of a Cloistered. It could just be its Fate affinity, but something doesn't add up. Unfortunately, I have too many variables and not enough equations to solve them." Her grin returns as she stares at him, and Olander soon sighs.

"Give me everything you have on Dungeon Thedeim, and I'll do an independent inspection of it once the roads clear in the spring." He knows she's just trying to play him to get what she wants, but he wants that information, too. Besides, doing it this way will get him a quest that mirrors what the king wants. The only thing better than completing a quest is being able to complete two quests with the same goal.

The coins dancing behind his eyes cease their revelry as she hands him the thickest dossier he's ever gotten for a dungeon. "All that for a dungeon that's been active for just a year?" he asks incredulously.

She smirks. "I've included the most recent dossiers on Neverrest, Hullbreak Harbor, Southwood, and Violet as well, as they are either affiliated or will give context to the report on Thedeim himself."

He hums as he glances through the thick set of files.

"Neverrest I know by reputation. Very aggressive, murderous dungeon, very persistent with its hostile expeditions. I know of Hullbreak because of the tragedy; not a lot of toyboxes suddenly go so staunchly belligerent. At least it keeps to itself. I'm also familiar with the Southwood, though I've never been there. It's one of the largest toyboxes known, with a wide variety of herbalism and lumber nodes rather than combat encounters." He pauses and frowns at the rather thin folder for Violet. He doesn't get to question it before the archivist speaks.

"The overview is that Thedeim subsumed Neverrest shortly before he got his own Voice. Despite that lack, he was still able to coordinate with the local adventurers to lead an assault on the cemetery dungeon and subsume it. After designating a Voice, Inspector Tarl came to Thedeim with a communication received from Hullbreak's enclave of merfolk.

"With the fall of the cemetery and the strengthening of Thedeim, the harbor dungeon could no longer sustain itself by raiding the other dungeons, and so had started to starve. They begged him to help, and Tarl passed it on to Thedeim. The dungeon then waged a careful war and infiltration, feeding Hullbreak enough to keep him going.

"However, when he tried to make official contact, the Harbor attempted to destroy the town, or perhaps was bluffing to make it appear like he would. Either way, Thedeim stopped the attack and vassalized Hullbreak Harbor. By all reports, the Harbor is doing much better now. As for the Southwood, it has been having increased invader activity and has asked Thedeim for aid with it. Unfortunately, the snows have kept any new reports from coming in."

"And this Violet?"

She grins wide. "His protégée. She is a deep toybox, so the guild is very interested in her growing up healthy and strong. I'm sure I don't need to remind you of all the resources deep dungeons can offer?"

He chuckles at her cheekiness. "The fancy title hasn't dulled me *that* much, thank you. And thank you for the overview. It looks like it'll take me a while to get all the details, but I should have plenty of time to go over them on the trip."

Her grin softens into a smile. "Then good luck to you, Crown Inspector, and safe travels."

He nods and makes his exit, heading home to prepare. He'll be going incognito for this assignment. He doesn't need to draw the eyes of the kingdom to the northern town of Fourdock. In fact, doing that would make his job much more difficult. Better to be a random adventurer than the crown inspector. Less politics that way.

Chapter 2

Alright, let me see . . .

Most of Silvervein is kinda handling itself as far as cleanup goes. I should probably ask Teemo to thank the Shield followers for how well they dealt with securing the town with minimal collateral damage.

A few of the . . . Are they technically buildings if they're carved into the rock with tunnels connecting them? Having windows and . . . I dunno, exterior walls seem like a pretty big requirement for a building.

Whatever they are, while a few have collapsed from the fighting, it's way fewer than if they were actual freestanding buildings.

Structural stability is not the only metric to measure a fight like this in, and I think they'll be cleaning up for a while. Broken things, stains, scorches, gouges, and more show that it wasn't a peaceful transition of power. From what information Leo and Honey are getting, the townsfolk are still trying to figure out where to go from here. Most of the people who were high in the Maw's clergy died when the Harbinger ate the Maw, so a lot of people are trying to figure out where they stand.

It's looking like sentiment for their clergy is . . . *unfavorable,* to be polite, and I expect any of them who aren't dead will want to vanish off into the tunnels before they get vanished by angry citizens. Silvervein isn't the only group of people needing to figure out what they're going to do, either.

Teemo heads back to Aranya and her party, looking to help sort out the kobolds, who are definitely going to need a lot of help. They've basically gone from being livestock to being actual free people, and that's a lot to try to take in. He pops in at what sounds like the tail end of Aranya explaining what happened since they all saw her last, with her grandpa sitting near her, and the other kobolds seated around her in the large central chamber.

Aelara, Yvonne, and Ragnar are working to get the chains off the rest of the kobolds, with the freed ones joining in the circle around Aranya as she speaks.

"—planned to attack the Maw and liberate us all, and not only has He done so, but He's been recognized as a true deity now! You all felt the energy of His apotheosis!"

"You're gonna make the Boss blush, talking about him like that, Aranya," quips my favorite rat, and Aranya smiles brightly at him.

"Well, it *is* my job to talk him up, Teemo."

The other kobolds put two and two together and shift to start bowing to Teemo, but he sticks a couple fingers in his mouth and gives a piercing whistle.

"No bowing! I know it's a lot different than what you're used to, but please. I'm just a normal rat."

Aranya laughs brightly. "No normal rat is a Herald, Teemo."

Teemo looks as confused at that as I am, and I can feel him checking his status just as I do the same. Just like she said, he's not only my Voice but also my Herald, as well as the Opener of Ways. *When'd you get that last one, anyway?*

"I think from trapping the Harbinger? But I want to know what's with the Herald title."

"You speak for Lord Thedeim, so of course you're his Herald," points out Aranya.

Teemo shakes his head. "I should have known you'd get some of that apotheosis on me, Boss. Gross. At least it seems like it's the same job as being your Voice."

"What's to become of us?" interrupts Aranya's grandfather, getting to his feet with the help of his cane. "Aranya has said so much of you, but . . . it's difficult to believe, after having been at the mercy of the Maw for so long."

Many of the kobolds gasp, with those nearest him quickly scooting away from the aged kobold, not wanting to be caught up in whatever violence he brings down upon himself. Their fear starts to slip to confusion as he continues to not be smote.

Teemo shrugs. "What becomes of you depends on you. The Boss wanted to free you, so now you're free. You can stay here or head out to the caverns, or join Silvervein or Fourdock. The Boss could even make an enclave for you . . . maybe? Can you do that, Boss?"

Uh . . . maybe? I don't have any options for it yet, but a lot of things don't really show up until they become relevant. If enough of them come back with Aranya, I'll probably be able to?

"I think you should all come with us," suggests Aranya. "It was difficult for me to believe at first too, but Lord Thedeim is a Sanctuary in the truest sense. Even if you don't decide to form an enclave with him, Fourdock would be a good town to settle in. Even with the people of Silvervein trying to find their feet after all this, it will take some time before they see us as equals."

Her grandfather peers at her. "Are you truly equal with the people of Fourdock? Our legends say the surface is not any kinder to us than the Deeps."

Aranya nods. "When Lord Thedeim found me, I was half starved and wore rags. He fed me as well as he could, clothed me, armed me, showed me the surface is not just a place of terror. I made friends. I even joined the adventurers' guild."

She pulls out her badge to show, which helps deflate the elder.

"I can see you're healthier than when you left. It's just . . . difficult to trust. It all just seems so unbelievable."

Teemo chuckles before slipping through a shortcut to perch on Aranya's shoulder.

"*Unbelievable* is basically the Boss in a nutshell, pops. I get that it sounds too good to be true, but if we were like the Maw, would we have bothered to get those chains off you? Would we be taking the time to try to convince you instead of just marching you off? The Boss likes to say actions speak louder than words, so what do our actions say about us and our intentions?"

The wizened kobold contemplates for a few long seconds before sighing. "Are we to be your followers, then?"

Teemo shrugs. "That's also up to you. The Boss didn't do this for followers. He didn't even know he'd be in a position to get more until not long ago. He's not here to put new shackles on your people, of any variety. You really are free to follow whatever path you think is best. You could all walk out into the tunnels, and the Boss wouldn't stop you, even if Aranya went with you. He'd be sad to see you all go, but it's your choice."

Aranya's grandfather inhales to reply, but Teemo interrupts him.

"You don't even need to make that choice right now. In fact, you probably shouldn't. The Boss will most likely be keeping a lot of his forces around here for a while so Silvervein can stabilize. If you want to try to get a look for yourselves about what's going on out there, this is probably your best chance to do it. Go see for yourselves how Silvervein has changed, and see if you want in on the kind of change the Boss likes to bring."

Aranya smiles as the kobolds start talking among themselves, some clearly wanting to explore, some worried about what they should do. She pats Teemo as she lets them figure out what they're going to do first. "See? You're already a good Herald, Teemo."

He sticks out his tongue, though he doesn't resist the pats. "Yeah, well, don't get used to it. I fully intend to leave that sort of thing mostly to you, thank you very much."

My High Priestess smirks. "But you're developing your own mystique with it, Teemo. Isn't that what you wanted?"

Teemo grumbles at that, and I chuckle before turning my attention to the last major thing that will need to be dealt with here: the Harbinger. Teemo's confident it can't wiggle out of the mobius trap, and though I believe in him, I don't like the idea of just sealing away ancient evils. They tend to escape after a millennium or two and get right back to wreaking havoc.

Besides, the thing has a veritable ocean of mana after eating the Maw. It'd be a shame to let that all go to waste.

As I prepare to start poking my scions to gather up to discuss how to lay a beating on the thing, I get a new pop-up. It's been a while since I've gotten one, and I don't know if I've gotten this one before.

Quest Received!
Deliver the Harbinger to an Agent of Order.
Reward: Mana, Fast Tracking.

"Fast tracking?" asks Teemo, which knocks me out of my thoughts.

You can see that?

"Yeah. Have you gotten a quest before?"

I don't think I have? I've given a few, but I don't think I've gotten one before.

"What's an agent of Order?"

A Follower of Order, Generally a Head Priest or Greater in Rank.

Teemo and I both squint at the new pop-up. ". . . What's Order?"

The God of Order, Overseer of the System.

"Boss, I think you might need to build a guest room if you're going to keep getting visitors like this."

At least the Shield has a place close enough not to need to couch surf.

Teemo chuckles at that as I consider the quest being offered. On the one hand, I would like to try to stay neutral and out of any dealing with the gods. On the other, that's looking less and less viable by the minute. I'm not against the quest, not by a long shot. I remember the weirdness of the Harbinger's actual name—or actual title, or whatever that was. That weirdness is why I don't want to take any chances with destroying the overpowered shoggoth.

Making it be someone else's problem is pretty appealing, though, especially since this specific someone else is probably a lot more qualified to not only end the Harbinger but also understand what shenanigans were involved with it. From all accounts, the Harbinger joined the Maw at some point; it wasn't a natural spawn like the Redcap. It doesn't take a genius to suspect there's more at work than meets the eye here.

The only reason to refuse would be if I don't trust the quest here, and the pop-up messages.

I let my paranoia chew on the possibilities for a few moments, but there's not a lot of meat on the bone for it. If the messages aren't from a god of order and are trying to trick me, why wait until now? Sowing confusion might have kept the Harbinger free if it'd happened earlier. It could be the Harbinger itself, somehow using its Mental affinity to mess with me, but that doesn't hold water either. It practically left a yellow trail behind when it fled from Teemo tossing around a few concepts. If it was peeking in on my mind, I think it'd probably be dead.

Not to mention that something like that seems to be against the rules. From what I've seen, anyone can talk to me, but if they want me to talk back, they need to do it through Teemo. The Harbinger possibly sending these messages seems like that would be breaking that rule, so paranoia doesn't get to win the day on this one. So now, I just need to make sure I'm making a good deal here.

"It says mana and fast tracking. How much mana, and what's fast tracking?"

Mana Reward Equivalent to the Mana the Harbinger Is Carrying, Plus Triple the Amount Its Defeat Would Usually Bestow.

That sounds like a lot of mana. Rocky brought back a pretty big pile the last time he defeated it, though it might have been inflated from the Harbinger killing Honey and Leo. Worst case, it'll be the amount Rocky came back with, on top of the net worth of the Maw.

"And fast tracking?"

Acceleration of Dungeon Options Gained from Age.

That gets my attention, and gets a raised eyebrow from Teemo. "Yeah? Like what?"

Acceleration of Dungeon Options Gained from Age.

Teemo squints at that, but I'm not too bothered.

He's probably restricted from detailing them by some other rule. Or he just wants it to be a surprise. Or he might not really like me. The Raven said I made him patch the library signs, remember? Besides, I'm fine with that part being a bit muddy. It's a positive on top of a bunch of mana, so I'm not going to look this gift horse in the mouth.

"Alright, Order. The Boss is willing to give you the Harbinger, but I can't just pick up the mobius trap and walk off with it. Just making it was about as much as I could manage."

An Agent of Order Has Been Dispatched. Thank You for Your Cooperation.

"When will they get here?"

An Agent of Order Has Been Dispatched.

Teemo grumbles at that, but I mentally shrug. It shouldn't take that agent long to get here. I imagine Order is chomping at the bit to get the Harbinger, and he said agents were priests. If he tells a priest to haul rear here to get a thingy, I imagine they'll make all haste.

So now, all I need to do is start rotating out my denizens and scions. We don't have mana from subsuming the Maw, but there were still a lot of denizens beaten up, and delvers saved. I doubt it'll be enough to pay my friends back, but it should be enough to make sure they know I appreciate their help with Murphy's Law.

Chapter 3

The next couple days are . . . Is it wrong to call them relaxing? Silvervein is working on rebuilding and figuring out what they're going to do, so it feels a bit wrong to be sitting back. I guess I'm kinda back to my problem of not really being able to do much directly outside my territory.

I'm starting to wonder how accurate that is going to be going forward. I haven't exactly been doing nothing these last few days. I've been tweaking and tuning things back home, feeling like I finally have the time and attention to spare for the home front. Everyone is doing fine, which isn't a surprise. My scions are all amazing and ensure things keep running smoothly, but there are always little tweaks that can be done, and little decisions that are really only on my shoulders.

I'm also running on scarcity spending at the moment, as most of my mana is going toward paying everyone back. I know they didn't do it expecting to get a return on their investment, but they still contributed a lot to this victory, so I'm not going to stiff them on the rewards.

And speaking of getting stiffed on rewards, when is that agent of Order supposed to show up?! Fluffles has already come back to drop off his mana, as have a lot of my other denizens. They might not have credit for the Maw or the Harbinger, but lots of little prizes add up quickly. I think once Nova gets back, we'll be close to being back in the black. And if I'm estimating that correctly, this quest for the Harbinger should give me a staggering amount of mana; enough that I'd probably want to share it anyway.

I'm sure the forest of four seasons that I want to make could probably drink it all in at once, but I like to let my new areas develop a bit slower. It helps them feel a bit more organic, and I can adjust if things aren't working quite how they should.

As for adjusting to new things . . . I'm starting to give some thought to what the Raven said when he asked me what it is to be a god. Because right now, I still don't have too much of an idea. I've been trying to figure things out the last couple days, but I still feel well out of my depth. It makes me wonder if the agent is taking his sweet time on purpose.

The afterlife seems like it's going incredibly well, which is a great relief. I'd hate to have tried my hand at heaven and only produced purgatory. Time is *definitely* weird in there, and I can sometimes see multiples of the same person walking around in different states of progress on a single project. Still, weird as it is, everything seems to be going smoothly.

Most of my fallen dwellers made some simple tools before organizing to make a proper workshop. The tools feel kinda ephemeral, a step toward a goal rather than the goal itself. It's hard to describe, but contrasting it with the workshop makes it pretty clear. It's fairly simple in construction, but simple doesn't mean shoddy. They're basically making a huge log cabin, trying to make sure it has room for whatever projects anyone who comes after might want to make.

It's kinda funny, but everyone who's not specifically working on the building itself are working on chairs. Seeing all the different ways they go about it is really interesting, too. One is carving theirs from a single large log, while another is piecing theirs together from worked branches; someone else is weaving one from wicker, and there's even a ratkin who is following a similar design to the spiderkin working with branches, but he's forging rods of steel, then heating, bending, and welding them together.

I can also see the changes in everyone as they work, becoming more . . . *them.* I don't know how else to describe it. Some of them is refined and purified as they work, and some of them just falls away like sawdust, or forge scale, or scrap fabric, or . . . something. The rules of reality here are definitely different from outside. Either way, the bits that are discarded are drawn to me, and gathering them up feels like holding sunshine in my hands.

I don't know what it is, but I can feel a lot of potential in it; kinda how I can feel how much mana I need to do an upgrade or a spawn. Is it similar to how dungeons work?

After a few moments, I reject the idea and invert it. I think the dungeon system is at least partially inspired by whatever this is. If Order is in charge of the system, why not crib notes from how the gods work?

Which then begs the question: can I make a spawner as a god? I seriously doubt it. My gut says it would be, at best, a bad idea. Maybe I can do magic with it instead? That feels closer; close enough that my gut corrects the semantics and wants to call it "miracles" instead of *magic.*

Bleh, "miracles" feels way too grandiose for what I think I'm currently capable of. Imma call it magic for now, and you can't stop me, gut.

I haven't tried doing anything specific with it yet, and have instead been giving Aranya a tiny sliver each time she does her own magic. It's definitely been making the kobolds more inclined to listen and trust I'm not going to just stuff them into new cages once they lower their guard. Her magic feels more impactful, more real, like there's more weight behind what she's doing. It's kinda weird to have that kind of effect, but it's also pretty cool.

She's been splitting her time between talking with the kobolds and helping in the hospital, with occasional breaks to give a sermon or two to my dwellers. It still makes me uncomfortable to be the topic of those sermons, as well as seeing more and more people who aren't my dwellers attending, but the message is still on point, so I try to just suck it up and deal. Still focusing on love, on helping, and now with positive change being thrown in the mix, too.

I probably shouldn't be surprised, but Aranya has also somehow learned at least the basics of what kind of afterlife I'm offering, and Vernew seems pretty excited by the prospect. Not the kind of excited that has me worried she might try to take the express route there, but the kind that has her doing far more productive things like organizing crafting get-togethers. Thing and Queen often come to either watch or participate, and though I'm still uncomfortable being the theoretical reason behind it all, the camaraderie is great to see.

They're even hoping to get a few of the people of Silvervein to give presentations on some of their food-processing techniques; things like making wine, making cheese, smoking meats, and such. It seems like a lot of people focus either on combat or on crafting, but very few people explore both options. Since my dwellers at Silvervein are mostly fighters, there's a lot of interest in creative skills now. I wouldn't be surprised if, once Aranya gets back home, the more craft focused dwellers start to dabble more in martial things, too.

A lot of kobolds are attending the sermons and gatherings, especially the younger ones. They were clearly chafing under the oppression, and now that they can actually get out and do things, they're soaking up all the freedom they can. The older ones are a bit more reserved, a bit more jaded, but even Aranya's grandfather is looking cautiously hopeful.

It makes *me* cautiously hopeful they'll come to Fourdock. I get the feeling they're not going to want to join a new enclave, but a new town might be just what they need. They've been trying to integrate into Silvervein, and while a lot of people are trying to be welcoming, there's a hanging cloud of awkwardness to the interactions that I've been able to see through my scions.

I think, in the end, there's just too much baggage for the kobolds to want to stay here, and too much baggage for Silvervein to properly integrate them, too. I don't see much lingering animosity from the pale elves and dwarves, but there is definitely a bit from the kobolds. Combine that with the guilt a lot of the Silvervein people feel about having not stopped how the Maw treated them . . . I put pretty low odds on the kobolds sticking around.

As for me sticking around, I'm looking forward to getting everyone back home. Silvervein's power vacuum is being filled with talks of a town council, and with all us outsiders making no moves to try to muscle in, the potential powder keg is defused before it could ever be lit. Honestly, we're just sticking around to ensure nothing can jump in and cause a disaster until they can get on their feet, and waiting for the agent of Order to show up.

It might not be the worst idea to have them give Silvervein a hand, too, after they deal with the Harbinger. Things might have technically been ordered here before, with the Maw in charge, but I'm hoping to go from one order to a new one, rather than letting the place descend into chaos. Change might not *always* be for the better, but I intend to get as close to "always" as possible.

Chapter 4

Kennith Ridgeward

It's difficult to keep himself focused as he travels. He's usually very aware of what he should do next, as his home in the Holds is delightfully stable and secure. Gnomes aren't especially common in the Holds, but as a Head Priest of Order, he enjoys a much-needed role in writing and enforcing contracts. In the Holds, it's easy to keep abreast of what is brewing, and so be prepared to enforce order so whatever happens does so smoothly.

Which only made the dream vision all the more strange. While he enjoys gazing upon his Lord's tesseract form, his Spatial affinity allowing him to appreciate it better than most, it was still a surprise to receive His direct attention.

"Go to the dungeon called Southwood, and from there, continue underground to the town of Silvervein. There, you will find the agent of a fledgling god, as well as a trapped being that is of interest to me. The fledgling has agreed to give me the being, though he is unable to deliver it himself. Finalize the deal."

As with the rare other occasions he's been able to meet his Lord directly, the meeting was short and to the point. When he awoke, a quick visit to the local Dungeoneer's got him the location of the Southwood. While he is positive Order has priests closer, it seems he's the closest with Spatial affinity, as the trapped being implies a need for such.

The journey will not be a simple one, but at least he knows ways to make it less complex. With winter quickly waning, normal travel is picking back up, but there are precious few routes to the Southwood, it would seem. He could trek through the Principalities and then through the Wanderlands, but going by road through the two nations can be tricky at best.

The Principalities are often the least stable at the end of winter and beginning of spring, with the factions probing and maneuvering, acting on plans forged in the cold of winter. The orcs of the Wanderlands are usually a friendly lot, but there are always a few tribes who failed to prepare properly for the cold months and look to make their mistake someone else's problem.

The more stable route is close to twice the distance, however. He could follow the Whitefall River past Meeting and up the Gofnar River, across Lake Gofnar, and up the Also-Gofnar River, but such a trip will be slow and expensive. His Lord may be patient, but Kennith would prefer not to test said patience.

Well, what sort of Spatial-affinity wielder would he be if he didn't have methods of getting where he needs to? For a journey such as this, he has just the answer. He really should try to reconnect with Syertly one of these days. The pair of boots they made together really are a wonder, even if the elf doesn't much care for Order. Nobody is perfect, and he has a unique sense of humor that Kennith sometimes misses.

Perhaps he can swing by the elven capital after this mission is over. If it goes smoothly, he should be able to spend almost a week there before he'll need to come back and bless any contracts. The dwarves prefer to prepare contracts over winter and sign in the spring, which should line up nicely.

The Leaguestride Boots do as the name implies: greatly lengthen the stride of the wearer. For many, it's an impractical enchantment, as the change in distance can easily throw people off. But Kennith is a master of space and can easily adjust. What's more, his affinity makes it possible for him to stand firmly on the ground while still well up in the air, making any ground obstacles meaningless to him.

The speed, combined with the elevation, lets him easily take the straight path through the Principalities and Wanderlands without worry of interference. By the time anyone can notice him, he's already well past them and vanishing in the distance.

Unfortunately, the view from above gets rather boring after a while, even for someone who most would say thrives in boring conditions. Which is why his mind wanders as he travels, thinking about the details of what he will need to do.

From the Dungeoneer's packet on the Southwood, it's a toybox that is rather friendly, so long as one gives the Voice proper respect. It also has a rather large territory, which is surely why Lord Order sent him there first. It will be a simple landmark to find, and he may even be able to get additional information from the Voice. If Lord Order has an interest nearby, the Southwood is likely to be at least vaguely aware of it.

Especially if a fledgling god is involved. Such a thing is usually far more important than the almost casual way his Lord spoke, possibly implying how much more important the trapped being is than the new god. He finds it difficult to imagine something like that, but it's the only thing that makes sense.

His thoughts wander to the mystery as he travels, often being the last thing he remembers before falling asleep, and the first thing in his head when he wakes in the mornings. As he nears the Southwood, he senses something that shoves aside his musings on the situation; something that might give him an actual clue as to what's happening: he senses a working of Spatial affinity.

He's glad he noticed it, too, as his thoughts had absorbed him enough he was actually off-course to find the Southwood! He had drifted southward, and would have missed the dungeon entirely if he hadn't found the interesting construct of space.

The working itself is simple, just a contraction of space to lessen the distance between points. The size of it, however, is impressive. He can also tell there was a mind toward concealment in its design. It would easily be unnoticed by most, but to someone with Spatial affinity, it's rather obvious.

He checks his map and sees it should take him right to the Southwood, so he decides to swap to a pair of more ordinary boots and sample the path to the dungeon. He has to make his own entrance, but he is courteous enough to close it up behind him. Whoever made it didn't want people to just barge in, so it would be rude to let others follow in Kennith's footsteps.

The path is pleasant and well made, and while the compression could be improved, the vast distance it spans makes it difficult to critique too harshly. In only half an hour, he reaches the end and is surprised to find a bevy of activity awaiting him in normal space. A train of wagons sits just inside the border of the Southwood, with dozens of people milling around. Ratkin and spiderkin abound, though there is also a healthy representation of elves, dwarves, and a smattering of other races.

Perhaps more surprising are the throngs of dungeon denizens milling around, too. The Dungeoneer's Guild didn't mention even half of the varieties present in their Southwood information packet. If it weren't for how casual everyone is being, Kennith would be worried. He's still wary, but the order of the gathering helps put him at ease. It could certainly be more organized, but an effort is being made, at least.

A fellow gnome notices Kennith and waves him forward with a smile, so he moves to see what information he can glean. As he nears, the other gnome speaks up.

"Hey! I hope you're not from the guild! You missed all the fun, snail!"

"Fun?" Kennith asks.

"Yeah! We beat the Maw like a week ago! You can still delve the Southwood if you want, but there's not a whole lot else to do now."

The Maw? "I'm sorry, but I'm not here for any Maw. Do you happen to know the way to Silvervein?"

The other gnome gives Kennith a confused look. "You want to go to Silvervein, but don't know about the Maw?"

There is clearly more going on than Lord Order said. "I've been sent by Lord Order to meet with a fledgling god and receive a delivery. I don't know much about the situation other than I should get to Silvervein."

The gnome whistles at that. "Order himself? Thedeim attracts a lot of attention. Well, the short version is there was a nasty dungeon deep in a hole past the Southwood, and Thedeim decided to help out and get rid of it. There's a town down there too, Silvervein, and the Shieldies are helping the people there get used to doing things without an overbearing crazy dungeon breathing down their necks."

"Can you guide me to Silvervein?"

The gnome shakes his head. "Sorry, I'm headed back to Fourdock for some relaxation after all this. You can probably find Rocky around somewhere, though. He can probably help. He's one of Thedeim's scions; can't miss him: zombie in bright shorts with big, padded gloves."

Kennith furrows his brows at that. "A Zombie Scion? And nobody is concerned about that?"

He shrugs. "Nah, Rocky's a great guy. You'll see." He inhales before speaking loudly enough for everyone nearby to hear. "Hey, anyone know where Rocky is? This guy needs help getting to Silvervein!"

"He's talking with the Stag! That way!" comes a voice from beyond where Kennith can see, but the pointing is copied by various people close by, giving him a heading. He nods and raises his own voice.

"Thank you!"

He heads deeper into the dungeon, and soon hears the gentle chiming of bells in the breeze, and a voice at a casual volume. He speaks up before he can understand what's being said, not wanting to appear to be spying.

"Excuse me! Is . . . Is Rocky there? I was told he could help me get to Silvervein!"

The bells take on a harsher tone for a few moments before they calm. Kennith can hear footsteps through the trees, nearing him, and soon, he sees the Stag, Voice of the Southwood, as well as what must be Rocky.

Despite being told about the zombie in bright shorts, his mental image could hardly have been further off. This zombie is no slow, shambling corpse. Instead of the usual emaciated form of a zombie, this one is fit and toned even with the obvious signs of being undead. It doesn't shamble but rather walks with a lightness that speaks of mobility, and rather than empty milky eyes, the ones peering at Kennith are full of intelligence, and oddly empty of malice.

The same can't be said of the eyes of the Stag, who seems unhappy at being interrupted. "What business do you have of Sir Rocky?"

It takes Kennith a moment to get over the contrast of the two scions before he answers. "I have been sent by Lord Order to retrieve something from Silvervein."

The Stag squints at him, but Rocky's eyes widen before he pats the Stag's withers with a gloved hand and grunts.

"He is expected?"

Rocky grunts again, and the Stag shakes his head.

"Allow me, then. I understand that the main tunnel is large enough for even my horns to pass without issue. You can take that mana back, and I can expedition to see what has transpired for my Lord to see personally."

Rocky grunts once more, and the Stag nods with a smile. "I am sure. You and Lord Thedeim have helped my Lord immensely. Guiding him is the least I can do."

Rocky grunts one last time and pats his withers once more before casually walking past Kennith, who is still trying to comprehend what he just witnessed. The Southwood should be hostile toward any undead, let alone a scion from another dungeon! Yet it seems genuinely fond of the scion, and appreciative of its master.

Kennith shakes his head and offers the Stag a bow. "I apologize for interrupting your discussion, but Lord Order personally asked me to do this, so I am anxious to see it done."

The Stag eyes him for a few moments before exhaling and nodding. "I understand. When my Lord gives me a task, I pursue it with all haste. While I would prefer to talk more with Rocky, I will doubtlessly see him again. I may even get to visit him at Lord Thedeim's territory soon." The Stag looks wistful for a few moments before refocusing on the gnome before him.

"For now, let us go. How quickly can you travel, gnome?"

"Give me a moment to put on different boots, and I am certain I can keep up."

The Stag smiles at that. "Excellent. If we make haste, we should arrive at the tunnel entrance in less than an hour. If you fall behind, I will return for you. Let me know when you are ready."

Despite himself, Kennith smiles as well. He really does need to get in touch with Syertly after all this, even if only to let him know how the boots compare to a powerful dungeon scion.

Chapter 5

Finally, the agent's here! Waiting for him was like waiting for a repair guy to show up. At least he can't show up while I'm gone, seeing as I can't really move. Teemo and Aranya both head off to meet him as soon as he leaves with the Stag, and I try to listen in through the Southwood's bond with him.

It doesn't work very well. I mostly get the feeling the Stag doesn't care for him much, but that doesn't really tell me a lot. The Stag is kinda grumpy and doesn't seem to like many people much.

Anyway, Teemo starts forging a shortcut at the outskirts of Silvervein now that we don't need to worry about hostiles overtaking it. It'll also help the locals dive the Southwood more easily and make things a bit smoother all around.

"You seem a lot less nervous about this guy than usual, Boss. He's an agent of Order, according to that quest. Feeling less nervous about dealing with deities?" asks Teemo as he and Aranya walk the shortcut. He's rushing it, and I can feel his dissatisfaction with his work, but he's as eager to get the Harbinger dealt with as I am. He can take the time to smooth it out after the agent is done.

I think technically being one has kinda worn away a lot of the mystique. Lowercase g's seem to be closer in power to what I was expecting of an angel, and not even an archangel at that.

Teemo pauses and scratches at his ear for a second before replying. "An agent of a god and a . . . strong agent of a god? Those two feel a bit fuzzy around the edges, Boss."

Probably for the best. Comprehending those fully would probably be way worse for your health than even the craziest scientific theories.

"If you say so. How do you think the meeting will go, then?"

I dunno. I'd expect him to be pretty eager to get the Harbinger, but I don't know what that'll actually entail. If he has to actually bring it somewhere, he'll probably just grab the thing and leave.

"Probably, yeah. What do you think, Aranya?" he asks, looking over his shoulder at my High Priestess as she follows in through the shortcut.

"I don't know. As part of my duties, I was looking into the other gods well before I ever left Fourdock, but there's not a lot of information to be had on Order," she admits. "He may be even less interested in empty ceremony than Lord Thedeim. He has a main temple in the elven capital, but it's supposed to be rather small and could be easily mistaken for an accounting firm or something similar. His adherents worship him through ensuring order in their daily lives and in keeping things stable. A lot of bureaucrats follow him, even though few bother proclaiming it. There's even a rumor the king himself is a follower."

Ugh, I hope we don't get a humorless paper pusher. Sure, that kind of efficiency is good when paperwork is absolutely required, but I don't want to have to submit a greeting in triplicate before he'll even acknowledge us.

Teemo snorts at that image. "Lots of boring soulless ink slingers, then?"

Aranya shakes her head for a moment, before reconsidering. "There's probably some, but the ones who are open about their devotion are supposed to be friendly enough, if often awkward around more ordinary people."

Sounds like introverts instead of misanthropes, so that'll be good. I'll take awkward friendliness over rigid regulation every day of the week.

The conversation drifts as they keep walking, since we don't really have a lot of information to go on. Teemo's looking forward to meeting someone else with Spatial affinity, while Aranya is looking forward to meeting a representative of a god. I guess they both want to talk some shop in their own ways.

While I'm pretty sure the guy isn't a High Priest like Aranya, he's still pretty highly positioned in a bigger and more organized institution. Even if I don't think I'll be running things anything like Order, getting a peek behind the curtain should help keep things from going sideways.

Even with the distance and having to go uphill, Teemo and Aranya are blazing through the tunnels toward the surface. It was a good two- or three-day march down, but they meet the agent at around sunset, as useful as that measurement is underground.

Putting that Opener of Ways title to work, eh, Teemo?

Teemo nods as the two groups approach, with the Stag giving a bow to my Voice and my High Priestess, and the gnome beside him offering one of his own before the Voice of the Southwood speaks.

"Voice Teemo, Lady Aranya. My Lord has asked me to witness what has transpired with my own eyes. I hope that's agreeable?"

Teemo *pshaws* and waves a hand. "Of course, Stag. The Boss is hoping you and Silvervein will get along well so you can get some extra mana and they can have some stable food and dungeon access while they get things figured out."

The Stag straightens and nods. "That would be most agreeable to my Lord. Your shortcuts to both Fourdock and Silvervein will be most helpful. He also hopes it's not presumptuous to suggest one to the Orcish Wanderlands at some point as well?"

Teemo taps his chin as he thinks about that. "It'll probably be a while for that. The Boss has plans for his part of the Harbinger's mana, and those'll keep me busy for quite a bit."

The Stag nods once more. "My Lord understands, Voice Teemo. He wished to raise the possibility, rather than demand anything."

"The Boss has added it to the list. Now, about your companion." Teemo turns his attention to the gnome, who despite wearing what looks like a traveling robe, its cut makes me think of a business suit.

"My name is Kennith Ridgeward, and I will be acting as Lord Order's representative. I have to admit, I didn't expect the fledgling god to be a dungeon." He peers at Teemo for a few moments before realizing how undiplomatic that statement is. "Er, not to insinuate—"

He's cut off by a giggle from Aranya. "The truth won't offend Lord Thedeim. He fully accepts he's new to this. I think he's doing very well, though I may be a bit biased," she says with a wink, and the gnome relaxes slightly.

"Ah, thank you. I'm more used to dealing with dwarves and contracts than with greeting new gods. Not that I think there are many out there used to something like that." Aranya nods as Teemo steps into the conversation.

"So you're going to take the Harbinger and complete the quest the Boss got?"

Kennith nods. "I am, though I think that may have to wait until tomorrow. Even with this Spatial working, I fear I'd be exhausted before ever reaching Silvervein. You're the one responsible for these shortcuts?" he asks my Voice, who nods.

"Yeah, I am, and yeah, I think we should relax and head back after some rest. I'm Teemo, no fancy titles needed. The Boss likes me to try to keep people grounded, especially himself. So, how's this going to work, anyway?"

The gnome pats a pocket of his robe. "I have the supplies for writing up a contract with me. Once I can confirm the entity and its imprisonment, I can formalize the exchange. The specifics will depend on the details, which I won't be able to get until I can see the situation with my own eyes. My Lord was rather sparse on details, and only said you have a being He is interested in, that you had agreed to transfer it, and that I would finalize the deal. You being a dungeon may complicate matters, though."

"Oh? How?" asks Teemo as he hops onto Aranya's shoulder and the group looks for a good spot to set up camp for the night.

"Dungeons are more tightly restrained by the system than people are, so there may be more things to consider than usual. I could give the details if you want, but there are shelves of tomes of the minutiae that could potentially become relevant, depending on the specifics."

Teemo and I both blanch at that, much to the amusement of Aranya. "I believe Lord Thedeim is content to wait and see what the actual complications will be, rather than listen to an exhaustive list of potentials."

The gnome smirks and nods. "I had suspected, but didn't want to presume. And speaking of presumptions: will the shortcuts stay stable indefinitely?"

Teemo shrugs. "Probably not *indefinitely*, but they don't seem to require much more maintenance than a normal road. I have a shortcut all the way from the Southwood to Fourdock, and just slapped together this one to Silvervein. Then there's the mobius trap I have the Harbinger in. They're all pretty stable."

"Even for a 'slapped together' work, this shortcut is impressive. Most Spatial magic is used to make internalized spaces larger, but you seem to focus on making distances shorter?"

Teemo nods. "Yeah. I started as a Scout for the Boss, making shortcuts around his territory for his denizens to get to wherever they needed to get to."

Kennith looks thoughtful before he replies. "I've heard of similar classes among rangers, though they call theirs trails. I've never had a chance to study them, however. I'm usually busy with contracts. Seeing compression on such a scale is very interesting, especially when combined with the warping inside to make it feel like level ground."

Teemo smirks. "If you like the warping, wait until you see the mobius trap!"

"What is that?" he asks, looking intrigued.

"It's . . . well, it's complicated. It'll probably be simpler to show you. If you're experienced with Spatial stuff, you should be able to handle it without any issues."

That earns a raised eyebrow from the gnome. "It's a complicated Spatial working, then?"

Teemo smirks as they find a small water stream coming from a wall and so can begin making camp. "It is, and it isn't. I haven't seen anyone else talk about something like it, other than the Boss. I haven't met many others with Spatial affinity, though, so I couldn't tell you how unusual it is."

"I'm looking forward to seeing it, then. Once we get camp set up, I should show you my Leaguestride Boots. It's not often Spatial casters can compare notes."

I smile at Teemo's eagerness to get a look at those, and settle back to doodle some basic designs and budget for my upcoming forest of four seasons. I do my best to keep my thoughts out of Teemo's ear so he can focus more on geeking out about Spatial magic. He doesn't get a chance to relax too often, so I want to let him enjoy it as much as possible when the opportunity arises.

Chapter 6

They all have a nice night camping, and I have a nice night roughing out where to put my Ant Enclave, and how to get started on the forest of four seasons. The Ant Enclave is easier to actually prepare for, and I even get some tunnelbores working to dig out an area near the exit from the labyrinth to the volcanic region. I'm pretty confident they'll have both the desire to explore out there and the ability to handle the temperatures involved, too.

My notes for the forest are a lot messier, and I don't bother much with cleaning them up; at least, not yet. I can already tell I'm going to need to upgrade my spawners to populate it properly, and depending on what I get with the expansion(s) required for the land, I might need to take up the Southwood's offer of a denizen or two. I can already think of uses for his foxes and bears.

I'm looking forward to getting into the weeds of proper planning for the forest, but I want to get that quest finished first, so I'll have an idea of what I have to work with. Not only will I get a bunch of mana, but I'm also curious what the fast tracking will give me. I know the Southwood has more options than I do, so I can't wait to get a chance to browse them for myself!

Even just the rough outline takes the night, so I focus back on the group as they resume their journey. Teemo opts to hitch a ride on the Stag for this leg of the trip, letting Mr. Kennith and Aranya chat about their respective faiths as they walk.

"So, even before apotheosis, he's been a catalyst for change?"

Aranya nods. "He very rarely does what people expect, though it's hardly out of spite. He likes to approach problems from different angles, and is very good at predicting possible complications. I think the scythemaw migration was a good example of that."

"Scythemaws?"

Aranya nods. "That's what Lord Thedeim calls them. Tunnel horror is the more common name."

Kennith jerks to attention at that name. "Ah, horrors! I've only ever heard tales of them from the dwarves. You say there was a migration?"

Aranya nods. "Right through Lord Thedeim's cavern layer, His spiderkin enclave, and His protégée."

The gnome winces at that. "I imagine that was an unpleasant mess and a brutal fight."

My High Priestess shakes her head and snickers. "That's what most were expecting, but Lord Thedeim had a different plan. From what I've heard from Yvonne and other rangers, His hesitancy to simply fight them was wise, and not simply because they are difficult to combat. They are an apex predator, so culling them from the area could have had countless unknowable ramifications on the underswamps and aquifer lake habitats."

Kennith looks conflicted at that. "I understand that, but what about the impact on his dwellers, his protégée, and his own territory?"

"It wasn't as severe as you might expect. The spiderkin were able to move off the floor of the caverns with little difficulty, and could largely continue their lives above the scythemaws. They count as delvers, not invaders, so Lord Thedeim was able to send ordinary encounters at them to continue getting mana for that section, and with a door erected outside her cavern, even Lord Thedeim's protégée was kept safe. She even got quite a boon of mana later, after they had left and she expanded outside. The scythemaws laid their eggs, and she got a significant sum of mana from it."

Kennith looks impressed. "So rather than a chaotic and costly fight against the horrors, he was able to take advantage in his own way, with minimal disturbance to the balance of nature."

Aranya beams, and if I could, I'd be sporting a bashful blush. It really did go smoothly; way more smoothly than it had any right to, especially considering how worried about it I was at the time.

"Is he interested in joining any pantheons?" Kennith asks, and my High Priestess politely shakes her head.

"He isn't against cooperating, but He prefers to minimize His dealings with other deities. I believe He'd like to secure His position before considering expanding it. His dungeon territory works similarly, with Him taking His time to carefully craft and utilize each section before moving on to another."

Kennith nods at that. "Understandable. The pantheons have been stable for quite some time now, but legends say that hasn't always been the case. A new deity is probably wise to come more into their own before trying to deal with divine politics."

Teemo retches all the way over from the Stag's head at that, earning a laugh from Aranya and a confused look from Kennith. "And I thought the Boss's idea of waste processing was disgusting! I can't imagine anything he'd want to stay further from than *divine politics*!"

My High Priestess nods. “I think He likes to stay away from those topics because He knows how chaotic changing them can be. Now that change is officially part of His portfolio, the potential for chaos only increases.”

It’s Kennith’s turn to look uncomfortable at that, and he quickly nods. “Yes, I see. There is wisdom in staying out of things that one knows could lead to disaster.”

Aranya titters and nods. “Though I think he’s doing a remarkable job of keeping Silvervein stable, even if the Shield is helping.”

“What happened in Silvervein? An adventurer mentioned a Maw and a large battle, but he was sparse on details.”

Aranya sighs and takes a few moments to gather her thoughts.

“I escaped the Maw and eventually found my way to Lord Thedeim many months ago now. Near the end of fall, the Southwood asked Lord Thedeim for help with strange invaders, and He investigated, eventually discovering the hostile dungeon was the one I hailed from. He allied with the Southwood and fought the Harbinger back, then fought the Maw itself. He knew about Silvervein, a town of emancipated dwellers from the Maw, and took steps to minimize the damage to the town and its people with the help of a group from the Crystal Shield. In the fight, the Harbinger consumed the Maw, and Teemo was able to trap it afterward.”

Kennith frowns in thought. “What *is* the Harbinger? And the strange invaders? I’ve not dealt with dungeons much, though I’m familiar with the required contracts involving them.”

Teemo speaks up from the Stag’s head. “The Harbinger and the invaders are definitely what Order wants to get a better look at. The invaders’ type is . . . weirdly wrong. The Boss calls it a corruption or an error, but there are connotations I don’t know how to explain. The Harbinger has a title with similar weirdness.”

Kennith looks concerned. “Would I be able to negotiate for information on those as well? If there is more to concern Lord Order than just the Harbinger, I would like to bring it to Him.”

Teemo shrugs. “I don’t see why not. Honey would be happy to share her notes, and I’m sure there’s a lot of bits and pieces of the invaders around.”

Yeah, we got a couple diced-up lessers and a few whole leasts from the group of scouts. They apparently have a really high-level field dresser. I don’t know how a whole corpse counts as being dressed, but they haven’t dissolved into background mana yet.

“Yeah, we can share, and the Boss is happy to. He thinks there’s more to all this than we know, and if anyone can figure out why it’s causing system weirdness, it’ll be Order.”

Kennith looks relieved, nodding as they round the last bend in the shortcut and are soon deposited back into normal space, not far from the milkworm fields. “That would be appreciated, thank you. Are we now in Silvervein? Can we go to where this Harbinger is being held?”

Teemo nods before focusing on the Stag. "You wanna come with us to see it, Stag? Or do you want to wander around a bit first?"

His ears flick as he listens for Southwood's answer. "My Lord would have a look at the Harbinger, if possible."

"I would also like to go," speaks up Aranya. "As Lord Thedeim's High Priestess, I should offer my help in negotiations, if He would have it?"

Teemo snorts. "Yeah, he'd like your help. Sounds like we're all going, then. We'll take the normal way; it's not far. The main tunnel is that way, and we can take it all the way to the Harbinger."

They make their way to the main tunnel, drawing some looks, and sometimes being ignored as the people focus on restoring their disrupted lives. A lot more looks are hopeful instead of fearful, so I can't help but be happy with how everything has gone so far.

As they near the Maw's temple, a wolfkin paladin approaches, and Teemo waves at him.

"Hey, Unsil! The Boss is thrilled with how your guys have been keeping the peace around here."

The grizzled wolfkin raises his shield in salute before smiling. "I think he can take at least a little of the credit with that spell of his. This whole situation could have been a catastrophe, but it went better than it had any right to." His smile slips a little when he notices the gnome, and he looks a bit uneasy as he continues. "So . . . you're all going to the Harbinger, then?"

Teemo nods. "Yeah. Is something wrong?"

Unsil shakes his head. "Not *wrong*, but . . . may I come with you?"

Teemo gives him a confused look. "I mean, the Boss isn't opposed, but it's a dangerous thing to get close to for idle curiosity."

"I know . . . but it's not idle curiosity. The Shield itself appeared to me in a dream and wants me to get whatever information I can."

Kennith gives him a suspicious look. "Is the Crystal Shield wishing to dispute Lord Order's claim on the Harbinger?"

Unsil quickly shakes his head again. "No! It doesn't want to interfere; It just wants a better idea of what we're dealing with. It can't protect people if It doesn't know what to protect them from."

Kennith still looks suspicious. "So long as you don't intend to interfere, I don't object."

"Cool. You might want his help too, Kennith. If you want to get a look at the Harbinger, it's going to try to hit you with a mental attack. Having a paladin keep your mind safe is probably a good idea."

The gnome looks even less happy about that, but relents as everyone gets moving again. "I haven't had much opportunity to test my mental defenses. I can comprehend a lot, but there's no point in taking risks just for my pride."

There's not much other conversation as Teemo guides them to the Maw's former Sanctuary, or rather, to the corridor just outside of it. Once they get close, Kennith starts looking all around like a tourist. Teemo's feeling of satisfaction makes it pretty clear why he's rubbernecking even before the gnome opens his mouth.

"Fascinating! You've folded a three-dimensional space down to two before twisting it onto itself to form a subspace!"

Teemo smiles wide. "I sure did!"

"How?!"

"It wasn't easy, I can tell you that. The Boss has some math for it, but it's the kind of stuff that would test your mental defenses, heh. I do more by feel than by math."

"Remarkable . . ." mumbles Kennith absently as he peers at the mobius trap. With normal vision, it looks like he's just staring at the hall, but with Teemo's Spatial sense, I can feel the twisting that is the Harbinger's prison.

"Ready to take a look at the thing inside?" Teemo asks, pulling Kennith from his inspection.

"Oh! Uh, yes, if the kind paladin is ready to keep my mind from being shattered?"

Unsil nods. "Crystal Shield, please offer your bulwark to this gnome to keep him safe in this task."

"You should probably be quick as you can while taking a peek, Kennith," warns Teemo. "It has the mana of a whole huge dungeon behind it, so you don't want to give it a chance to do anything too strong."

Kennith nods, standing straight. I can feel him carefully bringing his affinity to bear on the Harbinger's prison. He pierces a pinprick hole into it to see before slamming it shut. He and Unsil both stagger back, with the gnome sporting a fresh nosebleed and the paladin looking like he got his bell rung good.

"Queen's Balm," chants Aranya, and I give her a sliver of power to enhance the effect as orange mist settles on their heads. The two afflicted sigh in relief as they straighten, and Kennith quickly puts on his business face.

"Thank you for your help, Shield and Thedeim. That . . . That *thing* is absolutely what Lord Order is after, and I can only guess the danger it truly poses. Please give me a few minutes to recover, then I shall write a contract to seal its fate."

Chapter 7

Everyone sits around for a few minutes while Kennith and Unsil catch their breath before Teemo glances over at the Stag. "Did you still want to get a direct look at it?"

The Stag pales as his ear flicks, and he sighs in relief after a few moments. "My Lord is satisfied with simply knowing the Harbinger will no longer be a threat, and that all possible is being done to ensure that threat ends here. If you don't mind, I think I will take a look around Silvervein. My Lord would like to get a better understanding of what they might wish from delving him."

Teemo smirks. "Fair. It looks like the Harbinger is being more than a little rowdy right now. Can't imagine why it's so upset, heh." The Stag chuckles but doesn't give any other reply to that, giving Aranya a chance to speak up with her own curiosity as he goes, though at Kennith instead of the other Voice.

"So, what will the contract negotiations entail? I understand Lord Thedeim already has a quest. I wanted to be involved if there are negotiations to be had, but will they even be necessary?"

Kennith fiddles with the sleeve of his robe as he thinks. "Ordinarily, I don't think it would be necessary. The few times I've been involved in something like this, I'm basically just notarizing the completion of a quest. With this monstrosity, however, I'd like to be as official as possible. Can you bring a table and some chairs, someone? This could be awkward trying to work on the floor."

Teemo looks around the room for a few moments before agreeing. "Yeah, it looks like this place was decently furnished, but the fighting wasn't kind to the furniture."

Unsil speaks up. "I'll see what I can find. There should be a lot of my fellow followers nearby I can ask to help."

"A medium table and three chairs would be perfect, but even just a single table or a podium would be better than trying to sign on the floor," requests Kennith.

With that, Unsil heads out to find some help and some office equipment.

"So, what does official Order business entail, then? I think the last time someone tried to get fancy, it involved incense, chants, and maybe some holy water, back when that one guy tried to consecrate the cemetery."

Kennith smiles and shakes his head. "Lord Order prefers parchment, ink, and signatures. I'll need . . . let me see . . ." He starts looking through the pockets of his robe. From what Teemo can see, it's like he has a filing cabinet inside each one.

"Notarization of a completed quest, official transfer of . . . I think prisoner is most appropriate, witnessed authority to transport said prisoner . . ." He looks up to Teemo and Aranya. "You said the local authority is in flux at the moment?" At their nod, he resumes looking through his pockets and thinking out loud. "Can't appeal to the local government for any permits to strengthen anything . . ."

"Is all that really needed?" asks Teemo.

Kennith nods absently as he continues looking through his pockets, even pulling out a tome with a title of *Cross-Pantheon Agreements* as he answers. "In more ordinary circumstances, I would probably simply write you a signed receipt for the Harbinger, but as I said, I want to do this by the book. The more order that can be imposed on this, the more likely Lord Order will be to keep anything unfortunate from happening." He pauses to squint at the page, clearly reading some regulation or another before shaking his head and putting the book away.

"I think those three are the most I can do. Thankfully, I should be able to transfer the Harbinger directly to Lord Order thanks to my affinity, so there should be minimal chance for it to escape in transit."

"How's that work?" asks Teemo, curious about how someone else works with Spatial affinity. I'm curious, too. I can guess, but with him there, I don't need to.

Kennith looks like he's about to go into a long-winded explanation, but he pauses and smiles. "Right, you're Spatial affinity, and rather strong with it. The deities that have fully ascended exist in higher dimensions than we do. Even with my affinity, the specifics are complex, but the end effect is similar to one of your shortcuts, allowing me to connect and even move the space the Harbinger occupies into a space chosen by Lord Order."

Aranya looks a bit lost, but Teemo explains it.

"It's like how a piece of paper is basically just length and width, but no real height. If all you could sense was that paper, you'd never know when someone picks it up, because you can't sense up in that case. I basically put the Harbinger on its own piece of paper, and it sounds like Kennith will . . . basically be a courier to deliver it. None of us can really feel the paper moving around, so we don't notice anything besides the Harbinger being gone."

Kennith nods. "There are details that don't really translate well to our reality, but that's the gist of it. To extend the metaphor, I'll be sealing the Harbinger in a scrollcase to ensure it can't somehow break free, and placing a wax seal to not only further keep it contained but also to allow Lord Order to accept the delivery. The extra contracts help strengthen those."

Aranya ponders that, and I can feel Teemo chewing on the metaphor to try to glean some more insights. Kennith seems to be checking for parchments and inks in his pockets now, too. I bet he has fancier ones than normal. A contract written in pink ink on normal binder paper is probably still binding, but I bet something like proper vellum and some kind of magical ink will lend it even more weight.

It takes a few more minutes before Unsil returns, looking a bit embarrassed by what he's managed to find. "All I could dig up is what I think was a food or drink cart. The wheels can lock and it's nice and stable, but that's all I could find."

Kennith waves for him to bring it over. "That will do just fine. There's a rise in the floor here I can use to access the top easily enough. There are three . . . Oh, receipt!" He smiles to himself before continuing. "Four contracts I wish to invoke for this: A notarized witness of the other three contracts, a recognition of my authority to transport the prisoner, an official transfer of prisoner, and receipt of prisoner. Thankfully, as the Harbinger is not in the territory of any dungeon, the contracts can be deity to deity, and thus be transactional. If it was in a dungeon's territory, I believe a pact would be required with the dungeon."

Teemo smiles as he feels my relief at that. "That all sounds good to the Boss. He's trying to avoid any pacts."

Kennith nods at that. "As am I. They come with a whole slew of obligations and responsibilities that I don't think Lord Order is interested in at this time. First: the witness agreement. Do you, High Priestess Aranya, and you, Paladin Unsil, agree to act as witnesses to these contracts and verify that all parties involved freely agree to all terms involved?"

Unsil nods, and Aranya mirrors him after a few moments of consideration. Kennith produces what I'm pretty sure is magical vellum, because I can feel a weight to it through Teemo's senses, just as I can feel weight behind the ink and quill the Head Priest of Order produces next.

"Then please go over the wording here and sign directly underneath it to show your agreement. I will name each contract as we proceed, and you will sign again for each witnessed as freely accepted."

They sign, and quiet power thrums in just the witness agreement thing. I'm not usually one for this kind of legal formality, but it's pretty clear he wasn't kidding about Order being able to effect his power through the contracts. If that'll keep the Harbinger secure, I'm not gonna complain.

"This is the Recognition of Authority to Transfer a Prisoner. By signing this, I assert my authority to transport this prisoner, and Thedeim recognizes that authority." He places it on the food trolley and signs, then turns it for Teemo to read. For a "contract," it's very brief, with only a few more words than what Kennith said.

It looks legit to me, Teemo. Please sign it for me.

Teemo steps forward and pauses for a moment. "Do I sign my name, or the Boss's?"

Kennith smiles and shakes his head at himself. "Ah, of course. Sign it as 'Your name, representative of who you are representing.' I'll be signing as 'Kennith Ridgeward, representative of Lord Order' for the final notarization of the completion of your quest."

Teemo nods, and is pleasantly surprised when the quill shrinks in his hand. I get the feeling Spatial affinity is surprisingly useful in this kind of situation, not only for the quill being easily held in his hands but his writing landing large enough on the page to make it easily legible. Once signed, Aranya and Unsil sign the witness agreement, and I can feel the two pieces of parchment resonating with each other.

"This is the Transfer of Prisoner Authorization, dependent on the completion of the quest Lord Order gave Thedeim. Please double-check that all is in order, and sign if it is."

Once again, the contract is refreshingly simple, making me wonder if legalese makes things more or less legitimate to Order. I'm pretty sure Aranya said he's even less concerned with ceremony than I am, so simpler language is probably more binding than complex.

Teemo signs it again, Unsil and Aranya sign the witness form once more, and I can even start to feel the harmony of the contracts all the way by the field hospital, where Honey and Queen are organizing a dissection of the least and lessers.

"This is the Official Receipt of Prisoner," Kennith declares, and even though he doesn't raise his voice, it feels like it reverberates through the room. For a third time, the contract is straightforward, and signatures are added to it and the witness form. Kennith gathers up the papers and goes over them one last time.

"All parties declare they are aware of the stipulations of the agreements and will abide by the terms fully?" At the nods of everyone, he continues. "Then, as an official agent of Order, I declare these contracts in effect and ask Lord Order to invoke them to their fullest extent."

For a brief moment, nothing happens. Then I get a pop-up.

Quest Complete! Accept Reward? Y/N?

Of course I accept, and suddenly, I'm drowning in mana! Teemo grunts for me as I shunt almost all of it into the ally pool. I take a moment to try to recover from all that and the confirmation that, though there doesn't seem to be a hard cap to how much mana I can have, it definitely gets uncomfortable if I have too much.

I can feel surprise from the Southwood, Hullbreak, and Violet at the ocean of mana in the ally pool. There's definitely more in there than I want to hog to myself, and I trust them all not to just empty it out before we can all discuss what to do with it.

I can also feel there's more in my options, but for now, there's one last thing I'd like to discuss with Kennith.

"Whoof, that quest wasn't kidding about the mana gain. How soon do you need to get going, Kennith?" asks Teemo for me. The gnome hums as he considers, putting away the contracts into a pocket of his robe.

"I should probably leave soon; possibly tomorrow. Why?"

"Can you stick around for a while?"

Kennith looks confused at that, as do Aranya and Unsil. "Why do you ask?"

"Because the Boss wants to make sure Silvervein gets their political structure sorted without any major pitfalls, and you *are* an agent of Order, right?"

The gnome looks uncertain. "Yes, though I do have obligations back at Holdhome to attend to."

"Can your boss have someone else handle it? The Boss isn't going to ask for your help for nothing, of course. You still want the information on the least and lessers, right? I think Tarl of the Dungeoneer's is also investigating. If you stick around, we can give you a copy of what we figure out, and probably a corpse or two for Order to look at himself."

Kennith looks conflicted for a few moments before his eyes widen. "I . . . I believe Lord Order would want me to stay. I just received a quest to secure this additional information. There are others in Holdhome who can tend to my duties there, if they must."

Teemo grins. "Great! Sounds like you'll be sticking around here for a while, then. There are a couple inns and such around, so you can get yourself a room, then head to the field hospital once you're ready. If Tarl finds anything, that's probably where he'll go to let us know, and that's where Honey and Queen are, too."

Unsil smiles and claps Kennith on the back, nearly sending the gnome flying. "I'll make sure he gets settled in, Teemo."

"I'll come with you," offers Aranya. "I believe Ragnar and Aelara are at one of the taverns, with the latter trying to keep the former out of trouble, and I think Yvonne is also searching for any clues as to the mystery spawner."

"You guys have fun! I'll probably go hang out with Queen and Honey for a while, maybe get at least one of them to help with the search. See you guys later!"

I smile as everyone heads off to do their thing, and while Teemo checks in on my two eusocial scions, I'm going to see about plotting out a bit more for the forest of four seasons. With that windfall from the quest, there's a lot I can do, even while splitting the reward.

Chapter 8

Once Teemo gets to Queen and Honey, they promptly kick him out of the hospital and tell him to go bother Leo. The two of us probably should have expected them to want to dig around in the invaders and extract as much information as possible, so we have a good chuckle as Teemo heads to where Leo is.

He's using what was the scouting base as his command center for now. His current focus is on scouting the local area for other potential hostiles. While it seems like the Maw kept things pretty clean around here—at least as far as potential hostiles go—nobody wants to be caught by surprise by something sneaky. I'll eventually have to pull back everyone, so we need to be sure Silvervein can handle whatever threats might wander in.

Honestly, it's basically busywork for Leo, but it does keep him occupied. Even better, with his scouts still coming and going, he has a good idea of where Tarl and Berdol are. They're investigating what they think is the remains of the spawner for the Harbinger and its ilk, though the scouts don't have much extra information. But with a location, it's not difficult for Teemo to head over and have a chat directly with them.

He takes a bit of a scenic route there, the two of us poking around a bit to try to get our own sense for how the Maw built his territory. Big, mean, and ugly as the dungeon was, it was undeniably successful. I'm hardly going to go eating people, but I might be able to glean a few interesting ideas. Even just seeing what an "average" successful dungeon builds like could be good to know.

While I have to guess a lot—considering all the denizens, traps, nodes, and such are gone—the picture the information is painting isn't looking all that interesting. Where I tend toward open-yet-distinct areas, it feels like the Maw mostly just had a single theme to its territory. There are a few distinct sections, like the Kobold Enclave and quite a few kitchen areas, but it was mostly a complex series of rough-hewn stone rooms.

In fact, after getting a better look through Teemo's eyes, I'm pretty sure the temple complex was based off the design, just a bit more organized and more skillfully worked. We could even find where a spawner was, but I don't know if it was a fey or elemental spawner. It looks like a pile of slag or maybe forge scale, but I don't know what differences there would be between a fey or elemental spawner, or if those differences would even be apparent in this destroyed state.

When we eventually find Tarl and Berdol, it's not difficult to understand why they think this is the abomination spawner. The whole area feels unsettling, and the group of holes in the wall only add to it. They're hauntingly uniform and disturbingly dark, enough to make me wish I could remember what the term is for the fear of holes.

The two dungeoneers are examining the holes, and they jump a bit when Teemo speaks up.

"So, you think those creepy holes are the remains of the Harbinger's spawner?"

Tarl glances back at them before nodding. "I wouldn't stake my reputation on specifically that, but there was definitely something here. An unknown spawner is the simplest explanation right now."

"Can you tell anything about it? I found what the Boss and I are pretty sure was a different spawner on the way, but aside from it being something metal, we don't know if it's fey or elemental."

"The elemental ones will look like a collapsed forge, while the fey will be a heap of scrap. With this, though . . . there's not a lot of information to be had. The most powerful spawn available will usually have the greatest impact on the spawner. That's why the elemental ones look like dilapidated forges; forgemasters were the strongest," explains the elf.

Berdol nods and waves his floating clipboard. "We examined those first, and they looked almost exactly like the diagrams from the book. These holes could be from a cluster of nodes, but . . ." He trails off, and Tarl picks back up.

"If the Maw had nodes that would leave behind neat holes like this, we should have seen some. These are the only ones we've found this whole time. We haven't been here long enough for me to say definitively, but I seriously doubt they were part of nodes."

Teemo nods and peeks down a hole while I try not to imagine some horror reaching out and snatching him up. "So what *can* you say about these things?"

"It wasn't Metal affinity, for starters," declares Tarl with a tone of certainty. "That's strange, but not impossible. Scions will inherit a dungeon's affinity, but spawners don't always. The lingering unease points toward Mental affinity, which would be in line with the Harbinger."

"And the creepy holes," adds Berdol. "We saw a couple of the invaders, and they look *wrong* somehow. Even without them having the same holes as the spawner, I'd bet they're related."

Teemo leans back and looks around. "The mana here also feels weird. It feels thin in most of the territory, but here, it's . . ." He quiets, thinking as I take a look at the mana flow. It takes me a few seconds to realize why it looks so weird.

Teemo squints as he confirms what I'm seeing, even though it doesn't make much sense. "The mana's wrong because it's not moving."

Berdol looks confused, but Tarl looks *concerned*. "Are you certain?"

Teemo looks around for a few more seconds before nodding. "Yeah. It's slowly flowing in the territory I came through, but it's completely still around these holes."

"But . . . that's not how dungeons work, right?" asks Berdol.

Tarl nods with a deep frown. "It's not how they're supposed to work, no."

Supposed to?

"How *are* they supposed to work, anyway? I know the Boss does a good job as a dungeon, but that's mostly because he just focuses on keeping delvers busy."

Tarl chuckles and motions at Berdol, letting his apprentice solidify his knowledge by teaching. The catkin looks confused at the question for a moment before shaking his head.

"No wonder you guys are always calling him weird. I thought he was kinda weird before, but I get it now. Uh, anyway . . . while there are a lot of mana affinities, there are basically three mana states: turbulent, lamellar, and stagnant. Turbulent mana is . . . basically mana after someone uses it. It's excited and energetic, chaotic, and can make it difficult to keep using. Stagnant mana is still, and though it's pretty easy for people to use, it also makes wild monsters and invaders." He pauses and looks at Tarl. "I haven't been shown how that works just yet, though."

Tarl shrugs. "There are a lot of theories on the specifics, but stagnant mana seems to almost crystallize into invaders and other nasty things, like salt crystallizes from brine."

Berdol flips his papers to note that down before picking up where he left off. "Lamellar flows smoothly, and it's what dungeons do. They calm down the turbulent mana and energize the stagnant to get it moving."

Teemo frowns at that and looks back to the holes. "So, if dungeons are all about lamellar flow . . . what's stagnant mana doing here?"

"That's what has me worried."

No wonder Order wanted the Harbinger.

"What do you mean, Boss?"

The Harbinger, the least, and the lessers all seemed to have glitches in them, or at least in the status we could identify. What if the errors aren't just in the display? If they're somehow inverting how a dungeon is supposed to work, it'd explain why Order was so keen to get the Harbinger and whatever other information we can give Kennith.

Teemo's eyes widen at that before he focuses back on the two dungeoneers, who look interested in him explaining. "Boss thinks the Harbinger and its spawner were somehow making stagnant mana."

Berdol looks confused again, while Tarl looks like he doesn't like what he's hearing but can't offer much rebuttal. "I hope he's wrong, but that's what things are pointing toward. I already miss the days when Thedeim was the weirdest dungeon I'd dealt with."

Teemo chuckles at that. "Can you two get as much information as you can and give a copy to Kennith?"

"Who's Kennith?" asks Berdol, flipping through his notes as if they might hold the answer.

"He's the priest of Order who came to get the Harbinger. The Boss got a quest to hand it over in exchange for a bunch of mana and fast tracking, whatever that is."

Oh yeah! With all the mana, I forgot that was a thing! I start poking through my options as Tarl replies.

"Fast tracking?"

Teemo nods. "Yeah. It said it would accelerate things gained for dungeon age, but didn't say what they are."

Tarl and Berdol both look confused for a few moments before Tarl smacks his forehead. "Right, it's easy to forget Thedeim isn't even a year old yet! Considering what he's managed, I thought he had the enhanced control already."

"Enhanced control?" asks Teemo as I pay more attention. I can tell there's differences, but I'm not quite sure what they actually mean just yet.

Tarl nods. "There seems to be limitations on what a dungeon can do at first, to help young dungeons keep away from making huge mistakes. Rooms are severely limited, expansion options are predefined, and even spawners and their placement are already decided."

That helps explain why my expansion option is asking me to define an area instead of just giving me a selection to choose from. I also notice a few more rooms, but they don't immediately catch my attention, considering my expanded spawner options.

"For normal dungeons, they seem to get access to another room roughly each year. They also seem to get the ability to place additional spawners after five years, and after ten, their expansions become more focused."

I play around with spawners and expansions, not actually purchasing anything but seeing how they differ. One obvious change is how much cheaper expansions seem now.

"Why are the expansions cheaper? The Boss is toying around with the options, but it looks like even if he designates a section he could have expanded into before, there's a pretty big discount."

Tarl nods. "That's because they don't come with spawners anymore. The first couple expansions come with two to help get a dungeon on its feet. Very few dungeons expand enough to start getting single spawners until after they unlock the ability to create their own.

"After a decade, expansions don't include a spawner at all, allowing for more freedom to customize an expansion, but also more opportunity to make a mistake. If Violet, for example, were to be able to expand without also getting spawners, she could suddenly have huge swaths of territory she can't actually do anything with. With so much area but no spawners, she could be vulnerable.

"But an experienced dungeon will already have a plan for an expansion, even if they don't have the mana to fully realize it immediately. They can expand and place a spawner or two, and use the new area to increase their income and pay for the rest of whatever the dungeon wants to do."

Cool. That should make the forest of four seasons a lot easier to plan for! I won't have to hope I get appropriate spawners for it, at least. I can just buy what I want. I can probably even get a good discount if I trade for some of the Southwood's denizens and make them scions. Oh, and I'll need to trade for the climate control feature, too.

I hear Teemo chuckle as I prepare to dig into more planning for it. "Welp, we've lost the Boss to his new toys. He's not buying anything yet; I think he wants to talk to the other dungeons first. Hey, Boss! Anything you need done before you go planning?"

Hmm? Oh, uh . . . just to make sure Kennith gets the information he needs from everyone. If the Harbinger really is an agent of someone messing with the system, I want to give Order all the help we can.

Teemo nods. "Got it, Boss. Try not to have too much fun, yeah?"

I hum at him in reply as I start looking at my options and let the possibilities carry me away.

Chapter 9

Teemo

The Voice of Thedeim smiles as he feels his Boss settle in to dig through his options. He's been a bit on edge with the whole Maw situation, and it feels right for him to get back into planning. Just because the Boss *can* orchestrate the destruction of a dangerous dungeon and capture a crazy scion, it doesn't mean it's something he actually enjoys doing.

He sets aside what Thedeim is doing for the moment and refocuses his attention on Tarl and Berdol. "Do you guys need any other help here?"

Tarl shakes his head. "I don't think so. I'm going to take the time to detail things a bit more, but I think we're about done here."

"Would you like a second opinion from a ranger?"

"I wouldn't turn it down; they're much more experienced with stagnant mana than I am. Did you have one in mind?"

Teemo nods. "Yeah, Yvonne. I dunno how much experience she has with stagnant mana specifically, but she should know at least a little. I'm pretty sure she gave me and the Boss a brief primer on the mana cycle you explained a while ago, but I think we were missing the context to make it stick, you know?"

This time, Tarl nods. "If she's available, I'd love to have her perspective on this. Maybe she knows what these unsettling holes are from. I haven't encountered anything like them as a dungeoneer, but maybe a ranger has."

"Then I'll be back in . . . I dunno, an hour?"

Tarl nods and waves Teemo off as he motions for Berdol to come take a closer look at something. "Make sure you sketch this knot here carefully."

Teemo dives into a fresh shortcut as Berdol moves to comply, and the Rat Scion revels in how easy they're becoming. Usually, temporary shortcuts need to stay pretty short and small, or else they take too long or cost too much. But now, he feels like he can dash through minute cracks in the rock as easily as the tunnels everyone takes.

It's also nice to get confirmation that he's doing a good job with his Spatial affinity. The Boss has always been impressed, but he has a unique perspective that makes it hard to tell just how well he's doing. But after getting to talk with Kennith and seeing him so impressed with the mobius trap, Teemo can't help but feel a deep sense of accomplishment.

It's always easy to compare himself to Rocky or Fluffles and find himself severely lacking. But now, he has an independent opinion that he is, in fact, accomplished in his niche. He doesn't need to try to expand his affinities like those two scions, but knowing his hard work is paying off in its own way is more than a small relief.

It even has him wondering if he *should* try to expand his affinities, too. While he's pretty confident he understands what the Boss was trying to say now about how pressure, volume, and temperature are linked, he doesn't know if he wants to expand into the obviously linked affinities. Temperature would open up Ice and Fire, and those two seem pretty linked to Kinetic. Pressure might open up Wind affinity? But as cool as Fluffles and Rocky look slinging those around, they don't quite feel within Teemo's grasp just yet.

What *does* feel within his grasp is something he's heard the Boss deliberately try not to think too hard about where Teemo can hear. Not because he's trying to keep it a secret, but because he doesn't want to force the rat in a particular direction. While Teemo appreciates that, the possible affinity is intriguing.

The only issue is he's not certain if it's an actual affinity. He's not even sure anyone else has realized the concept yet. Still, with how Fundamental-with-a-capital-*F* the Boss says it is, Teemo can't see any way gravity *isn't* an affinity. It might just end up being Kinetic, but the rat's gut insists that, no matter how similar they might look in effect, the two should achieve the same thing very differently.

Fluffles could pick up something and move it around. A Gravity affinity on the other hand would make a thing fall upward before turning gravity off to allow the object to float. He's already been teasing at manipulating gravity inside his shortcuts, which is why he feels like he could break through.

Sure, it's just a matter of defining a different "down" inside a shortcut, but if he understands the Boss right, bending space basically creates gravity.

He'll need to toy with it later, probably after getting back home and meeting with the other dungeons. Boss will want to talk with them about how to distribute all that mana, and probably want to offer suggestions to everyone for what to spend their shares on.

A scion or two for Southwood is an easy guess, and a beach expansion for Hullbreak is also pretty obvious. The only uncertainty is with Violet. Having her designate a Voice is a no-brainer, but does she even have the option yet? Just another thing to bring up at a meeting of dungeons.

He sets aside the idea of a meeting for now as he pops out of a crack in the tunnel leading to the last bar he knew Ragnar and Aelara were at. Even if Yvonne isn't with them, they should know where she is. Thankfully, not only does it look like they haven't gone to a new tavern yet, but it also looks like the birdwoman is enjoying the spectacle of Ragnar participating in a drinking contest with probably a dozen or so pale dwarves.

With everyone focused on the carousing, jeering, and ribbing shouts of the participants, Teemo easily slips over to Yvonne's table, where she and Aelara are idly chatting.

"—and the milk from the worms is . . . Oh, hello, Teemo." Aelara smiles as she notices him, the elven woman looking dainty and posh, even with the pint of ale near her.

"Heya, Aelara, Yvonne. I hope I'm not interrupting?"

Yvonne shakes her hawklike head. "No, we were just talking about the milkworms. They're one of the biggest types of worms I've ever seen, and Aelara says their milk is at least as good for skincare as it is for making cheese."

"Yeah?"

Aelara nods. "I've found a few balms that use it, and they're lovely. They keep very well, too! I'm going to get plenty before we make our way back to Fourdock."

"Not today, I hope?" inquires the rat, and Aelara titters and shakes her head.

"I don't think we'll be leaving for at least another week. The earth here is more resilient than I'm used to, so it'll be good to train my affinity. And Ragnar hasn't had a proper drinking competition since he left his hold, I think."

"Cool, because I'd like to borrow Yvonne, if you don't mind me stealing away half your conversation?"

Yvonne smiles. "I don't mind. I've been exploring around a little, but the mana flows are difficult to sort out after the Maw vanished. I wouldn't be surprised if a new dungeon spawns somewhere nearby soon."

"That's part of the reason I want to have you look at something, Yvonne. The mana is weird. Tarl's been investigating a particular spot, and we both think you might have some new insights to offer on it."

Yvonne tilts her head in curiosity. "Oh? No offense, Aelara, but that sounds more intriguing than worm balm."

Aelara laughs and takes a drink of her ale. "None taken! Don't think you can escape me so easily, though. You may need to care more for feathers than skin, but that just means I'll get to experiment to find you something that will keep your feathers in the peak of health!"

Yvonne smiles as Teemo hops onto her shoulder. "I look forward to it. I don't usually care too much about that sort of thing, but a girl *does* sometimes want to feel soft and fluffy when not on a delve."

"That's the spirit! You two have fun!" Aelara waves as Teemo opens another shortcut, and the two vanish down it.

"So, what did Tarl find?"

"He's not completely sure. The Boss thinks it could be something dangerous. Well, something that implies something dangerous. The thing itself is pretty much inert, but if there are others, it could be bad. I'll let you take a look before I give you the Boss's take on it."

"Thedeim thinks it could be dangerous? That's concerning . . . though he is often more creative with things than most. Just because he can think of some dangerous option, it doesn't mean anyone else would. Still . . . I get the feeling it has something to do with the Harbinger."

"Got it in one. I guess it's not much of a spoiler if I tell you Tarl is pretty sure he found the remains of the Harbinger's spawner, which also makes it the remains of the least and lesser spawner."

Yvonne quirks an eyebrow at that, increasing her pace. "Oh? I would like to look at that even without a vague warning from Thedeim."

The two focus more on speed than conversation after that, and soon pop back into the chamber with the ruined spawner. Yvonne immediately frowns as she looks around.

"That's . . . unnatural," she confirms, her eyes settling on the unsettling holes near Tarl and Berdol.

"I thought as much," speaks the elf, "but I wanted a ranger to confirm. What do you think?"

"It's stagnant. Even more . . . there's a *snarl* of stagnation."

"Is that the weird mess of stagnant mana?" asks Berdol, showing his sketch. Yvonne takes a closer look at his notes before nodding.

"That's a snarl of stagnation. It's . . . how do I put it . . . It's like a spawner, but for stagnation monsters. While the smaller ones can simply coalesce in deep stagnation areas, there are occasionally these snarls that will give rise to stronger monsters."

"Can it be undone?" asks Teemo, eyeing the jumble of mana. When he last saw it, it just seemed like a mass of stationary mana, but looking closer, it really does look like someone tied it in a multitude of messy knots. The only question is if it was deliberate. Considering it's where the spawner was, it's difficult to chalk it up to coincidence.

Yvonne nods and examines the tangle. "It's a ranger technique. Some can slice through it, but I have a knack for untying them. It's like a beaver's dam in that if it's weakened enough, the natural flow can sweep it away. I've never dealt with one like this, though. I think it will unravel on its own eventually, since it's not deep in stagnation, but I don't see any reason we shouldn't try to speed it along."

Tarl looks thoughtful. "Can we help?"

Yvonne ponders as she continues examining the stagnation. "Ordinarily, I'd need to be guarded from the stagnation monsters while I work. Disturbing stagnant mana often triggers monsters to spawn. But with just this snarl . . . I'd like you to guard me, but it might not be required."

Tarl nods and draws his daggers, with Berdol levitating his blades a heartbeat later. "I think standing watch is a small price to pay to get to see something like this."

The birdwoman nods and starts drawing on her affinity, leaning on her Fate to find the weakest thread to start with. Teemo assists with Butterfly Effect, letting it guide him as he occasionally plucks at a strand. He loses track of time as they work, the meticulous job keeping his focus without being too much of a strain.

After what feels like maybe a few hours, Yvonne finally steps back with a smile at the weakened snarl. To Teemo, it looks like it's barely holding together, which Yvonne soon confirms.

"It's ready now. Tarl, Berdol, would you please use some mana? All it needs is a bit of turbulence to collapse."

Tarl nods and steps into Berdol's shadow as the catkin starts weaving his blades in complex patterns. Teemo watches as the mana around them starts bubbling from the use, and once the turbulence touches the snarl, it implodes.

The Rat Scion smiles for a moment before he hears a gasp from both Yvonne and Tarl. It only takes him a moment to realize why. He can see that the stagnant threads, the turbulent bubbles, and the laminar flow are all interacting! He can hardly comprehend the process, but the effect is pretty clear.

As the four watch, a tiny chip of jet crystallizes into reality on the floor in front of the holes, and Teemo can feel a tiny curious and frightened presence from it. He, Yvonne, and Berdol all stare for a few moments before Tarl stomps on a beetle scurrying toward the vulnerable little core.

"Defend it," he orders, and everyone scrambles to obey.

"I think it has spawners in the holes. Hide inside, little one," gently suggests Teemo, and though he can still feel fear from it, he can also feel it struggling to follow his suggestion. Teemo quickly dispatches any invaders that manage to slip past Tarl, Berdol, or Yvonne, all while a little worm wriggles from a hole: the dungeon's first denizen and scion, moving to secure the core. Once it reaches it, the worm coils around it while, at the same time, a small brass disk with four small limbs stumbles from a different hole.

Teemo watches the other denizen awkwardly gather the worm and core atop the plate before it bumbles back to a hole and into it with a series of clanks that indicate it simply fell in. Teemo can feel the little dungeon is still alive, still frightened, but feeling much more secure now as denizens start slowly milling around the holes.

Teemo's still trying to process what they all just saw as Tarl pulls out his note stone.

"Nascent dungeon coalescence witnessed. Unnamed dungeon, Shadow affinity. Worm and construct spawners, Worm Scion."

Chapter 10

The feeling of Teemo's concern pulls me out of exploring my menus. Once I realize what has him feeling like that, I understand.

A new dungeon?

"Welcome to the fun, Boss. Yeah."

You, Yvonne, and Tarl had a kid? I didn't even know Yvonne was pregnant!

Teemo does his best to give me a flat look. "That's not how it works, and you know it, Boss."

Yeah, I know. But it's fun to joke. You know just how many more I have ready to go, but we should probably figure out what to do before I make more gags at your expense.

Tarl and Yvonne eye Teemo, with Berdol scribbling whatever notes he can come up with. Yvonne speaks up before my favorite dungeon inspector can. "Thedeim has noticed, then?"

"Yeah, and he's mostly done making jokes about the situation now. So . . . what do we do?"

"Can he just take it as another protégé?" asks Berdol.

I'm pretty doubtful. It seemed like the system was pretty adamant about me only having one at a time. Still, the fast tracking might have given me room for another?

Release Protégée? Y/N?

Nope.

"Looks like he's still stuck with just one, and he's not ready to turn Violet loose yet."

Tarl nods at that. "I've only ever heard of dungeons having one at a time, but you never know with Thedeim." He taps his foot as he eyes the holes in the wall and floor, the little denizens swarming to keep any invaders at bay. "I'll probably need to stay here and keep an eye on it, and write a report of my own for Telar, too. The theory of dungeons forming from an interaction between mana states has been long accepted, but I don't know if anyone else has ever actually witnessed it! The way it went was different from the theory, but I don't know if that's how they always go, or if that's just how this one in specific went."

Tarl starts muttering to his stone about mana flows and whatnot, giving the others a chance to add their opinion, which Yvonne leaps on. "So . . . what do we do about it? Should you just subsume it, then?"

Teemo shakes his head and relays my reply. "That's being a bit hasty, especially if Tarl is going to be here to try to help guide it. The Boss also has an idea to help it along, too. I just need to go find the Stag. The Boss can't take another protégé, but the Southwood doesn't have one. He can ask the Boss for any advice if he wants it, too."

"Do you know where the Stag is?" asks my birdwoman resident. Teemo shakes his head.

"Not right this moment, but I doubt he'll be difficult to track down. It's not like there are two elk stags with crystalline antlers wandering around here. Anyone want to come help me look for him?"

Tarl speaks up from his stone. "Actually, if Yvonne doesn't mind, I'd like her help with a few small pieces of training for the nascent dungeon. It will be helpful for it to learn to recognize a delving party and understand a proper delve can give it a lot of mana, even with the loss of a few denizens."

Yvonne smiles. "I was hoping to just stay and observe, but I'd be happy to help the hatchling along."

Teemo nods and prepares a shortcut. "Then you two have fun being its parents. I'm gonna go find it an uncle to care for it more directly." The looks on their faces has both of us laughing as Teemo heads back to Silvervein proper. Our mood doesn't fade as he asks around for the Stag.

He's not hard to track down, as suspected, and Teemo soon finds him in the underground equivalent of a park, relaxing atop some long moss, with pale dwarven and elven children milling around him. Getting closer, Teemo and I can hear the peaceful chiming of his antlers as the children play, running around and generally being kids. A few are leaning against him, doodling in the moss or looking like they're going to take a short nap.

"You never said you were good with kids, Stag!" accuses Teemo with a smile as he nears, drawing the attention of the more sedate children. The other scion chuckles and shakes his head, more contented chimes coming from his antlers.

"I don't believe I've ever interacted with them before. It's easier to understand how protective parents can be, now. They're so innocent, so curious, even with how harsh things down here seemed to be."

"Did their parents dump them on you?"

The Stag shakes his head once more.

"No, at least not specifically. I found this place and decided to relax, only to discover that the parents of these children told them to go out and play, and this is their preferred spot. They gathered around and asked questions before deciding to play their games instead. The most curious ones are napping, else I would expect they'd have questions for you, too."

Teemo smirks at that. "I bet. So, have you learned what the Southwood wanted you to, about Silvervein?"

"Yes, or at least enough to understand he won't need to dramatically change anything within his territory to accommodate their needs. Some metal or stone nodes would not go amiss, but he expects they will be very interested in harvesting food from him."

Teemo nods at that as a dwarven lad with a stubbly beard flops himself over the Stag's back and asks a question. "Why're you so small?"

My Voice smirks. "Because I'm a rat!"

"But you talk! That means you're a Voice like the Stag, right? He said he's so big because he's a Voice!"

Teemo chuckles at that. "I'm Thedeim's Voice. I'm so small because he doesn't do a lot of things most people say he should."

The child looks hopeful as he responds. "Does that mean he doesn't eat his veggies?"

I laugh as Teemo gives my reply. "He does! But he also likes them."

The dwarven child sticks out his tongue in disgust. "That's not how that's supposed to work!"

"Exactly!" Confusion plays across the child's face before he shrugs and slides off the Stag to rejoin whatever game of chase or tag they're all up to, letting Teemo return his attention to the other scion. "So . . . do you want one?"

The Stag gives my Voice a look of concern and confusion. "I believe the city at large would object to that."

Teemo waves it off like it's not a big deal. "I don't mean one of these kids. I don't know if you could feel it from here, but a new dungeon just appeared in the Maw's old territory. The Boss can't take a second protégé . . . so does the Southwood want one?"

The Stag stares at him for several long seconds before his ears twitch. He blinks at what he hears before realizing he should say something. "Uh . . . my Lord is interested, but He wishes to know more."

"Then you should probably come take a look."

The Stag nods and gently prods the dozing kids with his antlers to wake them up. A few already don't want him to go, even after only knowing him for maybe an hour. Still, he needs to go, and the awoken kids organize their own game as he slips through a shortcut with Teemo.

"Is there anything my Lord should know about this nascent dungeon?"

Teemo shrugs from atop the Stag's head. "Probably, but we don't know too much about it. The little guy seems pretty healthy so far, but the circumstances of its birth are a bit concerning."

"What do you mean?"

"The Maw had somehow broken a spawner so that it made or maybe worked with stagnant mana. Yvonne said it made a stagnation snarl, something usually only found deep in stagnant mana areas, but she knew how to take it apart since that's basically what rangers do.

"Anyhow, she unraveled it, and the combination of that mana, the turbulence from her, Tarl, and Berdol, and possibly even a bit of lamellar from me reacted and condensed a little chip of a dungeon core made of jet. We fought off the initial invaders while the little thing took refuge in a hole in the floor, and now I think it's just trying to get its bearings."

The Stag hums at that as he thinks, his ear flicking occasionally as the Southwood voices his opinion. "That there was stagnant mana is concerning, but if the nascent dungeon is shaping the flows properly, my Lord doesn't see any reason to be concerned. What spawners does it have?"

"Worms and constructs, and it's Shadow affinity."

The Stag nods as they near the exit, and soon, he gets to lay eyes on the young dungeon himself. Tarl, Yvonne, and Berdol are carefully picking off a few denizens. I watch as several of the defenders sally forth from the numbers milling around the holes, clearly engaging them deliberately. The delvers don't even use any skills to deal with the attack before moving back from the holes to let the dungeon consider what it should do.

Tarl waves at the two scions as the groups meet. "So, what do you think, Stag?"

The Stag looks around with a measuring eye before nodding. "The flows are poor but already improving. Teemo told me of what you all found, and my Lord believes the new dungeon is performing normally, without any untoward strangeness."

The inspector nods at that. "That's what I think, too. I'm glad to have a second opinion. Are you going to make it a protégé?"

The Stag looks a bit uncertain, but he still nods. "My Lord wishes to offer it the opportunity, yes."

"Don't let us stop you, then," replies Yvonne, stepping to the side to give the Stag an easier path. He nods at the group as he passes by, while Teemo hops off his head so he can greet the new little dungeon as he sees fit.

When he enters the territory, the denizens all go still, even as the Stag lays down just barely inside its area of control. "Hello, little one. I represent the Southwood, a powerful dungeon far from here . . . or not so far from here, thanks to the shortcuts."

A slightly larger worm exits a hole and crawls out where it can easily be seen, though it doesn't make the long trek to where the Stag is. The Southwood's scion tilts his head as he listens. "Where are the protectors? They are safe. They are . . . my friends. They asked me to help protect you, too."

The worm wiggles more, and the Stag shakes his head. "They cannot always be here, and they don't have the ability to properly guide you. But my Lord can, if you will allow him. He would like to take you as his protégé, to guide and nurture you until you can protect not only yourself but possibly even others as well."

The worm slowly undulates before I feel the dungeon accept the offer. While I don't get any notice or anything like that, I *can* feel the cautious little presence be added to my allies, just like how Violet counts as one because of being my protégée.

The Stag smiles and stands, giving the worm a formal bow. "Thank you. For now, simply grow, young one, and be vigilant for any nodes you can spawn. You will probably get stone, gems, or metals. They will draw new invaders, so be prepared to repel them, but the delvers will also be drawn to them, and so generate mana for you."

The worm wiggles back to the hole as the Stag steps back, a peaceful smile on his face. I wonder if the Southwood was a bit lonely, way out here? If he was, I don't think he is anymore.

Chapter 11

I think pretty much everyone is eager to return home, but we also know things could collapse if we all just leave. There's a lot of little things to hammer down before letting the Silverveiners take the reins back.

Tarl is going to be staying, since there's not really anyone else around who is experienced with new dungeons. I think he did a pretty good job with me, so I'm not worried about the little dungeon going nuts, especially with the Southwood mentoring it.

I've started thinking of the little guy as Vanta, because I think it's cool. Teemo let it slip to the Stag, who asked the dungeon if it liked that name; I think it's still deciding. I'll probably still call it Vanta, even if only as a nickname, but we'll have to see. For now, its borders are still expanding, and Tarl expects it to solidify and stabilize at the size of the chamber there.

In related news, Silvervein has learned of it. It seems like there were still a few devoted Maw followers who assumed it was the Maw's reincarnation, but between Tarl and the Stag, any issues were dealt with before any of my scions could even get on the scene.

I think Vanta is confused about the hubbub, but I'll leave it to the Southwood to decide when and what to tell it. He asked my opinion, and I could only suggest trying to dumb it down as much as possible. Bad people exist just as much as good people do. Try to help the good and stop the bad.

Yeah, nuance is gone in that, but Vanta is too young to understand nuance right now. It might be too young to understand good and bad in all but the most basic of ways, even.

Still, while Silvervein is nervous about a new dungeon, especially one where Vanta is, they're willing to trust us all on this one. I think it's in no small part thanks to Unsil and Kennith working to help get people back on track. The Crystal Shield guys make rebuilding look easy, especially with Kennith handling the building of their new civic structure. The Shielders give hope for right now, and Kennith gives hope that things will be normal again soon, even if it's a new kind of normal.

I think Unsil is going to be sticking around for at least a while. He's gotten a lot of converts to the Shield, which isn't especially surprising. He's a great example of a paladin, and I hope Freddie has been able to learn from him.

Kennith is always busy, but even when he's dragging his feet in exhaustion, he has a satisfied smile on his face. Between meeting with Queen and Honey—with Teemo interpreting—and meeting with the burgeoning town council, he hardly has any time to sleep. It makes me wonder if I can make a stronger tea or somehow get ahold of coffee. Even with my new options to spend mana, I don't see anything too promising yet. Still, a bit of honey from Honey's bees helps him keep going long enough to make it to a bed to pass out most of the time.

Aranya is pretty busy, too, along with Vernew. The Shield wasn't the only one to get converts, which is still a strange thing to think about. The two, along with my other dwellers still here, are doing their best to help rebuild and encourage people. It even looks like a few of my dwellers will be staying here to form a little satellite church.

I take a moment to peek in and check on the afterlife for my fallen dwellers, and they're getting along great. They laugh and talk while they work, argue over designs and what's the best way to make something, and take the time to relax and just enjoy existence together.

I think I want to introduce some kind of challenge, or even hostile mobs or something, but for now, I'm not going to shake things up too much. Change keeps things interesting, but I don't want to make them overwhelming. Maybe once the workshop is more established, I'll introduce some more complex resources that will require them to overcome something. For now, I think all my fallen dwellers want peace more than excitement.

As for making challenges for those still living, I really need to figure out what to do with all the mana from the Harbinger.

Teemo manages to get a few minutes to ask the Stag about it, and he flatly refuses a simple twenty-five percent split across the board. He says he would not take so much of the gains, and even after I point out how much he gave for Murphy's Law, he only capitulates to accepting twice what he paid in raw mana. I am able to badger him into accepting paying for the cost of a scion or two out of the ally pool, but that's as far as he's willing to go.

Though Hullbreak and Violet don't exactly have Voices here to participate, I know they get the gist of the negotiations through the bond, and I get the feeling they are going to want similar terms as the Southwood. I'd happily pay them more, but I think twice their contribution and a couple purchases from the ally pool is as far as they'll be willing to go.

For Hullbreak, I'll definitely suggest he expand to try to claim a beach, or even some rocky cliffs; anything that will let delvers stay dry while still giving him mana. My suggestion for Violet is also easy, even if I don't know if she qualifies for one yet: get a Voice. She could probably also stand to expand again, but considering how much a Voice is compared to her mana pool, I doubt she'll accept both. She could probably use her college fund for an expansion, if she wants it. Or maybe for her Voice?

Hmm . . . see, this is why I want to talk with them about the mana. Hullbreak and Violet both will probably have tons of options to spend on, and though I'll leave the final decision with them, I'm not going to blow off the responsibility of taking care of my vassal and my protégée.

I'm also not going to shirk in my own development. Poe is running extra expeditions to the forest past the cemetery, and Coda is already planning where to install a fresh set of gates to lead outside. We've just been climbing a makeshift staircase over the wall! It's time for a serious long-term solution, because I want to expand that way.

There's plenty of woodland before the surrounding mountains start making an earnest climb for the heavens, so I should have plenty of space to build out there to my heart's content. With more detailed expeditions, I get a nice discount on the expansion. And if Rezlar builds the planned emergency hold in the mountains, it'll be easier to provide some kind of covert way for them to still delve even if the town is forced to evacuate. I'll probably need to expand underground to really do that, but the forest is still in the right direction to make that easier.

I think the hardest decision will be to figure out what kind of scale to build in. The manor is pretty big for a building, but it's still basically a house. The hedge maze is pretty big compared to that, but the tunnels have *way* more floor space, and the caverns have more than that! The lava labyrinth is even larger, too! Do I keep scaling up, or do I try to compact things? The price isn't really a problem, but I don't want to buy a square mile only for maybe a dozen people to get regular use out of it.

I can squeeze a lot of use out of not a lot of space thanks to Teemo, too. I want to achieve a bit of a dungeon crawl by having clearings connected by winding trails, which would traditionally take up a lot of space to be used for the paths between the rooms. But with Teemo's help, I could basically make longcuts and place the clearings a lot closer together, using the space more efficiently.

I'll run the idea by him once he gets back home and talks with Violet and Hullbreak. There's tons of forest out there, and I have plenty of mana to buy and use the space normally. If I want to do spatial shenanigans, it'll take more of Teemo's time, and he'll need to maintain it, too. I keep him pretty busy already just with talking to people and making what long shortcuts he's already done. I wouldn't want to take the rest of his time for something I have the resources to handle without bothering him.

I also need to consider what spawners I want to use for the forest. I think I can move the wolf spawner after I expand and finally give them a proper place to run around instead of trying to have quiet encounters at the back of the graveyard. The weaker wolves will still be mostly for expeditions, I think, but they can also be used in encounters basically in the entire forest. The later wolves are a shoo-in for the winter section.

I also want to buy the foxes and bears from the Southwood. I think the foxes would be a good fit for the fall section, and the bears might be good for winter? Or maybe summer, since the wolves will be well suited for winter. For spring, I have two ideas: One is to move some of my green undead in and give people besides the Shield followers a good chance to play with them. The other is to get a fey spawner. I'm pretty sure I could even give them Life affinity, which would be incredibly fitting.

I could also use a plant spawner, or maybe even several, depending on how much space I actually use.

Hmm . . . that gives me an idea. For a long time, I've had the option to expand upward, but I never tried it. After the earthquake from me expanding down, I didn't want to risk accidentally destroying Fourdock with something going up. Best case, the manor could expand in a crazy mishmash maze of a tower. Worst case, a real hurricane settles overtop Fourdock, and I'm supposed to build on the cloud.

But out in the forest, there's a lot less chance for a catastrophe. It's wild woodland; nobody is going to really be inconvenienced if a chunk of it decides it wants to float now. But I think the option for an upward expansion in the middle of a forest is a pretty obvious one: a huge tree. It'd even give me a good place to set a final boss: right in the canopy, or even deep in the roots. The branches will even give me extra space to work with!

While I don't want to count my chickens before they hatch, I can feel my Fate affinity resonating with the idea. I don't plan specifically for a tree as I start making sketches in my secret library, but I do make sure to leave a space in the center of the seasons for an upward expansion. Even if it's something more volatile, it'll still make a cool centerpiece for the forest of four seasons.

Chapter 12

As easy as it is to focus on a shiny new expansion, I can't go forgetting everything else I've built up. As my friends and denizens make their way back home, I take the time to ensure I haven't let anything fall apart while I was distracted with the Maw.

The manor is still running like a dream, with encounters designed for newer delvers. I think I've raised the average level of Fourdock quite a bit since I've come here, since it seems like even the dedicated craftspeople don't have too much trouble with the manor encounters. It's a little tempting to try to mix things up, maybe make the attic encounter tougher or even add in a rooftop boss before they can get to the belfry garden, but I don't think it's really needed. The encounters are my easiest, but the loot there is also the simplest. Besides, it still makes me a tidy sum of mana.

Similarly, the manor grounds are pretty easy, with the hedge maze being the standout attraction for the area. While I've opened up a bit of it for more lumber nodes, I might absorb it into the maze again once I expand into the forest. I'll have plenty of room for them out there. On the other hand, I could leave the industrial lumber production to the Southwood; I'm pretty sure he has those kinds of nodes, and with the shortcut getting shorter every time Teemo travels it, people should have a pretty easy time going there to stock up.

The tunnels underneath the manor could use some love, now that I look at them. They're not really a maze, but they're also not exactly simple to navigate. While I have the two challenge gauntlets in there to help draw delvers, the tunnels are really more to get people to other sections rather than being their own place for encounters. I have a lot of stronger spiders, snakes, and sometimes bats to fight down there, as well as some metal and gem nodes, but with the caverns and the lava labyrinth, I should try to brainstorm some better ways to use the space.

I wonder if I could dig out classrooms or something? Thing, Honey, Queen, and Coda all have pretty big brains, and I don't doubt that people would love to learn from them. I have a lecture hall room from the fast tracking, along with a few other ones I don't know what to do with yet, like a kitchen and a gallery.

The main problem with them teaching is that they'd need Teemo to interpret . . . right? Considering I'd be using a lecture hall instead of a normal room for it, maybe it will actually let them lecture? Who knows. I'll let that one percolate for a bit more before I try it. The tunnels do their job well enough for now, and it's not like basically having an underground roadway to my other sections is a bad thing.

The caverns are another section where things are fairly simple, but I don't plan to change much with them, at least for now. They have plenty of room for stronger encounters, not to mention my limestone quarry. I might put in a couple ore veins instead of just the scattered nodes, too. The tunnels have nodes, but the caverns should be able to support mining on a more industrial rather than individual scale.

I'll float the idea to Rezlar once Teemo gets home. After the disruption the nodes in the labyrinth made, I want to make sure I don't go crashing the steel market or something with a rich iron vein. I might make a smaller one even if he doesn't want it for the town, just for my dwellers.

The caverns are near the spiderkin, but my ratkin still frequent my ore nodes for their own crafting, and the two enclaves have been working very well together. The threat of the Maw got them even more coordinated than before, and with the threat in the past, they don't seem to see any reason to cease or even slow down that cooperation.

Past the Spiderkin Enclave lay the underswamps, which I haven't expanded into yet. When we first found them, I was going to mostly ignore them, since the spiderkin like to hunt there, but Coda dug out what was supposed to be a bypass tunnel for the scythemaws when we were worried about their mating migration, and the crazy reptiles never took the thing. It could give me a good route to expand a bit into the underswamps without messing up the hunting of my spiderkin. Maybe I'll look into it after the forest of four seasons is done. I want to do some stuff on the surface for a change.

Back to the tunnels, they also lead toward Violet, though my territory ends well before hers. They additionally lead to the crypt complex where my ratkin live in their enclave. My library and enchanting lab are in there, too, as well as my various undead encounters.

My zombies and skeletons are both specialized for resources, which for them makes them walking herbalism nodes, with the skeletons having more normal herbs and my zombies taking a fungal theme. The Shield followers love to fight them, since they're apparently pretty resistant to typical turning methods, and my undead are behaved enough that failing to defeat them doesn't mean joining the undead legions.

The complex then leads up to the surface, where the cemetery is, and where Grim keeps it quiet and peaceful. The peace is a little strained at the back of the graveyard, however, where the wolf spawner is. My awoos need a bit of room, and even the most respectful delver has a hard time resisting a fight against them.

I'll definitely be moving them out into the forest, probably before I do anything else with it. Whatever section I put them in will be the winter one, which I should probably put far away from town . . . or maybe closer to it? Could I even have each section go through the seasons, just on their own time? I'm going to need to play with the climate control option a lot once I buy it from the Southwood.

One last backtrack to the tunnels allows for the entrance to the lava labyrinth! My newest section definitely has my strongest encounters yet, both with denizens and with traps!

The entrance is pretty peaceful, with it looking more and more like a mall or a bazaar as I make adjustments. Jello's new metalworks is there, and it looks like she's even been included in the quests from the aranea kiosk. It's a bit bigger than most kiosks, and probably has a different design than most . . . I just think of it as a kiosk because kiosk is fun to say and is always used mostly to give out information.

Anyway, kiosks aside, Jello is where a lot of gathering quests in the labyrinth are getting turned in now, with the accomplished delvers sometimes getting silken wear from the aranea or some metal doodad from Jello. It looks like she's working with the aranea to give some of the shirts and pants some snap buttons to make them easier to put on as well.

The true entrance to the labyrinth is a sculpted gateway that looks like a huge wyrm, all three of its mandibles wide open to let delvers walk down its throat. I'd like to make it open and close some day, but it's pretty far down the list, honestly. Inside, delvers have to deal with more modest-size wyrms, and soon my basilisks will be able to wander the place instead of being shipped off to fight the Maw. I should probably look into diversifying the encounters a bit more, too.

The traps are working out as I hoped, but I don't want to make solving the labyrinth as simple as a good Fire Resist potion. I wonder if I could get my twinsnakes in here, possibly with a couple winter wolves to help regulate the heat. Cold-blooded critters need help to warm up, but they also need help to cool down. I wouldn't want my noodles to cook before they can play with the delvers.

I'll probably need to upgrade the snake spawner to get enough numbers for the twinsnakes, though. And I'll need Queen to get settled back into her lab at home if I want to give them the metal scales and Lightning affinity, too. Yeah, lightning, fire, and ice should be a good mix to lower the chances of delvers cheesing things.

There's probably a more general Elemental Resist potion they could take, but I'd expect the effects on each element to be diminished versus a single specialized potion. I just need to make sure the puppers and the sneks can operate down there without too much trouble.

Oh, I could also upgrade the Earth elemental spawner for some more fun things to fight in there! Some of the spawns already frequent it, but more variety will definitely be better.

I spend a little mana to move a couple groups of snakes and wolves there as a test before turning my eyes to a currently empty section of the labyrinth. I've been wanting to do this one for a while now, too. My ant spawner is maxed out, and the siren song of a new enclave has been in the background since before the fight with the Maw. Like with my spiders and rats, the final spawn straddles the gap between denizen and delver. They're smarter and have manipulators, and the final denizen for my ants are the magmyrm.

They did a great job as my own version of the red cross during the battle with the Maw, and I'm looking forward to establishing an enclave and seeing what an antkin looks like, or whatever the technical term is. I'll wait until they get back home, though. If the past is any indication, when I designate an enclave, a portion of the final spawn will get progress bars and get to work making their home. I don't know exactly how much they remember from being my denizens, but I want to reward my hard workers as much as I can. I want to make sure they have the chance to become the first generation of my ant dwellers.

I think I'll set the groundwork for the forest of four seasons, then designate the Ant Enclave. My other two enclaves grew up with me working on projects, too, so I don't think that will harm their development. They'll also have my ratkin and spiderkin to help them along, not to mention Aranya. There's no worry about them being neglected, even with a big project going on. In fact, if my ratkin and spiderkin are any indication, having a project is likely to help inspire them for their own ambitions.

Imagining my established enclaves working together with Aranya to guide the new one gives me a good feeling about the whole thing.

Chapter 13

Teemo and most of my dwellers return home, and my enclaves erupt in celebration. They mourn the lost and celebrate the hard-earned victory, giving me not only a bit more mana than their prayers used to but also giving me a bit more of that divine energy I still don't have a good term for. I also don't have much idea of how to use it, either, but giving little slivers to Aranya and the other priests and priestesses seems to work pretty well.

I'll need to experiment with the stuff later, because I have dungeon things to be doing!

Teemo touches base with Hullbreak first, and as expected, he refuses any deal more generous than what the Stag got. I suggest taking an expansion from the ally pool, which he's amenable to. He's going to take a couple days to look at his options, both for the expansion and for upgrading what he already has. Fishing is definitely going to pick up with winter finally pushed back by spring, so upgrading his fish spawner could be a great investment.

He's also considering upgrading his clam nodes for pearls, and his corals. I do my best not to be a backseat dungeon and let him make his own decisions, though I do encourage him to invest in what he already has before working on an expansion. I think he's feeling a lot more confident with taking risks and encouraging delvers now. He doesn't have to face things alone, and his merfolk have been flourishing ever since I had to force him to loosen his grip on them.

Violet, however, seems to be a bit more obstinate. Teemo talks with Onyx inside her secret sanctuary in the ceiling, which is looking much more refined than the last time I saw it. Back when she was just a little chip of a core, she was huddled in a shortcut in the ceiling. But now, the shortcut has faded, and she has a proper Sanctum dug out, probably thanks to Legs and Nose, if I had to guess.

Her little square-cut amethyst of a core is also not so little anymore. She's gone from a chip to about the size of a dinner plate. Onyx could probably move her around if she needs to, but honestly, her Secret Sanctum in the ceiling has plenty of room for expansion.

Anyway, interior design appreciation aside, both Onyx and Violet are being stubborn.

Teemo's resisting the urge to pinch the bridge of his nose as he tries to get through the two of them. "No, the college fund doesn't count! That's yours already, not a normal part of the ally pool. You got it from the scythemaws hatching, and the Boss shifted it there for safekeeping so you wouldn't feel bloated from it. You get that, twice what you contributed to Murphy's Law, and some other large purchase, probably either an expansion or a Voice."

I can feel Violet's opinion that that's not fair through the bond, and I imagine Onyx is trying to argue the same. Teemo doesn't bother translating most of what they're saying, but he does give them a curious look as they continue to argue.

"So she *does* have her eye on an expansion? Where's she want to go?"

Onyx covers her mouth with her claws like she accidentally said something she shouldn't, and I can feel a bit of guilt from Violet.

"Hey, no need to act like that, you two. I told you, the college fund is already yours. You don't need to feel guilty about spending it and also getting something else on top. You earned them both. Boss isn't just spoiling you, okay? So go on, where does Violet want to expand?"

The direction is so simple I don't even need Teemo to translate what I feel from the bond, though there are other potential problems with it.

"Up? Are you sure? Fourdock isn't all *that* far away, and if you expand up, you might cause even more of a quake than the Boss did when he expanded *down*."

Onyx shakes her head, and this time, I will need Teemo to translate, as I just get a chaotic mix of dim images and concepts. Teemo listens attentively, even as I feel growing concern from my favorite rat. He sighs when they finish, then speaks.

"So, apparently, Nose got a title while we were busy with the Maw: Explorer. It's similar to a Marshal, but it involves going out on expedition a lot yourself, too. He's been spreading Cappy's spores around, and the two have been getting a lot of information. Nose found what he says are some wet tunnels underneath Fourdock. He's also been listening in at the adventurers' guild and heard talk about sewer dungeons."

Sewer dungeons? You mean generally the worst dungeon in any game?

Teemo tries to suppress a laugh at that. "Don't let Violet hear you say that. Besides, sewer dungeons seem to work a lot differently to what you're thinking. They don't usually have encounters, for starters. Adventurers might be willing to go to all sorts of unpleasant places, but even the most curious ones are going to balk at traipsing through a sewer."

Then why were the adventurers talking about it?

Teemo shrugs. "Apparently, sewer dungeons are really common, and it's kinda weird that Fourdock doesn't have one. Neverrest probably ate them when they showed up, before anyone could discover them. Anyway, Violet's affinity should make her a perfect fit, even if I don't want to think about it very hard. I still remember you talking about treatment plants, bleh."

Her affinity? How does her affinity of . . . Her affinity of, uh . . .

Huh. What's her affinity?

Teemo can't suppress his laugh this time, even as I feel a bit of nervousness from Violet. He calms down pretty quickly and smiles at her core. "Nah, he's not going to be upset about it. I never realized he didn't know! Doesn't it say in her information or something?"

Well . . . probably. It just never seemed important, and it felt a bit like a violation of her privacy to look.

Teemo laughs again and shakes his head. "See, Violet? Affinity isn't important to him; he just wants to help you out. And, not to be mean, but you didn't really have any chances to capitalize on your particular affinity until now, anyway. She's Decay affinity, Boss."

I take a few seconds to chew on that, making sure to pat the bond with encouragement when I feel her nervousness again. *Decay is important to clean things up, ironically. I probably should have guessed, with the mushroom and centipede spawners, heh. So, she wants to become the sewers for Fourdock? How does that work?*

Teemo shrugs. "She was hoping you'd know."

Hmm. She should probably hold off on that for now, then. We wouldn't want to make another earthquake for Fourdock.

Teemo repeats my suggestion, only to get a shake of Onyx's head and an explanation I can't hear.

"Really? That might work. Onyx says Nose has dug into the sewers and is working on widening his little tunnel to be a proper access path for an expansion. Violet can't quite feel the details for it yet, but just like how you get details and a discount for sending expeditions, so does she. Once she gets a better idea of it, she wants to take the expansion."

That sounds fine to me. I'll get Coda and maybe Slash to help out with the access tunnel, and maybe you can go chat with Telar about how this works? Oh, and does Violet have access to assigning a Voice yet?

"Can you make a Voice yet, Violet?" Teemo listens for a moment before nodding. "It sounds like it, but she doesn't know who to designate."

It's a pretty big decision. I remember needing a bit of time to decide, too. Just tell her to think about it, and remind her she doesn't even need to do it before expanding. Teemo nods.

"No rush on designating one, Violet. You might even decide to make a new scion after your expansion and have them be your Voice. Boss is gonna send

Coda to come check Nose's path, and maybe have Slash help too, if it's needed. Imma go see if Telar has any advice on you taking over the sewers, unless you need anything else?"

Onyx shakes her head, and I feel Violet already deep in thought, probably about who to make her Voice. I pat the bond with more encouragement, feeling like a dad tussling his daughter's hair as she focuses on her homework.

Teemo heads for the surface and soon pops atop a bookshelf in the Office of Dungeon Affairs, or as it's actually known: the Dungeoneer's Guild. It looks like she and Berdol are already deep in paperwork for all the happenings with the Maw, so it's the perfect time to shovel even more work onto the two!

"Heya, Telar! I hope you're not too busy?"

The elven woman sighs and looks up to Teemo. "I am, thanks to you, and I get the feeling I'm about to get busier." For all her grumpy demeanor, there's still a brightness to her eyes, like she's never happier than when she has a dozen forms to update, collate, and file.

Teemo smirks. "Probably not too much busier. The Boss wants to know about sewer dungeons. Violet wants to expand up and take them over. Is there anything we should be careful about with that?"

Berdol looks up from his own papers with interest as Telar sheathes her quill in her inkpot.

"Sewer dungeons are one of the few types I'm familiar with, since they're more administrative than adventurous. I believe Fourdock's sewer system is a bit outdated compared to some, but they should still be perfectly suitable for her to expand into. She'll need proper access before expanding, or else she may take over the town proper, or cause an even worse quake than Thedeim with his downward expansion."

Teemo nods at that, so she continues.

"As for how they work, it's rather simple. The sewers are designed to allow easy access by the townsfolk, either via places to dump chamberpots or proper restroom facilities. A sewer dungeon will take the . . . *contributions* and deal with them in its own way. Some will turn the waste fully to mana for the dungeon; others will break it down before allowing the nutrients to wash out downstream—or to the ocean, as would be the case here. I've even heard of one that uses the processed waste to enhance herbalism nodes in its territory."

"And there's no problem with the local authorities about a dungeon taking over the sewers?"

Telar smiles and shakes her head. "Of course not. Most cities actively try to encourage sewer dungeons to spawn with their sewer design. A large, enclosed space close to active mana use is an excellent way to get a dungeon to spawn, even if the specific mechanics are still debated." She smirks over toward Berdol. "Though now there are a few eyewitnesses to grill for details, even if it's likely the situation was unusual." She shakes her head and focuses back on Teemo.

"Regardless, there will be no issue with her expanding to the sewers. In fact, the lord mayor will be actively incentivized to keep her happy and safe as the sewer. Whatever method she chooses to deal with the waste, it will help prevent disease and keep the harbor and docks clean."

"Cool. Boss has Coda helping with an access path. Violet found the sewers on her own, and even heard about sewer dungeons from listening in on the adventurers' guild. Once she has a path, she'll probably expand up that way. Oh, she will probably get a Voice sometime soon, too. Boss is sharing the wealth after the mess with the Maw."

Telar nods and glances at the shelf with the scrolls on the active dungeons in the area. "I'll keep that in mind. If there's nothing else, please have a good day. Berdol and I need to compile the information on the Maw and its unusual spawner, clean up Tarl's request for a new guild branch in Silvervein, and start the file for the new dungeon there, too."

Teemo whistles at that. "Don't let me keep you, then. And don't work Berdol too hard, either. Tarl's gonna need him back once he returns."

Telar simply smiles. "He's a good worker, and thanks to his affinity, he's the perfect assistant for copying forms."

Berdol snorts from his desk. Teemo looks to see several other papers laid out around him, parchment secured as metal quills hover over them. "It's not too bad when they're all the same thing. I never thought I'd be able to use my affinity for something like this." It's difficult to tell if he has a newfound respect for what goes into administrative work, or disdain. I'd wager both.

Chapter 14

Teemo returns and tells Violet the good news about the sewer expansion, and he gets roped into helping her get proper access to what's underneath Fourdock. I can feel how much he wants to be nowhere near the sewers, but Violet's scions are more than happy to hit him with puppy-dog eyes, so he can't just leave. Coda helps keep things on track, though, so I'm confident my protégée will have her expansion area soon.

I can also feel her poking at her mana and at the ally pool, trying to decide how she wants to pay for the upcoming expansion. I feel like I'm watching a kid counting their coins, trying to figure out the best way to get the most candy. Tempting as it is to try to give her free reign over the ally pool, it'll be good for her to learn to budget and understand the value of a dollar. Er, of a mana.

With her distracted with that, it's time for me to tend to my own distraction. I've been holding off on making my Antkin Enclave forever. I think it's finally time to pull that lever. My tunnelbores have been working diligently to make a separate section off the lava labyrinth for me to put them in, and though I think I'd like some extra shortcuts between all my enclaves, it's not anything that would require me to delay any further. And with my magmyrm returned from war, they can get their reward in the opportunity to advance to antkin.

I spend the mana, and the progress bars pop in over about a third of my magmyrm. As a ratio, it's a bit lower than my other enclaves, but I have more magmyrm than I had ratlings or aranea at the time I gave them an enclave.

They start gathering a lot of random things, which draws my curiosity. One group starts collecting from the underground herbalism nodes in and around the labyrinth, which isn't too surprising. I'm sure they can grow something to eat from them. Maybe not from the fool's coal, but there's plenty of other things.

Two other groups head to my Sanctum and start copying down the basics of enchanting and alchemy from Thing and Queen's labs, respectively. Though the two scions are still in Silvervein, I'm happy to see they won't need to worry about their labs being completely ransacked. Designs are meticulously copied to parchment, as well as recipes for the basics.

A fourth group even heads to Jello's metalworks to learn from her, too. They can't exactly hydraulic-press things into shape like she can, but with their natural heat, they can hot-work things like most others could only dream. Jello is happy to teach what she can, and I let my attention wander to the enclave itself as those groups gather. Because in the enclave itself, the rest of the magmyrm are working on making the place a home.

At first, it looks like they're all just milling around, uncertain what to do. It only takes a couple minutes to start seeing what they're up to, though. They start melting shallow lines along every surface, and it looks to me like they're planning where to put everything and everyone!

They draw a winding path through the main entrance cavern leading to the other tunnels, leaving several large sections unmarked for the moment. Then they all descend on one of the larger tunnels and work to expand it. They embrace their magma and scoop into the rock, liquefying it before carrying it back to the main tunnel, where they make a large pile for now.

As the other groups return from their gathering, they set their gains in their own piles, each in their own separate little clear spot, before either heading back out to get more or joining with the group to dig out the main tunnel. The whole design reminds me a lot of the Kobold Enclave. I wonder if they liked the design they saw, or if it's just a simple and efficient way to make a space. At the minimum, I expect my antkin will be much more comfortable than the kobolds were.

The gatherers return once more, this time with a few of my denizens instead of information and basic resources. They have a couple rockslides they're herding toward one of the side tunnels, as well as a tunnelbore ant that a few are riding! That one also heads for the tunnel with the rockslides, where they start widening it out a bit, too.

With everyone settling in to work on the enclave proper, things are starting to take discernible shape, too. I think the main tunnel is going to either be their working area or their residential. It's difficult to say just yet. Whatever they choose, they're clearly planning for plenty of foot traffic. If Coda wasn't already occupied, he'd probably like to take notes.

The entrance cavern is also seeing a lot more work, too, with the magmyrm starting to not only tunnel into the floor but also use the material they excavate to start shaping buildings! It makes me imagine how adobe houses might get made, though I think those usually had some kind of woven fiber core for the walls? No fiber interior for these ones, though. While I'm pretty sure I have some kind of plant around that could be used for that with the magma they're scooping and shaping, I definitely don't have enough to build a small town.

As the temperature starts to rise from all the magma they're slinging around, they seem to realize the issue with the scrolls and such they've gathered. The ones in the entrance chamber have a bit of a freak out before one just starts copying the information onto the floor. Nobody else seems to have a better idea, so before long, the interior floors of the budding buildings are covered in the hastily copied notes.

Man, and I thought my handwriting was terrible. Thankfully, they seem to be able to understand what they wrote, or at least aren't acting like anything was lost. In fact, the magmyrm look pretty satisfied with themselves, and a few even head for the exit, where they start carving the floor of the "road" with a mural. It's a bit rough, like their writing, but it quickly shows what looks like my core with countless ants moving about.

They move on to the next section, and I'm pretty sure that's Queen helping direct them, or maybe trying to protect my core like I had first planned for her to do? Nova they are not, so it's difficult to tell exactly what they're trying to portray, even if I'm pretty sure they're going for a brief history of their spawner.

It looks like the ants are intending to entertain plenty of guests, but if they do, they're going to need to figure out a way to cool things down a *lot.* I wonder if Teemo could teach them how to make pumice? I think that's a volcanic stone. And even if it's technically not, they just need to make the magma form a sponge and let it cool, right? It should give some nice insulation, though it might be a bit brittle for that. Stone with lots of tiny holes isn't exactly a good building material. I could try to suggest asbestos, but I'd rather not give my dwellers cancer, thank you. There might be a magical alternative? I should have Teemo ask Slash some time.

What else will my ants need if they want guests . . . Softer furniture is easy to suggest, but it's a bit early to do so just yet. They don't even have full walls up yet! Furniture can wait. Water will be a big thing they'll need, which is also a good way to sink some heat. I might be able to engineer some kind of aqueduct from the aquifer lakes, but then what to do with all the hot water after? We could try to vent it into the ocean, but I don't know that I want to potentially drain the lakes for that. Getting water *from* the ocean could work, but then, the antkin would need to have some way to deal with salt build up in the cooling pipes.

I don't know too much about saltwater, but I do know it's a pain to actually make it work. It loves to corrode metals, and though it's an even better heat sink than freshwater, the salt could just decide to start crystalizing wherever it pleases. And that doesn't even take into account the fact that the enclave is well below sea level. If something breaks, the whole enclave could flood. Heck, half of *me* could flood. I bet the First Mate from Hullbreak could help out, but it's probably a better idea to simply not do that.

I'm sure they'll think of something. There's plenty of time for them to figure it out, too. Heck, with the alchemy information, they could just make some kind of Heat Affinity potion, similar to the Aqua Affinity potion Old Staiven sells for people who want to explore Hullbreak properly. Or they could do something with enchanting. Or a combination.

It's definitely too early to worry about how my ants will socialize, considering they still don't have buildings set up yet. I bet Aranya will have advice for them once she gets back, too. She wasn't quite able to come back with Teemo and my forces, since she wanted to make sure the satellite church in Silvervein was properly established first.

Until she gets back, it'll be on Larx of my ratkin, and Vernew, Folarn, and Norloke of the spiderkin to help smooth any bumps in my antkin's road to independence. Larx especially has experience in guiding thanks to the spiderkin, and with their help, the antkin should be able to hit the ground running.

Chapter 15

My Ratkin and Spiderkin Enclaves have peeked in on the magmyrm as they work, but there's not a whole lot of new progress to be had there yet. They haven't progressed enough that I'm able to notice much in the way of physical changes yet, either. They're still pretty low slung and have graspers more akin to scorpion claws than hands, though now that I look closer, I think they're starting to get proper fingers and thumbs. They're not super dexterous with them yet, but I know they'll manage.

Which means I can take some time to get started with my forest of four seasons. I'm not going to buy the entire thing all at once. While I probably could, I don't want to drain the ally pool like that. And I want to take a bit of time to set things up properly. I'm planning to go really big here, too. I think the footprint will be close to a square mile once I'm done, and if the tree works how I think it will, it'll probably be close to a cubic mile of room, which is nuts.

The true upward expansion for the tree will probably come at or near the end. As with a lot of other expansions, a bit of prep work will make things a lot less expensive. I don't *need* a mile-tall tree right this instant, so I can pay a bit of time to nurture one for the role. I might even use multiple trees and wind them together. From the outside, it'll look like one huge tree, but if I can technically have it be four different ones, it'll be easier to specialize them for their specific season.

I had considered having the seasons rotate around, but I'm ditching that idea now. I don't want to have to keep moving spawners to stay in their season, and though I could use shortcuts to get the denizens where they need to go, it'll just be more hassle that doesn't accomplish anything but look cool. And . . . I mean, it *would* look cool, but it'd be too annoying to be worth it.

I plot out my first section for the forest of four seasons, which I'll be splitting into three parts. I'll have one wedge running along the cemetery wall and claiming a lot of the area just outside Fourdock, with the tip pointing out into the forest. I'll also take a large circular area from the tip of the wedge before extending out another wedge. The whole huge section looks like a two-blade propeller from a plane from above. The far section will be winter, with summer being the one closer to Fourdock. In the circular part, I'll start growing the tree. But what kind?

When planning out a huge tree, it's easy to think of something like Yggdrasil, but I don't want a world tree. For starters, I don't think it'll be big enough to hold worlds in its branches, nor would I want it to be, even if that was an option. For more mundane alternatives, a giant sequoia would certainly fit the bill, but they tend to grow straight and tall, where I want something that will be branching out and kinda bushy. I want my delvers to have a chance to run around in the canopy, and a sequoia just won't fit that.

Thankfully, magic should help bridge that gap. I think it'll be much more feasible for me to take a bushy tree and scale it up rather than try to make a sequoia have the kind of wide reach I want. Oaks and such are pretty bushy, but I feel like I can do better. I go through the different seeds I got from the Southwood, wondering if any of them would work for this.

Most of them are not for trees, and most of the ones that are, aren't very inspiring. There are two who stand out, though: yew and willow. They both have nice wide canopies that should be able to utilize the full space. The yew has great twisting branches where I can easily picture delvers running along, while the willow has the long drooping branches that remind me of vines. The drooping branches could be a great way to give access to the canopy without forcing everyone to use the main trunk.

The yew also grows slowly, while the willow is quick, and though the yew is an evergreen, the willow seems to like cold climates and is one of the last trees to drop its leaves come winter, and the first to bloom in the spring.

So, which to go with? Could I try twining them together? With the difference in growth rates, probably not. Can I make a hybrid? I'm pretty sure a suggestion like that would get me laughed at back on Earth, but with magic, maybe it can happen? The problem is that Coda and Queen have moved a bit away from just dealing in plants.

But if they aren't really cut out for that, who would be? I'll probably need a new scion . . . but they also might not have to figure it all out on their own. Those two might have drifted away from tending plants, but Grim definitely enjoys a bit of gardening. I think making a hybrid would be beyond him, but he could definitely be a helping hand for a new scion to work with.

The more I think about it, the more I like the idea. My Grounds Reaper helping with the central tree in my forest of four seasons just feels right. I can feel Grim's curiosity as my intentions percolate through the bond, and though he probably doesn't get the full picture just yet, he seems pretty interested with what he can perceive.

That's good enough for me. I solidify my intended area in my mind and spend the mana for it, taking a good chunk from the ally pool as I do. The new area feels . . . fresh and clean; a brand-new canvas to work with! My first order of business is to move the wolf spawner to the far section. It costs a little mana to move it, but nothing too bad. The stranded wolves in the cemetery jump the fence and make their way toward the far wedge, and I take a closer look at the other two sections while I consider what spawners I want to put in.

While I definitely want foxes and bears from the Southwood, the summer and tree sections are practically begging for different things. Or it might just be all the shiny new options dazzling me. There are just *so* many cool things to choose from! I stop myself before I can get lost swimming through the options, reminding myself of my goals: big tree, dungeon crawl.

I'm definitely going to need some kind of Life-affinity scion to help with the tree. Sure, Grim has it, but he's more about it being a balance or cycle. I think I'll need one who's all in on Life for this to work out.

Hmm . . . maybe even *two* who are all in on Life. I have summer and the tree section, so why settle for only one scion? That doesn't really help me narrow down the choices, though. So . . . what should be disqualified?

I think I'll start with eliminating all the other beast choices. I have a lot of beasts, and I'll be getting two more with the foxes and bears. I don't care how tempting the skunks are! Maybe if I expand somewhere beyond the forest eventually, but not for this. Second . . . I should reject the dragons. They're even more tempting than the skunks, but the magma dragon spawner is a ridiculous mana hog. I don't need another one that will happily drink in all my mana, even if they're cool.

Elementals I won't fully cross off the list, but a lot of them are complete nonstarters. Fate elementals sound cool, but I suspect that would be even more of a mana sink than dragons. Life elementals could be cool, or maybe Water or Wind, so I'll keep them in mind. Primal spirits could be neat, especially if they're aspected for Life, too. There are two other categories that are pretty hard to ignore, however.

First is the fey. I could get little bark pixies for a Life-affinity spawner, and if I don't get dryads from that eventually, I'll have to lodge a formal complaint with Order! The other major type I'm considering is plant. There's a lot of interesting things, but I'm liking the living vines the most. They have a lot of options, seems like, and though I'm probably going to specialize the plants and fey for resources once they're upgraded enough, I think they both have the versatility that I can give them combat specializations if I find I need to, once the time comes.

Yeah, I think fey and plants are the way to go.

I set my fey spawner about in the center of the summer wedge, and the plant spawner just slightly offset from the center of the forest as a whole. I think my plants are going to want to stick close to the growing tree, at least for the foreseeable future.

And, of course, I spend the mana to make two new scions. The first one out is my new Pixie Scion, who has a lot less bark than the normal bark pixies. She and her brethren all flit around, curiously poking at everything they find, often breaking off into other groups to explore or play.

The bark pixies look like tiny wood carvings with a flower on their head instead of hair, and butterfly wings. My new scion, though, has more ordinary skin, with bark at her hands and feet, which also coils up her limbs to cover her indecency. Instead of a flower on her head, she has vines thin enough to look like grass, and innocent pink irises in her large eyes, with big, pointed ears at the sides of her head.

I watch her and the others flit around as I consider what to name her. Calling her Tink would just be asking for trouble, same with Puck or Mab.

Man, most pixies are little terrors, come to think of it. Mine looks a lot more innocent, or she's already a good actor. Considering I feel mostly joy and wonder through the bond, she'd have to be a *really* good actor. Are there any other good fey names I could pick, hopefully with less mischievous baggage? Well . . . yes. I'm a bit hesitant after seeing Nova labor under the weight of her name, but I think she's come into her own now and isn't so worried about trying to live up to it. I'll have to trust my pixie is just as strong.

Have fun playing for now, Titania. Grim will be by soon to help you and your sister with a major project I have. Don't worry, I know you can handle it. I can feel a little uncertainty through the bond, but then she spots something and is off to explore before it can settle in. I smile and turn my attention to the other spawner, where my living vines are starting to spread out.

They're really weird, as they don't seem to have normal roots. Instead, they burrow around like a mix of snake and mole, with little tendrils that seem just as good at climbing as digging. For now, most of them are climbing the nearby trees to get at the sunlight, but my Vine Scion herself is situated near the spawner, with only a little bud above the surface.

Already protective, hmm? I think you'll like what I have planned, little one.

I can feel happiness through the bond as her bud expands into what I think is a little orange poppy. A couple other potential names for her drift through my mind, but I think Poppy will fit her just fine. She also makes me very optimistic about the chances of making some kind of willow/yew hybrid. I'm pretty sure poppies are not grown on little vines.

I let my attention wander to check in on the wolves, who all seem to be having a good time settling in, too. The winter wolves are relaxing their control over their Ice mana, lowering the temperature in the area already. They won't be enough to make the whole wedge feel truly wintery, but they'll probably help out with the maintenance for the area after I get the climate control.

I sit back and take a few minutes to just watch my denizens and scions in the new expansion, all of them settling in in their own ways. Soon, they'll be busy as I put in resource nodes and get the interesting seeds planted, but for now, I let them just take everything in.

The forest is nice and peaceful for now, and even though I intend to make it a good place for a dungeon crawl, I think I'll have enough room here to keep some of that tranquility, too. It'll be difficult to balance, but balance is a big part of the theme I'm going for. The cycle of seasons has a lot of change, but there's also a sturdiness to the balance of it. It's like a spinning top, where the balance looks delicate and precarious, but the constant motion is precisely why it's so stable. All I'll have to do is make sure I can keep it spinning.

Chapter 16

Olander Wideblade

The crown inspector does his best to keep his frustration in check. The king had asked him to inspect the new dungeon in Fourdock, though the crown had only become aware of it thanks to the fall tax reports. His Highness might not be expecting anything until late spring, but Olander had hoped to get there and back before the end of the year!

It's his own fault for getting his hopes up. Winter had started so mild, it wasn't unreasonable for him to think he could make it. But, almost as if deliberately thwarting his plans, winter seemed to condense its entire season into a month, leaving the roads and passes piled thick with snow, and leaving him stranded in a small town near Lake Gofnar.

While the town has a couple smaller dungeons, they're just no challenge to the tall elf. Denizen or scion, none could stand before his wide-bladed glaive. At least the dungeons got some good mana for it.

For the last month, all he's had to distract himself with has been the easy delving, the thick dossier he got from the head archivist, and what reports he could get of the new dungeon in Fourdock, or as it prefers to call itself: Thedeim. If it'd adopted the name from someone else, that'd be one thing, but by all accounts, it'd named *itself!* Most dungeons needed several years to be that self-aware, but this Thedeim had done it after only a few months!

If that were the only oddity, he wouldn't even bother leaving the capital, but that's probably the least of the strange things in the reports he was able to obtain. Many scions, close to a dozen by the time the official report was filed. If it had kept that pace, it should easily have over a dozen by now, and Olander wonders just how it can afford them all. Subsuming Neverrest would have given it a lot of mana, but it also claimed the territory, so should have had to spend everything to maintain it.

The only thing he can think of to explain the discrepancies is how active the scions are. There's hardly a delver account of the dungeon that doesn't mention directly meeting one or more scions. They can be seen working all around instead of either staying hidden or being bosses guarding lucrative rewards. Thedeim seems to really only have a single scion that fits that description, and even that one stays in a large maze of shrubberies, hunting delvers and delivering them outside should he capture them.

Yes: capture. Despite all the combat encounters, there is not a single death attributed to the dungeon. There's even a report of a group actively being saved from a tunnel horror by the Skeleton Scion. Olander suspects they must have missed something in the fight, as they don't describe a *fight* at all! Instead, the charging monster seemed to simply collapse at the feet of the skeleton.

Even considering how wounded the delvers were, they should have been able to see some kind of attack. Even with the skeleton having access to Life, Death, and Fate affinities, they should have noticed *something*. The power implied by them missing it makes him eager to square off against the scion. What a fight that would be! Though the other reports indicate it could simply refuse to engage with him.

Despite its clear strength, the skeleton apparently prefers to keep the cemetery, tending to the graves and the grass. There is a mention of a Zombie Scion that the dungeon seems to be grooming to be a true boss encounter, but the details are sparse with the reports so old. He doesn't have much hope for a Zombie Scion to give him a good fight, but it could be possible. With the speed Thedeim was growing, even a slow, shambling zombie could get tough enough to resist him for a time.

Most of the rest of the reports aren't especially concerning, aside from the speed. An enclave of ratkin would be more fitting for a dungeon at least a decade old, if not a century, but fits with the level of advancement. A resident isn't surprising, either, though a kobold is rare.

One thing that *is* concerning is the report of an *undead* resident. It's being quietly kept out of the public records, and though there are rumors, the very idea is so insane that people are usually well into their cups before they entertain it. But the official record is resolute: undead. She even paid taxes! As he understands it, there was a bit of tomfoolery in claiming her old worth as an inheritance, naming herself as her next of kin, but nothing egregious aside from rampant abuse of loopholes. He's no tax elf, so he'll take the word of the ones who are.

He wants to speak with her and get more detail, for himself and for the crown. And with the roads finally declared open, he will soon get to ask his burning questions.

He meets with the merchant caravan as they prepare to set north and finds there are far more people than he would have expected to just move cargo. He has his traveling glaive and ordinary armor on, rather than the more opulent trappings of his office so as to easily be hired on as yet another guard. It's not much compared to his salary, but he'll take a bit more coin along the way.

The number of people is explained by just a little listening: there are a lot of craftspeople heading for Fourdock. That, in and of itself, already answers one of the questions of the king. The increased taxes from Fourdock don't seem to have been from any extra tax burden but from a genuine boom triggered by the new dungeon. Considering the number of smiths and shipwrights, Olander will definitely need to get the updated reports before he does his own inspection.

He meets with the caravan master and is told to simply keep alert. The roads are rather safe, but it never hurts to be careful. He doesn't see a need to assign specific watches or positions around the caravan, instead trusting the guards to handle that.

Olander decides he'll be walking along one side of the caravan, letting him stretch his legs a bit when he goes alongside, and rest his legs a bit as he lets it pass him once more. He starts his patrol as everyone else gets their final preparations, and in doing so, he meets an elf who sticks out among the gnomes and dwarves and beastkin.

She doesn't look like a crafter; not even an enchanter or alchemist. Instead, she looks like a librarian separated from her tomes. Or perhaps a scribe. She looks rather young, too, probably in her early twenties. Her robes are simple grays, and her hair is set in a neat bun. She wears thick spectacles, and overall looks quiet and mousy. It's not until he gets closer to the wagon she's sitting on that he notices the simple wooden holy symbol around her neck: the open hands of Laermali, matriarch of the elven pantheon and goddess of magic.

He probably should have pegged her as a follower from her robes. While hers are much simpler, the goddess is said to enjoy the color and style for easy movement, casting, and reading of tomes. Book dust doesn't show very easily on such a color. Still, her faith doesn't explain why she would be part of the caravan. He dons his best friendly smile and speaks up as he gets near.

"Hello, ma'am."

She starts when addressed, surprised to be spoken to. "Oh! Uh . . . hello? You're one of the guards for the trip?"

He nods, still smiling. "That I am. I couldn't help but notice you're a bit of an outlier compared to the others riding the wagons?" She stammers as he continues. "Not to be rude, mind you. You just caught my eye, is all. You don't look like a smith or a shipwright."

The explanation seems to calm her down a little, and she shakes her head. "Oh, uh . . . no, I'm not. I . . . I guess I'm on a pilgrimage?"

That earns her a raised eyebrow of curiosity. "A pilgrimage? I didn't know the Great Mother had any holy sites this far north. And you only guess? I'm not exactly devout, so please excuse my ignorance, but don't most people *know* if they're on one?"

She stammers a bit before sheepishly nodding. "I'm not sure what else to call it, I suppose? I heard the Great Mother's voice telling me to go north and seek the Ice Sage, but that's all. I don't know what She wants. I'm barely an acolyte . . ."

Olander's smile returns as he nods. "Ah, that makes more sense. I'd probably be confused about what I'm doing, too, if She told me that. What's an Ice Sage?"

"I don't know. But this was the first caravan north after winter. If they're related to ice, I should probably try to get north as soon as possible, right?" she asks, hoping for a bit of reassurance, which Olander is happy to give.

"Makes sense to me. I imagine you'd know Her better than I do, but it seems reasonable. She didn't give you any other advice?"

She shakes her head. "No, she didn't. Which is why I'm not sure if I should even call it a pilgrimage. She might just be trying to help me get somewhere I should be to have a better life. After hearing all the crafters talk, it sounds like Fourdock is going to be bustling soon."

The male elf nods. "That's what I hear. I'll be staying there for a bit after the caravan arrives, too. The new dungeon is supposed to be pretty interesting. Oh! I never introduced myself. Please, call me Olander." He offers his hand to shake as she eyes the blade over his shoulder; he has to suppress the chuckle at such a familiar sight. His weapon is well-known, as is his name. How many Olanders can there be who use a glaive? On the other hand, what are the odds of actually meeting the crown inspector, especially so far outside the capital?

She jumps as she realizes she's been leaving him hanging, and accepts his hand to shake. "Sorry! Uh, I'm Tula. Pleased to meet you."

"Likewise, Tula. I'm going to get back to my patrol, but would you be unhappy if I seek you out once we stop for the night? I don't know anyone in the caravan, and I'd wager you're in the same boat?"

She titters and nods. "I wouldn't mind. The crafters seem friendly enough, but I think they'll be a bit loud for me to want to join their groups in camp."

"I'll see you later, then. Gotta go make sure everyone's safe and stays that way," he finishes with a wink and resumes walking down the line of wagons.

His earlier frustration already feels so far in the past. Soon, he'll be able to get to work, and he'll even have some friendly company along the way. He has no idea what an Ice Sage is, but he'll try to keep an eye out for one. Just because he's not devout doesn't mean he'd try to impede a follower of the Great Mother. Besides, it could put another pretty smile on Tula's face. They may have only just met, and may not meet for long, but pretty things are all the prettier when fleeting.

Chapter 17

I'm not the only one around here doing some renovations. Violet, Hullbreak, and the Southwood all get working on their own projects as I let the forest of four seasons get settled. Southwood designates a new Bear Scion and offers me a trade, which I'm surprised to see. I thought I'd need to send Teemo to talk to the Stag, or at least Leo or Honey, but it seems that being allies makes trading things a lot simpler.

He wants some extra mana to make sure he won't have troubles paying for his bear, and exchanging the climate control ability will definitely get that for him. I take the climate control, but I still don't trade for a bear of my own, nor a fox, though they're near the top of my list.

I think once Leo, Honey, and Thing head back, I'll do the exchange so they can all travel home together. I'm pretty sure the Stag is still hanging out with little Vanta, who seems to have accepted the name now that he's had some time to chew on it. So yeah, once they're ready to head home, they can check in with the Stag and have that trade waiting for them once they pass through the Southwood.

As for its Bear Scion, he's still getting used to the new responsibilities, but I can feel the Southwood getting more information about beyond his borders now, so it looks like it'll be slow and steady. I bet the Stag is going to ask Leo and Honey details about scouting, probably once Vanta's borders stabilize. There's also more of the Southwood's denizens wandering around Silvervein, ensuring the Shield followers won't be the only line of defense if anything nasty shows up.

Closer to the home front, Violet has her expansion going now, too. Coda and Slash helped make what I'm thinking of as a water main from the sewers down to her territory, though they put it pretty high up; it's not like sewer water will help her bunnies or ore nodes, but it gives her a proper expansion path, which she eagerly takes. Her new denizens are interesting, too.

The first is an alligator spawner, or maybe crocodile? I think she technically only has caimans right now, which I'm pretty sure are their own thing separate from crocs and gators. I would complain, but I still remember how I changed Neverrest's wasp spawner to bees despite how much difference there is between the two bugs. Either way, she has moderately sized biteylizards wandering the sewers now.

I think Nose and Legs are already looking for ways to make the water main a bit more accessible so the things can possibly come populate the rest of Violet's territory, but it's not a big rush. I'm kinda glad there's not a lot of ways to travel down to Violet from the sewers, thanks to her other spawner: Decay elementals.

The fresh spawns are called putrid oozes, and they look like a slime mold made from sewage. Yeah . . . not difficult to see why adventurers tend to stay out of the sewers. As much as I don't really like looking at the things, they're shooting Violet's mana up quick. Right now, I think she's turning the sewage straight into mana, but I can also feel her poking through her own options and thinking about the other things she could do with it. I even manage to give her a quest to decide what to do.

She's also still following my lead and making new scions for each spawner. Her names for them are still pretty simple, but Teeth for the small crocodile and Slimy for the elemental gets the point across. Slimy is taking to the sewers well and is more than happy to deal with the new flies and rat invaders. The caimans can help out with the rats, too, but I think Teeth wants to get down into Violet's territory for delving and sink her teeth into the stoats that go after the bunny nodes. Violet deals with them well enough for now, but a few teethy things couldn't hurt.

And how could I almost forget she's chosen her Voice? I was kinda hoping for Cappy. The potential for jumpscares alone would have been amazing. Of course, he wouldn't be able to go out and talk to people and dungeons far away, so I can't really blame her for not choosing him. Nose wouldn't have been *terrible*, but he's out on expedition so often now that he'd rarely have the chance to talk to anyone.

Legs is more of a homebody, but he's also probably the least social of her scions. So yeah, it's not really much of a surprise that she's chosen Onyx to be her Voice. The little shadow spirit is already in the spawner, ascension bar ticking up. I wonder if she'll have a large change like Fluffles gaining wings, or if she'll be basically unchanged, like Teemo.

Not to be outdone, Hullbreak got his expansion, too. I think if he stretched, he could have gotten all the way to the stony beach I invaded him from so long ago, but he wouldn't have had much leftover to actually build with. Instead, he's claimed some cliffs not too far away.

It'll take some work to make them a place to actually delve, but he's already testing those waters. His crabs are having a go at the cliffs below the waterline, but even after he upgrades the spawner to get more of them, I don't think they're going to quite be cut out for the job. They're making some progress, but it'll take a long time before they have anything suitable for people to delve in.

He's too old to get a free spawner or two, so I think he's mulling over a new one and maybe a new scion to help with it, but he hasn't made any decisions just yet. Personally, I think he should use Water elementals. He *has* to have access to them by now, and they should be pretty easily able to dig out a cool oceanside cave. Still, he hasn't asked for advice, so I'll refrain from giving it, even if I really, *really* want to. He's a smart dungeon; I know he'll figure something out.

He also has new invaders, which seem to be evil seagulls. They try to snatch up catches from the fishermen or snap up fish and denizens that get too close to the surface. They can't take anything big, but they are very annoying. The Quartermaster is marshaling the troops to counter them, so I don't think they'll be too much of a problem for much longer.

My own new invaders have shown themselves, and they're rather insidious, especially considering what I want to do with the big tree. I'm getting boring bark beetles. I don't mean boring as in uninteresting; I mean boring as in holes. Holes are not good for trees, generally speaking. Thankfully, my chosen spawners are perfectly suited to thwarting the things. My bark pixies might look cute, but so do ladybugs, and just as the ladybugs have a voracious appetite for aphids, my pixies have an unquenchable desire to eradicate the bark beetles.

The living vines, on the other hand, help heal the trees and plug up the wounds, ensuring nothing happens to the lumber. I'm definitely going to want to make a lumber node later. For now, I'll leave it alone until I can talk with the Southwood about what kinds he wants, and what kinds I should use. I think I might focus more on firewood and wood for making charcoal, and he can have the more structural timbers, but we'll have to hash that out later.

My new scions are stepping up, too. With the climate control option, I designate both the summer and winter quadrants, and Titania and Poppy leap at the chance to get the bounty of fancy wild seeds into the ground. The little pixie even starts commandeering my fruitbats to ensure the seeds grow healthy and cost me just a song to officially designate some new herbalism nodes.

Poppy also gets a few fruitbats, but she's more interested in wrangling a couple ratlings to help her plan out the central tree. Thumbs and garden tools are going to be a big help for her project. I don't know if she managed to hear me musing between willow and yew or if that's just the actual best choice, but either way, she's growing a few small saplings of each in the central area.

I mean, even "sapling" is a bit grandiose for what they are right now, but they're growing quickly; even the yew. I don't know if she's going to hybridize them or maybe graft, but either way, they will need to grow a bit first. I really hope she can somehow magically hybridize them, giving the elegant beauty of a willow and the twisting branches of the yew. I bet if she can't on her own, Thing and Queen would be more than happy to help with alchemy or enchanting.

Even with Poppy boosting the growth of the little trees, she has plenty of time to promote growth elsewhere, too. I think she's taken some inspiration from the hedge maze and wants to make the sections of the forest similar to that, but on a much grander scale. I think that'll work perfectly, too. There won't be a Tiny hunting people in the forest of four seasons, but that just means they can focus a bit more on the encounters.

I need to work on them more, too. It'd be easy for me to make the whole place a wonderful little hiking trail with nodes and such, but I can't forget that I want to make a dungeon crawl for the stronger delvers around here. I think it's time to take a good hard look at my spawners and see what I can do to give the people the fights they crave.

Chapter 18

So.

I need some denizens that are fun to fight. I need ones that will make the delvers shout, "Oh, yes!" rather than, "Oh, no . . ." I have some pretty strong ones, sure—I couldn't have beaten the Maw otherwise, but there was also a bit of a tactical outmaneuvering in that victory, too.

So, can I adjust any of my current denizens to fit the bill of a good fight? My dragons are certainly qualified for that. In the lava labyrinth, the delvers seem to love fighting the wyrms and the basilisks, even with the significant burns they can inflict. The problem is I don't know how good of an idea it would be to have those Magma-affinity dragons cutting loose in the forest. While I'm pretty sure Titania and Poppy can keep conflagrations to a minimum, I don't want one mistake to set the whole forest ablaze. I might let a couple into winter, but I think, for the most part, my dragons are going to be staying in the labyrinth.

My other good potential for a good fight are the twinsnakes. The default variety has a good combo with the Poison-magic head and Kinetic other head, and it gets even better when upgraded with the metal transmutation and Electric Affinity potion. I bet they'll be able to wander three of the four seasons without much difficulty, and the tree shouldn't be a problem for them, either.

The only real problem is they're slow to spawn, and the alchemically boosted ones are even slower. They keep some of the buffs between spawns, but need pretty regular maintenance to keep everything going. I'll probably try to encourage Queen to step up production of alchemy soon, which I doubt she'll be upset about. I can also upgrade the spawner to speed up the twinsnake rate, and maybe even get whatever's next! I think I still have a type before the semi-intelligent capstone denizen, too.

I'll wait to upgrade the spawner until I get the tree growing or grown, I think. I want to make sure there's more than enough room for them to wander around.

Unfortunately, I don't think snakes are going to do it for the entire forest. They'll be good anywhere except winter, but I want a bit more variety. Bears will be the bruisers for their season, probably fall, or maybe spring. Maybe even both. They could be a big presence on the ground with my noodles more in the tree. Wolves will also be big on the ground, I expect, and especially prevalent in winter. In fact, I take a moment to upgrade the wolf spawner to get more tundra wolves to fill the place out a bit.

Let me see . . . can I do anything with my other established spawners? It's kinda tempting to buy more, but I shouldn't buy some fancy shiny new thing when I already have something that can do the job.

Let's see . . . rats? No. Spiders? No. Or . . . maybe? They've been living in the tunnels and caverns, but they could certainly have a good place in the forest, on the ground and in the canopy. They're not tough enough to be full frontline fighters, but they should be good for ambushes and skirmishes. I might even get them to weave safety nets so delvers don't plummet to the ground from the branches.

What else? Snakes? Just did that. Birds? Hmm . . . it *has* been a while. I think the bird spawner has two new denizens before the capstone. They're specialized towards resources, so they probably won't be the best fights. On the other hand, there should be rewards for the best fights, too.

They go on the list to upgrade once the tree is up.

Ants? Leafcutters will help; otherwise, it's maxed already. Which does remind me to take a look at the enclave.

They're starting to look a *lot* different now. I think their earlier lack of change was just a lack of *obvious* change. They were probably rearranging their innards, as they're starting to stand up. I'd call them bipeds now, but they still walk on four legs, with one set of arms as their crude hands. They keep the two legs on each side pretty close most of the time, only really spreading their stance if they need stability or leverage for something heavy.

That aside, they're still building their enclave, and occasionally chatting with the leaders of my other enclaves. It's good to see them all working together like that. It makes me feel better about focusing on the forest, knowing they're all fine.

Other spawners to check on . . . my three undeads? The skeletons and zombies will fit right in with spring, thanks to their verdant and fungal natures, respectively. It'll be good to let them play with people besides just the Shield followers; they're not the only ones who need experience with the undead. Sure, anyone can head into the crypt complex to rumble, but the Shield definitely has a strong presence in there. In the forest, I think there will be a bit less of a monopoly.

The hands will probably spend a little time in the forest, but I don't think they're going to be a major force there. My slimes? Nah, they can stay in the underground, helping my nodes and veins. In fact, I should upgrade them and see if there are bigger ones who can significantly boost the limestone quarry.

Wolves? Already planning on using them. Dragons? Already planning on *not* using them. Earth elementals? Hmm . . . maybe. When preparing for the Maw, I was considering upgrading them to be heavies to plop on the front line and really mess with whatever it might do, but I ended up using the basilisks for that instead, and never did upgrade or specialize them. Those would be easy to slot in as good, tough opponents, and they should be able to handle any of the seasons, too. I keep them in mind as I continue down my list.

Bats? Already specialized for resources, though I should probably upgrade the spawner. The forest is going to be gigantic, so I'm going to want plenty of fruitbats to keep things running smoothly for herbalism nodes. Their spawner is also pretty woefully out-of-date. I basically specialized it and forgot about it. But even that is better than what I've been doing with my bees.

When I took Neverrest's territory, I immediately swapped the wasp spawner he had over to bees, made Honey my scion, then . . . never touched it again. Maybe an upgrade or two, but it's not even specialized! They make honey just because that's what they do, but they're not actually specialized toward resources at all.

I could change that right now . . . or I could try something. I don't want to move them away from making their honey, but that doesn't mean they can't be specialized toward fighting, too. I could even specialize them toward magic, and as fun as it would be to have spelling bees, the idea of fighting bees is growing on me the more I think about it.

And I can't forget my two newest spawners. If I upgrade the fruitbats, they might be able to handle all the nodes out there with the help of the leaf-cutter ants, leaving my fey to potentially be specialized toward fighting or magic, and similar with the vines. I think it's too early to plan ahead for them just yet, though. They're going to be major parts of the forest, but I don't need to cram them into a niche just yet. For now, I'll wait and see how they develop, and fill the gaps with my other spawners.

Alrighty . . . sneks and birbs are on the list for upgrades, but need to wait for the tree. I can let some of the twinsnakes migrate to the forest, along with probably most of the widow spiders, too. Undead for spring, but that can wait until I actually buy the land for spring. Earth elementals, bats, and bees, however . . . are all on the short list for upgrades. Earth elementals are classic tanks for a reason, and even if I specialize the spawner for bruisers, I should still get plenty of my sneaky little rockslides to scout out any other things like the Maw who might need to be dealt with.

I take a closer look at the spawner to see if there's anything that catches my eye for options on that path, and see something interesting: Soil elementals.

While they don't have the raw defense of their rockier cousins, they seem to have a lot of regeneration and gain Life affinity, too. The more I look at them, the more I like them. Rockier elementals basically require things like hammers or picks and are a hard counter to any kind of blade. These, however, can take a good beating no matter the weapon.

I smile to myself and spend the mana before watching a Soil elemental flow out of the Earth elemental spawner like it just emptied a wheelbarrow. It mounds itself up and starts wandering the caverns for now, so I let it find its bearings. I'd poke Titania and Poppy to come take a look, but I'm not done yet!

I pump mana into the bat spawner, too, upgrading it until it gives me a new option as well: a rainbat. It looks a lot like the flying foxes I already have, but a dull blue color. It also seems to like the day more than they do, and it takes off from the belfry, leaving a faint colorful trail behind it. My new bat has Water affinity, which is cool, and it's not difficult to guess what it will do with that. It starts with a circuit of the manor, watering the herbalism nodes and perking them up before it makes its way toward the forest. *Good bat, you know what you're doing. Keep it up!*

And for my last trick for now, I specialize the bee spawner for fighting, upgrading it until I get a new bee, too: the bumblebee. Back on Earth, they don't even get as big as a thumb, but my bumbles are about the size of a fist . . . and also have the kinda derpy adorability bumblebees entail. They start meandering around the cemetery as I finally nudge Titania and Poppy to come take a look at the new friends for their forest.

Titania radiates excitement as she rushes to meet the new bees; I can already picture the pixies riding them into battle. Poppy works her way toward the caverns, quickly digging her way toward the Soil elementals with great interest. I watch them both as they go, wondering if I might specialize their own spawners to harmonize with the bees and elementals.

My two new scions make it to the denizens quicker than I would have expected, but watching them makes it easy to see why they were so eager. Poppy starts digging through the Soil elemental once she gets there, which doesn't seem to harm it, while Titania is trying to help the bumblebees find good places to make their own little hives. I hum to myself as I watch them all, enjoying how life sometimes can just . . . fit together.

Chapter 19

Berdol

This has probably been the busiest winter of Berdol's life. Usually, the tabby catkin spends the snowy months in and around the adventurers' guildhall, enjoying the warm hearth, good drink, and loud company. If he's ambitious, he'd commission a new blade or armor or something else, but in general, the winter months are a time to relax.

Of course, life rarely lets a good routine like that continue for long. He had expected to be busier this winter, thanks to apprenticing to Tarl and joining the Dungeoneer's Guild, but that busyness was supposed to be spent learning, reading information on dungeons, maybe taking the inspector exam or filling out forms; the kind of busyness that can be satisfying but not exciting.

But then Thedeim declared war on a distant dungeon no one knew about. And he formed an alliance between himself and the Southwood, which is a status the guild vaguely knew about but had basically been a legend until now. And that doesn't take into account his apparent *apotheosis!* He and Tarl could hardly miss the orange wave that signified Thedeim's true ascendance, though the catkin had been perplexed when the elf didn't even mention it into his note stone.

"Aren't you going to mention that?" he'd asked, which earned him an immediate shake of the head from the elf.

"Nope. The guild doesn't have any regulations for this. Dungeons are often worshiped by their dwellers, and sometimes even get a following among delvers, but there's no guides for what to do if one achieves true divinity."

"Shouldn't we tell them, though? It seems important," he'd insisted to the shrugging elf.

"If it were a different dungeon, maybe. But I don't think Thedeim will really change much because of it. His changes for getting all the mana from the Maw will have a more direct impact on the guild. You can note it if you want, but I don't think it'll really do much."

Berdol had, but after seeing the aftermath of the subsumation of the Maw and learning the convoluted nature of how it actually fell, not to mention the efforts put into building up Silvervein, he has to admit Tarl was probably right.

Even if it feels weird that the guild would be more interested in his account of the creation of that little shadow dungeon than a dungeon achieving godhood. If he had the kind of mana sense Tarl or Yvonne do, he'd have something useful to put to parchment. Instead, he's putting to parchment duplicate reports to send back to the main guild. It'll probably be fall before they need to be sent, but better to get on it now rather than let it all build up over the year.

He sighs as he sets aside the iron quills, his affinity letting him easily make as many copies at once as he can get quills. He stretches and groans as his joints pop, before sighing in relief this time and looking over to Telar.

Even with him being able to fill multiple forms at once, the elven woman's efficiency lets her far outpace him in administrative work. He had heard Tarl accuse her of being a bureaucramancer, and seeing her stack of finished forms compared to his, he's inclined to believe his mentor. "I think that's all the reports from the winter delvers you wanted me to copy?"

Winter saw the creation and expansion of the section Thedeim dubs the lava labyrinth, a twisting multilevel maze with transportation traps mixed in with more ordinary ones, though they are all designed to mimic the typical death traps of other dungeons, usually using a sleeping effect to incapacitate delvers.

Telar looks up from her tea and nods. "Take a break for now, Berdol. I think copying the new reports can wait until after lunch."

"Do you, uh . . . still want me to start running the inspections on Monday?" he asks, still uncertain about taking that kind of responsibility. He's only an apprentice, after all. On the other hand, Tarl is still busy with Silvervein and establishing not only a new guild office there but also gently guiding the little dungeon he, Tarl, Yvonne, and Teemo got to see coalesce.

Telar nods over her cup. "I do. With Tarl indisposed, the responsibility falls to you." She smirks at him before continuing. "At least, all the local dungeons are friendly. Inspecting Neverrest was especially stressful for me, hoping his stealth would be enough to let him return safely."

Berdol shudders at the memory of the murderous dungeon that used to inhabit the cemetery before Thedeim subsumed it. He never had a chance to delve it before the guild sealed it off, but the stories of the ones who did were generally the kind to earn drinks of sympathy rather than celebration at the guild.

Thinking of how the dungeons around here have changed since Thedeim happened makes him feel a lot better. Telar happily shatters that feeling with her next words.

"You do realize you'll need to delve the sewers if Violet has claimed them, right? I already have a few reports from delvers who say she has new denizens."

The very idea of delving a sewer makes Berdol very glad that catkin don't share in their ancestors' aversion to water baths. "At least Violet probably won't deliberately throw anything at me in there."

"Indeed. I'm also getting reports her Gremlin Scion has gone missing. She may have a Voice for you to speak with, too."

"Onyx? She'd make a good Voice, yeah. And it'll make it easier to teach her how to fight, if she still wants tips with that."

"She may advance to a shade or shadow from the new title, or she may stay a gremlin. Teemo didn't advance his form, so it's difficult to say. I'd imagine a shade wouldn't be able to learn too much more from you."

Berdol chuckles and nods. "Probably not. At that point, she'd probably be able to spar with Rocky, though, so she's not going to stagnate."

Telar nods before continuing. "I also have reports of Hullbreak expanding to encompass the Overlook Cliffs. He seems to be moving slower than Violet, but you should expect at least one new variety of denizen when you inspect him."

"I need to make sure I get a fresh Aqua Affinity potion from Staiven, then. I think I have an old one from the start of winter, but I never got a chance to go delve before everything happened. I dunno if it's still fresh."

The elven woman shrugs. "I wouldn't know. Make sure to get a receipt from him for the delving potions used for inspections. Those will be guild expenses, not yours."

"I don't suppose the guild would pay for my new blades, too?" he asks with a smirk, knowing the answer before she even opens her lips.

"Only if you exclusively use them when on an inspection," she replies with a smile, playing along. "Though we *will* reimburse you for damage done to them on the job, provided you don't deliberately damage them to take advantage of the situation."

Berdol nods at that. "I forgot about the damage reimbursement, actually. I'll keep in mind to have my stuff appraised before I go inspect, then. Thedeim especially can be rough on gear."

Telar finishes her tea before standing and organizing the scrolls on her desk. "Speaking of him, I'm also getting reports he's expanded beyond the cemetery and created two new spawners, along with two new scions. Estimates have the expansion at close to a mile long."

Berdol gives a low whistle. "He's not wasting time, is he? At least I can talk to Teemo and hopefully not get blindsided by whatever he's cooking up in there. Any hints for the new denizens and scions?"

"I have an account of a colorful new variety of bat seen leaving the manor, as well as new, larger bees buzzing over the cemetery walls. I only have a report on one of the new scions: a bark pixie, so he has at least a fey spawner now. There are also a few sightings of strange things moving just under the ground, but nothing confirmed yet."

The catkin taps a finger against one of the double-ended blades at his belt as he considers. "Bark pixies should be Life-affinity fey, I think. The new bat means he's upgraded that spawner, and it also sounds like he's upgraded the bees, too. With bees big enough to mention, I don't think he specialized them for resources, but I don't know what he would have done with them. The underground has me stumped, though. He might have picked up worms to go along with his wyrms, or maybe Violet upgraded her moles. I'll have to ask when I go inspect."

Telar idly nods as he speaks, organizing the scrolls before pausing at one. "Ah, I almost forgot. I have a few secondhand accounts that Thedeim has established a third enclave, this time using his ant spawner. A few traders with the established enclaves overheard them talking about the soon-to-be antkin."

That gets the catkin's attention. "Antkin? I don't know that I've ever met one before."

"Neither have I. I believe the Principalities have a population of them, but they seem to be reclusive, or at least don't trust those outside the Principalities. Either way, it would be a good idea to try to get a look in the enclave, if Thedeim doesn't object."

Berdol shrugs. "I doubt he will, but I'll ask before doing anything. Anyway, where should we eat?" he asks as he stands and goes around the desks, capping the inkwells.

"I've heard of a new café by the docks that's supposed to be good. Seaspray Café. They're supposed to serve a lot of fish from Hullbreak there."

"Oh, that sounds good! I tried a little fishing, but I don't have much of a knack for it, so I haven't had any dungeon fish before. I might need to hire a fisherman to help me with delving Hullbreak next week, come to think of it."

Telar smiles and leads the way out of the guild, setting a sign to let everyone know they're out to lunch. "You should consider officially pursuing it as a skill, especially if you end up enjoying the meal. I understand most adventurers try to have at least one crafting or gathering skill."

He nods as they start walking. "Yeah, I can do a bit of mining, but that's mostly because of my affinity rather than any real desire to mine. Fishing could be nice, though. Relaxing on a boat, reading, while I wait for something to take the bait."

The two idly chat as they walk to the docks, where the fish is even better than they could have hoped. Even the bustle of the boats doesn't distract them from their meal, no matter how excited the workers are to soon have new sailors and wrights. The caravan bearing more should arrive any day now.

Chapter 20

Olander

The tall elf hums as he walks down the street, taking in what meager sights Fourdock has to offer. It's hardly a run-down slum of a town, but it doesn't compare well against the capital, unfair as the comparison may be. He might have found the town more interesting if he was still with Tula, but the two parted ways at the town gate. She had her pilgrimage to get to, and he technically needed to follow the caravan to their destination in town.

At least he was able to let her know he'd probably be found at the adventurers' guild if he was not actively delving.

After getting his pay as a guard, he is now making his way to the guild he knows the way to: the Dungeoneer's Guild.

Not only does he need to touch base and get the full up-to-date packet on Thedeim, but he should also make them aware he's in the area. He's technically retired, and they should have no reason to be unhappy at him delving, but he finds it better to let whoever is in charge at the local guild know he's there and who he is, even if he's intending to keep a low profile. It tends to keep misunderstandings to a minimum.

And he *does* intend to keep a low profile for this mission. The presence of the crown inspector can make dungeoneers and adventurers nervous, never mind the ordinary townsfolk. It's best to keep things subtle when he still has a duty to perform. If he feels the need, he can reveal himself and show off after, giving some flowery speech about how good or bad a job everyone is doing, blah blah.

But that's putting the experience before the fight. For now, he focuses on the sign down the road, proclaiming the Dungeoneer's Guild's presence. He always finds the sign says a lot about the interior, and it is already speaking well of the local guild. The paint is a bit worn and dulled from the sun, but the sign is clean and hung straight. They could probably use more funding, but they still take pride in their work.

A bell rings as he opens the door, and the elven woman at the desk speaks before looking up, putting the last couple lines on whatever paperwork she's doing. "Welcome to the Dungeoneer's Guild. How may I . . ."

She trails off when she looks up, clearly recognizing him even without his trappings of office. That makes it easier, at least. He smiles and steps forward.

"Hello, ma'am. Please, just Olander. I'm hoping to not make too much noise about my mission here." He offers his hand to shake, yet the woman continues to simply stare at him. He might even say she's starting to glare before she finally replies.

"Then you can call me Telar. I'm the leader of this branch of the Dungeoneer's. How can I help you?" she asks, setting aside her quill and capping her inkwell. She must have a powerful Ice affinity to be acting so coldly. It makes business easier than being fawned over, though it's been long enough since he's had that kind of reception that he's a bit thrown for a few moments.

He retracts his hand and awkwardly scratches the back of his head. "Well, I'm here to get as much information on the dungeon called Thedeim as possible, Miss Telar. The income for the town as a whole seems to be up sharply, with the dungeon getting the credit. If it really is an economic powerhouse, the crown will want to invest in the town and the roads. If it's not, then it'd be a waste to do all that."

She gives a short nod at that. "Understandable. If I hadn't been here to witness it, I'd be suspicious of the growth, too. Standard price for the in-depth packet, which includes unverified updates if you're so inclined."

"Unverified?" he echoes as he pulls out the requisite coinage, to which she nods.

"Thedeim's growth makes it difficult to keep the packet fully up to date, especially with him seeming to be starting a major project right now." She accepts the money and hands over more of a booklet than a pamphlet, which earns Olander's curiosity.

"So much to know? It's not even a year old yet, is it?" he asks, feigning ignorance to see if he can get her to reveal anything.

"As far as we can tell, he's about a year old now, yes."

He nods at the official line. Getting a proper age for a cloistered dungeon like Thedeim seems to be difficult. And if the Dungeoneer's chief archivist's hunch is correct, it's even more difficult to properly date a Lost dungeon. Either way, it's easier to simply give a date since discovery.

He takes a moment to check the overview, and gives a low whistle at the number of scions. He expected over a dozen, but not that many.

"It really has so many scions?"

Telar nods. "There are also reports of a Pixie Scion. If he continues the pattern, he probably has a Living Vine Scion as well, though I haven't gotten any reports of one yet."

"He, huh? He's already advanced enough to think so complexly?" He skims the nodes and territory features as he talks, feeling like he's scouting a dungeon that's closer to a hundred years old rather than one.

"He was capable of rudimentary communication even before getting a Voice. He was able to coordinate with a group of adventurers to aid in attacking Neverrest, subsuming it before it could subsume him."

Olander nods at that. "Hence him being considered Cloistered. He'd need to be at least a decade old to be that coordinated. Just quietly hiding in that manor, then?"

"That's the simplest explanation, yes."

He finishes skimming the overview and closes the booklet for the moment. "Where is Inspector Tarl? I'd like to ask his opinion on the dungeon."

"Inspector Tarl is currently indisposed."

"Is he hurt?"

Telar smirks and shakes her head. "No. He is currently establishing a Dungeoneer's Outpost in the subterranean town of Silvervein. It had a murderous dungeon that called itself the Maw and was worshiped by the emancipated dwellers that make up the town. It was making hostile moves against the Southwood, a different dungeon just barely within the jurisdiction of my branch. Thedeim was approached by the Southwood, and they allied to stop and eventually subsume the Maw. Not long afterward, a new dungeon coalesced, so Inspector Tarl is tending to it in the hopes of steering it toward a more beneficial attitude."

Olander frowns at that. "He didn't just subsume the new dungeon, too?"

Telar smirks again and shakes her head. "No. That's not how he operates. Besides, it'd be exceptionally rude to subsume his ally's new protégé."

"He didn't want his own protégé?"

"He already has one."

That earns a surprised look from Olander, who reopens the booklet to examine it closer. "A protégée *and* a vassal?" He keeps up the act as he scans the booklet, squinting in suspicion as he finds new information. "And a recognized ally. Not just a temporary arrangement? I don't think I've ever seen that before."

Telar's smirk turns predatory. "I would recommend getting the full packet on the other local dungeons, too. Thedeim has a close relationship with all of them."

Before Olander can contemplate the damage to his wallet or business stipend, the bell dings again as a catkin enters.

"Alright, Telar! I got everything apr—Oh! Uh . . . hello?" The catkin quiets as he steps in properly, more like an employee who doesn't want to interrupt his boss rather than someone recognizing who Olander is. The elf smiles and offers his hand to shake.

"Ah, hello! Are you one of the inspectors? I'm Olander."

The catkin takes the offered hand. "I'm Berdol, and I'm just a junior inspector, apprenticed to Tarl."

Telar speaks up from her desk, looking calculating as she does so. "Mister Olander here is a retired inspector, and I believe he's looking to do a bit of dungeon tourism. If he agrees to be your subordinate on the upcoming inspections, I can waive his fee for information."

The crown inspector doesn't know what to say, which gives the junior ample time to offer his own input. "Oh, that'd be great! An outsider's perspective will help me make sure I'm not missing anything, and if he's strong enough to retire, he should be able to put the dungeons through their proper paces better than I can!"

Now, wait just a moment! He raises a finger to start listing his objections, but falters in the face of Telar's utterly unflapped gaze. He's supposed to just be looking into Thedeim, not all the other dungeons around here!

But . . . what about his cover? He doesn't want to draw any attention, and if he contradicts Telar on this, it will definitely come out that he's the crown inspector. Then he'll be crushed under the need to make appearances, give speeches, and generally have to be a public figure! He glares at Telar as she sips from her cup of tea. Where did she even get that?

He's experienced enough in a fight to know when he's beaten, and so tries not to sag as he turns back to Berdol. "That sounds like just the thing to help me knock the rust off. What're your plans?"

Berdol smiles with excitement. "Then let's get your gear appraised! And how are you at fishing?"

Olander gives him a confused look at the non sequitur. "Fishing?"

Berdol nods as he leads the way toward the exit; Olander can feel Telar's eyes on his back. "Yeah. Hullbreak has a lot of fishing nodes, but I'm a terrible angler. If you can fish, that'll make it a lot easier to delve him."

". . . Isn't Hullbreak a rather nasty belligerent?" he tries, glancing back to the elven woman sitting at her desk, who looks like a lioness watching her cub take down a wounded gazelle.

"Berdol will fill you in on the details, Mr. Olander. I'll have your reimbursement and other reports prepared by the time you return."

He lets Berdol drag him out, feeling less and less abused by Telar's manipulation as information pours from the eager catkin. Thedeim basically rehabilitated Hullbreak, even after it threatened to wipe Fourdock off the map? Not only that, but his Conduit somehow redirected the energy of the hurricane back onto the scion that summoned it, before Thedeim vassalized the older dungeon. He's getting a lot more details than the reports, which lends credibility to the chief archivist's theory.

That kind of cunning and creativity is beyond a cloistered dungeon, even a Fate affinity. Maybe she wasn't insane by entertaining the theory of Thedeim being an ancient Lost dungeon. Communicating before a Voice, forming a recognized alliance, and wielding magic like that . . . There is definitely more to this than he was expecting. He hopes he and Berdol delve Thedeim last. He'd like to have a bit of time to try to plan how to handle him, and delving the other dungeons should help with that.

As long as his influence isn't *too* impactful on the other dungeons. He gets the feeling he won't be that lucky.

Chapter 21

Tula

Here she is: Fourdock. The trip here was thankfully quiet and peaceful, possibly because of Mr. Olander. He looks a lot like what the crown inspector is supposed to look like, but she finds it difficult to imagine someone as prestigious as that taking a job as a simple caravan guard to such a distant town. While fun to imagine she spent her evenings chatting around a fire with someone who personally knows the king, such a thing definitely belongs in the imagination rather than reality.

And the reality is that he's just a nice, handsome elf, and the trip was better for having met him, if a bit chilly. She'll need to get used to chilly, if this is where the Great Mother thinks she should be for a while, possibly even her entire life. And if this is where she can find an Ice Sage, she'll *definitely* need to get used to being cold.

At least she'll get to have a warming spring and all of summer to try to prepare for a cold fall and colder winter. But . . . how should she prepare? She didn't really have much of a plan besides getting here. She has a bit of coin saved up from living with her parents, but she doesn't know how long that will last her. It's too bad there's probably no library here for her to assist with.

Or maybe there is? She doesn't have any better plans right now than to try to ask a few of the locals. She starts following the flow of traffic toward the center of town, taking a few moments to ask the passersby if there's a library that needs scribes. Most of the townsfolk shake their head at her, but a rather burly minotaur man seems to be better informed than most.

"No real public library, I'm afraid. There's a scroll and book store a couple blocks that way; the Tattered Scroll. I think they do more enchanting and magic stuff, and cater to adventurers. I've never looked inside, honestly. The Church of the Crystal Shield has their historical archives, but that's probably not what you're after, either," he says with a chuckle, glancing at her holy symbol.

She shakes her head politely. "No, probably not. While the Shield and the Great Mother get along well, I'd imagine their own acolytes are more than able to tend to their histories."

He nods at that, reaching a hand up to pick at the tip of one of his horns as he thinks. "Well . . . the various guilds have their collections. The Dungeoneer's Guild probably won't let you at their knowledge without joining or paying them handsomely for the privilege. Hmm. You might try the local adventurers' guild: Slim Chance. I hear their collection of monster knowledge could use a dedicated hand. Yvonne tends it as best she can, but she's an active adventurer, too."

Tula considers the options and smiles at the minotaur, giving him a small bow of respect. "Thank you, sir. You've been most helpful."

"Any time, little lady. If you ever need flour, come find me at my mill. It's the only one well inside town, since I can mill by hand!" He smiles jovially before taking his leave, letting Tula chew over the options as she continues to follow the traffic.

The shop could be a good place to try, but she is very likely to be unqualified. Even as a follower of the Mother of Magic, her enchanting ability is . . . lacking, to say the least. Such a shop would want her to enchant scrolls, not copy ancient tomes. Should she try the adventurers' guild, then?

The idea of her joining such a guild makes her smirk at the absurdity. She's no adventurer. Although, if the kind miller minotaur is correct, they might specifically *not* want an adventurer to tend their library. She should probably stop by eventually anyway, to see about the price of creating a quest to find an Ice Sage.

Her musings are interrupted by the realization that the traffic is growing thicker as she approaches the center of town, with much of it seeming to flow toward a large, creepy-looking manor. Is that the dungeon everyone is so excited about? She can't imagine any other reason for so many people to be headed that way, though the type of people is not what she would usually expect from adventurers.

While she can pick out a few individuals and small groups who look like seasoned veterans, most of them look like ordinary townsfolk, or maybe crafters of varying professions. She slips out of the flow and into the calm of an outdoor eating area just outside a bakery of some kind. The wondrous scents coming from inside call her to enter, but she resists for now, choosing instead to try to listen for any details.

She's heard of active dungeons in the center of towns before, but this is the first she's ever seen. Most are at the outskirts, or maybe in the sewers, but this one seems almost in the dead center of town! That implies it used to belong to a local lord, possibly a founder. They must have been deposed in disgrace at some point, if the new lord decided to not move in.

The questions as to the origin of the manor urge her to try to find the adventurers' guild. Surely, they would have information on a location that became a dungeon! The temptation of knowledge makes her drool a little, or maybe it's the bakery she's standing outside of. A rumble from her stomach confirms the cause, so she gets in line to purchase something.

Inside, she finds a very rotund troll woman tending the ovens, while a tall, thin troll man works the counter. Most people are getting what's apparently called cobble bread, with the option of cheese or no. It looks like a bunch of small rolls baked in too small a pan and fused together, which seems like an odd choice to Tula, until she sees someone enjoying it. The little rolls can be easily pulled from the whole, giving a nice bite-size morsel to enjoy.

She is so getting some with cheese.

When she reaches the counter, the troll smiles at her with a twinkle in his eyes. "Ah, you're new! Gonna have some lunch then delve Thedeim?"

"Um . . . Thedeim?" she asks, knocked from her thoughts by the question.

His smile simply gets bigger. "Ah, *very* new, then! Welcome to Fourdock, miss. If you're delving, we recommend the fortified cobble bread. Guaranteed to help you tough out a hard fight! If not, the normal cobble bread is just as tasty, minus the buff and markup, heh."

"Oh, uh, no delving for me, no. I wouldn't know what to do in a fight. Normal cobble bread please. Uh, with cheese!" she quickly adds.

The troll nods and offers her a clump, as well as a small sweetroll. "No charge for the roll, miss. It always pays to give a new customer a little something extra. Anyway, if you're going to be in the area for a while, you should try delving Thedeim at least once. He's a dungeon unlike any other!"

Tula smiles awkwardly and nods as she pays. "I'll uh . . . keep that in mind. Oh . . . do you know where the adventurers' guild is? I've heard their book collection is in need of a practiced hand," she explains, not wanting to give the impression that she's interested in delving after all.

The troll simply laughs away her awkward explanation before responding. "The Slim Chance is about five blocks away. Just turn left and fight the flow; you'll eventually find the guild at the headwaters of the people coming to delve, heh."

"Thank you, sir, for the directions and dessert!" She grabs a simple wooden plate and takes a seat outside to enjoy her bread and roll as she tries to get over her social awkwardness. At least the people of the town are friendly. Usually, if a town is having a boom, there are some who resent outsiders, not wanting their own slice of the pie to be thinned to make room. From the attitudes she's seen so far, the prevailing opinion is there's plenty for everyone.

From how many people she watches enter the dungeon as she eats, it's probably because of the dungeon. Plenty of people enter, and most of the ones leaving seem to be in high spirits, even the ones nursing injuries. She shakes her head as she watches an elf with a broken arm laugh with his companions. Only adventurers could be so blasé with their lives. How many enter those gates and never get the chance to walk back out? She can only guess.

Her melancholic mood only lasts as long as it takes her to reach her sweetroll. The honeyed treat knocks such dour thoughts clean out of her head and lets her simply enjoy the treat. The adventurers know how dangerous their line of work is, she supposes. They would probably balk at the idea of organizing a messy shelf of books just as she would balk at the idea of facing some slavering monstrosity. To each their own.

She feels much better with a full stomach as she returns the wooden plate, then follows the directions to the adventurers' guild. It looks like the stream is fading, making her imagine she witnessed a change of shifts in the dungeon, as ridiculous as the notion sounds to her. Inside, the guild looks much like a tavern, though with one wall occupied with quest notices, and the space behind the bar full of trophies as well as bottles of liquor. Also behind the bar is a thin orc, clearing away a few dishes.

His eyes land on her, and he nods before turning to his sink, silently acknowledging her presence and letting her know there's no rush. He'll be washing dishes until she needs him. She gladly takes the time to try to gather her thoughts and look over some of the posted quests. Over half of them are for something in Thedeim; it looks like there's a lot more to that dungeon than just the abandoned manor. Most of the other quests are for other dungeons, with a few not specifying which to delve at all. There are also bounties for criminals, requests for scouts, requests for more mundane help like getting firewood, and more.

Seeing the variety helps her feel more confident in the odd request she'll be making. While most of the quests are in dungeons, it's not a requirement. Her Ice Sage may be a special encounter in a dungeon, or it may be something else. Either way, she makes her way to the bar, where the orc is already drying his hands, waiting for her.

"Hello, miss. Are you here to sign up, or are you looking to post a quest?" he asks with a smooth confidence.

". . . A bit of both, I think? I've heard you have a library in need of a scribe, or even librarian?"

He chuckles at that and nods. "It wouldn't be a terrible thing to have someone else working on it. Yvonne does a good job when she's here, but she can't always be. I can probably afford to hire an actual librarian. You also had a quest to give, yeah?"

Her confidence at tending books wavers in the face of needing to explain her quest, but it needs to be done. She takes a moment before explaining. "The Great Mother sent me north to seek the Ice Sage, but I don't know what that is. I'd like to set a quest for help, but I don't know how much I can pay."

"Hmm . . . an Ice Sage? Haven't heard of that one. If it's a monster, I don't think it's in my books. If you're gonna be the librarian, you'll soon know better than I will, though. If it's not in there, I'll take your quest personally. I know a few people who know things. We can discuss payment if they turn anything up."

Tula gives him a confused look. "The bartender will take my quest?"

He mirrors her look of confusion before laughing. "I'm not just the bartender! I'm Karn the Slight, master of the Slim Chance guild!"

She pales at the revelation, worried she insulted who she was hoping would be her boss. "I . . . guess that's my odds of getting the librarian job, then?"

He laughs again and shakes his head. "Our motto is to defy the odds, young miss . . ." He trails off, and she belatedly realizes she never told him her name.

"Tula! Tula, Mr. Karn."

"Well, Miss Tula, I think you'll be a fine fit for a librarian. It won't pay as much as adventuring, but there's a small office off the library you can use as a room, if you need one. Do you have anything you'd need to move in?"

She fights a blush of embarrassment and shakes her head. "Oh . . . no. I have some coin to purchase what I need, but nothing else. I thought it best to travel light."

"Probably a good idea, yeah. Well, let's get you settled." He steps out from behind the bar and motions for her to follow him up the stairs and to the library. Honestly, she's seen worse. Although . . .

"Are those bees?"

He smirks and nods. "Yeah, I'll explain later. Just shoo them out of the way if you need to; they're friendly enough. Anyway, you can get a look at the library, and I'll see if my contacts know about this Ice Sage of yours."

She nods absently as she traces the source of the bees to a corner where it looks like a mouse or maybe a rat chewed a small hole near the ceiling. She can't imagine why bees would be in here, but if the guildmaster isn't concerned, she should try to listen and not bother them too much. Instead, she heads to the catalogue, hoping to get a better idea of how the collection is organized, and what improvements she can make.

It doesn't take her long to hope she gets to meet this Yvonne in person soon. The methodology of organization is fascinating; one she hasn't seen before. She'd love to talk with whoever came up with it.

Chapter 22

Today is looking to be pretty busy. Onyx should be coming out of her spawner soon, Hullbreak seems to have decided what spawner he's going to add to his new cliffside section, my own new section is starting to see curious delvers go deeper and deeper, and it looks like Berdol is getting ready to inspect Hullbreak. He even has a new friend, if the expedition reports are to be believed.

And that's just on the home front. Vanta's borders have stabilized now, so the Southwood is giving the little guy some more advice on how to set up nodes and trying to give advice for encounters. Vanta loves numbers, never sending one of his little denizens when he could instead send a swarm. I doubt he's able to specialize his spawners yet, but I bet he'll be aiming for every swarm variation he can get.

The idea of swarms has even had me digging through the complex web of options for my spawners, wondering if I could do anything interesting. My bees are probably the best suited for that, but I don't know if I want that for them; at least not yet. The bumbles have had a few fights with the more curious delvers, but I don't know if I'd call a swarm of them a fun fight. Honestly, once I get the next tier of spawn, I'll probably have the bumbles join the rotation in the manor and on the grounds.

It's difficult to keep focused on my own things right now, though. I kinda want to tag along on the inspection for Hullbreak, but I also don't want to miss Onyx emerging and possibly saying Violet's first words! Thankfully, though I can't personally be in multiple places at once, I have scions who can do it for me.

"I'll go hang out with Berdol and his new friend, Boss. I've been meaning to ask the First Mate if there's anything her Captain needs for the lighthouse. Light, probably, but you know what I mean," he finishes with a smirk as he lazes not far from my core. If my core keeps getting bigger, I'm going to need to ask him to expand the space in the Secret Sanctum. Or just dig out more area.

"And I think Rocky'll be more than happy to wait to greet Onyx. She's been kinda looking up to him, and once she's a Voice proper, they'll have all sorts of things to talk about, I'm sure."

Works for me.

I poke Rocky with the idea and feel eagerness, even as he winds down his training. I dunno if a cooldown is required for scions or for undead, but the routine seems to be working pretty well for Rocky, so I'm not going to force him to speed it up. There's enough room on Onyx's progress bar that he can afford to take a bit of time.

Oh, and make sure to ask if Hullbreak needs anything elsewhere, too. It's good for him to be fully in charge of his new expansion, but there's nothing wrong with getting some help.

Teemo just waves me off. "I'll ask him, but I doubt he'll take it. You have your own expansion to plan; don't go taking on planning his, too."

I grumble as Teemo chuckles before darting through a shortcut. How dare he be reasonable, and even worse: right! Still, goofing around aside, I should make sure I'm not mistaking procrastination for patience. I focus on the . . . I dunno, line of two seasons? Propeller of two seasons? Whatever my half-a-forest is.

Titania and Poppy are working hard, as are my denizens. I upgrade the spawners while I'm at it, upping the spawn rate but not going so far as to get a new tier of denizen yet. While I can see a lot of work still to be done, I don't want to rush it and ruin the whole project. The pixies are settling into their niche of defenders against the boring beetles, while the living vines are spearheading the efforts to plant new herbalism nodes.

They're spreading and growing quickly, and though only a couple of the new nodes are ready for harvesting yet, the more adventurous delvers are definitely jotting down every patch they can find for later. I'm not too worried about them potentially mapping out the place. The lava labyrinth is the section designed to test their pathfinding; the forest is going to be a test of their martial and magical might. I don't mind parties plotting a route to hit whatever nodes they need. The challenges will be in getting there, not in navigating.

I make sure to pat Titania and Poppy's bonds with plenty of encouragement and happiness at their progress. They're both doing a bang-up job already, and Poppy even tries to draw my attention to the yew/willow project. Poppy has a whole pile of seeds for what should be true hybrids that she wants to test, and I give her my blessing to see what they have to offer. I don't know if any of them are viable yet, and judging from how it looks like she's still working on cross-pollinating, I don't think she quite knows yet, either. Still, it'll be interesting to see if any of them will sprout, let alone hybridize into the kind of tree I'm looking for.

If they don't, there's already a pretty strong contender among the experiments in growing the trees together. There are several variations on grafting, but the process seems a bit labor intensive and doesn't quite give the look I want. One that looks very promising is a tree where Poppy is coaxing the willow to grow almost more like a vine than a tree, winding around the yew as a base. Above the ground, it's very promising. The roots might be an issue, though.

Poppy has a handful of vines constantly tending the roots of the two trees, ensuring one doesn't overcrowd the other. I think it'll still work at scale, even if I have to upgrade the vine spawner to have the numbers for it, but I'm not ready to commit to it yet. It'll be a solid plan B while Poppy experiments with the hybrid seeds.

The sudden chill of Teemo diving into the ocean derails my train of thought, and I feel his smug satisfaction as I focus on him. "Ah, the Boss is paying attention now! Done playing with plants for the moment?" he asks. While Queen's version of a water-breathing potion makes it a bit awkward to speak underwater, Teemo is still a Voice, so it's easy not only for me to understand, but the others as well.

Said others are Berdol, who is looking like he's trying to stay professional and not laugh, and a tall elf who looks mildly uncomfortable about the whole situation.

"So, the new guy is Olander, Boss. He says he's a pretty experienced delver, and the ODA hired him to help Berdol with the spring inspections."

The elf looks more confused at that, and is easily able to express it thanks to the Aqua Affinity potion he must have gotten from Old Staiven. "ODA? The Dungeoneer's Guild contracted me."

Teemo waves him off. "That's just what the Boss likes to call you guys. He came up with it before anyone ever told him the real name, so he tends to still use it because he thinks it's funny."

The elf looks more confused while Berdol abandons his professional demeanor for a moment and laughs. "That's just Thedeim. He's a bit odd, but easy to get along with." Olander still doesn't look like he gets it, but he doesn't try to belabor the point. Berdol takes a few more seconds to compose himself before addressing Teemo with a more businesslike tone.

"Voice Teemo, would you be willing to ask the Voice of Hullbreak if she would like to accompany us on the inspection? She seemed inclined to, once we were done fishing." I can feel a ping from Hullbreak, which Teemo interprets before I can really process it.

"Yeah, she's on her way. You can get started on the nodes until she gets here?"

Berdol nods and checks his clipboard, making me wonder just how Staiven's Aqua Affinity potion actually works. There are a lot of complex things that have to be going on to allow paper and even *ink* to function properly. Queen probably would know, but I don't think I could torture Teemo with having to sit through her trying to explain it.

"Let's get a sample of the corals first, then. It looks like most of the seaweed and clambeds have defenders, so we'll chip off a few pieces while we wait for her." He looks over to the elf, who nods with a faint smirk as he replies.

"You're the boss on this one. I'm the hired muscle, heh." Olander pulls a pick from his bag while Berdol produces just a pick head, and everyone swims down toward the nearest coral. The elf quickly slices off a chunk, while Berdol spots one of the sea cucumbers and makes a note, which Teemo shamelessly swims up to read.

"'The sea cucumbers appear unchanged and are still specialized for resources, helping the corals grow. Coral nodes appear to be slightly richer since last inspection, so are likely upgraded. No new varieties spotted as of yet.'"

Berdol yanks away his notes as soon as Teemo starts reading, but my Voice continues from memory until done, and even blows a raspberry at Berdol for his fruitless effort. "Still verbose. Tarl would have probably said, 'Cucumbers unchanged; coral nodes upgraded; no new nodes.'"

"I like to take more detailed notes so I don't forget anything," counters Berdol, on the defensive.

Teemo eases up a bit and smiles. "Fair enough. You wouldn't believe the notes the Boss takes sometimes to try not to forget something. Then he forgets where he put the note, or even that he made it in the first place, and makes a fresh one."

Hey!

Berdol cheers up at that, while Olander still seems a bit confused by a dungeon having banter with an inspector.

A shadow passes over the group as the First Mate appears, smiling at the good-natured ribbing. "The Admiral seems like he has so many things bouncing around the hold of his mind, I'm surprised he hasn't capsized. Still, it works. The Captain is doing better as his vassal than he has in a long time."

Teemo grins and nods. "That's why he has all of us scions, to keep things stable! I can't imagine what would happen if he tried to do all this on his own."

Neither can I.

Teemo's cheeky smile falters, and the First Mate laughs as I turn the tables on him.

"No fair agreeing with me, Boss! How am I supposed to talk smack now?"

You're not.

Teemo sputters for a few moments while I do my best to grin at him before he changes the subject. "Anyway, you wanted to tag along for the inspection?"

The First Mate bobs up and down in the water in a sharky nod. "I do. The Captain also invites the inspector to his Sanctum once he's done." Her eyes manage to twinkle with mischief as she glances at Teemo. "I suppose you can come, too."

"No respect . . ." gripes Teemo for a few moments before he can't hold the charade any longer and bursts out with a laugh. "Alright, enough shenanigans!

Berdol has an inspection to do; he doesn't need color commentary from us in the peanut gallery. That includes you, Boss."

Hey!

"I'll clam up and let you guys get to it. I'll let you know if anything interesting happens, Boss. It feels like Rocky is trying to get your attention."

I curiously turn my focus to Rocky; Teemo's right. Rocky is right outside the crack that hides the shadow spirit spawner, and it looks like Onyx's progress bar is about finished filling.

Time to hear what my protégée has to say!

Chapter 23

Onyx

Being chosen as Voice fills Onyx with conflicting emotions. On the one hand, being chosen is an incredible honor. On the other, it's an honor she would have expected to go to Legs or Cappy; they've been with Violet from the start, whereas she and Nose came after her first expansion. She feels a little guilty getting the title over them. Or she would have, if they didn't seem to be fully onboard with her receiving it.

Legs is much happier tending to his metalworks, creating things for the denizens and delvers. She can't forget the wonderful metallic claw gauntlets he made for her, and she hopes they'll still fit once she finishes adapting to her title.

Cappy seemed interested in the title, but he's enough of a thinker to point out the obvious flaw with giving it to him: he can't easily leave. They've all seen Teemo go on long expeditions to negotiate for Mentor Thedeim, and though Cappy could probably manage to spread himself to the points of interest inside Fourdock, something like a trip to the Southwood would be beyond him.

She even asks Nose if he might want the title, but he seems to have his claws full with just being an Explorer now. He's more interested in going out and looking at all the interesting things around. While that would make it easy for him to go on long expeditions to other dungeons, it would make it harder for him to communicate with the delvers and Mentor Thedeim.

While Onyx is still uncertain about the decision, Violet seems happy, even *excited* to see the gremlin become her Voice. With her new expansion, Violet will surely have a lot to say to the world at large, and maybe even need Onyx to explain to the two new scions how things will work in detail. She's tempted to delay her ascension to meet the two new scions properly, but she can feel the *need* to return to the spawner. She doesn't know what will happen if she doesn't, but she's not sure she even *could* resist for much longer.

She settles for trying to greet them through the mutual bond they all have with Violet, hoping Teeth and Slimy won't feel snubbed as she enters the crack in the wall that holds her spawner.

She hasn't been here since her last lesson with Berdol, and she's looking forward to learning more from him once she emerges. Inside the spawner is so much different than outside, like some peacefully dark version of one of Teemo's shortcuts. Reality works differently here, in ways she can't describe.

She settles in, though she can't quite wrap her mind around how, and feels her thoughts start to drift. She can feel herself changing, feel her *senses* changing. It could be terrifying if not for the bond with Violet slowly growing more and more clear, her happiness and excitement providing a stable bedrock for her shifting form and perceptions.

She wonders how Teemo sees Mentor Thedeim, as his Voice. She and the other scions know Violet is much simpler than he is. She's so much younger, so it makes sense. She can already tell she'll need to interpret a lot more than Teemo probably does. The swirl of emotions she senses from her dungeon is growing clearer, not more complicated. Delvers are fun, invaders are painful, sewage is . . . tasty?

Even in whatever state she's in, Onyx shudders at that thought. It's good for Violet to have a stable source of mana, but it just feels *wrong* for her to think about it like that. She'll try to explain it to her once she emerges, maybe. Should she potentially deprive her dungeon of a good source of mana just because she personally doesn't like its source?

. . . She won't try to make Violet reject the sewage mana, but she can hopefully get her thinking in terms of it being useful instead of tasty. Time seems to pass in a haze as she tries to think of a way to do that, until a question drifts through the bond, quiet as smoke and as easy to miss as a shadow.

What should I say first?

It's not said in so many words, but rather a swirling mix of impressions and memories. Mentor Thedeim is eager to hear her say something, and Rocky is even waiting outside the spawner to greet her once she's done. They expect something, but what should Violet say?

The expectation seems to trigger a slow anxiety in her dungeon, which Onyx is quick to try to address before it can get out of hand, even with her still in the spawner, her ascension not fully complete.

"What would you like to express that you couldn't before?" she asks in her mind, the concept moving through the bond with only slight resistance. The anxiety is waylaid as Violet tries to think, more memories and emotions spilling out of the bond as her ascension nears completion.

First is a memory of fear, of great things beyond Violet's power prowling just outside her territory. Freddie and Rhonda, the orc and goblin that Violet still likes to think of as mushrooms sometimes, her first delvers. First, she thought them overwhelming invaders, but they created mana from fighting her denizens rather than stealing it away. Invaders, but not? Then Teemo and Aranya. The terror of first seeing them is so at odds with how Violet sees them now, and Onyx can feel a bit of shame from her dungeon at how she first perceived them.

Then the offer of mentorship, and the gratefulness of Mentor Thedeim's guidance. He protected her from the scythemaws, encouraged her with her nodes and spawners, even helped teach Onyx how to fight! Fighting is still scary to Violet, but a little bit of challenge isn't *too* bad.

Onyx sends her own feeling of relief through the bond at that. She knew her desire to fight was something Violet wasn't comfortable with, at least at first, but it seems like she's coming to accept it, in moderation.

She's also come to see the necessity of fighting at times. She was elated to see Hullbreak also come to learn from Mentor Thedeim, even if she's having trouble understanding the difference between protégée and vassal. All she knows is her Mentor is helping a dungeon much older than she is. Even old dungeons can learn, so they both should learn as much as possible from Mentor Thedeim.

Then came the problem with the Southwood. While she was happy to see an ally, even if she still doesn't quite understand the distinction, the new invaders were absolutely terrifying! Violet knew she couldn't fight them directly, but when Mentor Thedeim started that big Fate spell, she saw a way she could finally contribute.

The happiness at helping sticks with Onyx as she finishes ascending and makes her way out of the spawner. Her movement is different now. While she could always slip through tiny cracks, she feels like she has to slip *everywhere* now! Her senses come into focus, and she takes the time to examine herself and the extensive changes she's undergone.

Gremlins are small shadows who mostly retain their shape. But now she's a shade, able to freely change her form, to become a darkness clinging to surfaces or to become a figure standing wherever she pleases. She explores the ability before suddenly needing to check something.

Her gauntlets are lying just outside the crack, and she's relieved to see she can form her hands inside them and move the gifts from Legs around freely. She even takes the time to copy something she's seen some Shadow-affinity delvers do and encases the claws in shadow, allowing her to easily move them wherever she pleases.

"That's a good trick, Onyx."

She jerks against the wall in surprise, holding her claws up defensively before she realizes it's just Rocky. She deflates and reaches a claw toward him before thinking better of it and swapping to a hand without a weapon. "Hello, Rocky."

He grins and bumps her fist. "A shade now. You're going to make the delvers jumpy, especially if I start teaching you how to fight properly."

Onyx is utterly unaware of how creepy her grin at that idea looks, especially with Rocky looking just as eager to start training. Before he can lead her to a better place for it, however, he pauses and nods. "Right, Coach wanted me to watch for you to come out, in case Violet had anything she wanted to say to him. Teemo would be here, but there's a new inspector or something that Coach wants him to keep an eye on. So, anything to say?"

The anxiety from Violet starts creeping back in, but Onyx smiles as she speaks up. "Yes. I think, most of all, Violet wants to say, 'Thank you.' Things are still confusing for her, and she wants your help to understand it, and she also greatly appreciates everything. I do mean *everything*, too. She knows there's been a lot of things you've protected her from, dangers she could vaguely see but had no idea how to combat. You've kept her from the overwhelming things, and let her grow with the challenges she can handle. So, thank you."

Rocky is quiet for a few seconds before he dons a small smile. "I don't need to be a Voice to know the Coach is happy to hear that. He worries about a lot of things, but now, maybe he has one less thing to worry about. Or one more thing, heh."

Onyx smiles as she feels Violet's happiness settle over her like a warm blanket, though the new Voice isn't without her own concerns. "That reminds me, though. I want to train, but I should probably try to explain to Violet the difference between tastiness and usefulness."

Rocky looks confused at that, making Onyx sigh and continue. "Sewage. It's good mana, but . . ." She trails off as Rocky snorts in amusement.

"Fair enough. I'll be in the Coach's caverns for a while, or at the arena. Come find me later, yeah?"

Onyx nods. "Yeah. See you around, Rocky." She waves as he takes his leave, then melts into a pool of blackness to more easily make her way to the Sanctum. She can feel Violet's curiosity about what she wants to talk about, and tries to organize her thoughts. Sparring with Rocky would probably be easier than explaining this, but it needs to be done.

"Alright, Violet. Uh . . ."

Chapter 24

Teemo

He may have promised to keep quiet for Berdol's inspection, but a Voice has more ways to communicate than with just sound. He watches Berdol go about his duties, with Olander following his instructions, trying to figure out what the elf is up to.

What do you think of that guy? he asks the First Mate, using body language and a strange something else that seems to be a major part of shark speak. It's not harder than pheromoning back at Queen when they talk, but it is another odd form of communication.

He's suspicious, agrees the First Mate, her own eyes watching Olander's every move.

Don't stare, he directs her with a smirk. *He might think you hate him, or even worse, that you like him!*

He chortles as she glares at him, but at least she's being more subtle with her observations now. *He's very high level. I can't get a better read than that.*

The Rat Scion absently nods. *Yeah, same. He seems friendly enough, but he's definitely slumming it out here. So why?*

The First Mate bobs in a shrug. *Who knows. Delvers are even more complicated to predict than the Admiral.*

Teemo nods to that as Berdol and Olander engage a small group of fighter crabs, which Olander dispatches with a single attack.

"Parting Thrust!" Teemo's pretty sure glaives aren't really built for thrusting, but this guy didn't get the memo. The motion looks like a thrust, but it sends a tall blade of force through the salty water that easily bisects the two crabs. The Voice can't help but whistle, impressed.

Berdol seems to feel the same way, as he turns to the experienced elf. "That was strong! Are you used to fighting underwater?"

The elf smirks and shrugs. "Not exactly 'used' to it, but I've done it before. Nobody ever expects a glaive thrust, so it's become a staple of my style. A good control of Kinetic affinity lets me project and focus the energy without needing a spike to do it for me."

Berdol nods at that, flipping his notes to a new page to jot that down for his own use before returning to his inspection notes.

"How different is it from the last inspection?" asks Olander, looking at the floating clipboard.

"Tarl inspected Hullbreak not long after Thedeim vassalized him. Thedeim got him back up and running, but most of the nodes and spawners were pretty basic in the last inspection. The kelp nodes were a lot less bountiful, for example."

Olander nods, looking unaware of Teemo and the First Mate subtly observing him. "And the crabs?"

Berdol takes a moment to check the notes before responding. "I think you're stronger than Tarl, so it's hard to gauge the difference, but I think they've only had one, maybe two upgrades. Or he's using the basic crabs for the nodes and keeping higher ones for the lighthouse."

The elf hums at that. "It really wasn't there in the fall?"

Berdol shakes his head as he gathers a few samples of kelp. "Nope. Thedeim was preparing construction, but I believe it wasn't started by then. It's not quite finished yet, but it should be operational. Right?" He turns to look at the First Mate, who quickly nods.

"Aye. The Captain is still tuning the encounters, but I doubt they'll prove much of a challenge to Mr. Olander."

He tries to wave off her confidence in him. "If it's cramped, I'll have a lot more trouble than even under the waves. The blade makes a good rudder, but I still need room to bring it about. Just because I *can* thrust with it doesn't mean it's the best way to use it."

Teemo's not convinced, but doesn't see any point in arguing, nor does the First Mate. "Then I hope you don't mind if the Captain sends a few sharks to defend the clam beds. I don't think he was able to send any at Tarl in the last inspection."

"That'd be very helpful, if you don't mind?" adds Berdol. "We only have an estimate of the strength of the shark denizens. I think the only delver to deliberately challenge them was a dwarven ship captain who wanted to fish them."

The First Mate rumbles in mirth at the memory. "I hope he comes back soon. I haven't had a personal challenge from a delver before. He took the loss well, and I can't wait to see what he plans to do better."

Olander gives her a bit of side-eye before shrugging. "I should be able to handle a shark or two. Any specializations I should worry about?"

"Not especially. We're focused for fighting, not for any real trickery."

"Boss should see if Queen can make some go-juice for you guys. Or your eels. Both would fit," comments Teemo.

"Go-juice?" asks Olander, prompting Berdol to explain.

"It's what Thedeim calls the Lightning-affinity serum his Alchemist can produce. In delvers, it behaves much like a hastening potion. For denizens, however, it grants Lightning affinity. I think it needs to be reapplied between spawns, but it's very common to see Lightning denizens in and around the manor."

"Huh." Olander seems to chew on that information as the inspection continues toward the clam beds, with his focus returning as a pair of tiger sharks move to intercept him and Berdol. Where he seemed pretty relaxed against the crabs, he's focused on the sharks. He interposes himself between the catkin and the incoming fish, glaive held ready.

The sharks don't seem impressed as they part, moving to circle the two in opposite directions. Olander moves decisively as they approach, as if he knew exactly how they would position themselves. He wasn't kidding about the blade making a good rudder, as he slashes it upward toward one shark before turning his grip and pushing against the weapon to position himself properly to bring it down at the other.

"Twin Crescents!" he shouts, two blades of force hurtling toward the sleek predators. The first is cleaved through before it can do much, but the other manages to twist and lose only a portion of its tail.

It may have avoided the fatal blow, but with the loss of maneuverability, it can't get out of the way of Berdol's flying blades. "Lacerate!" The catkin doesn't have the raw force behind his attack to finish off the wounded shark, but its remaining fins are disabled, allowing Olander to swim up and casually behead the denizen. He brings the trophy back to Berdol, who works to remove as many teeth as he can before the rest disperses back into mana.

"I think you could handle more than just a couple sharks, my guy," comments Teemo, which only gets another shrug from Olander.

"On my own, sure. While you don't seem the type to try to sneak in and get Berdol, I should still keep on my toes."

Berdol manages to extract an even dozen teeth before the shark disperses, and speaks as he moves to gather a few clams. "I think I'm with them, Olander. You'd probably have to fight the Quartermaster or First Mate to have a challenge."

The elf looks very interested in that notion, turning his attention to Teemo's current ride. "Would you be interested in a fight, First Mate?"

She shakes her head. "No. I'm strong, but I'm not especially interested in fighting delvers. Nor is the Quartermaster, I'd wager. The Admiral knocked the desire to fight out of him very effectively."

"Oh?"

Teemo nods. "Yeah. When the Boss vassalized Hullbreak, it wasn't as smooth as he would have liked. Hullbreak pulled a desperate gambit, selling off basically everything to make an Albatross Scion: the Quartermaster. He's Storm affinity, and pretty good at it, too." Berdol leads the group toward the lighthouse as Teemo continues.

"It was a pretty clever plan, for how desperate it was. He was going to attack Fourdock directly with the scion and a bunch of gulls if we didn't back off, leaving them both to starve. Of course, the Boss isn't that easy to outmaneuver. He sent Poe to stop him. He was doing a good job, until the Quartermaster dug deep and created a hurricane."

Olander frowns at that, "How did you rebuild so quickly?"

Berdol snorts as Teemo grins. "What, you think the Boss can't stop something little like a hurricane? He sent Fluffles, his Conduit. He ate the storm and obliterated the Quartermaster with it, getting a title to boot. Stormeater."

Olander's frown deepens at that. "Stormeater? Did he not have Storm affinity before?"

"Nope." Teemo grins wide, refusing to elaborate, much to the unhappiness of the experienced elf.

"We got a lot of reports from the incident," offers Berdol. "There were more than a few adventurers with Storm affinity in the area, and they all said the same thing: that Fluffles somehow stole the energy of the hurricane and turned it back on the Quartermaster."

"That's not how that works . . ." grumbles Olander, only further cementing Teemo's grin. The elf is deep in thought until they get to the lighthouse, where Teemo has to part ways with the First Mate.

"Let me know if the Captain needs anything for the cliffs, yeah? Boss says you're in charge of it, but that doesn't mean you have to do everything without help."

The Shark Scion nods. "I'll pass on anything he might wish to ask. I think he wants to give the new eels the chance to carve them, but he might ask for guidance with his spawners. The lighthouse will be limited to crabs and gulls for now. He wants to see what the delvers think of the encounters before adding anything else."

"Fair enough. We'll meet back up after they finish with this part?"

She nods, and the three continue into the lighthouse. Teemo thinks Coda really outdid himself with the design, and can only imagine how much the delver masons learned in the project. He doesn't let himself get too distracted, though, keeping an eye on Olander as they climb through the battles with the crabs and gulls.

The elf is distracted, and Teemo doesn't think it's with the architecture. He's not even using any skills to quickly dismantle the encounters. While the demonstration of skill is more than a little intimidating, he can't help but be encouraged by how thrown the elf seems to be. He might be experienced, but he still hasn't seen everything. When it comes to the Boss, he hasn't seen *anything!* If one of Fluffles's titles has him thrown off this badly, Teemo can't wait to see his reaction to some of the other things the Boss has done.

Chapter 25

The rest of Hullbreak's inspection goes pretty well; I might have missed a couple details while listening in on Onyx trying to explain why sewage is not tasty, but it's very heartening for Hullbreak to invite the inspectors to his Sanctum.

He's told the merfolk about it, as they are working on a temple hidden in the kelp cave. They're still working on carving the walls, but the pedestal for his core is pretty nice. It's a triangular column fit for his size, though they'll need to expand it soon, or find some other way to display the core. It's come a long way from being able to fit in the First Mate's mouth. It's . . . about a yard on each edge, now? It'll be difficult for them to make a pedestal for something like that.

Oh, they could make a recess in the pedestal and display it point down. I dunno if his core has a designated up or not. My sphere doesn't, because that's kinda the point (or lack thereof) in a sphere. I'd have Teemo ask, but I don't want to interrupt the little ceremony. Showing your core is a big deal, and Berdol and Olander understand that. Hullbreak is pretty nervous about it, but I also can feel resolve and relief in putting that kind of trust out there. He's not going to be holding guided tours of his Sanctum to the ordinary delvers, but this should go a long way toward repairing relations with the guild proper.

I also consider Teemo's suspicion of Olander. He's easily the strongest person I've seen. Miller, Rezlar's butler, gives me strong vibes, too, but nothing as clear as with Olander. Even if Miller is stronger, he's not going to delve me, so I'm more than happy to chew on the problem that could actually *be* a problem.

While I don't exactly expect he'll be like the trio when they first showed up, trying to attack residents and scions without a care, I don't know if I'll be able to give him the delve he wants. At least not yet.

I want to make the forest hard enough for him to need to pay attention, though I don't want it to be strong enough to be a challenge for him yet. That kind of level of encounters would be *way* more than the other delvers can handle.

He might have some fun with the gauntlet, or playing with the traps in the lava labyrinth, but as far as combat encounters go, I think I only have one that could interest him: Rocky.

If any of my scions are going to give him a proper encounter, it'll be Rocky. Just thinking about it has my Boxer looking excited, his fists a blur as he shadowboxes. He taps into his affinities as he has a proper workout, blending and transforming his known affinities in all sorts of interesting ways. Losing to the empowered Harbinger did nothing to dampen his spirit, and I'd wager he's already working on techniques to counter the combo-breaker moves it liked to do.

Hmm . . . I should make a thing of this. Like a *whole* thing. Rocky's bouts with the delvers have been pretty impromptu, spur-of-the-moment affairs. What if we publicize it a bit? I can already feel Teemo's approval, even as he keeps quiet in the tail end of Hullbreak's inspection.

What will we need? What does any good prize fight need? We need the fighters, sure, but we also need spectators. There's plenty of seats, but I think they can be improved on. It's been a while since the arena was put in properly. The stone benches aren't terrible, but I think we can do more. In addition to seating, we also need concession stands. The smiths and smelters have been making me some good mana working in the mall area outside the labyrinth. If it works for that, it should work for people making food, right? I even could put in that kitchen I picked up.

I poke around the arena, looking for places to put in a few amenities until Teemo, Berdol, and Olander get back to Fourdock proper.

Teemo easily rides Berdol's shoulder as they walk back to their guild, speaking up as they get close.

"So, you guys are going to delve Violet next?"

Berdol nods. "Yep, probably in a day or two. Telar will want to update Hullbreak's packet, and that usually takes a couple days."

"Cool. You know Violet claimed the sewers, yeah? And she got her Voice, too?"

Berdol looks happy, while Olander looks alarmed at the news. The elf can't get his thoughts in order before the catkin replies, "That's great to hear! Well, not about her taking the sewers, but about the Voice. Who did she pick?"

"Onyx. Legs isn't very sociable, Nose is usually off on expedition, and Cappy isn't exactly mobile. Her other two scions are still getting settled, so she didn't want to overburden them."

"How many scions does she have?" asks Olander, looking concerned. Teemo smirks at him, having fun teasing the high-level elf.

"Six. They grow up so fast."

"But how? The upkeep . . ." He trails off as he runs the numbers, which only increases Teemo's smile.

"She's learning from the Boss. And she hasn't upgraded them too much yet, so there's not too much in the way of upkeep anyway. But I wanted to ask about after Violet's inspection. The Boss will be after, yeah?"

Berdol nods while Olander still looks distracted, but Teemo's next words get his attention quickly.

"Then the Boss would like to invite Olander there to a prize fight. I can tell you're strong, and Rocky's just *itching* to fight someone as strong as you."

Olander looks very guarded at that invitation. "I don't know . . ."

"Why not? You'd probably give Rocky the best challenge he's ever had from a delver!" exclaims Berdol, to the frown of Olander.

"That's the zombie, right? I've faced a few Zombie Scions before. They can be pretty good at taking a hit, but they're always so slow."

Teemo snorts as Berdol smiles. "Trust me, he's not slow. He's a strange sort of fist fighter with a mastery of a wide range of affinities. Which ones does he have now, Teemo? I think the official pamphlet is a bit out of date."

Teemo takes a moment to gather his thoughts and totally not to increase the dramatic reveal. "Let me see . . . well, Fate, but that hardly counts. Kinetic, Fire, Ice, Sonic—or Thunder, if you prefer—and Mental."

Olander stares in disbelief as Berdol simply makes a note. "Mental?"

"Yeah, he picked it up from defending against the Harbinger. So far, it's all defense, so don't worry about him messing with anyone's mind."

"That's . . . How . . . *Picked up*?!" sputters Olander. "That's *not* how that works!"

Teemo shrugs. "Rocky has the title Affinity Savant. Argue with the title, if you want. Anyway, are you in?"

"In?"

"For the prize fight. I'm sure Grim himself will be there to make sure nothing too bad happens. He takes the Boss's reputation for safety seriously. So, are you in?"

Olander looks like he wants to argue a couple points with Order, but he takes a minute or two to pace a bit and calm himself down before answering. "So . . . a challenge from the dungeon itself?" He looks to Berdol. "Would the Dungeoneer's Guild have any problem with this?"

The catkin shrugs. "I doubt it. Most of Thedeim's scions aren't really meant to fight, but Rocky is a major exception. There's even an arena in the tunnels specifically for fighting Rocky. The closest ones to winning so far were Freddie, Rhonda, and Larrez. Rocky still knocked all three of them out, but they dug the deepest and were rewarded. Most of the other challengers either thought they could get an easy win or have been using the bouts as a test for new skills."

"Are there any rules?"

"Mostly, just stay in the ring, and stop if the bell rings. There are specifics for groups, but if you're solo, that's it."

"So I can use a weapon and my affinity? Armor?"

Teemo nods. "That's all fine. Rocky is training to be able to handle things like that. The Boss made him to be a proper boss fight, and Rocky has been having fun with it the entire time."

Olander folds his arms, considering. It's not difficult to tell he's very cautious about accepting a fight with my scion. I think he's been in more than a couple dungeons before, so I wouldn't be surprised if other ones might use something like this as a trap. On the other hand, you don't get as many levels as he has by avoiding challenges. I dunno if Rocky can give him a good fight, but even the prospect has the elf sorely tempted.

Eventually, he sighs and straightens up. "I accept."

Teemo and Berdol both smile wide, though I imagine for different reasons. Berdol will get to see one heck of an exhibition match, where Teemo may have just secured me a big pile of mana. "Great! Swing by the manor when you get the chance, then. One of Boss's aranea should have a quest plaque for you. You can even do a bit of normal delving if you want. The Boss has a lot of stuff to interest a delver."

Olander looks uncomfortable once more when Teemo mentions a quest, but he's not backing down. "I just might. I've heard a lot about him, but I haven't had a chance to delve yet. That won't be a problem, right?"

Berdol shakes his head. "That'll be fine. The dungeoneers are pretty friendly with the local dungeons, so I can't imagine you doing anything to change that. Heh, just take the time to read that booklet you got from Telar. Thedeim does a lot of things differently. If you're used to belligerents, it'll be a pretty significant shift."

"I'll do that, and probably stick around the guild to ask questions, too. There's a lot of things I haven't seen before." He looks thoughtful as he and Berdol head inside the building, and Teemo hops into a shortcut back home.

None too soon, honestly. Onyx has gotten through to Violet about how sewage isn't delicious, but now, she seems to be comparing the delvers to sewage. It's in the nicest way possible—she likes them both—but Onyx could probably use a hand straightening that out.

Chapter 26

Aranya

It's times like these that make her appreciate just how much work Larx, Vernew, Folarn, and Norloke do. She likes to think she's been doing an admirable job of learning to delegate without just being lazy, but she's had precious few to delegate to with regards to her people.

At least, Lord Thedeim's second church is going smoothly. The ratkin and spiderkin priests have been providing a wonderful example to inspire the townsfolk, and thanks to how well they get along with the Shield, the people of Silvervein don't feel the need to be concerned about any power struggles between the churches.

The Shield has been getting the greater share of new followers, which Aranya fully understands. It has no connection with a dungeon, and after getting out from under one, most of the pale elves and dwarves are wary about joining up with another. She wonders if they would have been driven out of town if not for the clear wave of divinity released from Lord Thedeim's ascension.

Curiosity about that event got many feet through the door, and His message of love and self-improvement kept many there. From what she's been able to tell, the Shield has been gathering those possessing more of a martial bent, while Lord Thedeim is attracting those more inclined toward crafting of differing types. Here in Silvervein, that mostly means a variety of cooks, though many are starting to branch out now.

And though Lord Thedeim's influence is growing smoothly, her own people are having a much more difficult time adjusting. A few kobolds have decided to follow Him, but a great many more are having difficulties deciding *anything*!

Right now, they're still trying to figure out what to do without the Maw. A few stubbornly want to stay in Silvervein, but the vast majority are in favor of a clean break, a chance to direct their own path. Unfortunately, it seems like *everyone* has their own idea for what path they should all take.

Some of the more rebellious youth think they should try to take over Silvervein, which at least, nobody else is taking seriously. No, the real discord is over where to go and what to do once there. She, of course, argues they should come to Fourdock and join one or more of Lord Thedeim's enclaves. Unsurprisingly, there's resistance to that idea.

Much like the rest of Silvervein, the kobolds are not eager to bind themselves to another dungeon. Most of the elder kobolds seem interested, recognizing how different Lord Thedeim is from the Maw, but her own grandfather is among the voices that dissent from the idea. Aranya is starting to wonder if he just likes being contrary, as he doesn't have any other suggestions for where to go, recognizing the lack of other options.

They could go to Fourdock and attempt to formally immigrate, but considering how closely they work with Him, the kobolds at large don't see much distinction between Fourdock and an enclave. But what else can they do? Just wander off into the Deeps?

They know how poorly they get treated out there. Her grandfather was among the first kobolds born under the Maw, and he knows well the tales of how much worse the outside was for them. Many others would have simply killed the group of kobolds instead of keeping them in captivity. The youth argue what is worse, while the older ones accept that a sliver of hope is better than nothing at all.

Aranya sighs as she sits in the Kobold Enclave, watching them mostly go about their lives. They're stuck, without understanding how much better things are beyond the rut they live in. They've survived there for so long, leaving it is still frightening, even with the opportunities at their fingertips.

She spots Tarl entering the enclave, but can't even muster the energy to wave as he approaches. Trying to convince her people has just been so frustrating.

"Hey, Aranya. Looks like you're doing well," he greets with a sarcastic smile before sitting against the wall next to her. "Still no progress?"

"No," she sighs again. "Everyone has their own ideas for what to do, but it feels like there's no desire to actually follow through on them! They'd rather have the stability of misery than risk what little they have on hope."

Tarl nods at that. "Sounds about right. I've seen delvers consistently come back from delves with broken bones but refuse suggestions to do something different. 'I know how to deal with a broken arm. Trying something else could be even worse.'"

Aranya perks up slightly, as Tarl at least understands how she feels in this. "Do they ever change?"

He thinks for a few moments before shaking his head. "Not often. They think it works, as much as that kind of pain is 'working.' Usually, it takes something forcing them out of the habit. The shop being out of potions, or maybe a delve goes wrong and shows them how thin their margin of victory was, or any number of other things that force them to change."

The kobold leans her head back against the wall, her eyes closed. "I don't like the idea of forcing them, but I'm not sure what else to do. How can I force them without making the decision for them?"

Tarl snorts, earning a brief glare from her as he replies. "You really are fit to be Thedeim's priest. You both can miss the obvious sometimes. Give them a deadline."

"A deadline?" she echoes, not liking the idea of that kind of ultimatum.

He nods. "They know your offer, but there's no urgency to it, so they can keep doing whatever they're doing. Give them a deadline to decide on whatever they want to decide on, then go home."

"But . . . I don't want to abandon them!"

"I know, but you also don't want to force them, right? You've shown them the chest and explained there's no traps. Now, it's on them to open it and get the rewards, or abandon it for fear of repercussions."

"But what if they decide to stay? Or leave into the tunnels?"

Tarl shrugs. "Would you stay with them?"

She opens her mouth to say of course she would, but realization draws her up short. Would she abandon her friends to try to help her people, especially when they would refuse to *be* helped? Would she never see Yvonne or Aelara or Ragnar? Never get to see Freddie and Rhonda grow stronger? Never see Lord Thedeim's new expansions?

"I . . ."

Tarl smiles at her. "It's not really a fair choice, but I wouldn't worry about it being a choice at all, honestly. They'll come with you, even if they complain every step of the way. They're smart enough to see their best option is with Thedeim and Fourdock."

"And if they don't?"

He shrugs again. "Then they're opening the chest you told them is full of traps. Best you can do at that point is make sure you're not in range."

She sighs again and leans forward slightly, sitting up rather than lounging against the wall as she opens her eyes. He's right, even though she doesn't like it. Leaving them to their fate seems cruel, but would she accomplish anything by letting them destroy her, too?

A spark of resolve lights within her, and she nods.

"You're right. I've made Lord Thedeim's case, and they're not stupid. They're just scared. Most times, it's good to comfort someone in their fears, but there comes a time to confront it. Do you need me to take anything back to Fourdock?"

The elf nods. "I have a few reports to send back to the guild, if you don't mind waiting for me to do them. Kennith should have the structure of the town government stabilized soon, too, and I know the townsfolk want the Dungeoneer's to keep an eye on their new dungeon. The Stag should probably head back to the Southwood soon, and Honey and Leo are probably ready to go home as well. Maybe a week to tie up all the loose ends?"

"A week." She nods at that as she stands, her orange pendant giving off a warm illumination that echoes her rising mood. "That should be plenty of time for them to get ready to move. I'll let them know I'll be leaving in a week, with or without them. Hopefully with. I . . . I don't want to lose them again."

Tarl smiles and stands, putting a reassuring hand on her shoulder. "I don't think they want to lose you, either. You've shown them things can change, and despite how much I bet they'll complain about it, they don't want to miss out."

She smiles at him before taking her leave, the elf returning to relaxing against the wall and letting her do her duty to her people. Thankfully, it's not difficult to find who she needs to give the message to.

Her grandfather is still in his small dugout hovel, sitting on a basin of gravel as the most comfortable thing he has. With scales, it's not bad, but her friends were not impressed with it before they headed out to explore outside for a couple days. The aged kobold looks up from his own contemplations and smiles warmly for her.

"Ah, Granddaughter. I was worried the others had badgered you clear out of the enclave after the last meeting. I hope you're not too discouraged," he probes as he reaches a hand up for her to help him to his feet.

She shakes her head as she pulls him up. "At first, but they've made things clear for me."

"Oh?"

She nods. "I won't make the choice for the entire enclave, but I *will* make them *make* a choice. I'm leaving in a week, along with the rest of Lord Thedeim's scions. I want you all to come with me, though you are all free to stay here or go somewhere else, if you wish."

Her grandfather's eyes widen. "A week? Surely you can give us more time?"

"No, Grandfather. I've given you all time, given you all the information I have to give. It's on you now to act on it."

"But only a week . . ." he tries before getting shut down.

"We've had more than long enough to discuss it, and you know it." Her hard look softens as she meets his eyes. "I know how uncertain everything is if you all come with me. But can you honestly tell me you'd rather stay here where the ghost of the Maw shades every memory? Don't you want to see something new, something *better*?"

"We'd be on our own out there . . ." he quietly replies, echoing the hardships told of the times before the Maw.

"We *wouldn't*—that's the whole point. I'll be there. My friends will be there. Lord Thedeim will be there. We don't have to be isolated."

He puts shaking arms around her and holds onto his granddaughter for support. "It's all so much . . . So many horror stories of outside. Even you had a harrowing journey after escaping the Maw, only barely surviving . . ."

She wraps her arms around him, supporting and comforting him. "I know . . . but you know what I think the most important thing to learn from that is? Alone, I was miserable. Together, things improved. Lord Thedeim found me, fed me, saved me. Yvonne, Aelara, and Ragnar gave me friendship. Fourdock in general gave me acceptance. We can't close ourselves off from others, even when we make a mistake in who to trust. I've found people to trust. Now, you all need to learn to trust *yourselves* enough to accept help without fear of misjudging once again."

She kneels with him as the tears flow, a lifetime of hardship and dashed hopes pouring out of her grandfather. She holds him close as he clings to her, desperately holding onto the hope she offers, and she supports him the whole while. Even if his grip should falter, he doesn't need to be the only one holding on. Her own strength won't be enough to drag him up to a better tomorrow, but she knows what he's struggling to accept: they're not alone.

Not anymore.

Chapter 27

Looks like everyone will be home in about a week. Well, probably not Tarl, but everyone else. I'm looking forward to it. Leo and Honey haven't been home in forever, feels like, and Queen and Thing seem pretty eager to get back to their home labs, even if their latest titles suggest they should be out and about, saving lives.

Personally, I'd love to see those titles gather dust, but I'll probably need their medical talents again eventually. I even have projects that will hopefully not involve surgery and triage, and not just for my Enchanter and Alchemist. Those two I want to have look into the composite armor more, and see just how much they can enchant it, especially with full access to my nodes and plenty of time.

Leo, I want to organize more expeditions to keep an eye on the forests and mountains around me. Seeing the Southwood get to patrolling his borders makes me realize the fog of war has probably crept back in around my own territory. Poe does a great job still, but having them work together gets me so much more information.

And speaking of information, Honey is going to have a field day when she gets back. She apparently gave some of her bees standing orders to keep an eye on the library and report to Poe if anything happens, and it looks like something has happened. There's a new librarian! She looks every bit the shy nerdy scribe according to the reports, and also looks good enough at tending books to not just go and reorganize everything on the first day.

In fact, she seems to be gearing up to do the opposite. Yvonne has been working to implement a version of the Dewey decimal system and impose order, which has been slow going but effective. I don't remember the specifics of all the categories, but the basic concept of organizing by categories and using numbers to make it theoretically infinitely expandable is easy enough to remember. Actually putting the numbers on the books is a bit more difficult, but Honey's bees are able to write clearly at a small scale. It's not laminated-printer quality, but it'll definitely work.

While I don't exactly have projects for Aranya, Yvonne, Ragnar, and Aelara, they're still intending on coming home at the same time, and bringing the kobolds with them. If those four aren't careful, maybe I *will* be able to rope them into something to help out the kobolds. Or maybe my antkin, come to think of it.

The kobolds are still arguing a lot about what they specifically want to do, but Aranya is feeling pretty confident they'll want to join with the ratkin or spiderkin, with only a few expected to want to live on the surface. Sure, they'd like freedom, but the surface is so open and scary! Underground might also be scary, but at least it's a scary they understand. So yeah, with the kick in the pants of having a deadline, it looks like most of them are deciding to give me a chance.

I wonder if they'll want to help with the antkin, or maybe feel special kinship with them. My newest enclave is still trying to find its proper place, with the progress bars stagnating at about the twenty-five-percent point. I'm pretty surprised about that. They seemed pretty on the ball to me, but that's way earlier than when the spiderkin were having problems.

It's not too difficult to see why, however. My ratkin and spiderkin seemed to have a pretty good idea of what they were when advancing, but the antkin are having a bit of an identity crisis. While they seem pretty interested in the idea of interacting with outsiders, they are all over the map on how to actually do it.

They've basically split into factions, though I haven't been able to identify any leaders among them. Maybe that's why they're having troubles? The leaders of my other enclaves don't seem too worried, but I still think I should find out if there's anything that can be done, so I ask Teemo to pop in and see if he can figure out if anything is wrong, or if I'm reading the room wrong.

"At least it's cooled off in there a bit by now," comments Teemo as he makes his way to the enclave. After their initial construction blitz with magma, they've eased off a lot on building, letting the heat slowly dissipate. I wonder if they'll try to tame a couple tundra wolves or something. I'm pretty sure that'd be a solution that flies in the face of the laws of thermodynamics, but what is magic for if not at least mocking the natural laws behind their back?

Whatever long-term solution they can come up with, they don't seem to have one just yet, or at least not one Teemo notices as he starts wandering the enclave. The larger central receiving room is a lot less busy than it was, with most of the magmyrm having split into tunnels for their own little factions.

There's a ranching faction who seem to be mostly concerned with domesticating . . . basically every denizen they can get their little pincer-hands on. The tunnelbore ants aren't a surprise; they were using those from day one to expand and shape the colony, but they've also picked up several slimes, a pair of wyrms, and what looks like a swarm of spiders. I imagine they were using the wyrms to help with construction, but I don't know what they have planned for the slimes. The spiders are easy enough, at least: they're also after silk.

I doubt they're going to be able to compete with my spiderkin. In fact, judging by the simple togalike robe they're wearing, I'd say the spiderkin have already been by to clothe them in the basics. Still, more clothing manufactory is not a bad idea.

They might not be looking to make clothes, though. The next faction Teemo looks in on are clearly the ones from my medical brigade. My antkin seem inclined to make their own bandages and trade for clothing. I also see what the ranchers might want the slimes for, as the medics definitely have a few domesticated healing slimes tucked away in little alcoves, idly bubbling in contentment.

They also have surgical tools, which I'd bet they got from the ratkin. We still don't have medical-grade steel, but a little bit of magic does the trick to close that particular gap. They also have a lot of carvings on their walls, ceilings, and floors. Teemo even spots a room with what amounts to rows of shelves detailing the anatomies of my dwellers, as well as the more common delvers.

While the medics look like they want to take a scientific approach to healing, the alchemy faction is looking to blend it with magic, a lot like Queen runs her own lab. They also have carved shelves, but this time full of alchemical formulae or diagrams of plants and critters, and how to extract whatever bits they need.

They are probably the ones most using their affinity, at least so far. They've made little Bunsen-burner things that have a small blob of rock instead of a burning flame. They use their magic to turn it to magma and have all the heat they could ask for. It looks like they're studying the go-juice right now. It works differently on delvers and denizens, so they're probably taking advantage of their transitional state to see if they can get anything interesting to happen. Nobody seems to have exploded, so at least they appear to be following good lab safety guidelines.

From the fusion over to pure magic, there's an enchanting faction, too. They're definitely taking more after Thing's lessons than Queen's. They're also the only ones I've seen who are using carved tablets to store information instead of leaving it immobile on whatever surface is convenient.

That's probably because they're also carving their runes into other tablets and realized they could make their text mobile. From what Teemo can understand, they're working on a cooling enchantment, as well as a different form of a durability enchantment that would be good for roads. I guess they must have been hanging out with Coda some, too.

Which leads me to the last faction: the engineers. They're working on defenses, and it looks like they remember helping set up the lava labyrinth. At the moment, they're working on prototyping axles, gears, and other assemblies, making sure they'll handle the loads of whatever they need them for. I bug Teemo to look over their designs, and though he can't make heads nor tails of it, it looks like they want to use a lot of resetting pit traps with a drawbridge to secure the entrance to the enclave.

It reminds me of some of my designs for defenses in *Dwarf Fortress*, though they're missing the large, serrated disks. Probably for the best, honestly; those kinds of traps are pretty messy in the game, and I don't imagine they'd be any less so in real life. I'd rather not have to deal with invaders being splattered all over every surface. Besides, pit traps are a lot less lethal, and I imagine the medic faction would have a problem with the more lethal options.

Unfortunately, while the factions themselves seem pretty stable, the memberships are constantly changing. I don't think anyone is trying to specifically be a part of all of them at once, but there's definitely a lot of turnover between them. The medics seem the most stable, but also get the fewest recruits. Medical knowledge is a lot to take in, so a lot of the magmyrm never even make a serious attempt at it.

"Well, that's a mess."

Yeah. And you didn't see any leaders for the factions? I could have missed them.

Teemo shakes his head. "Nah, Boss. You think leadership's holding them back?"

It seems like the most obvious answer, right?

"Sure, but what's the obvious solution? There are a lot of groups wanting to do their own thing, so we probably shouldn't just put one of them in charge, right?"

I chew over the situation, feeling like something about it is familiar. Is there an overarching theme the antkin can unite behind? On the surface, there's not a whole lot to go on. Ranching, medicine, alchemy, enchanting, engineering. Some will make things, but not all. Some are more of a service, some are more magical, others more scientific . . .

Hmm.

"Feels like you've got something. Care to share with the rest of the class?"

Pfft, you already know what I'm thinking of if you're putting it that way. They're all trying to learn in their own fields. It's like a big, disorganized school. Well, a disorganized college. Some have already chosen their majors; others are still trying to figure it out.

Teemo nods at my train of thought. "So, organize them like a big school?"

Couldn't hurt. Five colleges, each headed by a dean, with a sixth acting as headmaster. Probably pull that one from the undecided so nobody gets too much power. It'd allow for ties, but that'll just mean they need to argue it out more.

Teemo hums as he processes the basic idea. "That sounds like something they can work with. And if it doesn't work, Aranya'll be back before too long anyway."

He heads off to suggest it to the ants, who are pretty eager to try it. They're all smart enough to see *something* needed to change, but couldn't think of anything that would still let them have their burgeoning identity.

I chuckle to myself as they get to work, jokingly calling it Antpimple Academy in my mind. Teemo perks up at that, making me quickly respond.

Don't you dare *suggest that name to them!*

My Voice chuckles. "Who, me? I'd never! That's a terrible name, anyway. It should definitely be Ratblister instead."

Chapter 28

Olander

He hasn't felt this apprehensive about a delve in a long time. On paper, he should have nothing to worry about. Looking around his suite and all the notes, though . . . that's a *lot* of paper trying to reassure him.

He shakes his head, trying to clear it as he prepares his pack. Knowing each and every piece of gear he's bringing helps him focus on what has him so uncomfortable with delving Thedeim. He's not worried about dying, at least. Even if the dungeon has been playing some kind of long game, even if it turns murderous on him, he's confident he'll be able to get out.

It's the rest of the town that he'd need to worry about. Thankfully, while his gut is telling him to be wary, it's not screaming at him about danger. Ironically, those are the situations he does the worst in. If some dungeon just needs to be knocked down a couple pegs and quarantined, that's a simple—if dangerous—task. In a murderous dungeon, if he were to somehow fall, someone else would be able to take his place, or a group of people. Either way, the threat *would* be handled.

The upheaval from Thedeim isn't that kind of situation, unfortunately. He can't slash and fight his way out of accidentally destroying the local economy if he upsets the dungeon.

"Just a normal delve," he tries calming himself, going over the myriad of reasons that won't happen. He's hardly inexperienced with dealing with dungeons, even if most of his experience is with belligerent and murderous ones. He won't accidentally upset it by fighting. The dungeon even *wants* to fight him, wants him to face the zombie Rocky.

He'd spent some time going over the detailed report on the Zombie Scion, and he's very glad he did. With any luck, he'll get to watch a few adventurers have a match with him so he can get a feel for what he'll be up against. No matter how many reports he reads, they won't compare to getting to see the scion fight with his own eyes. A lich that fights with its fists is a difficult concept to wrap his head around, but there are far too many reports for him to ignore it.

He could go to the local adventurers' guild and ask them directly, but why not go to the dungeon itself? Which is why he's preparing his adventuring kit. He's not bringing his full gear, much as he's tempted. His cover as an experienced adventurer will let him bring a lot of things, but his best armor and weapon will be dead giveaways for his identity, as well as some of his more potent trinkets. No, better to bring his well-used things, the sort of stuff that bears the marks of use, wear, and repair.

The memories that come with them will also sell his cover, as well as help calm his nerves as he comes close to finishing his preparation. He could go to the guild, maybe interview a few of the members before he delves, but that'd just be putting it off. He has a mountain of notes scattered around and over the desk in his room. No, the time for the accounts of others is over. If he wants more, he's going to need to get some firsthand experience with the dungeon Thedeim.

He'll probably still visit the guild after his delve, though. That kind of rowdy atmosphere is just the thing to help him cool down after a good delve. He smiles at the rising sun as he exits the inn, enjoying the cool sea breeze. The morning still has a bit of a bite to it, but the locals don't let it slow them as they go about their jobs.

There is one last temptation to face before he enters the dungeon, and he is not strong enough to resist it today. That troll definitely knew what he was doing when he gave Olander a sweet roll with his order the other day. The thought of sweet cobble bread has been bouncing around his mind ever since, and it'll be just the thing to give him the energy to have a productive delve!

He gets it fortified, of course. One doesn't turn down a good buff, no matter how overleveled they might be for a dungeon. He's had stronger buffs, but he can't offhand remember having a better breakfast. Hopefully, the baker continues to level. Considering the line as he leaves for the dungeon, there's no fear of her stagnating.

He enjoys the treat as he enters through the gates of the manor, mentally noting the subtle change in the air that denotes a dungeon's territory. It's only his training and experience as an inspector that keeps his stride steady as he feels the attention of the dungeon settle upon him.

He's felt malevolence, felt cold calculation, emotionless weighing of how much mana he'll make. He's felt the joy of a toybox, and the hunger of a murderous, but never something like this. Warmth is the simplest way to describe it, with a strong undercurrent of curiosity. Other dungeons always seem to wonder how much mana he'll give them, but this one feels like it wants to see his *reaction* to what's in store.

He tries not to swallow his current bite too heavily, but can't hide the look of caution as the Voice crawls out from under the porch, making a direct line toward him.

"Ah, Olander! Come to officially accept the quest? From that pack, looks like you're here to do more, too."

He slowly nods, trying to find his footing with the Voice. "Yes. I've heard a lot of things about delving you, so I figured I should get a look around before joining Berdol for the official inspection."

"Cool. You want a guided tour?"

Olander eyes the rat cautiously. "Is that . . . normal?"

Teemo shakes his head. "Nah, but you're not normal either. I don't know exactly how strong you are, but the Boss says he doesn't have much that could challenge you. He figures the best way to keep you from being bored is to show you around a bit."

He fights the urge to squint at the rat, suspicious of how self-aware the dungeon is. "What would that involve, exactly?"

Teemo shrugs. "Mostly me following you around, pointing out things the Boss thinks are cool. Oh, and helping you get around. The Boss has a lot of territory, so it's easy to miss things if you don't know what to look for."

"I've read the packet . . . though they did say it might be out of date. That's the whole point of doing the official inspections, right?"

Teemo smirks and nods. "That's what they tell me, yeah. So, is there anything in particular you want to see?"

"I think I'd most like to meet as many scions as possible. The packet says over a dozen scions, but . . ." He trails off as Teemo nods.

"Yep, Boss has a lot of them, though a few are still out on expedition. I don't think it'll be difficult to meet the ones still here, though. I'd suggest starting with either Poe or Tiny, since they're the closest."

Olander takes a moment to recall the information on the scions. "That's the Raven and Spider Scions, correct?"

"Yeah. Tiny is over in the hedge maze, while Poe is just up on the roof." Teemo points, and Olander can see Poe peering over the edge at him. The cold calculation that's missing in the presence of the dungeon itself is there in full in the look the Raven Scion is giving him.

". . . I don't think he likes me much."

Teemo just scoffs and waves off his concern. "He's not nearly as mean as he looks. I'll head on up and meet you there? You can have some fun with the encounters in the manor, or head straight for the attic. There'll be a boss there, but I don't think you'll have much trouble with it."

He heads for the porch before stopping and turning back to Olander. "Oh, and don't forget to take the quest from the porch! I know you said you accept, but the aranea are making it an official quest. If any others catch your eyes, feel free to accept them, too. Just take the plank with you. Simple." He parts ways with Olander with one more wave before vanishing under the porch, leaving Olander alone with only a few other early delvers.

With little else to do, he approaches the porch, letting him read what's on the multitude of hanging signs. A subtle glance upward lets him see the aranea stationed in the rafters. A few are looking through peepholes to see the gates and approaching delvers, while others tend to the dangling threads holding up the plaques like strange decorations. He browses them for a couple minutes, surprised to see ones even suggesting delves in Hullbreak or Violet. None catch his eye, until one drops down to dangle right in front of him.

Prize Fight Rocky

That's the one. He stares at it for a few long moments, wondering if he should accept or not. He *wants* to, no doubt about that, but he's walked into enough traps over the years to be suspicious of something he wants so badly. Because if Rocky is as strong as the locals believe, Olander the retired adventurer might not be victorious. He could take the loss without worrying for his life, in theory, but could he personally accept that?

Could he let a challenge like that pass him by, let a chance to truly cut loose slip through his fingers just to try to avoid politics? He takes the plaque, already knowing the truth inside himself. Blowing his cover is worth it to have a real fight, to have to try, to *strive* for victory. Accepting the quest pop-up is hardly an afterthought as he pockets the little piece of wood. It looks like he has a little over a week before he'll get a chance to really get the measure of this dungeon.

Until then, there's delving to do.

He can't keep the smile off his lips as he explores the manor, even with how massively outclassed the denizens are. Even with the vast disparity in power, they manage to keep his interest. Though the first encounter could have been straight out of the Dungeoneer's handbook, they quickly step it up with the encounters constantly coming from new, unexpected angles. He doesn't need to use any skills to deal with them, yet if he were too slow, he'd start taking hits.

This dungeon knows how to *challenge* someone! If this is what the lowest of the dungeon has to offer, what about the scion made to fight? He eyes the timer as he climbs the ladder to the attic, wondering if he'll be able to wait that long. The anticipation is already more painful than any delve he's had in a long while.

Chapter 29

If I were still limited to just the manor, I'd probably be concerned with how Olander is tearing through my encounters. But, having more than a bit of experience with delvers now, I'm smiling right along with the elf as he rampages through my denizens.

I'm pretty impressed with them, too. Yeah, they're getting cut down in droves, but they're taking advantage of all those shortcuts Teemo's sprinkled around to really keep Olander on his toes. I think it's a point of personal pride for him to not use any skills on them, which only makes him have to lean on his innate talent with his glaive all the more.

Hollywood wishes they could manage this kind of fight choreography. With my denizens able to pop in from basically any angle, Olander is constantly moving to intercept them all. He flows seamlessly from spear-like forms—stabbing and slashing at his full reach—before shifting his grip and spinning the weapon like a staff, striking with the blade and butt in equal measure. He's even forced to add in the occasional sweeping kick as he dances through the manor.

I think he's produced more mana for me in there than the place has generated in any single day so far. He actually looks a little disappointed when he finishes off the trio of electric dire rats in the attic before realizing he's cleared this section and earned a nice chest to loot. He dumps it all into a bag of holding without looking too closely. I'd be annoyed if I thought there was anything in there he might actually be interested in.

He's looking much more relaxed as he exits onto the roof compared to when he first entered my territory, and it doesn't take him long to spot Poe and Teemo over by the chimney. My Voice waves from beside the large corvid, speaking up as Olander gets near.

"Boss says it looks like you were having fun in there!"

Olander nods. "I was, actually! Most dungeons don't bother sending low-level encounters at me after I clear a few, but the denizens were determined to give me a proper warm-up. Just how many shortcuts have you made?"

Teemo chuckles as Poe watches the two. "One or two here and there. I was a Scout before the Voice, so I had plenty of time to make sure the denizens can get where they need when they need."

"Indeed." He takes a few moments to simply look around the roof before speaking up again. "So, the roof is a bit of a cooldown area, then?"

Poe nods as Teemo explains. "Yeah. Fighting up here is a bit tricky. We wouldn't want delvers falling off and breaking their necks or something. Besides, the only thing of interest up here besides Poe is the belfry garden."

"Does he get challenged often?" inquires the elf, turning his attention on my Marshal.

"Not really. He *can* fight, but he prefers to direct the expeditions and keep the local map accurate."

"I heard he has a pair of titles that make him quite the challenge?"

Teemo snorts and nods. "Marshal of Murders and Lord of Unkindnesses. He wiped the floor with a trio of delvers who were being annoyances. Boss even imprisoned them and created the gauntlets to wring a bit more mana out of them as they worked to earn their freedom."

"Oh? How strong were they?"

Teemo shrugs. "Before you, they were easily the strongest delvers we've had. Vnarl, Mlynda, and Hark. They were getting more than a little cocky, so the Boss knocked them down a couple pegs. But the punitive gauntlet gave them the attitude adjustment they needed, and they're regulars around here now."

"Hmm. So easily forgiven?"

Poe caws in mirth as Teemo grins. "Easily? You should go ask them if getting free was easy, heh. Boss is willing to let bygones be bygones if people show improvement."

Olander looks thoughtful about that for a few moments before refocusing on Poe. "Do you have Death affinity? Every other Raven Scion I've seen has it, but you are a lot subtler with it than them."

Poe shakes his head and caws, which Teemo translates. "No. He doesn't have much interest in it, honestly. He prefers to observe the delvers and manage the expeditions. Between him and Leo, there's not a lot going on that the Boss doesn't know about."

"So a friendly battle would be out of the question?" he presses, which Poe nods to.

"Yeah, he says no thanks. If you tear through the crows and ravens like the manor denizens, he won't have anyone left to send out."

Olander looks disappointed at that but doesn't press further. "Then who is the next scion I should meet?"

Teemo points off the roof to the large tangle of greenery and webbing that is the hedge maze. "Tiny, definitely. Do you want to meet him properly, or run the maze?"

Olander rubs his chin in thought as his eyes follow Teemo's finger. "What would be the difference?"

"If you run the maze, you search for chests and try to avoid Tiny as he stalks you, while avoiding the thieving dire rats. If Tiny catches you, he'll web you up, lighten your load, and dump you outside the maze. I dunno if he could get the better of you, though."

Olander hums in reply, still thinking. "And if I just want to meet him?"

"I'll let him know and guide you to his lair. He doesn't get many visitors, honestly. Mostly Vernew, or sometimes Rhonda, Freddie, and Larrez."

It takes Olander a few more seconds of thought before he nods to himself. "I think I'd like to simply meet him, if I can. I don't think I've ever had the chance to just talk to a Spider Scion before."

"Then I'll go let him know and pause the runners. Shouldn't take me long. You can have some more fun in the manor or wander the grounds if you want? I dunno if you do much herbalism." At Olander's headshake, Teemo nods. "I'll meet you at the maze entrance, then!" With that, he vanishes through a shortcut as Olander gives Poe a measuring look.

"Vnarl and party, hmm? I should try to talk to them later. You're sure you don't want a scrap?"

Poe briefly embraces his titles and caws, the sound echoing unnaturally as every crow and raven on the roof stops what they're doing to stare at the elf. Rather than looking cowed, the elf looks excited, but he pushes it aside and holds his hands up.

"I'm not going to force it, don't worry. I'm sure you're a formidable fight, but I wouldn't want to strain relations with your dungeon. It might make Berdol's inspection more than a little awkward. Still, let me know if you change your mind? Commander titles are rare and powerful. I'd love to see them in action."

Poe seems a bit uncertain what to make of Olander as the elf hops off the roof and lands with no more impact than if it was a simple step down. That elf has some serious Kinetic affinity. Rocky's gonna have quite a fight on his hands.

I watch Olander wander to the maze, the yard denizens mostly ignoring him. They've proved their point with the swarm ambush tactics. In fact . . . I wonder if I could do something like that as another attraction. I likened his fighting to dancing, but what if it was actually put to music? I bet Slash could do something cool with that if he works and practices with the denizens.

I doodle in my library a couple notes and potential routes through my different sections, imagining delvers basically doing a rhythm game through my territory. Yeah, I definitely need to run this by Slash and see if he's interested.

For now, though, I turn my attention back to Teemo and Olander as they go through the maze. It looks like they didn't need to wait too long for the runners to finish, so now they're taking the short route through to Tiny's lair.

Even the experienced Olander pauses when he sees Tiny relaxing just outside his personal silken home. No matter how tough and fearless you are, a spider approaching the size of a bus is going to tickle a couple instincts. Olander loosens slightly as Teemo calls to my largest scion.

"Tiny, I brought a guest! Don't eat this one, yeah?"

Tiny chitters more quietly than his size would indicate, fixing Teemo with enough eyes for at least two full sets of glares.

"Aw, you're no fun. I'll ask him, though."

Olander is still looking wary as Teemo addresses him. "So, I'm sure you know the Boss is Fate affinity. Tiny here is the one of us who's most been delving into that. The spiderkin even call him the Reader of the Web, and he has a title for it, too. He wants to know if you'd let him read you."

The elf looks taken aback at that, even as Tiny settles in. I think the elf was expecting a tricky scion full of malice and deception instead of a big, fuzzy, friendly fortune teller. "What would he be looking for?"

Teemo shrugs. "I dunno. The only Fate stuff I've messed with is playing around with chance. Fluffles has a good grip on the affinity as a whole, but Tiny here is the undisputed master of actually looking into what could be. I don't think he'll look too far or deep, though. He says looking too hard tends to change things, though if there's anything specific you'd like him to check on, I don't think he'd mind."

Olander looks equally cautious and curious, clearly wanting to hear what Tiny might see, but also uncertain he wants to let the big spider poke into whatever secrets he might have. It looks to me like curiosity is winning out in his head as his look shifts to one of figuring out a puzzle. After over a minute, he finally speaks.

"Will I find what I seek?"

Teemo smiles like he just landed a big sucker, but Tiny looks much more serene as he reaches two of his legs forward. A gentle orange glow emanates from them as he waves them slowly around Olander, seeming to draw thin orange gossamer into reality for him to examine. The gargantuan spider works in silence, with Olander staying still to not interrupt, and Teemo sent into silent appreciation of watching a master at work.

Just as it seems like the threads are starting to make some kind of odd sense, Tiny waves a leg and wipes them back from whence they came, chittering with an amused glint to his many eyes.

"He says you seek a lot; some for yourself, some on behalf of others. The things you think are important are easy to find if you know where to look. It's the things you've given up on and forgotten that are truly important. Pay attention, and you might find a few of them, too."

Olander listens quietly, though he's frowning by the end. Teemo gives him a couple seconds to process it before he smirks and continues. "They never give a definitive answer, eh?"

Olander snorts as Tiny mocks looking offended. "He gave a better show of it than others, at least. Why don't they ever speak it plain?"

Teemo shrugs. "Fate stuff. I dunno how else to explain it. Boss and Tiny both say looking too close can change it. Anyway, you want to go see the next scion? I could probably get Coda to meet us at the maze entrance."

Olander nods absently as he muses over what Tiny had to say. I dunno how good of a read he got on Olander, but I think it's good advice, no matter who you are.

Chapter 30

Olander meets with Coda at the manor porch, but they don't have all that much to talk about. My nerd bat isn't exactly a powerhouse in a fight, and I think the elf is still a bit distracted thinking over what Tiny had to say. Coda isn't bothered too much, however. He's been taking trips down to the Ant Enclave ever since they started organizing like a college, interacting with the engineer caste of antkin. Olander goes ahead and cuts his delve short for today, freeing Coda to go hang out with his fellow nerds and giving me a chance to take a closer look at how they're all doing.

Their progress bars are moving once again, which is great to see. They are all happy about it, and now that they're progressing again, I'm able to see them going through more physical changes. Much like a normal anthill will have castes like worker, major, etc., my antkin are literally growing into their chosen specialties.

The undecided make me think of worker ants, a bit smaller than most of the other castes but versatile to do whatever needs doing. Their hands are bulkier than most of the other antkin now, but I think that's more because several of the other castes focus more on very fine manipulation than grip strength, where the worker antkin are jacks-of-all-trades.

The other easy comparison to make to normal ants are the rancher caste. They're a lot like majors, significantly bigger and bulkier than the other ants so they can handle whatever critters that need it. They also have one large hand and one normal one, reminding me more of crabs than ants in that respect. The large hand still has fingers, though they are definitely specialized more for gripping than manipulation.

Interestingly, their right hands are the larger ones, making the ranchers what I would consider to be left-handed. They're not going to be writing with their rights, that's for sure. They definitely look strange right now, but I'm expecting they'll get better as the changes solidify. Teens are often awkward, and my growing antkin are no different.

The medical ants are probably closer in look to teens, in that lanky, stretched-out way they sometimes are. They're also changing the color of their carapaces, which is interesting to me. While they're *all* looking less like they're made of magma these days, the medical ants are growing more and more pale, and I think they're soon going to shift from looking washed out to looking actively white. Probably to make it easier for them to tell if they need to scrub up better.

Their lankiness is also aimed toward their medical profession, with the thinness extending to their hands as well. The joints in their hands are weird, looking more like the ball and socket of a shoulder than the simpler hinge of a finger. It's like not only are their thumbs opposable, but each individual joint in their hands, too! They're definitely the undisputed kings and queens of manual dexterity among my ants, and I'd imagine among the people of the world, too.

The alchemical ants have their own unique adaptations as well. Their proportions are closer to the worker ants, but they all have big gasters, making me imagine them as the ant equivalent of having beer guts. They need those bigger gasters, too, because they hold several individual . . . I forget the term for ant stomachs. Ants usually have two: one for themselves, and one for sharing. These guys have several more, each connected to their own proboscis thing in the ant's mouth.

I don't know why ants' mouths don't disturb me as much as the spiderkin ones do. Maybe they're just too alien, whereas the spiderkin mouths nestle firmly in the uncanny valley. Whatever the reason, I stick around for a full checkup on one of the alchemist ants by a medic, and see multiple tubes poke out as they make sure everything is working correctly.

I'd be a bit nervous about storing alchemical substances in my body, but the alchemist ants clearly don't share my unease. Seeing them in their lab would make a lab tech back on Earth either faint or have a fit, but after watching for a while, the only thing that looks unsafe is them constantly swigging and spitting out liquids. If I ignore the specifics of where they put everything, I can see they keep everything organized and meticulously measured. I'll probably need to just chalk it up to magic ensuring the alchemists will be fine and try not to twitch too much about the antkin drinking things most people definitely shouldn't.

The enchanting ants probably have the most subtle changes from the worker caste, though time will tell if they stay subtle. Where the medics are changing to have white carapaces, the enchanters are tending toward blacks with subtle dark greys. I think they're either naturally forming runes or carefully engraving them when I'm not looking. However they're getting there, they are helping the ants manipulate the flows of mana as they ply their trade.

Aside from the coloration, they are physically almost identical to the workers. If I only had a silhouette to judge on, I wouldn't be able to tell the difference.

And lastly but not leastly, are the engineer ants. Their hands are probably the weirdest, even compared to the medics, because they have two thumbs on each hand, with the second where the pinkie would normally be. The pointer and ring fingers have the similar opposable weirdness that the medic fingers do, but the middle has a few extra joints and is definitely specialized for grip rather than manipulation.

It's a really weird configuration, but *wow* is it effective for tinkering. They practically have two hands on each hand, letting them fiddle with something while checking the design notes, or really go to town when they bring both hands to bear on a project. As for the rest of the ant, they're a bit bulkier than a worker, but nothing like the ranchers. The heavy things an engineer has to wrangle generally don't fight back, I suppose.

None of the castes have leaders yet, but that's because of how they're going to choose them. It's looking like a kind of democratic meritocracy, which is interesting. Every ant in the specialized castes is working on a project in their field, which looks like it'll be judged by the others. Whoever does the best thing will get to be in charge, though I can't tell for how long just yet.

A few projects catch my attention, like the rancher trying to domesticate a couple of Violet's gremlins. I don't know what they intend to use them for, which is what has me taking a closer look. I still can't figure it out, though I think there's a nonzero chance of them simply being pets, but I dunno.

Most of the medic projects are over my head, similar to the alchemy and enchanting, but the engineers are right up my alley. I think my personal favorite is a simple quick release and lock for the pit traps. It's a self-resetting mechanism that uses a counterweight to close it up and be ready for the next unfortunate to wander by. I like it because it's the kind of mechanism that will be useful in a lot more than just pitfall traps. Time will tell if the ants recognize how useful it is.

The worker ant projects are looking a lot different than the specialized ones, though. While they focus on individual tasks, the workers are redoubling their efforts on the enclave itself. Infrastructure, architecture, even art; if it's something that would generally be considered public property, the worker ants are competing to make their own little parts of it the best they can be.

The whole thing is organized chaos, and I enjoy watching them work. There's a renewed sense of purpose to them as they finally have a direction to follow to meet their goal. It's not difficult to imagine them feeling a bit discouraged when their bars stalled out. Being the earliest to have progress issues isn't an accomplishment to generally brag about.

On the other hand, blazing a new trail is definitely something to brag about. Sometimes, you end up only having taken the scenic route; sometimes, you discover something completely new. Either way, you get a journey to appreciate, each step leading to the next, building on the last.

I'm not worried for them, and I hope they're feeling more confident for the task ahead. They'll hit other roadblocks, before or after their bars fill, and I know they'll handle those, too. Not only because they have the tenacity and drive of their tiny brethren but because they will have the support of friends.

Normal ants generally don't play well with others, but my antkin have been working from the ground up to make friends outside their own enclave, and outside my other enclaves, too. Ordinary ants might crave sugar, but my antkin understand that friendship is so much sweeter.

Chapter 31

Berdol

He's been looking forward to this inspection.

Inspecting Thedeim is still intimidating to the catkin, and he's not certain he'll be able to do it justice, but the dungeon's protégée is another story. He's had fun sparring with Onyx, and now that she's apparently the Voice, he can't wait to be able to hold an actual conversation with her.

With the paperwork finally sorted after the inspection of Hullbreak, he's ready to check on the youngest dungeon in the area. He's not so sure he can say the same thing about Olander, though. If Violet wasn't a toybox, he'd be concerned about how distracted the elf is. If he's supposed to be a bodyguard, he should probably pay a bit more attention.

He can guess as to why, at least. The elf had been very apprehensive about Thedeim, even planning to do a solo delve or two before Teemo waylaid him with the suggestion to fight Rocky. He did his first solo delve the other day, and there's probably only a handful of people in all of Fourdock who don't know he accepted the quest.

A lot more people probably don't know that he actually got a reading from Tiny, though. Berdol didn't even know that was a thing! He was vaguely aware that people with strong Fate affinity could do something like that, just as he was aware Tiny was supposed to be the scion with the most Fate expertise. He just never put those two threads together.

He eyes Olander as the two make for the sewer outlet to the sea, wondering what's going on in the elf's head. There's probably no harm in asking, right?

"Worried about fighting Rocky?" Berdol would be, even if it were an ordinary challenge. He's read the reports of other challengers and has no idea how someone is even supposed to fight the crazy zombie.

At least the question seems to knock Olander out of his own head, earning a confused sound before he processes the question. "Not worried. More . . . intrigued. I've faced a lot of scions from other dungeons, but I don't think I've ever heard one talked up as much as Rocky. With the average level of Thedeim's denizens, it'd be easy to think the townsfolk lack perspective on how strong scions can get . . . but with how odd Thedeim behaves, underestimating Rocky would be a fast way to lose."

Berdol nods at that as they near the shoreline. The sewer outlet isn't exactly by the docks, but the geography makes it simplest to have the outlet near there. Thankfully, not near enough for the smell to travel far. "Yeah, if you don't take the fight seriously, he'll knock you out without much preamble. I get the feeling he'll want to make a show of the fight with you, especially with the notice on the board about it."

Olander snorts. "I've never seen a dungeon *advertise!* Sure, more people will come to watch, but how did he even come up with something like that?"

Berdol echoes his snort as the outlet comes into view. "That's a question I hear around the guild a lot. We don't really have an answer, and I think both Tarl and Telar have given up on finding it."

"How about you? Do you have any ideas—or hopes—of figuring him out?"

The catkin shrugs. "Not really. I don't think it really needs an answer, and the surprise is part of the fun of delving him."

"I understand that, at least. Teemo mentioned Thedeim wanted me to not be bored, but I didn't think he'd be able to give me any kind of a challenge. Then he chained encounters at me throughout the entire manor, keeping me constantly moving. I've never had so much fun against denizens I so outclassed."

Berdol nods absently as he levitates out the key and unlocks the grating, though he pauses as he notices something. He levitates his notes as Olander gives the air a few tentative sniffs.

"I don't smell much sewage. Either there's a clog or Violet is already working hard in there."

Berdol hums as he makes his notes, agreeing. "Yep. Her expanding is all but official in our records, so part of this inspection will be in making it *actually* official." With his note made, he uses his affinity to open the grate rather than touching it directly. Violet doesn't seem to own the sewers all the way to here, and even if she did, it'd take more time to clean it enough for him to touch.

"I'm glad towns started designing with sewer dungeons in mind," comments Olander as they enter, the elf lighting a torch so they can easily see.

"Oh? Haven't they been doing that for a long time?"

Olander nods as he looks around. "Yeah, but some of the really old cities have sewers that weren't designed like that. When the dungeon gets subsumed, they upgrade, but the really old sewer dungeons don't like delvers trying to reshape their territory. I think most town leaders would rather have an upset murderous dungeon than an unhappy sewer, so they don't bother pressing the issue. I was an escort in one where we had to have Aqua Affinity potions as well as disease and poison protection, too."

The catkin shudders at the idea, and even the elf looks haunted by the memories for a moment before he continues. "At least this one has plenty of headroom."

Berdol makes a note to get some disease protection potions the next time he has to do a sewer inspection. He doubts he'll need them for this one . . . hopefully. The air isn't exactly pleasant, but considering they still haven't found Violet's borders, it could be a lot worse. If she wasn't actively cleaning things in her area, the stench would probably be intolerable.

He pauses as he feels the change that signals entering a dungeon, looking back at the exit with a measuring eye. "What would you say? About . . . a hundred feet from the outlet?"

Olander glances back before nodding. "About there, yeah. What sorts of spawns is she supposed to have? Do you know?"

"Teemo mentioned putrid oozes and caiman, but nobody was crazy enough to try to come in here to verify on their own."

"That glamorous duty is all yours," replies Olander with a smirk as they continue walking, both appreciating how quickly the air is clearing. He bars Berdol's path with the blunt end of his glaive when he spots movement in the mostly-clear water. "Looks like a caiman to me. How do you want to handle it?"

Berdol makes a note of the denizen as he considers, then gently pushes the offending haft down and out of his way. "For now, we'll leave it alone. If it follows her usual methods, it's mostly there for invaders. If it attacks, deal with it, but otherwise let it do its job."

Olander tenses for a moment as Berdol moves his spear before releasing his breath and shaking his head with a smile. "Right, toybox."

The catkin smirks as they walk past the denizen, letting it lazily swim along its patrol. "Do they even make belligerent sewer dungeons? I don't think I've seen any examples in the books yet."

"Eh, a couple, but you're right. They're mostly cooperative. Some are just more . . . *cooperative* than others." He doesn't get a chance to elaborate as they round the corner and seem to hit a wall of stench. The source is obvious, as a large stagnant pool can be seen ahead of them, writhing with movement.

Berdol shudders at the sight, making a note as he comments, "They don't call them putrid oozes for nothing."

Olander shrugs, seeming to only be bothered by the smell. "I dunno. I think the slimes are kinda cute. I had a friend when I was a kid who had a domesticated one as a pet."

"A domesticated putrid ooze?!" Berdol recoils at the thought of what kind of parent would allow that, with the image only getting more ridiculous as Olander laughs.

"Not a putrid one! A normal one. We liked to go out and gather a bunch of flowers to feed it to change its color. We got in a lot of trouble one time when we took some flowers that weren't wild, heh." The elf chuckles at the memory even as Berdol tries to usher them away from the wriggling pool. His eyes twinkle in mischief as he continues. "I've heard of adventurers sometimes keeping putrid oozes, though. Just put it in a box or other container and have a bottomless chamber pot!"

Berdol gags at the idea, much to Olander's mirth. A second voice joins the echoing laughter as the sewer tunnel darkens, cutting off the elf as he raises his glaive.

"A portable ooze! I wonder if I could get Violet to send them on expeditions like that, somehow." The shadows lengthen as the elf takes a defensive position, though Berdol's laughter cracks his focus for a moment.

"Relax, Olander! It's Onyx!"

Olander does anything but relax as he keeps his eyes on his surroundings. "That's not a gremlin."

"Not anymore I'm not, no. I'm a shade now. It's a lot easier to get around like this." She slowly steps away from the wall in front of Olander, respecting the distance he can easily reach with his weapon. Where she used to hardly reach Berdol's waist, now she's noticeably taller than him. Two holes in the darkness mark her eyes, letting the two delvers see the tunnel beyond her, and a mouth cuts through the shadows when she speaks.

"It feels like it's been a while, Berdol! Too busy to come give me more fighting tips?"

He chuckles and nods. "A bit, actually. There's a lot that goes into learning to be an inspector, and your mentor causing mischief doesn't help things."

Onyx's grin stretches her face, making Olander tense up again, but Berdol ignores him and simply steps up to get a closer look at his friend and scion as she replies. "Mischief is part of the fun!" Her smile slips a bit for a moment before she sighs and lets the smile shrink back to more ordinary proportions. "Violet says it's only sometimes fun. Are you going to be okay? She was worried you might freak out if I kept teasing," she asks Olander, who slowly lowers his glaive. He takes a few moments before replying.

"Sorry. I haven't had good experiences with shades before."

Onyx slumps a little. "Ah, sorry about that. I'm still getting used to being a shade. There's just so much more I can do now!"

"On top of being a Voice," points out Berdol, earning a happy nod.

"Yes! That's actually why I'm here. Violet knows the Mentor usually has his Voice along for inspections, so I'm here! Is there anything I can help with?"

Berdol nods and consults his notes. "I have a whole list of things, if you don't mind." She smiles at that, urging him to continue. "Well, to start with, are there any new scions?"

"Yes, Slimy and Teeth. They're both a bit busy, but Slimy is just back that way, dealing with a pool. Let me introduce you!"

Berdol starts to protest but is cut off by a smirking Olander. "He'd love to! It's his duty as an inspector to personally meet as many scions in a dungeon as he can, after all." Berdol's look of betrayal earns another peal of laughter from the elf, who follows along as Onyx leads the way.

Being an inspector is not always easy.

Chapter 32

Aranya

It will be good to get back home. Not only is she looking forward to getting back to what has come to feel like her proper place in the world, but being able to bring her people there as well makes all the difficulties of the last week worth it and more. It makes the difficulties of the past at large worth it as well, but the most recent trials are simply more fresh in her mind.

Despite her resolve when she delivered the ultimatum, she questioned the decision countless times over the ensuing days. The heart-to-heart with her grandfather tipped the balance to get the kobolds moving, but after being stuck in their situation for so long, getting moving is an arduous process.

Honestly, if she hadn't given the deadline, they would have found some other reason to drag their feet. But with her grandfather's support, too many are going now for the reluctant to want to stay behind on their own. She received more than a few irate visitors the first day or two, but after that, everyone was simply too busy to waste time complaining to her in specific.

She's been helping them pack what meager belongings they have and get what food they can for the journey. She had expected food to be difficult to acquire, but if anything, there is more than they can reasonably carry! While the local industry is finally shifting away from mostly food production, the people of Silvervein are still very accomplished at it, and leapt at the chance to provide some kind of aid to the kobolds they'd ignored for so long.

She'd be more bitter about it if the food weren't so good.

And so now, she looks at the throng of kobolds and legion of Lord Thedeim's denizens, standing beside Leo and Honey along with her friends, as the few last-minute things are done. The Stag, Tarl, Kennith, and Serd are there to see them off, with the pale elf being the official representative of Silvervein in this.

Everyone can feel the subtle shift in the atmosphere that signals the time to go, where there really is nothing left to do but get moving, so Aranya approaches those who are staying and smiles at them.

"It looks like it's time for us to get going."

"My Lord should offer Lord Thedeim the trade as you all pass through. He has a bear and a fox ready for you, and is eager to see more of the odd forest you're cultivating."

Honey buzzes, and Leo gives a wolfy grunt in reply, to which the Stag nods. "I'll be returning to my Lord soon, but not quite yet. Tarl has asked that I help guide Vanta directly for a little while longer. The bear is doing . . . well enough in his duties that I should be able to stay here for a few more days, and I enjoy helping the young one. Give your lord my and my Lord's regards."

His piece said, Tarl steps forward and hands Aranya a leather-bound ledger. "This should be everything the guild needs to establish a branch here. The Southwood was already a long trip, but Silvervein and Vanta are way too far away for me to properly inspect regularly. They might even move Southwood to the jurisdiction here."

"Perhaps, but I hope you'll still delve my Lord on occasion, Tarl. You always have the most interesting news to share," comments the Stag.

Tarl snorts at that, the corners of his mouth hinting at a smile. "It'll be nice to come do a more casual delve every so often. The official ones take so *long* with all your territory. But with Teemo's shortcuts, it'll be a lot easier to swing by for a respite from Thedeim's nonsense."

Most smirk, fully understanding Tarl's joke, but Kennith and Serd don't join in the humor, both still a bit removed from Him to know the kind of things He gets up to. The gnome speaks up next, offering his hand to shake to Aranya.

"It's been an interesting experience, coming here and meeting all of you. I'll still be sticking around to ensure the council understands their duties before going back to Holdhome, I think. Lord Order may have more in plan for Silvervein, but I don't think His potential plans involve me. I'm looking forward to getting back to the more boring matters back there."

Aranya shakes his hand and nods at that. "That's fair, and thank you again for your help with the Harbinger. Lord Thedeim was more than happy with the compensation, and even happier still to know that beast is well and truly handled."

Serd steps up to shake her hand next. "We're in Thedeim's debt for all he's done for us, Priestess. I wish we could help your people more, but after so long, distance is probably best for everyone."

"I think we mostly need some time to come to terms with everything. We've *all* been freed, and I think we'll all need a bit of time and space to figure out what that really means. Once things have calmed here, definitely send some traders to Fourdock. They're good people, and I'm sure they'll be happy to engage in a bit of commerce."

The Stag interjects before Serd can respond. "There are also the wandering orcs to the south. They only have a single true settlement, but they're some of my Lord's more common delvers. A bazaar would certainly get their attention, and get my Lord more mana."

Serd looks thoughtful about that. "I'll float the idea of establishing caravans once things are stable enough for that. A lot of people are curious about what the surface has to offer, and the surface is apparently interested in the goods we have to offer, too. In fact, there'll probably be unofficial caravans before long. Merchants always follow coin, even if they're not always completely ready for the trip."

Aranya nods as a few snickers are had at the expense of overeager business types. "Sometimes, being *completely* ready is just an excuse to delay. While there's probably more we could do to prepare for the trip, I think delaying would do us no good. May Lord Thedeim smile upon Silvervein and see it prosper, and keep us all safe on this journey." Her pendant glows a soft orange as she feels a small sliver of Lord Thedeim's might empower her prayer. High Priestess or not, it's still humbling to be entrusted with that kind of responsibility.

"Warm meals and cool tunnels to you," replies Serd in farewell as Ragnar whistles for the attention of the kobolds.

"Slash's Projection," mutters the kobold in a quick prayer, enabling her words to carry to all involved without her needing to raise her voice. "It is time for us to go. We will have the protection of Lord Thedeim's denizens for our exodus, and that includes against more than just bandits or monsters. If anyone is having troubles with the journey itself, please let one of the denizens know. They'll inform Leo or Honey, and they'll inform me. We'll be utilizing shortcuts the entire way, and though they are odd at first, they will shorten the trek significantly. I'll call for halts as needed."

She pauses for a moment before continuing. "And thank you all for joining us. I know it's a difficult decision and the road ahead is full of uncertainty, but this is a change we all desperately needed. It can be scary, I know, but please believe that each step along this path is one toward a better tomorrow."

She smiles at the scattered cheers she gets for her impromptu speech. Most of the kobolds are still apprehensive, but quite a few are optimistic about the future now. Even *scattered* cheers are better than scattered jeers, so she'll take this reaction with a smile. It's difficult to make people happy about a long march on foot.

She waves her goodbyes before joining her brethren in their walking, her friends at her side.

"Did you practice that?" asks Aelara, earning a laugh from the red kobold.

"No! If I did, it probably would have been a lot longer and a lot more boring."

Yvonne nods sagely at that. "Indeed. Practicing speeches is a good way to stumble down the path to becoming a noble."

Ragnar shudders at that, only exaggerating his disdain for politicians slightly. "Yer already walkin' a narrow road wi'bein' a High Priestess."

Aelara shrugs before Aranya can respond. "You met Kennith, and he's fine. And that paladin from the Shield. Most of the Shield people are pretty good."

"S'a fair point," concedes Ragnar.

"I intend to keep things as casual as possible, at least as long as I'm the High Priestess. He's not big on ceremony, and after having seen Kennith channeling Order and talking with him about their hierarchy, I'm confident in keeping at least empty pomp to a minimum."

"I think you're doing a good job so far," compliments Yvonne, with the smiling agreement of Ragnar and Aelara. They let her writhe under the praise for a few moments before Ragnar changes the subject.

"So, where're they gonna go?"

"I think most of them are hoping to settle with the ratkin. Some want to join with the Spiderkin Enclave or Fourdock proper, but the majority favor the ratkin."

"How did they make such a good impression on the kobolds?" asks Yvonne.

"I think it's more that the spiderkin can look a bit intimidating if you're not used to them, especially the large tarantulakin."

"Aye. 'Ave y' seen Folarn's axe? I bet it's 'eavier'n me!" They laugh and chat as they walk, settling in to debate which enclave they would join if they had the need. Ragnar and Aelara prefer the ratkin, while Yvonne would join the spiderkin. Aranya can't bring herself to choose, and the conversation wanders as the day marches on.

The first break is called later than Aranya had intended thanks to the happy distraction of talking with her friends.

Chapter 33

I have a bit of fun at Berdol's expense as I watch him meet Violet's other scions and do the rest of the inspection. Olander looks like he's mostly having fun, too, but I don't miss the fact that he always keeps Onyx within his line of sight. He might have found Slimy to be cute, but Violet's shade definitely puts him on edge.

As the inspection winds down, I think Olander is looking forward to being done, but Berdol and Onyx seem oblivious to his unease. The last thing Berdol does for the official inspection is check the hatching chambers for the scythe-maws. They've long since cleared out, but they're still an interesting thing to look into.

"I think that's it, Onyx. From what I can see, Violet is a thriving toybox and will only get better as she gets used to the sewers."

"Great! Mentor Thedeim seemed pretty confident, but it's good to hear she's doing well by delver standards, too." Her confidence and happiness at hearing the report slip a bit as she continues. "So . . . that's it for official inspection things?"

Berdol nods. "Yep."

"Then, do you want to spar some? I really want to see what I can do now!"

Olander's eyes bug out, where Berdol only looks a bit uncomfortable. "I mean, sure, but I don't think I'll be a good spar for you anymore. I can try to give you a couple more pointers, but I don't know how much they'll help you."

Onyx slumps a little at that. "I was kinda afraid of that, yeah. Maybe it'd help you out, though?"

Berdol laughs. "Maybe some, but I think I'll need to do some more regular delving to close the gap enough to really make a difference. Maybe you could spar with Olander?"

Onyx turns begging eyes upon the experienced elf, but he's having none of it. "No."

"Aw, why not!" comes the reply from both Onyx and Berdol, earning an exasperated sigh from him.

"I already told you: I've had bad experiences with shades. If I fight her, it'll be a *fight*, and one I intend to finish quickly."

Onyx tries to turn up the charm with a big wobbling lip, but Berdol has a better idea.

"What about Rocky?"

Olander raises an eyebrow at the tabby catkin. "There are still several days before the prize fight."

Berdol shakes his head. "I don't mean you. Her!" He points at Onyx, who is looking surprised as well. "If anyone can keep up with her, it'll be Rocky, and you can get an idea of what fighting him will be like if we get to watch." He turns his focus to the friendly shade. "We'll get to watch, right?"

"Er . . . maybe? Mentor Thedeim has a secret training room in the caverns, but I don't know if delvers are allowed to see."

I can feel her trying to figure out my opinion through Violet's bond, and though I don't mind her and Rocky showing off, I don't want to show them any of the established shortcuts. Thankfully, that's an easy fix. I hardly need to think of the solution before Teemo is on his way. I think he's looking forward to a bit of an exhibition between Onyx and Rocky.

"I think Teemo's on the way? His reaction isn't exactly negative, but there's more to it than just a yes."

Berdol nods at that while I think Olander is trying to contain his eagerness. No matter how strong the elf is, only a fool would pass up the chance to size up an opponent before a fight, and I doubt fools get the chance to be semiretired adventurers.

They don't need to wait long before Teemo pops up, seeming to emerge right from the shadows that make up Onyx's right shoulder.

"Alrighty, Boss says you guys want to watch an exhibition match between Onyx and Rocky?" All three nod, despite Onyx wanting to participate, which makes Teemo smile. "Yeah, I think we can use the training room. It'll be more of a spar and coaching than a match, but I still think you'll all have fun with it. The Boss wanted me to make a temporary shortcut there instead of using the established ones. Gotta keep things secure, you know?"

Berdol nods again, while Olander looks suspicious of me understanding security measures like that. He doesn't speak his thoughts, however, and soon, the three are heading through a simple shortcut to the training area.

Rocky's already there. While he often likes to train in the ring when on his own, he bolted here as soon as he got an inkling of what's planned. He seemed pretty eager to teach her a few things after she ascended, and now, he not only gets a chance to do so but also show off a bit to who will certainly be his biggest challenger yet!

He grunts and waves in greeting as the others arrive, and I can see the disappointment in the faces of the delvers. The "training room" isn't an official room . . . I should see if I can trade for one with the Southwood, come to think of it. Anyway, the room is mostly just an empty cave with a circle carved into the floor. It's used equal parts as a place to test attacks and to spar between my scions, so there's not a lot of room for things like weights, punching bags, or target dummies. The walls should be able to handle whatever attacks my scions come up with without breaking, and the ring gives them a good field to stay within for their fights.

Teemo makes his way to an outcropping in the wall to watch as Onyx heads for my zombie Boxer.

"Thanks in advance, Rocky! I've been wanting to ask you for tips, too, but didn't know the best time." Rocky grunts, and she giggles. Olander looks like he's desperately trying to process the dissonance in his mind at a *shade* giggling. "You *did* say any time is a good time, but I've also been busy. Anyway, please teach me!"

Berdol goes and leans against the wall next to Teemo, with Olander belatedly following, still trying to sort out his feelings about this situation. He gets a bit of time to process as Rocky grunts and Onyx listens, even donning her spiked gauntlets.

"Looks like he wants her to shadowbox a little so he can get a feel for where she's at, first," comments Teemo for the benefit of our guests. Berdol levitates his clipboard with a fresh bit of paper, probably hoping to glean a few pointers himself as Onyx begins.

She starts off pretty simple with a few slashes, a few stabs, before she starts to look comfortable. She leans back, lunges forward, slips to the side, parries imagined attacks and counters, all while mostly keeping her form stable. She soon starts lengthening her limbs and even sends them on impossible arcs to harry her invisible foes, finally finishing with a series of strikes launched from the shadows in the room, coming at angles that would surely catch any delver off guard.

Judging by Olander's look, that's how a lot of shades fight. I imagine that, while it looks cool when a friend does it, it'd be terrifying to try to actually fight a foe like that. I'm not the only one who notices, either, as Berdol looks over at him.

"Is that . . . how shades usually fight? I don't think I'd do very well against one."

The elf nods. "She still has a long way to go, but yeah. When fighting a shade, it's always the attack you don't see coming that gets you. And with a strong shade, there's *always* unseen attacks."

Rocky nods at his assessment, grunting an explanation that Teemo only partially translates.

"He says she's not bad, but she needs to get more used to her Shadow affinity. Leo can give her some tips on that once he gets back. For now, he thinks he can give her a good spar to get her thinking about how to better attack and defend."

Olander looks doubtful. "He's going to teach *her?* I've read the reports, but still . . . a shade should have no problem at all dealing with a zombie."

Rocky's laugh is echoed by Onyx, making it sound way creepier than I think they mean to. "Are you kidding? Rocky would wipe the floor with me if this wasn't a friendly spar."

Even Berdol chuckles and nods at that. "Just watch, Olander. You'll see."

He still looks doubtful, but the elf quiets to focus on the spar. Rocky sets his mouthguard and takes his stance, looking light on his feet and ready to rumble. Onyx tries to mimic him, but he grunts a negative at her. While I think she could adapt a boxing stance to work with her claws, she should use what skill she already has rather than trying to improvise on the basics.

Her stance makes me think more karate than boxing, with her hands at different levels, slightly open. It's a versatile stance for attacking, blocking, or parrying, but I think the boxing stance is better for absorbing blows or ducking around them. Onyx takes a moment to focus herself before launching forward with a diagonal slash of her claws.

Rocky easily steps back before stepping in and catching her off guard with several body blows before he steps back out. She tries a couple more slashes before she figures out what my zombie is telling her with the pulled punches, and she starts letting her shadowy form shift to try to avoid the attacks.

She looks awkward doing it, but Rocky nods in approval. Getting the idea is often the hard part. The rest is just practice. He grunts, and she changes from slashes to stabs, which he easily parries with his raised dukes—letting the gauntlet sail just past his head—or ducks and weaves to launch counters.

She gets plenty of practice with her own dodging, but she doesn't seem to get any ideas for how to tighten her form with the stabs. In frustration, she tries to grab his raised hands, only to get a firm rebuke in the guise of a headbutt that sends her staggering back a couple paces. Rocky grunts as she recovers, and Teemo once more gives Olander and Berdol the gist.

"He says it's a bad idea to grab someone if you don't know what you're doing. He might try to teach her a couple techniques that could work well for her, but a lot of it will require her to figure it out on her own. The Boss calls it judo. He only understands the basics, but the basics were all Rocky needed to build his boxing style. Now he wants her to do that shadowy strike, the one that comes from weird angles."

Onyx looks a bit winded, but the determined smile on her face makes it plain she's having the time of her life, even if she hasn't landed a solid hit yet. "Here it comes!"

Her gauntleted hands vanish into her body as the shadows seem to lengthen, casting the room in an eerie umbra. The attacks come without warning nor shout, one from behind and above, one directly from the side.

Olander and Berdol's breath fogs as the temperature in the room plummets, Onyx's shadowy limbs freezing solid as Rocky flexes his affinities. A heartbeat later, light and heat wash over the area, the shadows beaten back. The temperature and lighting quickly normalize, revealing Rocky standing before Onyx, a glove with a lick of flame not even an inch from her face. She stares at it for a few moments, needing the time to process what just happened, before she smiles wide.

"That's amazing!"

Berdol looks like he agrees, but Olander looks flabbergasted.

"But . . . that's—"

"Not how that works?" interrupts Teemo with a knowing grin. "Trust me. That's *precisely* how that works."

Chapter 34

Olander

Back in his suite, the elf pores over his notes, trying to make sense of what he saw from Rocky. Never in his wildest dreams did he think the Zombie Scion could do what he witnessed. He's never seen *liches* do something like that!

His thoughts are even more jumbled than his workspace, though the mess of ink and papers is making a valiant effort to keep up. He looks mad as he scribbles, writing at a pace to make any trained scribe jealous as he records his thoughts. He calms as he goes, letting the questions remain on the paper he placed them on, to be taken in turn without worry of forgetting anything.

He sighs as he finally puts the quill away and gets to organizing. Much of his scribblings are either outlandish worries or wild theories, and can be easily put aside for later. In fact, looking over his thoughts now, he sees only two immediately important things: Thedeim provided the seed for Rocky's fighting style, and Rocky's affinity prowess is unheard of. Put side by side like that, it's not much of a leap to guess that Thedeim has a deep understanding of affinities, too.

It lends all the more credence to the insane theory he is somehow a Lost dungeon, sealed away and only recently opened to the outside world once more. It's a crazy idea, that he would be somehow trapped beneath Fourdock for ages, but he can't imagine any other explanation for not only his growth but the power of his scions.

Power he seems to be willing to share with his protégée. He doesn't know what judo is, but if it's as strong as Rocky's boxing, Onyx is going to be the strongest scion from a toybox ever recorded. Her being a shade already makes her rare, and even if she genuinely seems friendly and a little innocent, she'll be a true nightmare to anyone unfortunate enough to earn the ire of her or her dungeon.

He jots that thought down and turns to his notes on Rocky's fighting style, recalling how the zombie moved. His dexterity rivals the nimble fey, while his raw power is at the level of the strongest beast, and his magic . . .

It's hard not to be in awe of it, even after all Olander has experienced. On the other hand, it's so impressive *because* of all he's experienced. Among scions, he's only seen archliches wield opposing affinities with any amount of control and skill, and only a handful of mages can do the same. He recognizes the difference between Arcane-affinity tricks and actual opposing forces, and Rocky was using the real deals.

Even more, he wove and utilized them like they were the same affinity! Teemo's teasing words echo in his mind, but he can't accept them. That is *not* how Fire and Ice work. He's fought alongside enough friends and against enough foes with those affinities to know how they're used.

And, if the pamphlet from the Dungeoneer's is correct, those are not all of his affinities. How can a single zombie have more affinities on his own than most entire parties?! A *zombie*, of all things! If he was a lich, it'd make at least a little sense, but no.

He grumbles and stands, beginning to pace to try to burn off some energy.

He hasn't felt this apprehensive since his final trial to become crown inspector. And just like back then, though there is some fear, there is a lot of eagerness, too. Sure, Rocky could cause untold devastation if he decided to, but any Conduit could probably do even more. Even more important to Olander, however, is the *challenge* Rocky can give.

The way he moves, the way he uses his affinities! There are going to be a lot of people trying to mimic him in the coming years, Olander is certain of it. A fighting style like that should be translatable to delvers with minimal issue. If he wasn't so used to his glaive, he might even try to dabble. Unfortunately, from everything he saw in that fight, the style is almost exclusively punches, with the occasional headbutt thrown in for good measure. Olander needs both hands on his glaive to use it properly.

He stops pacing as he remembers something. It doesn't take him long to find the paper in his notes, and he nods at the forethought of his past self. He *should* interview some of the adventurers. They'll have a different perspective on Thedeim, but also should have better details about Rocky. He's supposed to accept challengers, so getting to talk to them could give him a better understanding of how to get the most out of his impending fight with the surprising zombie.

He cleans himself up a bit before heading for the adventurers' guild. Looking fresh from a delve is one thing among adventurers, but showing up covered in ink rather than blood sends a certain message, no matter the glaive at his back.

It doesn't take him long to look presentable as a semiretired adventurer enjoying a bit of down time, and soon, he walks through the doors of the guild.

He gets a few curious glances, but most don't pay him much mind. The thin orc at the bar watches him for a few moments longer than the others before returning to preparing drinks and food for the relaxing adventurers. Olander is moderately certain Karn the Slight knows who he is, but the rogue is polite enough to not go spreading that around.

As much as he'd like to leave the guildmaster to his business, he really does need some advice about who to ask for tips on fighting against Rocky.

He takes a seat at the bar next to some variety of birdkin with a smoking pipe. An eaglekin, perhaps? He's never been good at differentiating the birds of prey. He's smoking an interesting blend, which makes the wait more pleasant than he expected, until Karn stands before him.

"Olander, yeah? I hear you're helping out the Dungeoneer's Guild?"

The elf nods casually. "I am. I also have a quest in the local dungeon."

Karn grins at the understatement. "Oh, really? I've heard a couple rumors, but I'm definitely not running a betting pool on how it'll go."

Olander snorts at that. "Well, who would I talk to to improve my odds? I got my first hint of what he's capable of yesterday, and I'm hoping to learn a bit more."

"You can ask pretty much anyone, really. I think only Aelara's and Vnarl's groups have resisted the urge to go a round against him. If you want my advice, though . . . I think it'll take a different Olander with a glaive to beat him, and even that wouldn't be a guarantee."

The smoking birdkin chuckles at the absurdity of the crown inspector visiting Fourdock, nodding at the sentiment. Olander raises an eyebrow at that and addresses him.

"Really? Have you faced Rocky, then, friend?"

He nods and takes a drag from his pipe, savoring it before exhaling and elaborating. "I thought I could handle him once. I have both Wind and Fire affinities, and I've never seen an undead withstand my conflagration spell." He chuckles at himself, taking another drag before continuing.

"I felt like a fledgling again. What portions he didn't simply dodge, he suborned to his own use. He danced through the spell, gathering what portions he wanted, before darting forward with a punch. I barely knew it was coming before I woke up in a healing slime. The spectators tell me I was launched clear out of the ring and into the strange denizen."

He smiles at the memory, tapping out his pipe onto a provided tray. "It's good to be reminded there are still greater heights to soar to." Olander eyes the birdkin as he talks, getting a feel for his level. He's certainly not new to adventuring.

"Just one hit?" Olander asks for clarity. The birdkin nods.

"One hit. Many of his fights are decided in one, though he'll sometimes take the time to soften people up before going for the finish. His fight with Rhonda, Freddie, and Larrez is one everyone remembers."

"A party? Did they win?"

He squawks in a laugh. "Goodness, no! But they put up a spectacular fight. You should try to get them to share the tale themselves." He turns to look out into the rest of the guild. "I don't think they're here right now, though."

"Do you know where I can find them?"

"Respect their privacy, Jirt," interjects Karn. The birdkin nods.

"I'm sure you'll bump into them around town. A goblin mage of a sort, an orcish paladin, and an elven swordfighter. They're young and more casual than most of the adventurers here, so they don't really want publicity just yet. But mark my words: they're going places."

Karn nods at that description, and Olander does his best to commit that to memory. "What about the groups that haven't fought him yet?"

Karn nods at Jirt before walking off to tend to other adventurers, leaving the two to chat. "Both groups have their reasons, though I can only guess."

"What do you guess?" asks Olander, quietly placing a coin next to the adventurer's pipe. He casually scoops both up and starts idly packing the pipe as he thinks.

"Well, for Aelara's group, it'd be a bit of a conflict of interests, I think. Aranya and Yvonne are both residents. I'm hardly a dungeoneer, but I understand those with close ties to a dungeon don't generate as much mana as those unfettered? They get plenty of adventuring out in the wilds, scouting or dealing with ranger business. As for Vnarl's group . . ."

He pauses, using a finger to create the flame for his pipe. "I think they've had enough of Thedeim's scions. They provoked Poe to a fight by threatening Yvonne. After knocking them out, Thedeim imprisoned them until they could escape through the gauntlet. Their relationship is warmed now, but I think they've had their fill of fighting his scions."

"Are they here?" asks Olander, eager to hear their side of the battle. Jirt looks out over the guild once more and nods.

"They're in the middle there; the troll, halfling, and wood elf." Olander follows his gaze and nods before standing.

"Thanks. Enjoy your pipe." The birdkin nods and settles in as Olander approaches the group, earning a squint from Vnarl as he gets near.

"Do I know you? You seem familiar."

"Probably not. I've been mostly around the capital for years now."

Vnarl's squint intensifies before he shrugs. "So were we. We probably bumped shoulders somewhere. Anyway, you need something?"

"Well, I have a quest to fight Rocky, and I hear you've tangled with some of Thedeim's other scions? I'm trying to get a better feel for what I'm up against."

The halfling snorts, whereas the other elf looks a bit sympathetic. For his part, Vnarl just grins. "Hah! Maybe that's where I know you from, then! Thedeim has your face plastered everywhere he can put those notices!"

"So, can you help me?"

The troll shrugs and motions for him to take a seat. "I probably shouldn't; I bet on Rocky, but I'll do what I can. We've steered clear of Thedeim's scions after Poe."

Olander gratefully takes a seat. "I heard a little about that, but would you like to explain? Oh, I'm Olander, by the way." He offers his hand, and they shake it in turn, introducing themselves.

With that out of the way, Mlynda speaks up first. "We were stupid and thought we could take on the world. If we had taken the time to gather info like you, we'd probably still be in our old guild."

Hark chuckles and elbows her. "At least that worked out well for us. Slim Chance is way better."

Vnarl nods. "And Thedeim's a way better delve than anything in the capital, too. Anyway, there's not all that much to tell about the fight, honestly. We had the bad luck to discover Poe's titles. Even before he embraced them, he took Hark out of the fight."

Hark winces at the memory and nods. "He swooped down from the roof, grabbed me, and bounced me off it, a tree, I think a second tree, and then the ground."

Mlynda continues. "He directed the crows and ravens around to attack us, and even with a combination attack, Vnarl and I were pretty beat up by the time we dealt with the other birds. Then the expeditions returned. We never stood a chance."

"Is that why you haven't challenged Rocky?"

All three laugh, with Vnarl explaining. "A bit, yeah. Mostly, though, we've seen him fight. Whenever someone gets the idea to challenge him, we try to be there to watch."

Hark finishes the thought. "I don't know if we'd even lose in an interesting way. We're kinda midrange specialists. Even without the ring keeping things close, I think he'd close the gap no matter what we do."

Olander hums and nods at that, recalling what Jirt said about Rocky dancing through his conflagration. "Any other advice?"

The group shrugs as Mlynda speaks up. "You could try the guild library, if Karn doesn't mind. It has a lot of accounts of delves in Thedeim, and pretty much everyone writes about their bout with Rocky."

Olander nods at that and stands. "I think I will, and I'll pay for your next round, too."

The trio grin and raise their mugs in salute as he goes. It's not difficult to get Karn's attention once back at the bar. "The next round at Vnarl's table is on me, okay? And can I check out your library?"

Karn nods at the first, and after a few seconds' consideration, nods at the second. "That should be fine. Just try not to get in the librarian's way. She's been busy organizing, and I don't want you to mess her up. It's just up the stairs; can't miss it."

He nods and places a few coins on the counter before following the directions, surprised to see a familiar face among the tomes. "Tula! I didn't expect to see you here! How goes your search?"

She brightens and smiles, placing her books on a counter so she can greet him properly. "Olander! I still haven't found whatever an Ice Sage is, but this library makes up for it! The organization is . . ." She trails off and blushes a bit, realizing he probably doesn't understand the intricacies of handling books. "Well, it's novel and incredible, but I won't bore you with the details."

He laughs. "Well, I'm glad you're enjoying yourself! Hang on, you have a fly in your hair. Let me . . ." He reaches toward her, only for her to flinch away and stop his hand.

"No! She's . . . Well, they're all assistants, I guess?"

Olander gives her a confused look. "Assistants?"

She nods. "I think the local dungeon is into books! I've tried asking around, and apparently, he has a Bee Scion, and these are some of her helpers. They're very polite."

Olander still looks confused, but now that he looks over the small library, he can see a small hive developing in one of the high corners. "If you say so. Heh, Karn said to not mess with your system, so I'll trust you. Do you have the book on the fights with Rocky? I'm doing a bit of research of my own."

Tula is more than eager to show him where it is, and he lets her guide him. In a dungeon, he may be king, but this is Tula's domain. He'll follow her lead.

Chapter 35

Aranya and everyone should be getting to the Southwood soon, so I should make sure I'm ready to accept the trade once they're there. Poppy and Titania have been working hard on the sections of the forest I've purchased, and I think they're about ready for me to purchase the rest.

I'll hold off on expanding upward there just yet, though. While Poppy is having some good success with a yew as a base and the willow growing like a vine, she seems convinced she's close to a breakthrough with hybridizing the two. She's been getting more viable crossbreeds lately, and though they don't have the qualities I'm looking for, they're a good proof of concept for the work she's doing. She just needs to select for the traits I want, and we'll be golden!

She's commandeered more than a few of the small bees to help keep track of everything, and when combined with the leafcutter ants and her own magic, not to mention the rainbats, she gets through a generation of plants a day.

A couple of the more outdoorsy adventurers have wandered into her lab/farm, seeming pretty confused at everything going on, but Poppy bullied them out pretty quickly, not wanting them to disturb her experiments.

It was interesting to see the Soil elementals in action with the living vines. The basic style and challenge is pretty similar to the wyrms, except the wyrms can only really target a single delver. With the vines and the elementals, however, they practically become living AoE attacks. They don't do the most damage yet, but they make it practically impossible to have firm footing and move how you might want. The buzz of incoming bumblebees was what made the delvers decide to get while the getting was good, and I got a bit of mana for defeating them.

While Poppy is taking to a research and support role, Titania is more on the path of becoming a warrior queen. I'd call her a warrior princess, but I wouldn't know where to even begin with making a chakram. Jello probably could, but unless Titania expands into Metal affinity, I don't think she'll get much use out of it.

I'm sure she'd try, though.

She's been going through the various denizens and testing how they'd do in the forest, and most seem to do very well. The crows and ravens are more than happy to hide shinies all over the place, same with the packrats. I should sprinkle around some chests once I have a better idea of the layout for the forest as a whole, too. I think it'll really help incentivize delvers to come have a look.

Most of the denizens that have been working out haven't been a surprise, but there is one I didn't expect to be able to contribute as much, though it is already opening up some interesting opportunities: the tunnelbore ants.

They need a bit of help from the vines and Earth elementals to stabilize things, but Titania is already making an interesting tunnel system through the forest. It almost makes me want to ask Violet about trading for moles or gremlins . . . or centipedes or mushrooms. There's a lot of potential for them there, but I'll hold off. I don't want to go stealing her niche. Even more than making tunnels, Titania is using the tunnelbores to landscape a lot, too. There are a couple creeks and such running through, and I think she has a plan in mind to divert them.

Rerouting waterways can be tricky business, but she and Poppy are both confident, so I let them work on their project without me interfering. Coda stops by occasionally to give his own opinions. While the two are definitely going for a more natural look, it's never a bad idea to have a better understanding of fluid dynamics when dealing with water flow.

I think it's time to buy the rest of the forest now. It's another big chunk of what I got for the Harbinger, but this is what I've been planning for, so it's not exactly a surprise. Titania and Poppy are both excited with the new area, and I think glad they didn't have to try to manage the entire thing all at once. It's good to take things in steps to avoid getting overwhelmed.

They've mostly worked out the kinks with the first section, so now they take to the second section with gusto! I upgrade their spawners a bit, too. I don't go far enough to get a new creature yet, but faster production for the pixies and vines will ensure they don't get stretched too thin.

Grim is helping out, too. He nods at the expansion and heads to the spawning crypt, opening the doors to lead a large group of fungal zombies and verdant skeletons to what will be the spring section. A handful have been out to help Titania and Poppy before, but with the new room, they might as well get used to filtered daylight and open spaces.

Some of the people in the cemetery give the procession curious looks, but they're not bothering anyone, so the delvers leave the undead to whatever it is they're doing.

Time gets away from me as I watch everyone work, spending a bit of mana to put in some nodes or spawn some more denizens, and before I know it, I can feel Leo and Honey both trying to get my attention. Looking through their eyes, I can see the border of the Southwood not far ahead; I can hear and smell my denizens and the kobolds behind, too.

Right, I also need to make sure everyone is ready for them. Larx is aware of a lot of them wanting to join the enclave, so the ratkin have been working to ensure there's room, as have the spiderkin triumvirate. They're not getting quite as many, but they're just as excited to have new neighbors as my ratkin. I haven't looked as hard at Fourdock's preparations, but all they really need is a couple spare houses—which are pretty easy to find—and they'll be ready to rock.

Speaking of being ready to rock, the Southwood seems pretty eager to trade with me, and I suspect the pile of mana he'll be getting is only part of it. Now that I have the entire footprint for the forest of four seasons, it just needs the climate control enabled to make the name fit. The central tree will be important, too, but it'll be this upgrade that really sets the area apart and gives it the theme I want.

Soon, I won't need to just imagine what it'll all look like. Leo's tail wags in anticipation, and Aranya pats his head as they all get closer.

"Lord Thedeim is looking forward to the transaction, I can tell. Not only a special upgrade, but two more scions as well. You'll make sure to help them adjust, right, Leo? You know how it feels to transfer to a new sanctuary."

His tail wags harder in agreement. I think Leo has adjusted well to my nonsense, though he also wasn't exactly happy under Mlynda's control. Still, they've both grown, and he didn't even growl at her on the occasions they met during the attack on the Maw!

I'm curious about the two new denizens and scions I'll be getting, too. I wonder what it's like for a denizen to be upgraded to a scion? Do they suddenly have complete thoughts? Did they not before? Is it more gradual? Or have they always been as smart as a scion, but just never had the drive or other reason to actively make decisions?

I'd ask, but I'm even less of a psychologist than I am a biologist.

Leo, Honey, and Aranya enter the Southwood's territory, the throng of kobolds following behind, with Yvonne and her party bringing up the rear. As they gather, my scions break away from the group to meet with the Southwood's other scion: the bear.

I think he's a grizzly, but he's closer in size to a polar bear. Despite this, he seems more relaxed than threatening and easily takes a seat before making bear noises at Leo and Honey. Whatever he's saying has them feeling amused, which I think can only be a good sign. They exchange some pleasantries before another bear and a fox step out from behind him.

They make their own noises, and they all chat as I get the much-awaited pop-up for the trade. The window is pretty simple, and though I think I can expand it to make a counteroffer and maybe try to get a training room, too, I'll save that for later. Maybe the Stag can come visit and I can ask about it then. Either way, he's offering the two denizens in exchange for mana.

By the raw numbers, it's a pretty hefty sum, but I get the feeling he's asking as little as he can get away with by the system. I briefly consider countering with more, but then simply accept. I feel like trying to pay more would be like arguing about the bill at a restaurant. Best to accept the first offer rather than start unneeded drama about who will pay what.

Besides, I don't think either of us is getting screwed with this deal. He gets a nice injection for his projects, and I get what I need to finish my latest one. It's win-win!

I accept and upgrade the fox and bear to scions, only to meet a hurdle.

Denizen Must Be Within Territory to Ascend to Scion.

I pout at that but have to begrudgingly admit it makes sense. Otherwise, some crazy dungeon that's definitely not me could spend the piles of mana I definitely don't have to just upgrade denizens on expedition and ambush someone with a huge threat!

Fine, Order, ruin my fun. Or delay it, I guess. I pat the bonds with Leo and Honey, and they move forward to greet the latest additions to my growing menagerie, with Honey doing a little dance of greeting on the nose of the bear, and Leo licking the top of the fox's head. That'll have to do until I can upgrade them and pat them more directly.

I'm already looking forward to getting them to their new home, and not just for the new spawners. Soon, they'll get to meet everyone, make new friends, and come to the realization that I do things a *lot* differently than the Southwood. I'm pretty sure they volunteered for this, so really, they'll only have themselves to blame for the chaos ahead.

But they're not the only thing I've gotten! I let Leo and Honey welcome my new denizens as I return my attention to the forest of four seasons, preparing to make it live up to the name I've been giving it the entire time.

I select the entire forest for the upgrade and take my time to adjust everything how I want it. I could brute force it to make the sections fit their seasons, but even I wince at the upkeep that would take. But, if I adjust the flows, moving the heat around instead of just deleting it, the price plummets.

I even see why Titania and Poppy were having Coda advise on the redirection of the waterways in the territory. Water is a great place to sink heat. I think I'll need to change where they're moving the creeks and streams a bit, but with putting the excess heat into them, I also get a discount on adjusting the humidity, too! I'm sure I'll need to have Fluffles or maybe even the Quartermaster swing by to help guide everything and fine-tune it, probably at the direction of Poppy or Titania, but the discount will definitely be worth it.

I look over the adjustments once more before paying the cost, and smile as the denizens and scions in the forest pause to see the mana flows start working. Sure, I could have gotten a dramatic, sweeping change all at once, but that'd be the brute-force option. Slow and steady is the clock of the seasons, and I see no reason to rush it.

Chapter 36

With the return of the group only a day away, things are busy while everyone tries to finish some last-minute bit of prep to welcome them home. As if this last week wasn't already a busy one.

My enclaves are a flurry of activity, with every last dweller either preparing to welcome the kobolds in general or welcome home Aranya in specific. The ratkin have been digging out their area of the crypt complex, expanding their enclave to ensure there's room not only for the kobolds but for the first wave of true births among my dwellers, too. There are still a few months before anyone expects to give birth, but expectant mothers are starting to show, encouraging the fathers to ensure there's enough room for larger families.

As far as I can tell, the spiderkin aren't that far along just yet. I do my best to give them their privacy, but gossip is easy to hear. Things are more focused on who is courting who rather than when someone is supposed to be due. I wonder if the spiderkin have live birth or do some kind of egg sac or something? I guess I'll learn eventually.

The only enclave not preparing for the return is the Antkin Enclave, though they still need to fill their bars. They've certainly heard of their return, and I think they're delaying picking their leaders until everyone is back. Or they're taking the time to fully examine each project presented. The resetting latch has gotten some buzz, but the most popular among the engineer ants looks to be a Stirling engine. It's mostly a proof of concept, but considering the ambient temperature of the enclave, it makes sense to explore it.

My scions are also working diligently to ensure everything is prepared for the triumphant return of everyone who's been out on expedition for so long. Fluffles is helping the bees organize and file their current projects away to make room for the vast swaths of knowledge Honey will surely have them working on. Poe is tending to the war room, ensuring he'll have everything he needs to get Leo up to speed on the situation on the home front.

Tiny is helping out in the forest of four seasons, tidying things up and providing moral support for Titania and Poppy. They're going to have two more scions with whom they're expected to work closely together, so they need to make sure they're ready to contribute and help them adjust. My Pixie Scion is practically a blur as she rushes to-and-fro, while Poppy is nervously churning the ground enough to possibly endanger some of her experiments!

The big guy doesn't have any trouble snaring Titania in a web nor in plucking Poppy out of the ground, gently setting the two on his back as he starts meandering the forest. I can't hear anything, but the manic energy I can feel from the bond with my two newest scions starts to settle and calm to something more manageable. When he finally lets them down, their movements are a lot more confident.

My denizens pitch in as they can, with most in the forest following the command of the two sister scions. The only ones who are really doing their own thing are the tundra wolves. With the climate control option, they're eagerly working to make the winter section match its season quickly. I imagine they'd change what they're doing if asked, but Poppy and Titania are more concerned with setting a solid baseline for the seasons right now. At the moment, they only intrude into the winter section to direct the placement of the appropriate herbalism nodes.

Spring is also seeing quite the transformation, probably because it's actually spring right now. Fruitbats, rainbats, verdant undead, leafcutter ants, and more swarm over the section, making it already bloom with vibrant life. In fact, seeing all the denizens reminds me that I should upgrade a couple spawners to keep with the idea of making the forest a challenging delve!

I still expect my foxes and bears will play a pivotal role in that, but they're not the only combatants I expect to have.

I start with upgrading the plant spawner, which pushes up a little sprout that a bumblebee quickly scoops up and flies off with to plant somewhere. The menu calls it a dreambloom, and from what I can gather, it's no surprise the bumblebee was interested in it. It grows into a huge blue-and-white flower with a shape similar to a sunflower, but the central head is supposed to mimic the phase of the moon.

Bumblebees are a primary pollinator and are able to use the plant's unique property to help them out in a fight, too. It's not called a dreambloom because of the flower but because of the pollen. It can be a pretty strong sedative, and I think it'd be a cool challenge to have the occasional patch of them the delvers have to get through. Sure, I want them to mostly need to fight, but a good environmental hazard can make the fights more interesting.

Upgrading the bees will probably also make things more interesting, so I do that until the bee spawner starts spitting out rumblebees. It looks like these ones are kinda solitary, more like carpenter bees than others. And they're big, about the size of a cat? They're also clearly made for fighting.

Each one is different from the last, with some having longer stingers, others having clubs at the end of their limbs, or small claws, or spikes, or . . . It's like they got into a random pile of weapons, and each one fused with something different. Those are definitely going to make fighting interesting. Melee delvers are going to be important to have around to keep these guys off the ranged fighters and casters.

Where the bumbles seem to prefer the spring section, I think the rumbles like the summer more. That, or they aren't as good at tending to the nodes as the others. It'd make sense. They're specialized for fighting, not resources. I imagine all bees will have at least a bit of proficiency in tending herbalism nodes, but these guys are definitely ready to rumble.

And lastly but certainly not leastly, I upgrade the fey spawner until I get a new one: a sprig. They look like a slightly-anthropomorphic stick bug with a few leaves sprouting at random joints. They have big eyes that stick out from their narrow heads; I'm not sure if they're adorable or creepy. They're also a fair bit bigger than the pixies, about two feet tall if they're not bending over or anything. They move slowly, and I watch as one goes to a tree and seems to just merge into it.

I can tell it's moving around, but there's no indication on the surface until it opens its big eyes. This one soon spots a boring beetle and slowly extends a limb out from the bark; the invader doesn't notice until the sprig strikes. It cleanly impales the beetle, holding it to the trunk of the tree as a second limb extends from the surface. I'm pretty sure it's a proboscis, though only after it, too, impales the beetle and makes little slurping sounds.

That's . . . really effective against the invaders, at least. I don't know if I want to see them attacking any of the delvers, though. It finishes drinking the beetle and flicks the corpse away, letting the empty shell disperse into mana as it uses what it drank to nurture the tree. Creepy as the sprigs are, I can already see the use in having them around the central tree. Poppy has noticed, too, and she calls the sprig out of the tree to probably talk about the specifics of what it does.

I don't doubt she'll be recruiting more than a couple of them to help with her botanical experiments. They might even be a key in solving the root problem with the climbing willow around a yew. That's still plan B for the tree, but it's good to see the backup plan stabilizing. A good backup gives the more ambitious plan room to experiment and take risks. Even if Poppy can't get a hybrid just right, the big central tree can still happen.

The sun soon sets, and I get the chance to appreciate the dreamblooms in their natural glory. I think they'll be most common in the spring and fall sections. They seem to like it cool, but not cold, and definitely don't like hot. Every single one the bumbles have planted have been in cooler, shaded spots. The little buds dimly glow, seeming more like hidden little stars than representations of the moon.

I think it inspires my packrats, because they change how they start hiding things. Instead of using places where people would have to deliberately look, they hide some things under leaves and in the shade, making the forest at night twinkle like the sky. Teemo even takes the time to take in the scene, looking up through the trees to compare.

I don't notice any familiar constellations, and though I do see a single moon, it's more blue than white. It looks smooth, too, so maybe it's fully submerged? With magic, it might even be literally a ball of water all the way through. What better thing to command the tides than water, right?

Teemo chuckles at my thoughts but doesn't voice his own. Instead, we both just take in the night and all the things around us, from denizens to delvers. So many points of brightness, so much change over a single year. Tomorrow will be another day full of people, but for right now, it's nice to sit back, relax, and reflect.

Chapter 37

The sun rises with Teemo and I still kinda chilling. It's weird to think that I can't see the sky unless I'm looking through the eyes of my scions, but Teemo's cool enough to give me a good view of the sunrise.

Aranya and everyone are only a couple miles out right now. They were tempted to push on to get here last night, but decided it'd be better to keep to the camp schedule and wake up fresh, and have basically the full day to try to settle in, instead of trying to stay up late marching further, then stay up even later trying to get settled. Probably the right decision, all things considered.

It also gives my dwellers just that much more time to have their breakfast and prepare to welcome everyone. Their path will have them enter the forest of four seasons, so Teemo ensures my enclaves know the shortcuts to get there. He waits on a branch while my other dwellers mill around, eager and anxious to do what they can to help make the kobolds feel welcome.

I didn't even realize how anxious I was about everyone getting back safe until I see Aranya and my scions leading the march. My High Priestess's eyes brighten as she notices Teemo and everyone, and she waves alongside a happy howl from Leo.

"Welcome back!" greets Teemo and the gathered ratkin and spiderkin, my Voice soon hopping onto Aranya's shoulder as she finally reenters my territory. Leo and Honey soon follow, as well as Queen and Thing, each having a good pile of mana saved up for me. I embrace the bonds to let them know I'm glad they're back.

"It's good to finally be back. I can tell Lord Thedeim is happy to see us all return, too. He hasn't been idle, either. This expansion looks . . . big."

Teemo laughs at that but doesn't get much of a chance to comment. Much as it'd be nice to just sit and chat, there are a lot of people who need to get settled, and a lot of denizens to sort out. The latter are the easiest to deal with, excepting my new fox and bear. Aside from those two, they all know where to go, heading off to their respective territories with minimal guidance. The kobolds need a lot more help, though.

Larx and Folarn are good at directing people, and soon, there's a stream of nervous kobolds and plodding wagons making for the shortcuts to my enclaves. The ones who are planning to live in Fourdock proper are sticking near Aranya and Teemo for now. They've got a few valuables they intend to trade for some temporary lodging before they find some kind of job.

It looks like they're mostly young adults who are interested in independence, so I wouldn't be surprised if they want to try adventuring. I certainly wouldn't mind the mana. For the ones staying in my enclaves, my denizens already know to leave them alone. My more dangerous ones get a few concerned looks as they pass, but the kobolds don't get too much of a chance to dwell on it. My dwellers are eagerly chatting away as they guide everyone, lending the processions a vibe like a big school field trip rather than a careful walk past dangerous beasts.

They're only technically dangerous. It's fine, I promise.

Since they seem to have everything well in hand, I turn my attention to my two new denizens, getting a better look at them before I make them scions. They both look a bit out of their depth, which is fair enough. The Southwood doesn't often deal with this many people all at once, and though I think the forest should feel familiar to them, I'm also pretty sure they can't forget how different it is from their former home.

The fox is a male with an orange-and-white coat, black tips on his ears, and white feet. His fur is pretty fluffy right now, but I expect he'll be shedding soon now that spring has sprung. Or maybe he'll hang out in the winter section. Either way.

The bear is a female black bear, and though she looks a bit more stoic than her fox companion, her nervousness is given away by her ears and nose all wiggling and taking in as much information as possible. Leo and Honey are sticking close to them, trying to help them feel at ease, but I think it might be time to take them somewhere a bit more private before making them scions. *Teemo, if you would?*

"Sure thing, Boss. I'll be back in a couple minutes, Aranya. The new recruits are looking a bit overwhelmed."

The kobold smiles and nods, reaching up to rub a finger under his chin. "Alright. I expect Yvonne, Aelara, and Ragnar will be here by the time you're back so you can greet them as well."

He nods at that before hopping down and scurrying over to my gathered scions and soon-to-be scions. "Let's head to Poppy's garden, guys. It should be quiet enough that we can talk without having to dodge any feet."

Thing, Honey, and Queen trip over each other as they try to respond, which earns a laugh from Teemo. "You guys can head off if you want, sure, but I think you'll want to meet Poppy. Titania's around, too, but I think Poppy's current project will get your attention."

Leo chuffs in a chuckle as the three brainy scions look interested in their own ways. They and the two new denizens follow Teemo through a shortcut to the garden, where it looks like Poppy is in the middle of organizing the latest set of seeds, which quickly earns the attention of Queen and Honey, and Thing's curiosity. Teemo smirks and waves for them to go.

"Go ahead and play, guys. Poppy will love to have some people to talk to about this project who will actually be able to keep up. A lot of it goes over my head. Talk shop and see if you can offer her any help."

They eagerly do just that, leaving Teemo and Leo with the new recruits. My Voice turns to my Warden before speaking. "So, have you tried to give them an idea of what's in store for them? You've been through this before."

Leo nods and woofs.

"Ah, good. Now, for you two, I'm sure it's difficult to understand all he's tried to impart, but there's one last thing the Boss wants before he makes you scions. Are you sure you want it? No hard feelings if you two want to go back. The Boss wants new spawners and scions, but you don't have to be how he gets them."

The two look surprised at that, exchanging a look before the bear grunts and the fox squeaks their reply, earning a smile from Teemo.

"Great! Now when the Boss shows you something crazy, you can't blame anyone but yourselves!" Leo lets his tongue loll out of his mouth in a quiet wolfy laugh as the two denizens try to look brave despite their apprehension.

Welp, they'd better get used to change, because here comes the first hit of it!

I spend the mana to make them scions, which doesn't actually have much external change on them just yet. I'm pretty sure Leo had to spend a bit of time in the spawner to get everything to stick, so they probably need that, too. Now, where to put their new spawners . . .

"Do you two have any preference on a season? Summer and fall are fully open, but if you're set on them, I'm sure the Boss can make room in winter or spring for you."

I don't need Teemo to translate the confused looks on their faces at the offer. He gives them time to recover and give an answer. They both look nervous as they reply, like the teacher just asked a trick question yet demands someone answer it.

"The bear is interested in summer, and the fox likes fall."

Works for me.

I settle the bear spawner in a nice new dug out cave in the summer section, and set the fox spawner in a smaller cave network in fall. The two new scions look surprised to feel their spawners in the area they requested. I intend to surprise them at least once more before they head to their new homes to let the new title solidify.

"Alright, now, for names . . ."

The two look stumped and dumbfounded at the same time, which is fine. I like figuring out names for my scions. They'll be a challenge, too; all the bears I can think of have been guys! I could call her Mamma, but that just feels weird to me. It does, however, lead me to a tangent that could work. She's hardly a blonde, but I like the name Goldilocks for the bear. I'm sure she'll fit in just right.

The fox is even more of a challenge. If he was a vixen, I'd have no shortage of names to pick from. The only guy fox I can think of is Nick, which doesn't quite feel right. I could go for the homonym and call him Guy Fawkes, but I get the feeling that if anyone is going to introduce my concept of explosives to this world, it'll be Queen who does it. What other foxes could I name him after?

Hmm . . . Oh! He's not a fox, but he's definitely named after one. It might be like naming a dragon "Draco," or a bit meta for naming him after a guy named after a fox, but I think Zorro will be a perfect fit for him!

Teemo shakes his head at me. "You come up with the weirdest names, Boss. Goldilocks. Zorro." He points at the two, smiling at the look of surprise at their names. "Yeah, they come with a bit of history attached, but don't worry about it too much. For now, just head to your spawners and get some rest. Once you're done, I'll give you the grand tour. Things can get pretty hectic around here, but we're all in this together. If you need any help with anything, just ask someone. Now, go get settled, okay?"

They both still look a bit lost, but perk up when Leo grunts and motions for them to follow, making more wolfy sounds along the way. I pat the new bonds with encouragement as they go, Leo giving them more advice as they vanish into the undergrowth.

I take a look at the new spawners to see what my options are, but I don't get further than seeing the basic bears and foxes before Teemo urgently demands my attention. I focus on him to see Poppy, Queen, Thing, and Honey all looking eager about something, but Teemo is trying to contain his panic.

"Boss! Please tell them you were joking about the explosives!"

Chapter 38

Rhonda

The goblin girl scrutinizes her spell as she cycles it, ensuring every last detail is correct. On the cluttered table nearby, her familiar—Lucas the jumping spider—stands ready with a bit of charcoal to take any notes she needs. He watches the spell as well, interested in what his master has created.

Rhonda tries to slow the spell further, which has been the truly difficult part of studying it. In theory, it's a pretty simple spell, at least for her. In the entire world, maybe only she and Thedeim's scions understand the principles behind it, but once you get them, it's not difficult to apply. The spell is a cycling hot explosion/cold implosion, the small fireball transitioning to shards of ice as it dissipates. The shards converge back to the origin point, where the low temperatures combine back to a hot temperature, and then just a lick of mana is all it takes to reignite.

The efficiency still surprises her, even after having seen Rocky weave fire and ice together effortlessly. She feels like she's getting closer to that now, thanks to the advice of Vieds, the changeling pyromancer. Ice has always come naturally to her, but with the examples he's given her on the few delves she and Freddie have been able to tag along with, Fire is feeling more and more natural, too.

Even better, she can feel something else, some secret in the explosive force fire can sometimes produce. Is this how Rocky expands his affinities? She's still missing something, but the more she watches the mana cycle in her spell, the more she feels like there's something *important* there, if only she can figure it out.

"Ah, my prize apprentice, stuck," comes the voice of her mentor, Old Staiven. The wizened ratkin smirks at her as he descends into the basement lab, her pout at his words only egging him on. "Such potential, and she's wasting it in the basement."

"Master Staiven, this is important!" she protests, only for him to grin.

"Oh, I'm sure it is. But how long have you been staring at that spell? It's been doing wonders for your control, which is why I haven't tried to stop you, but you're at a wall, I think."

Rhonda winces at that. The old ratkin's smile softens as he moves to put a hand on her shoulder. "It happens to all of us eventually. You'll get through it, I'm sure. But not down here." He waves a hand through her spell, disrupting her concentration and ending the cycle. "You need a break. Go get your friends and do something fun; get your mind off this. You'll come back refreshed and ready to try something new."

She brightens at the thought of hanging out with Freddie and Larrez. It really has been a while since they were able to hang out and go on a more casual delve together. "Do you think they'll be available?"

Old Staiven waves off her concern as he moves to his shelf of alchemy recipes. With the new forest expansion from Thedeim, the ingredients for some of his old favorites might finally be available once more! "Torlon won't begrudge the lad of a break, I'm sure. Larrez might be a different story, but you can at least go ask. Maybe you three can go pester Rocky about his upcoming fight."

"Upcoming fight?" she asks, turning to see if Lucas knows what he's talking about. Her familiar gives her a couple shrugs all at once while Old Staiven laughs.

"You really have been down here too long. Focusing on your studies is all well and good, but you can't let the world pass you by, Rhonda! The Dungeoneer's Guild has contracted a semiretired adventurer to help with the spring delves, and Thedeim has officially challenged him to fight Rocky." His eyes sparkle like he knows something she doesn't. Which he probably does, the wily old rat. "I think he'll be Rocky's biggest challenge yet. You'd do well to make sure you watch the fight, Rhonda. Getting to see him go all out can only help your studies."

Her eyes widen at the idea of Rocky being able to go all out, especially against a delver! Thedeim doesn't kill, but it's difficult to imagine anyone strong enough to go toe to toe with him at his full strength. "When is it?!"

"In a day or two. There are flyers all over Thedeim's territory with the details. Go get your gear and your friends and see for yourself. Ah, this one should do." He smiles as he plucks a book from the shelf. "I'll be going over some old recipes while tending the shop today. If you can get any information on what will be in the new forest expansion, it'll help me decide what new formulae to dust off."

She nods as Lucas hops onto her head, forgoing any hat while in the basement. "I'll do my best! You know how his new expansions can be, though."

He nods and waves for her to head up the ladder. "Yes, yes, I know. Have fun, and make sure Freddie brings any new monster pieces by once you're all done. I'm sure the lad would like the extra coin, and I'm always looking for fresh ingredients."

With that, she scampers up the ladder then up the stairs to the living area over the shop. Her adventuring robes and hat are looking a little worn, and the robes are looking a bit small now, but they'll be fine for this.

"Lucas, please make a note to look into getting some new robes. I wonder if Miss Norloke would help make a new set . . ." She trails off as Lucas holds up her notebook with the words "New Robes" underlined two times. "Two extra times? I really have been distracted lately. Hopefully, the others won't mind us taking a trip down to the Spiderkin Enclave, then."

Lucas chitters from her wide-brimmed wizard hat, taking a few moments to ensure his little foci are all still where he left them before settling down as she dons the hat. "Alright, quick check before we go. Foci?"

Lucas chitters an affirmative as she holds up her own staff, the red and blue gems sparkling as she sends just a trickle of mana through them. "Check! Potions?"

She pats her belt and checks the pouches, frowning at the color of one of the potions. "Hmm . . . The Lightning Resist potion is starting to wash out. I'll make sure to use it today and replace it later. Check! Pack?"

Lucas chitters once more in the positive as Rhonda gives it a quick look before slipping the straps over her shoulders. "The rations are *still* good? I know they're supposed to last for a long time, but wow. Then I think we're ready!"

With a spring in her step, she heads down the stairs, waving at her mentor as she nears the door. He doesn't look up from his book as he waves back. "Have fun! Keep her out of trouble, Lucas!"

The goblin giggles at that before leaving the shop, stepping out into the wonderful spring day. She takes a deep breath and smiles as she starts walking. "Definitely was too focused for too long."

She nods at people while she walks to the temple of the Shield, noting that there's more people around than usual. Well, with spring here, it's not really a surprise that people would want to immigrate. She even spots a group of kobolds walking around, too! She nods at them with a smile as they pass, and soon, she's at the steps of the Church of the Crystal Shield.

The older wolfkin who is usually sweeping the steps isn't there; instead, a young elf lad is doing the job. They nod at each other as she enters, the boy needing to focus a lot more on sweeping than the experienced wolfkin, and she makes her way through the church. She greets priests, clerics, acolytes, and more on her way to Freddie's room, before a dwarven scribe points her toward the archives to find her friend.

As she rounds the corner to get there, she spots Torlon, who smiles and waves.

"Ah, Rhonda! I was about to suggest Freddie go get you and go delve or something. He's been going over tactics a lot lately and focusing on his prayers. Improving himself is all well and good, but he can't forget the people around him who he should be doing that for."

Lucas makes spidery noises as Rhonda nods. "Master Staiven basically told me the same thing. I'll drag Freddie and Fiona out to get Larrez, and we'll go delve. Is there anything you need in there?"

He shakes his head as he opens the door for her. "Not especially, no. I might ask Freddie to welcome High Priestess Aranya back for me, but that's all. The Shield is very interested in a closer relationship with Thedeim, and that begins with a proper friendship with his High Priestess. Truly, It gives me the heaviest burdens to bear," he jokes, Rhonda fully aware how well he and Aranya get along together.

They walk in comfortable silence through the archives until Lucas spots Freddie, hunched over a book and looking enthralled. Fiona, his own larger spider companion, spots the group and waves as Lucas darts forward, jumping over benches, tables, and acolytes. Fiona's mandibles twitch in a smile as he dashes across the book Freddie is reading, causing him to jerk back in surprise, then have to lean back further as Fiona gives chase.

"What the—Rhonda! Head Priest!" He smiles and stands, accepting a hug from his friend. "What are you guys doing here? Er, you and Lucas, I mean. Torlon can be here if he wants without a reason."

The gnome chuckles. "I came here to get you to head outside, get some fresh air, maybe delve, and let High Priestess Aranya know the Shield is glad to see her safely home once more."

"Old Staiven said I should get out of the basement and do some delving, too, so here I am! Get your armor!"

Torlon smirks even as Freddie looks reluctant. "You heard the little lady, lad. It'll do you some good to get out of these walls." Before Freddie can respond, Lucas bounces in, ricocheting off him and Torlon before Rhonda grabs him out of the air. Fiona isn't far behind, a web raised in several of her legs as she gives chase.

The young orc laughs as he scoops Fiona into his arms, the ogre-faced spider pretending to glare at her elusive friend. "I think it'd do Fiona some good, too. Alright, let me go get my armor, and we can go see if Larrez is available."

Torlon waves at the group as they exit the archives, and Rhonda waits outside Freddie's room as he changes. "How's your armor doing, by the way? My robes are getting a bit small, so I'd imagine your armor is the same? You're not only getting taller; you're getting all buff from training, too."

She can hear Freddie snort at that from inside his room. "I think 'buff' is a bit far, but . . . yeah, my armor is getting kinda tight. I should try to commission some chainmail or maybe splint mail? Chain will probably be slower to grow out of, but splint is definitely better protection."

"Do they not have any here in your size?"

"I mean . . . they do, but some of them are pretty old. And if I buy some and grow out of it, that'll just be a new set for the next paladin in training, right?"

Rhonda nods at that, despite the door between them. "That makes sense. Do you think the ratkin might be able to help you with that? I want to ask the spiderkin for some help with new robes. Maybe even Thing will want to help me with the runes."

Freddie grunts, either in agreement or just in trying to get into his armor. "Maybe. Oh, Jello might be willing to help me, come to think of it. She's a metalworker now, apparently. That's not an armorsmith, but if we can get her the materials ourselves, she'll definitely be more affordable."

"Mmm! If she's anything like the aranea, we'll probably need to do a couple quests to pay for it, and maybe a couple to pay Thing, too. Do you think Larrez needs any new gear also?"

Freddie opens the door, fiddling with one last strap as he answers. "I don't think so? He's a bit older, so he doesn't have as much growing to do. We can always ask, though. Even if he doesn't, he'll probably get some good experience just mining Thedeim's more exotic ore nodes for materials."

Rhonda nods as Fiona helps Freddie with that last strap. "Then you're ready to go?"

He nods, patting his Simple Hatchet and shifting his shoulders to ensure his shield won't fall from his back. "Ready! Let's go get Larrez!"

Chapter 39

Freddie

The young orc paladin hums a quiet hymn as he walks down the street with Rhonda, both of their minds more on the upcoming delve than in making conversation right now. Of course, that doesn't extend to Fiona and Lucas, who are constantly chittering at each other as they ride their masters.

Honestly, he prefers Fiona chatting with Lucas to constantly fussing over his shield. She seems to have decided that the bottom half will feature one of her webs, and aside from the occasional check to ensure it's in pristine condition, she doesn't fiddle with it as she rides his back.

Once they near the mayor's manor, the guards out front spot them and wave. With their frequent visits to their friend, the other guards all recognize them on sight. Not that Freddie imagines that would be difficult. He, Rhonda, Fiona, and Lucas are a pretty unique group, after all.

As they get closer, Mr. Miller steps out to talk with the guards, who head inside before the group can get there. The ashen elf cuts an imposing figure, and a lot of the adults are clearly intimidated by the man, but Freddie can see the glint of amusement in his eyes with every interaction. He's definitely more than just a butler, but what's the point in calling him out on it? He's some special guard for the lord mayor, and he's certainly not evil, so there's no point in starting drama over something he can't even prove in the first place.

"Hello, Mr. Miller!" greets Rhonda. Freddie echoes her a moment after. The elf smiles at them and their spiders before speaking.

"Ah, come to steal away one of the young master's guards once more?"

Freddie smiles and nods with zero shame. "Yes. If he's available, that is?"

Mr. Miller gives a small smile and motions for them to come through the gates. "His shift will be over shortly. Would you mind accompanying me while he finishes up?"

Freddie doesn't mind, and a glance at Rhonda shows she's not opposed, either. Returning his attention to the tall elf, he nods. "That's fine with us. Did you need anything, Mr. Miller?"

His eyes sparkle with mischief as he gives a small nod. "Just to talk, young sir and miss. At my age, an elf often finds himself wanting to hear the sound of his own voice and is generally discouraged from simply talking to the mirror."

Rhonda giggles as Freddie nods, and the two fall in behind Mr. Miller as he leads them around the grounds of the manor.

"Thank you for indulging me. I wanted to thank you two, actually, and now I get the chance to be verbose about it."

"Thank us?" asks Freddie, with Rhonda looking just as confused. Mr. Miller takes their confusion in stride as he nods, still walking.

"Indeed. Though the young master is taking a more active role in the management of the town, it's my personal duty to see to the management of his household, and that includes the guards. Most are rather rough and tumble, you see, the sort that I would think would intimidate young Larrez. He's skilled and observant, but you two know how quiet he can be around those he doesn't know."

Freddie nods at that, as does Rhonda, with the goblin finding her reply before he can. "And high-strung! When we first met him, he was so jumpy and nervous!"

"Yeah, he was usually pretty focused in a fight, but after, he'd be jumping at shadows and stammering whenever we'd try to talk with him."

Mr. Miller agrees with a fond smile. "Indeed. But thanks to you two, he's become much more confident in himself. He's taken to his duties with aplomb, and is much happier for it. Not to mention how well you five all work together while delving. I used to worry he'd have a nervous breakdown and never leave his cot in the barracks, but now, I find myself wondering if he'll simply take up the mantle of an adventurer fulltime!" he jokes before letting his mirth fade.

"You two really have been a great help to him, and through him, to the young master. While I know you two befriended him simply because that's who you are, I find myself still in your debt." He holds up a hand as the two try to protest, the ghost of a smirk at a corner of his mouth. "I don't do something so extravagant as gifts, and I think young Larrez would perish from embarrassment if I were to offer something like that besides. Still, I have my own honor."

He stops and turns, meeting their gaze with an air of authority and significance. "If there is anything you two ever need, ask me, and it will be yours." The sudden shift in mood vanishes like smoke in the wind as he smirks at the two. "Within reason, of course. But you two are reasonable, so I'm sure there won't be any issue. I'd offer the same to your two arachnid companions, but spiderspeak was never my forte, I'm afraid."

He turns and resumes walking, with the two rushing to catch up after trying to figure out what just happened. "Oh, and please don't mention this to him. Young Larrez would feel awkward about this at best, you understand."

The two nod, able to process at least that with ease. Larrez always looks uncomfortable whenever they offer to cover his meal or get him some potion or other thing that might help him. Freddie thinks he doesn't like having debts, maybe from living on the streets or some other harsh upbringing. A gift from a friend isn't a debt, but that's all Freddie can think of for why Larrez always looks guilty for accepting help like that.

Larrez doesn't talk about his past much.

Freddie doesn't get to speculate much either, as he soon sees the wood elf hurry out the door to the gardens. Shock, then happiness, then more shock flash across his face before he heads for the group.

"Miller! Uh, sir! I hope my friends haven't been bothering you? I wouldn't want to throw off your schedule."

Mr. Miller chuckles and shakes his head. "Think nothing of it, young Larrez. I can show them the winter tulips while making my own rounds. They are most agreeable company, as I'm sure you'd agree."

"Then, uh . . . interior patrol concluded; nothing out of the ordinary, sir." Larrez stands at attention, and Mr. Miller runs an appraising eye over him before speaking.

"*Nothing*?"

Larrez slowly nods. "Yes?"

The older elf frowns for a moment before shaking his head. "Ah, that was rescheduled to seven. You're dismissed. Go have fun, and don't mention that to the others."

Larrez looks concerned about whatever is going to happen at seven, but Freddie steps up to help distract him, easily greeting his friend. "You heard him; let's go! I hope your shift wasn't too strenuous?"

Larrez shakes his head as he lets his friends lead him toward the front of the manor and the gate. "No, not really. There are a few auditors from the capital, but they're polite . . . almost to the point of boredom," he admits.

"Better than them being jerks, right?" asks Rhonda, but Larrez doesn't look so sure.

"Maybe, but shouldn't they be at least a little hostile? The crown doesn't call an audit as a favor to whoever's getting audited."

Freddie shrugs. "Maybe they just don't see any point in making the process more painful than it needs to be. And it's probably a good sign that they haven't found anything. If they did, they'd probably act like it at least a little?"

Larrez sighs. "Maybe. Either way, I shouldn't worry about it, right? Anything wrong will be on the mayor, not me."

"Do you think he'd try to sneak anything through the ledgers?" asks Rhonda, earning a quick shake of the head from Larrez.

"No!"

"Then there's nothing to worry about," points out Freddie. "Anyway, if you're not too tired from your patrols, we were going to go do some delving."

Larrez brightens at that. "That does sound nice. Can we stop by the guildhall first? I'd like to relax and maybe eat something before we go." The two are fine with that. Larrez continues as they exit the manor. "So, are you two excited for Rocky's challenger?"

Freddie gives him a confused look while Rhonda brightens at the reminder. "Oh yes! Master Staiven suggested I go talk to him! I'm feeling comfortable with Fire now, and I can feel there's something I'm close to . . ."

"Someone is challenging Rocky?" asks Freddie, apparently the only one not in the loop. Reading the histories in the archives is interesting, but he guesses it's easy to miss out on things happening now if he stays down there.

Larrez nods. "There's a retired adventurer helping the Dungeoneer's with their spring delves. He's supposed to be really strong—stronger than the other adventurers—so Thedeim challenged him to fight Rocky. There's even a betting pool at the guild."

"Huh." Freddie has trouble imagining someone who could actually fight Rocky. The zombie is just too good! "What're the odds like?"

Larrez shrugs. "I haven't been keeping track too much, but I think they're an even split. Everyone knows how strong Rocky is, but Olander is supposed to be one of the strongest delvers to come through Fourdock in a while. They say he's more used to belligerents around the capital, so to be from there and be able to basically retire . . ."

He leaves it unsaid as Freddie and Rhonda both nod. You don't get to retire from adventuring by being weak. Some people even say adventurers only retire once they run out of things to challenge them! If there's nothing to compete with him in the capital, can Rocky step up to provide it?

"If any dungeon can give him a challenge, it's Thedeim, and if anyone can give *Rocky* a challenge, it'd be someone who can handle the dungeons around the capital," comments Freddie while his friends agree.

"I think I'll check the challenge book while we eat, see what tricks he's picked up since we last saw him."

Freddie nods as they enter the guild, finding it pretty quiet at this time of day. The most active delvers are already off to Thedeim or the other dungeons by now, with only a few stragglers relaxing in the common area. Guildmaster Karn waves at the group as they enter, smiling and motioning for them to have a seat at the bar.

"Hey, strangers! You three finally found room in your schedules to come do a delve?"

Freddie chuckles as they all three nod. "Yeah. Rhonda and I have been busy with our studies. But you know, keep a blade at the wheel too long and you'll have nothing, so we're taking a break."

"Winter is a good time for extra training and drills at the manor, too," offers Larrez, which Karn accepts without comment.

"So, you three looking for a quest before going?"

"Lunch, actually," corrects Freddie, earning a wide smile from the guildmaster.

"Ah, of course! You two are probably eating your mentors into the poorhouse, heh. Well, the evening stew is still morning soup, but there is one upside to getting here at this time." He pauses for dramatic effect before turning and reaching into a basket behind him, revealing what he has with a flourish.

"It's not hot and steaming, but it's still a long way from stale! Even stale, I'd take a Cobble Bread roll over any of my cooking, heh. Three soups and three rolls, then?"

The group all agree before Rhonda makes to hop off her stool. "Imma check the library before we tuck in."

"Hold up a second, Rhonda," says Karn, much less jovial than before. Rhonda awkwardly tries to get back onto the stool properly as Karn motions for the three to lean in, where he lowers his voice. "There's a new librarian, and she's looking for you."

Rhonda and Larrez look confused, but Freddie frowns, his protective instincts already kicking into gear. "Why?"

Karn shakes his head. "I can guess, but I won't say it out loud. She doesn't know she's looking for Rhonda, though. She's a follower of the Great Mother, who told her to seek the Ice Sage."

Rhonda's eyes widen at that while Freddie fights the urge to draw his hatchet. Even Larrez has to consciously move his hand away from the hilt of his rapier. Karn nods at their reactions before continuing.

"She doesn't know what it is, and doesn't know about you. I don't think she's bad news, but it's on you how to handle this. Heh, just without violence. She's a good librarian; you'd probably all get along with her. Just making sure you know."

With that, he quickly gets their meals in front of them, though they all eat slower than usual as they think. A follower of the goddess of magic? Freddie doesn't understand the specifics of Rhonda's class, but he's not surprised a deity like that would be interested in his friend. He glances at her as they all eat, trying to figure out what she wants to do about this.

Whatever she decides, he'll be there for her.

Chapter 40

Rhonda

The goblin's mind races as she slowly eats the soup; even the nice bread can't distract her from her thoughts right now. How does that new person know about her? About her being an Ice Sage? As far as even Old Staiven knows, hers is a completely new class!

She's seen how the Church of the Crystal Shield has treated Freddie and his unique class: with friendly interest and a desire to help guide him, but she doesn't have that kind of support network. It's enough to tempt her . . . but the acolyte life just isn't for her, so she only has her mentor's advice to go on: be careful who you share with.

Karn doesn't seem to be too worried about what she might do, which is a relief, at least. If Rhonda knows anyone who can get a good read on a person, it's the retired rogue leading the guild. Still, while the librarian herself might be friendly, she's apparently a follower of the Great Mother. Is she looking to recruit Rhonda? It's not difficult to imagine the goddess of magic would be interested in her class, just like how the Shield is interested in Freddie's.

The Great Mother isn't as actively helpful as the Shield, and she's not exactly the most actively benevolent deity out there. She's hardly a plague on the land, but her priesthood seems more interested in pushing the bounds of magic without worrying too much about the consequences. Some of the most amazing and most terrible magical developments can be laid at their feet, and so at the feet of the Great Mother.

Does she even have the option to try to avoid her? Could she somehow take away Rhonda's magic? That concerning thought is easily quashed, at least. Taking someone's magic, if it's even something she can do, would only diminish the deity's own power. More people doing magic strengthens her domain, right? She might need to ask Freddie about that later, but the logic seems pretty sound to her.

The more she thinks about trying to lie low, the more she thinks the goddess is deliberately trying to give her that option. She clearly knows Rhonda is here, and she must know the only Ice Sage is a goblin, at least. But according to Karn, the librarian doesn't even know Ice Sage is a class, let alone one belonging to a goblin girl.

The newcomer's presence feels more like an invitation rather than a demand. She can reveal herself or keep her secret. So, which will it be? The shy part of her from before she got her class thinks she should keep quiet. Better to not attract attention. But she's grown a lot since she got her class . . . and keeping it a secret forever would be hindering her. She's a student *and* a teacher. She helps Master Staiven as she can, of course, but even he admits he's a bit too stuck in his ways for her suggestions to be much more than interesting theories for him to experiment with against his own established knowledge. If the new librarian is still inexperienced, she might be able to teach someone from the beginning!

And if she's making a mistake in trusting the outsider, she has plenty of friends to ensure nothing too bad will happen.

She nods to herself as she finishes the soup, her mind made up.

"I'm telling her."

Freddie and Larrez both give her surprised looks. "Just like that?" asks Freddie, with Larrez following up.

"Are you going to just go up there and introduce yourself and your class directly?"

Rhonda's resolve shakes at that question but doesn't crumble. "Well, maybe not quite like *that*, but I do want to tell her. I think by not giving her much information, the Great Mother is kinda letting me decide how and when to share, or even *if* to share at all."

Freddie considers that, slowly nodding. "She should know more than what she apparently told the librarian. If she wanted to force the issue, she has a *lot* of followers in the kingdom. That she apparently sent a single acolyte with sparse information does point at her trying to be diplomatic."

"Maybe she's not actually that interested?" suggests Larrez, earning a shake of the head from Freddie.

"She'd have delegated the message through a priest, but Karn didn't mention anything like that. If she appeared directly to the librarian, it was important to have her personal attention; important enough to attempt subtlety instead of being direct."

Rhonda nods. "I'm glad, too. If her High Priest or something was wandering around asking about me, I'd never leave the shop again!" Larrez makes a face at the idea of being sought out like that while Freddie snickers and nods.

"So, how are you going to go about it? Should we all go up there and chat with her?"

Rhonda thumbs the jewels on her staff as she thinks. "I think I'll go up there on my own and more or less do what I originally wanted: check out the book on Rocky's fights. If she really is a follower of the Great Mother, it shouldn't be hard to pique her interest with his fighting style. I might try to invite her along for our delve, if you two don't mind?"

Freddie smiles while Larrez shrugs. "I don't have any problem with it. Thedeim is pretty good about not overwhelming new delvers, so we should be able to escort her without issues."

Rhonda smiles at her friends and stands. "Then I'll be back before too long! You guys can check the quests for anything interesting while I'm at the library, if you want?"

Larrez and Freddie nod at that and stand, the two gathering the dishes as they do so. "I need to ask Karn if he knows any craftsmen who are available for commissions, too."

"The mayor's estate has a couple good armorers on retainer, if you want me to ask them later," offers the elf.

"Do they work with rare metals? I was thinking of trying to gather some today and offset the cost." The two chat about gear as they head off, and Rhonda heads up the stairs to the library, Lucas relaxing on her hat.

Once inside, the quiet hum of bees fills the air, lending an oddly calming atmosphere to the place of learning. The new librarian isn't difficult to spot; the elf in dust-colored robes is sitting at a table, reading a book. It looks like she's deep in her studies, too, and Rhonda wonders if that's how she herself looks when in the middle of something interesting.

If it were any other day, she might let her keep reading, but the ice needs to be broken. She raps the end of her staff on the floor, not loud enough to be disturbing but enough to get her attention in the quiet room full of books and bees. The elf moves a finger to mark her spot as she looks at Rhonda, clearly used to being interrupted in her studies.

Instead of looking sour, she smiles and stands. "Ah, sorry. I was engrossed in my book. How can I help you?"

Rhonda's shyness tries to surge once more, but she forces it down as she speaks. "Uh, I'm looking for the book on Rocky's fights? I want to place a bet with Karn, but I want to make sure I'm up on his techniques, first."

The librarian looks confused before turning her attention to the bees. "Rocky's fights?" The bees buzz, and several mill around in the air over one of the shelves. "Ah, delving logs. Is he a strong delver?" she asks as she leads the way, with Rhonda following along behind her.

"Oh, he's very strong, but he's not a delver. He's one of Thedeim's scions."

That draws the librarian up short. "The guildmaster bets on people's lives?" she asks, sounding like she can't believe it. Rhonda giggles and shakes her head.

"Lives? Nah. Rocky is undefeated, but he hasn't killed anyone. None of Thedeim's scions do. In fact, there's no recorded deaths at all. He works pretty hard to keep it that way, too."

"No . . . Wait, undefeated?" the elf asks, trying to process what she's hearing. Rhonda clearly isn't the only one who's been hitting the books too hard to keep up with the local goings-on. She nods as the librarian remembers she's supposed to be getting a book, and they chat as they go.

"Undefeated, yeah. He's Thedeim's Zombie Scion, and he fights like nothing else. His mastery of affinities is second to none."

"Affinities . . . in a *zombie*? Not a lich?"

Rhonda laughs at the common confusion. "Not a lich! He likes to punch things, but he infuses them with his affinities with skill and precision. My friends and I have fought him a couple times, though only once for real." The goblin snorts at the memory. "He knocked us out with ease once we stopped holding back, but it's good to have something to aspire to."

The librarian doesn't look like she shares that opinion. "If you say so? I've never tried adventuring. It seems too dangerous, even for all the benefits it can bring."

"You should give Thedeim a try, then. The manor and grounds are designed for new delvers."

The elf shakes her head, smiling at the absurdity of the idea. "I don't think it's for me."

"Are you at least going to go see Olander and Rocky fight?"

The elf's hand freezes in the middle of taking the book from the shelf, her eyes wide with concern. "*Olander*?"

Rhonda raises an eyebrow at her and nods. "Yeah? The retired elf adventurer with the glaive who's been helping the Dungeoneer's Guild. Why, do you know him?"

She takes a deep breath before pulling the book down and handing it to Rhonda. "He's a friend of mine. We met on the way here. He was a caravan guard."

Rhonda nods at that as she leads the way back. "That makes sense. He's supposed to be really strong. That's why Thedeim offered him a challenge."

The librarian pauses and slaps her palm against her forehead. "*That's* why the book sounded familiar! He wanted to look into it, too!"

"Did you go over it with him?"

She sighs and shakes her head. "No, I thought he was checking on a local legendary monster from the past, not something he was getting ready to fight himself!"

"Well, want to go over it with me, then? Your friend will be safe, no matter what we see in here, so don't worry about that. We could even go and meet

Rocky directly so you can see how friendly he is. My friends and I are pretty good at delving."

Rhonda watches the conflict reflect on the elf's face as she tries to make a decision. It's not difficult to follow her thought process. If Rhonda didn't know anything about Thedeim, she'd be really worried about Freddie challenging an undefeated scion, too! She's not sure which way the elf will decide, so maybe she should bait the trap a bit more.

"You're a follower of the Great Mother, right? Your robes are in that style."

The surprise question knocks the wagon of her thoughts off the trail, and she nods. "Yes, but—"

"Then you'll definitely want to hear about how Rocky fights. My mentor says he shouldn't be able to do half the things he does with his magic, and he's the smartest person I know!"

The allure of a magical oddity tips the scales in the elf's mind, and she agrees. "I . . . suppose? I haven't been making any headway in my studies, and I *would* like to know what Olander will be up against."

"Great!" With that, they arrive back at the front. They move aside the book the librarian had been reading, and Rhonda realizes she hasn't introduced herself yet. "Oh, I'm Rhonda, by the way."

"Oh! I'm Tula! I'm sorry I didn't introduce myself earlier. I've been a bit frazzled with my studies lately, you see."

Rhonda waves off her apology and takes a seat, opening the book. She takes a few moments to find a fight she's not familiar with and turns to the page as she chats. "I know how easy it is to get distracted with research, and to be frustrated when you can't make progress."

Thankfully, the details of the fights make it easy to ignore past frustrations as Tula and Rhonda go over Rocky's record. He's gotten a *lot* better after tangling with the Maw, and Rhonda is feeling confident in placing her bet on the scion. For Tula, what started out as simply listening turns into furious note-taking as she tries to comprehend how Rocky does what he does. By the time they reach the last fight, she's taken more notes than she took on her other research project!

She goes over them as Rhonda smiles in triumph, knowing she's got the librarian right where she wants her. "So, you want to go meet Rocky? I promise it'll be safe, and he might even be willing to give you a demonstration if you ask nicely."

Tula's instinctual refusal dies before it ever reaches her lips, a burning curiosity making its move. She's still uncertain, but despite how brutal each fight was, the difference in penmanship gives credence to the fact of them all being first-hand accounts from the challengers. So much power wielded perfectly to defeat but not kill.

"If . . . you're sure your party won't mind?"

The goblin smiles wide. "They'll love to! Do you have any focus or anything like that? Just because Thedeim is safe doesn't mean he won't make you work for it!"

She reaches into the neck of her robes and produces her wooden holy symbol. "I have this?"

"That should work fine. Let's go get you introduced to Freddie and Larrez!" She takes Tula's hand and makes for the door, the elf resisting only a little as she looks back to the safety of the books and shelves. The bees swarm together and swing side to side, waving goodbye as the Ice Sage drags the invitation off to adventure.

Chapter 41

It took a bit of convincing, but my nerd squad is finally willing to leave the topic of kaboom for later. Thing, Honey, Queen, and Poppy are back to working on how to help with the tree, and acting like it's just a coincidence they're looking into fertilizers.

Well, joke's on them. I don't know much about what goes into making some proper boom. Honestly, I don't think that particular part of Teemo's explanation held too much water for them, but the safety concerns did get through their eager heads that it should be something to explore later, and in *very* small scale. Because it's not difficult at all to make something that explodes—the trick is in making it only explode when you want it to.

Still, I'm content to let everyone pretend nobody knows about any ulterior motives. Unless they get into the *really* big booms, I think magic's existence will make them more parlor tricks than weapons. Fireworks could be cool, though.

Anyway, I'm just glad they're back on track, and Teemo is relieved to have headed that particular disaster off at the pass.

My new scions have settled into their spawners, letting their new status set in. I don't think they're going to change too much, at least on the outside. Leo didn't. Teemo didn't. Fluffles is the outlier, honestly. Though speaking of scions who might change, I take a moment to track down Nova to see what she's up to. She's not in her spawner but rather deep in the labyrinth, toying with some magma.

I still don't know why she didn't get a title for beating the Redcap. He was a Conduit, and she beat him! That should earn a title, right? It seems unfair to me, but maybe the real credit went to the Harbinger, since it subsumed the Maw? Either way, I might be indignant about it, but Nova isn't. A mix of concentration and happiness bubbles from her bond with me as she works the magma like a sculptor might work clay.

I'm pretty sure she's gotten Fire affinity, and a quick peek at her stats confirms that. I would have expected Earth first, but from what I can tell, she's focusing on controlling the heat to only let the magma solidify exactly where she wants instead of letting it solidify mostly in place and use Earth affinity to add the finishing touches.

She's probably not far from making that leap, though. She's working on little figurines of the other scions, and though she's getting a lot of detail into them, it'd probably be more accurate to call them statuettes. I think she's limited in what kind of scale she can manage until she can start manipulating the solidified stone directly. Still, they look great. If she keeps this up, I'm going to start decorating the labyrinth and beyond with her work.

She pauses as she feels that idea, but pushes her worry aside as she continues working. Her small Tiny is her most intricate yet, so she can't afford to let distractions keep her from making it just right. I pat the bond with encouragement before turning my attention to my High Priestess as she works with the antkin.

Right now, she's meeting with the newly elected leaders of the enclave. The antkin were waiting for her input before they chose, but she had to admit most of the thesis projects were beyond her. She did at least encourage them that it seemed like a fine way to choose leadership to her. They still wrangled her into being the one to read the names of the winners, though.

The rest of the enclave is partying, with my other dwellers mingling and chatting, too. The leaders and Aranya are gathered in the city hall, which the new worker dean and headmaster worked on. It's not the only city hall candidate, but the others will be used for things like a library, a school, a church, and so on.

His name's Ed; I think most of the antkin have single-syllable names. Ed sits at the front of the table with Aranya, with the former looking like he maybe should have thought about what being the headmaster meant before volunteering for the role.

And though I say head of the table, it's a hexagon, so each of the deans could be considered to be sitting at their own head. Going around clockwise is Tam the medical dean, Jeb the ranching dean, Nik the engineering dean, Zac the alchemy dean, and Liv the enchanting dean.

Jeb, Nik, and Zac are guys—along with Ed, of course—while Tam and Liv are ladies. They're a little bigger than the guys, but not nearly like I was expecting. The spiderkin have a way more pronounced size difference between the sexes, and I don't think the antkin are going to be changing much more. While they've all filled in a bit, the only real obvious change has been in the enchanter ants.

The subtle runes now dimly pulse with power, and I think the color correlates to their affinity. Magma is still the most common, but there's still a lot of others represented. I'd examine everyone closer, but Ed decides it's time to start.

"Well, welcome to city hall, Deans. Is there any business we need to discuss right now?"

"Food," says Jeb simply. Aranya nods at that.

"Now that you have your leadership sorted, you need to be self-sufficient to complete the transition from denizen to dweller."

"Can we just eat the things you ranch?" asks Nik, probing the obvious solution.

Jeb thinks for a few moments before shaking his head. "Some of 'em are good for eating, but I don't think we have the space to scale up ranching for food."

"Perhaps as a supplement, then?" suggests Tam. "Having a variety of food sources will make it easier to deal with anything unfortunate in a single method."

"Some kind of farm, then?" mentions Zac. "We have some small gardens for reagents, but we also don't have the room to scale up to feed everyone."

"We should consider hunting, too," suggests Liv. "The other enclaves hunt outside for food and other interesting things. While we appear to be losing some of our heat resistance, we should still be able to hunt deeper, especially with some proper enchantments."

"I'd love to learn the construction of the bows and spears Lord Thedeim showed the other enclaves. It'd give us a good starting point for things beyond defensive traps," adds Nik.

Ed nods at the suggestions and carves a few notes on a slate. "I think the workers can easily expand the ranching and gardening areas to include some food production. I imagine the alchemists would like us to handle that portion of the growing?" At Zac's nod, Ed turns to Jeb. "And the ranchers?"

"Hmm. We could use a hand with some of it, but I think we'll be able to handle being in charge of livestock. Some of the more exotic beasts are a handful. Livestock should be easier to handle for the ones still learning, and for the more experienced to be able to relax with."

Ed nods and jots down a few numbers. "Who will handle the hunting?"

The antkin look conflicted as they weigh their individual faction's ability, even Ed. Aranya steps in and speaks up with an encouraging smile. "If there's no clear choice, try comparing notes."

They nod to that, and Ed organizes his thoughts first. "I think the workers *could* do it. We're very versatile, but I don't know if we'd have what it takes to be proficient hunters."

Tam speaks next. "The medics prefer not to shed blood, but I think we would be able to identify weaknesses in potential prey. Unfortunately, I don't know if we'd actually be able to take something down."

"The ranchers should be able to handle anything out there," proclaims Jeb. "But we're not exactly stealthy. I'm pretty sure anything we could take would see us coming and make themselves scarce."

Nik takes a few more seconds to think before answering in turn. "I think we could make something to make hunting easier, but most of the engineers will probably be preoccupied in our workshops and only be able to go out to hunt when testing a prototype."

Zac and Liv both nod at that, with the former speaking up first. "The alchemists will be the same, and by the look on Liv's face, the enchanters are similar?"

She nods. "Indeed. We could outfit someone very well, but time spent hunting would be time not spent creating improvements."

"Perhaps you should try small, mixed teams?" suggests Aranya. "A worker, a rancher, and a medic, equipped with gear from the other three factions." The ants seem to like the sound of that, so Aranya continues. "After the meeting, you should talk with the other enclaves, especially Vernew. If anyone can help you figure out hunting, it'll be her."

Ed nods and speaks up. "Then I think that's all we need for the moment, unless anyone has anything else to bring up?" Heads shake, so he continues. "Then, meeting adjourned. Jeb, Tam, let's go see if we can find Vernew in the celebration. Crafters, please bring up the need for hunting with your factions tomorrow. Otherwise, let's go have some fun."

The antkin and Aranya cheer to that, though she stays behind for a moment as they head out to join the revelry. "I'm glad I was able to get back for this. It's so fulfilling to see them grow into themselves." She smiles toward my core, not caring about the distance and caves and such between her and it. "No wonder You do things the way You do."

Chapter 42

While my enclaves are having a nice social gathering/party, the delvers are having their own kind of fun. In fact, I notice a particular group has just arrived, and they brought an extra friend along this time. Rhonda, Freddie, and Larrez—along with Lucas and Fiona, of course—are also leading an elven girl probably about Larrez's age who looks like a scribe who got lost.

It's pretty apparent she knows she's in a dungeon by the way she looks around even just the yard with wide, nervous eyes. Teemo heads there as the group takes their time, chatting and trying to put the scribe at ease.

"See?" says Freddie, gesturing at the calmness that is the walkway to the manor and the front yard. "No crazy traps or brutal denizens. Thedeim likes to let adventurers choose just how much adventure they want."

The elven lady doesn't look too convinced, but she's at least following everyone to the porch. She doesn't step onto it, though, as she spots the aranea and freezes in her tracks, staring. Teemo picks that moment to pop out of a shortcut behind her and speak up.

"Never seen a questboard before?" he asks, startling the poor thing, who whips around but can't find the speaker. "Down here," he helpfully provides. She fearfully glances down, probably expecting some horror, but looks confused when all she sees is Teemo.

"A talking rat?"

Teemo puffs himself up and stands on his hind legs. "I'm *the* talking rat, lady."

The scribe only looks more confused as the others laugh at Teemo's antics. "Tula, that's Teemo. He's Thedeim's Voice," informs Rhonda. I can practically hear Tula's train of thought derail multiple times while she tries to process that.

"The dungeon? The same dungeon that's supposed to have an undefeated scion? Has a rat for a Voice?"

Teemo nods before slipping through a shortcut to land on her shoulder. "Yep, there's only one Thedeim, thankfully. I don't think the world could handle two of him, heh. First time in a dungeon, hmm?"

Tula nods at that, still trying to process what she's learning as Rhonda takes her hand and guides her onto the porch. "Don't hurt yourself trying to figure him out, Tula. I'm pretty sure even Mr. Tarl has given up on that, and he's an inspector!"

While Freddie and Larrez chuckle, Tula absently moves a finger to rub Teemo's chin, who accepts the tribute with zero grace and leans into it.

"That's the stuff."

"But he's so . . . cute! How can a dungeon have a cute little rat for a Voice and also have some crazy powerful Zombie Scion, too?"

Teemo pulls himself away from the pets with visible effort to answer her. "The Boss doesn't standardize us. I'm his Voice, so I'm good with people, and I tell it like it is. Rocky is his fighting scion, so he's a monster in a fight, and a good teacher for anyone else looking to learn their way around combat. Pretty much all of us have our own niches, and the Boss lets us be ourselves."

Tula resumes petting Teemo as she thinks, earning a happy squeak from him while the others look over the quests.

"Did you want to get a quest, Tula?" asks Freddie, eyeing a couple kill quests.

"Um . . . no? I've never done much fighting, and I don't really do gathering, either . . ."

"Do you know any runework?" asks Larrez as he peruses the mining quests. "There are a lot of ways to get reagents for it here."

"I . . . can do scrolls and other inscriptions, but I haven't really practiced it," she admits, earning a smile from Rhonda.

"Herbalism is probably the best way to get ingredients for magical ink and dyes. I'll show you the basics, if you want?"

Tula still looks uncertain, but she doesn't refuse, so Rhonda points her at a quest to gather some ochredill. "Ochredill is a staple, great for neutral bases for all kinds of things, and easy to gather, too."

The elven woman cautiously reaches for the indicated plank, finding it easy to pull down and claim for herself. "Are you going to gather anything, Rhonda?" she asks.

"Nah. I need to talk with Rocky and probably Norloke, Freddie needs to visit Aranya for a couple minutes, and looks like Larrez wants to do some mining."

The indicated elf absently nods as he continues looking over the mining quests. "Freddie mentioned having a piece of an odd anthill from the labyrinth, layered with steel and orichalcum. I think if we can get more, I can convince the mayor's armorer to try to do something with it." He pauses as he spots a plank that sticks out. "Hmm . . . damanascus? Is that what it's called?"

Freddie shrugs. "I dunno. I don't have enough right now for anything, so I didn't bother taking it to a smith."

Larrez shrugs and takes the plank. "If it's the wrong thing, we can sell it."

"I'm pretty sure that's what you're after," supplies Teemo from Tula's shoulder. "That's from one of the crucible anthills in the labyrinth. Anyway, what brings you all here today? Just showing your new friend the fun of adventuring?"

Rhonda shakes her head. "That too, but we've been cooped up all winter, and they said we should get out and have some fun. And I need to get some new robes."

"The ones Rocky gave you don't fit anymore?" asks Teemo, giving her a look over. I don't think she's grown *that* much, has she?

Freddie perks up at the mention of that robe. "Oh yeah! That robe looked cool. It's too small already?"

Rhonda looks bashful before replying. "I, uh . . . haven't really checked. They just look so good! I wouldn't want to ruin them on a delve!"

Teemo hops to her shoulder as Lucas moves to the other, and both flick her ears. "They're made for delving, Rhonda, just like Freddie's hatchet. You should go grab them. If they fit properly, great. If they are a little small, I'm sure Norloke can let them out a bit, especially if Thing and Queen come help."

"Speaking of the other scions, how's Jello with armor?" asks Freddie. "I'm outgrowing mine, which is why I'm looking for materials and a smith."

"I'll be right back, guys. I'll get my robes," interjects Rhonda before she rushes off while everyone else keeps talking.

Teemo smoothly transitions over to Larrez's shoulder before answering. "I'm sure she'd like a new project. I think Queen and Thing are going to have her occupied, though. The Boss has a new kind of armor that they're still prototyping. It worked well enough against the Maw, but it has issues with lasting longer than a couple battles still. You could help test it if you want, but I'd probably stick with the guy Larrez knows if you want something reliable."

"Maybe I could do both? Gather materials for a traditional set of armor, and volunteer to test whatever you're making. How is he making special armor, though? I've seen the weird bows. Is he going to put a bunch of ropes and pulleys on the armor, too?"

I briefly wonder if I could do something with that for mechanical advantage, like a medieval power armor, but Teemo laughs and shakes his head. "Nah, the Boss is just making it out of weird stuff. I'll see if I can't get a sample for you to look at later. How about you, Tula? Anything you were hoping to get done in here today?"

"I . . . I want to meet Rocky," she admits, surprising me and Teemo both.

"Yeah? You want to learn how to punch things?"

She shakes her head. "No. It's . . . His magic is strange. From the accounts I've read, it's like he can switch affinities on the fly. It should be impossible, but there are way too many reports for people to just be making things up. If I could figure it out, I'm sure the Great Mother would be happy with me."

"Great Mother?" echoes Teemo.

She nods, pulling out a little pendant depicting open hands from her robe. "Laermali, the Great Mother of Magic."

Oh? Oh. Ooohhhhh . . .

Teemo has a better poker face than I do. "Ah, makes sense. Did she send you to talk to the Boss?"

Tula looks confused. "No? Why would She?"

"Because the Boss showed Rocky how to do it. He showed all of us, really. It's just that Rocky is really good at it."

"But . . . how . . . ?" stammers Tula, trying to wrap her head around how a dungeon of all things could start breaking magic like I have. Then Teemo goes in for the kill.

"That's why I thought you would be here to talk to the Boss. She sounds like she'd be too busy to come chat with her newest coworker herself, so sending an acolyte would be the obvious step."

Tula looks equally confused and offended, and Larrez interrupts. "Uh . . . I don't think Thedeim counts as a . . .'coworker'? The enclaves revere him, sure, but he's not—"

"He is," corrects Teemo, to the confusion of the elves. Freddie, though, looks like he's figured it out. "He apotheosized and everything after the Maw. The Raven himself visited, we had a chat, the Boss went a bit sideways, and I exploded in orange." He smirks at the reaction to his description of events. "I got better, but the Boss is stuck with being fully fledged now. Poor guy."

Tula and Larrez stare, jaws slack, while Freddie chuckles and shakes his head. "No wonder Torlon wanted me to welcome Aranya back. I bet the Shield wants to make sure everything is still fine between you two."

Teemo nods at that. "Oh yeah. While the Boss wants to officially keep a bit of daylight between himself and any other gods, the Shield has good people working under it. He's happy to continue working together like that."

"I'll make sure Torlon hears that." Freddie smiles as the elves continue to stare, not even reacting when Rhonda bursts through the gates with her robe in her arms. She hurries to the group, oblivious to the bombshell Teemo dropped.

"Whew, I'm back! The robes might be a *little* tight in the chest or shoulders? I'll definitely want to ask Norloke to check the fit. Anyway, what'd I miss?"

Chapter 43

Rhonda looks at Tula and Larrez with curious eyes, wondering why they look so shocked. Freddie rescues them from saying it themselves, even if that probably only reinforces reality for them. It kinda does for me, too. It's still weird to think about.

"Thedeim's a god."

Rhonda tilts her head in confusion. "Hasn't he been for a while? Aranya and the enclaves have been worshiping him."

The orc chuckles and shakes his head. "Being worshiped doesn't make someone a god, even if someone's faith is strong enough to focus their magic through them."

Larrez's mind finally seems to grind into gear, though he's still clearly trying to process things. "I asked Torlon about that a while ago. I just . . . never expected to see the difference become moot."

That gets Freddie's curiosity. "Oh? What were you two talking about?"

"It was not long after I first met Aranya. Teemo said Thedeim didn't worry too much about it and said he was pretty sure he wasn't a god. I asked Torlon, and he explained the difference between gods and focuses of faith. For people like us, the difference seems a bit . . . academic."

That seems to help get Tula on track, too. "There's . . . a lot of arguments about it, but . . . that seems right. Actual deities have more power and can thusly empower their worshipers directly, but even that is usually reserved for people like Prophets or High Priests. But for him to be an actual deity . . ."

Tula and Larrez look haunted, while Rhonda and Freddie seem pretty nonchalant about the whole thing. Teemo speaks into the quiet, hoping to keep any worries to a minimum. "He's just Thedeim to you guys, so don't worry about it. I think you all are more worried about his status than he is. He tries to mostly just keep doing what he's been doing. You wanted to learn about Rocky's affinity stuff, right, Tula?"

"Er . . . I wouldn't want to impose on—"

"It's no imposition. The big lug is eager to show off and hear opinions for some of his latest tricks. Don't go trying to make things all formal. If Laermali wants to make something official, she can send someone with a more direct line. If *you* want to learn, all you have to do is get to him." My Voice smiles at the gathered party. "And it looks to me like you have a good party to do that. So, where are you guys gonna go first?"

Freddie looks over the group before answering. "I think Tula and Larrez are still recovering, so maybe it'd be best if we visit the spiderkin first? Unless Miss Aranya is closer?"

Teemo shakes his head. "Nah, she's still in the Antkin Enclave, helping them adjust. They've finally sorted their leadership, so now they need to secure food for themselves. I'm sure I could get her to come meet you at the training room, though. She'd like to see you guys again, and I bet she'd like to get a preview of what the fight will be like, too."

Rhonda nods at that. "That sounds perfect! I don't think I should be too long with Norloke. I can give her the robes and see what she thinks of the fit, then leave it to her to adjust." She pauses as she realizes something. "Uh . . . what should I pay her? Do you think she'd accept potions in trade?"

Teemo shrugs. "Probably, but you'd have to ask her. I think she'd normally not charge you anything for it, but the spiderkin are sewing up a storm after their deal with that cloth merchant. I think they want to try their hands at the new composite armor, too. I'll get you that sample so you can check it out while she plays dress-up, Freddie. You guys want a shortcut?"

Freddie shakes his head. "No, but thanks. I think we could use some time to process, or to let a couple encounters take our minds off of things." Larrez looks relieved at that suggestion, though Tula still looks nervous about the whole thing.

"Alright. You guys have fun. I'll go get that sample and let Norloke know to expect you guys soon." He gives them a wave before slipping through another shortcut, but I keep watching, curious to see how they do. It'll be an interesting challenge to give them some fun without scaring Tula to death. It's always difficult to plan encounters when there's a big level disparity in a party.

"Um . . . maybe I should go . . ." quietly suggests Tula, earning the focus of the group.

"It'll be fine," assures Rhonda. "He didn't tell you to leave or anything, and we can keep you safe, don't worry."

"It just . . . feels a lot bigger than what I should be sticking my nose into. I thought I'd be looking at a weird scion, which is already something really big! But now that weird scion is working for a new god?" She shudders. "I just don't want to mess this up. It sounds like something the Great Mother should have sent a proper priest for at least, not just a little scribe . . ."

Freddie rests a hand on her shoulder. "She didn't. She sent you. She thinks you're the right person for the job." His gentle smile shifts to a humorous one. "Besides, someone with actual authority would be the last person to send to Thedeim. He likes things informal. You'll do fine."

Tula looks encouraged, but not enough that she's going to just go charging in. "I . . . You think so? You think She sent me for this?"

Freddie shrugs. "I follow the Shield, not her, so I won't try to say what she'd do. It just seems to me that she *could* have sent her High Priest but didn't. I think it was a deliberate decision."

"Besides, I don't think you could make a worse first impression than the Shield did," points out Larrez with a grin, earning a laugh from Freddie and a confused look from Tula.

"What?"

"I'll tell you the story while we move. Let's take the access shaft," suggests Freddie, and soon, they're moving. I go ahead and send a stronger probing encounter than usual: an electric dire rat and a spitting viper. Tula gulps when she sees them, though Rhonda hands her a potion.

"Drink that. It should help with the lightning attack."

"Lightning?!" Tula stares at the potion before chugging it while Freddie and Larrez get into position to keep the denizens at bay.

"Anyway, the story," starts Freddie, taking his stance with Fiona and Larrez at his side. "There used to be a murderous dungeon in town called Neverrest. It was in the cemetery. It started encroaching on Thedeim, so he fought it, beat it, and subsumed it, making the graveyard available again."

The viper and rat attack at once, with the viper spitting at Freddie and the rat whipping its tail to sling electricity at Larrez, hoping to arc into the others using him as the base. Freddie raises his shield without hardly missing a beat in the story, while Larrez maneuvers his sword and watery duplicate to intercept the bolt. "Levee Parry!"

Much like a levee helps guide rivers, his rapier and water combine to channel the lightning to the ground, stopping the attack in its tracks, much to the disappointment of the rat.

"Attack the tail!" suggests Tula, even as Freddie keeps telling the story while he and Fiona keep the viper occupied.

"With the cemetery free, it just needed to be reconsecrated before people could be buried again. I still didn't have my class at the time, but I'd delved with Rhonda a few times, so I was sent along to help keep everyone safe during the ritual."

Rhonda looks like she's trying to keep her magic more subtle than usual, and she quietly heats Freddie's hatchet as she summons several icicles to hurl at the rat, aiming for the tail like Tula suggested. It's not an easy target to hit, but with Larrez attacking, she manages to hit it right at the base. Sparks fly as it loses control of the current, giving Larrez plenty of time to pierce it through the eye, cleanly finishing it off.

"The acolyte in charge tried to consecrate the cemetery in the name of the Shield, but was rebuffed. I didn't know it at the time, but doing it like that tries to form a pact between the dungeon and the deity. There's a generic version that the acolyte was supposed to do, but he didn't. Searing Slash!"

He interrupts his own story to step forward and swing at the viper just after Fiona gets a web net onto it. It wouldn't hold the viper for long, but his buffed attack lets him quickly decapitate the dangernoodle and finish the encounter.

Tula looks relieved when the fighting is over, taking a few moments to process both the encounter and the story Freddie was telling. "Wait, a pact? And the dungeon rejected it? But I thought Teemo said Thedeim liked the Shield?"

Freddie shrugs as he inspects the head, seeing if he can get the venom glands out without too much damage. "He did and he does, but he didn't want to make a pact. Then the acolyte tried to *exorcise* Thedeim."

Tula's eyes widen at that, but Freddie's not done with the story just yet. "So Larx, the elder of the Ratkin Enclave, consecrated the cemetery instead while the acolyte was preparing a stronger ritual to exorcise him. He made a big ruckus shouting at Larx, so Grim—Thedeim's Skeleton Scion—came over to investigate. Then he tried to turn Grim, but the magic had no effect on him at all. And you know what Grim did?"

Tula looks nervous as she replies. "Attack? I mean, it sounded like the acolyte was doing everything in his power to anger the dungeon."

Freddie smiles and shakes his head. "Nope. He shushed the acolyte. After that, we left before he could embarrass himself anymore, heh."

Larrez chuckles at the story and looks at Tula. "See? I can't picture you doing anything worse than that."

She titters at that, looking relieved to know I'm not going to just sic my scions on her for an accidental insult, or even a deliberate one. "That does make me feel better, at least."

Freddie returns to the viper head and pulls out a small knife to try to dress it for the glands, giving Rhonda a chance to speak up.

"So, how'd you know about the tail? We've fought them a few times, but mostly just use potions to deal with the lightning. Good parry by the way, Larrez!"

He smiles at the compliment. "Thank you. I got the idea from the lightning rod at the mayor's manor. I had to clean it with Mr. Miller's guidance, and he talked about how lightning always seeks the ground. I'm curious about how you knew about the tail too, Tula."

She looks bashful at the attention, but doesn't keep the secret for too long. "Well . . . I don't really do adventuring much because I have Knowledge affinity. Can't really hit harder with it, but I can analyze and find weaknesses. Not that I can usually take advantage of them, but still."

"Sounds useful," comments Freddie as he works on the glands. I think he's going to manage it, too. They're pretty tricky to get out, but he's taking his time and doing it right.

Rhonda and Larrez both nod their agreement. "Maybe we can get you to come adventure with us more often, then?" asks the elf. "We're pretty good at adapting to whatever attacks come our way, but having a better idea of what to expect would make things easier."

". . . Maybe? That was still frightening, but . . . was it really useful?"

"Definitely," assures Rhonda. "In fact, if we fight another one, I think I'll try to avoid the tail and see if Freddie can get it off in one piece. I bet Master Staiven can use it for Lightning Resist potions at the least! Oh, that reminds me!" Rhonda turns back to the house and points at the herbalism nodes growing along the back.

"You need some ochredill! Let's grab that before we head to the enclave."

Freddie stands, knife cleaned and put away, and glands securely in a vial in a pouch. "Works for me. I hope we get to fight another electric dire rat just for the look on Old Staiven's face when I slam a big rat butt on his counter and ask for money."

They laugh at the image as they head for the nodes, and I smile to myself, glad to see them making friends.

Chapter 44

I keep watching as they delve, carefully picking what denizens to send their way. If they were doing a more ordinary delve, I think they'd get overwhelmed. Tula does her best, but there really is a significant gulf in her power compared to the others, and I don't know that they'd be able to pick up the slack if I treated them like a larger party adventuring in the cavern layer.

Luckily for them, they're headed for the enclave, so I make sure the denizens take it easy on them. They still need to pay the toll, but I have no intention of cutting my spiderkin off from the surface. By the time they reach the enclave, Tula is looking a bit haggard, but at least not traumatized.

"I can't believe you all do that for fun . . ." she grumbles, much to the others' amusement.

"Aw, it wasn't that bad, was it?" asks Freddie, forcing Tula to sigh and admit the truth.

"It wasn't as bad as I feared, but . . . I don't think I'm coming back without all of you, or maybe Olander."

"Hard to argue with the experience, too," adds Larrez, earning another grudging nod from the scribe.

"Let's go find Norloke. The enclave is as safe as Fourdock, so don't worry." Rhonda nods at the guards as the group enters the enclave, giving Tula her first sight of my spiderkin industriously going about their day.

Right now, they're focused on ensuring their capture baskets are properly repaired for the harvest. The cave lobsters are about ready to be culled and distributed to the live wells of the residents, making room for the next generation of tasty little pinchers.

Larrez is the first to notice the reason, or at least the first to voice it as they head for Norloke's home. "It looks like they're getting ready to harvest their lobsters. Have you guys had them before?"

The others shake their heads, with Rhonda replying first. "I hear they used to be a pretty common food back before Hullbreak went nuts, but they've been too rare for orphans like us to try."

"I've had crayfish, but there are no lobsters where I used to live," adds Tula.

"I've had them before," admits Larrez. "They're alright. Well, sea lobsters. I haven't tried the cave ones. They're supposed to be pretty easy to cook."

"Maybe we should come back later to see if they have any extra to sell," suggests Freddie. "The spiderkin seem to really like them, so they can't be terrible."

Rhonda looks uncertain about that. "They look weird. But I guess a plucked chicken looks weird, too. I'd be willing to give it a try, at least."

"I wonder why they always leave the head feathers on . . ." muses Freddie as they arrive.

Rhonda knocks on the door to the ground level of Norloke's elaborate home. While many spiderkin are starting to take to making stone or brick homes on the floor, Norloke and the other weavers especially still like to weave their homes up near the ceiling of the cave. Of course, they still have guests, so they have at least a small room or two built on the ground floor, and generally keep their live wells there.

The knocking gets the spiderkin's attention, and she pokes her head out from her silken abode in the ceiling, smiling and waving as she recognizes who's come to call.

"Ah, Freddie, Rhonda, and Larrez! And Lucas and Fiona, too! Oh, and a new friend? Give me a moment to get these last few stitches, and I'll be right down!"

They oblige, with Tula looking around the enclave at the busy spiderkin. "I've never been in an enclave before. I'm not sure what I was expecting," she admits.

"I wonder if they could make you some silk robes," ponders Freddie. "Rhonda's going to be asking about some, so you could, too. I don't think them dyeing it would be a problem, either."

"I'm not sure I could afford it. These work well enough."

"No harm in asking," points out Rhonda. Tula shrugs in defeat at that as Norloke exits her silken room, nimbly climbing down to greet the group.

"Thank you all for waiting! Now, to what do I owe the pleasure?" she asks with a smile as she opens the door, ushering them all in. The room itself may be made of stone and bricks, but the weaver has covered practically every surface in soft silks, lending it an elegant, almost ephemeral atmosphere. She waves a hand for them to all take a seat as she takes her own, eagerly awaiting their answer.

"Well, we wanted to visit and catch up some," starts Rhonda before pulling out the nice robe Rocky had made for her. Norloke's eyes twinkle in recognition as the goblin continues. "And to ask if you can do adjustments on this? I'm kinda outgrowing my current robes. I was going to ask for something new, but Teemo reminded me of this. It was just too nice to wear for ordinary delving, but . . ."

Norloke laughs brightly as she holds out her arms for the robe. "Oh, it is a very nice robe. I remember when they were presented to you! I hope you weren't worried about ruining them somehow? Rocky had these made specifically for delving, just like Freddie's hatchet and Larrez's rapier."

"Did you help him make the robe?" asks Freddie. Norloke shakes her head.

"No, he kept it a secret until the reveal. We probably should have realized he was up to something when the aranea started watching us for a while, same with the ratlings at the ratkin forges." She chuckles in hindsight as Rhonda hands it over; she starts examining it.

"Oh my, they even used widow silk! Remarkable. I hope Jeb domesticates some of them soon; their silk is remarkably strong." Her fingers flow over the garment as she observes out loud, her attention moving from the guests to the piece of clothing. "Oh, you can feel Thing's runework, too. Clever. I think he used some of the metal transmutation elixir to reinforce the threads as well. Hmm . . ." She pulls and pushes on the fabric before nodding. "I think I can let it out some without disrupting anything."

She turns her attention to Rhonda, her hands measuring on the fabric as she analyzes the goblin girl. Rhonda speaks up as she watches her work.

"How much will it be? And how much to get some simpler silk robes for Tula here?"

"Oh, it shouldn't be too much for either. We can talk about the details while I get your measurements. Freddie, Larrez? Do you two know the way to the armory? Teemo stopped by and asked about the new composite armor. Folarn is in charge of that, or at least our part in it. I believe she wants to get some pieces to Rocky so he can put them through their paces. Honey had a whole book of things she wanted tested."

Freddie and Larrez laugh about that. "Sounds like Honey," comments Freddie as he stands. "Do we take them to Rocky's arena, then?"

"I think Teemo wants them down in the secret training room. He should be waiting in the armory for you, though, so he'll tell you there."

Larrez nods and stands as well. "Then I guess we'll meet you two there once you're done?"

Norloke nods. "It shouldn't take us too long. You boys help move the armor, and they should be along by the time you're done."

The guys nod at that and go, and I follow them, giving the girls a bit of space to themselves. At the armory, Teemo meets with the guys, showing them the armor suits, and they get to work without much complaint. Freddie is pretty incredulous about how light they are, but Larrez just chuckles about more of my nonsense.

The harder part is in moving a few dummies in to put the armor on, but once Rocky sees everyone hauling things around, he lends a hand. True to Norloke's word, Rhonda and Tula arrive as the guys are getting the last of the armor set up. The elven woman looks curious, but Rhonda is the one who gets to voice her curiosity first.

"Is that the armor? Is it dipped in glass or something?" she asks, poking a set designed for a ratkin. Rocky snorts in amusement as Freddie shakes his head.

"Teemo says it's some kind of lacquer?" He looks to my Voice, who shrugs.

"Resin, but I'm still a bit fuzzy on the actual difference. It's tough, but it doesn't dent like metal does. Go ahead and give it a few attacks; you'll see."

Freddie smiles and pulls up his hatchet. "I've been wanting to give them a test since I picked up the first piece. Ordinarily, I'd expect to chop through it easily, but there's definitely some Thedeim weirdness going on. *Hyah*!"

Despite his words, he doesn't seem to put any special skill into the attack as he swings for the chestpiece. The hatchet digs in slightly, leaving a good scratch in the finish as he pulls away. The orc shakes his head before taking a closer look. "How's it do that? It almost felt like wood, but it took a hit that should have dented normal armor at least."

Curious, Larrez gives a testing jab with his rapier and finds that, though he can make a pinhole in the outer layer, he can't get much deeper without using a skill. Teemo elaborates as the guys give the armor a couple other experimental whacks, stabs, and slices.

"The Boss calls it composite armor. It's like . . . You know how silk is supposed to be really strong but is too flexible to make a good plate out of? The resin makes it stiff, and you can embed a bunch of other stuff, too. He says that, if done right, each material adds its own strength to the whole. The design is pretty complicated, considering how, in the end, it looks like they just paint the resin onto a very impractical robe, or even a bedsheet."

"It seems pretty effective to me. Why does Thedeim want to test it more?" asks Freddie, looking like he's ready for a suit of his own.

"Mostly, it's in the maintenance. Metal can be bent back into shape, but this can't. It accumulates the dings and scratches until something finally gets through, or the layers come apart and the whole thing becomes useless. It also doesn't handle most affinities too well. Things like Kinetic and Metal are pretty easy to stop, but Fire, Ice, Lightning, and such are still a problem."

"Is . . . Is that why you have Rocky here?" timidly asks Tula, eyeing my Zombie Scion and clearly thinking about his long list of affinities. He grunts and nods, then gestures to Rhonda with a questioning look.

"I'd like to help too, if that's alright? I really want to see you work with Kinetic first, if you don't mind. I'm close to a breakthrough; I can feel it."

Tula looks confused, where Freddie and Larrez are trying to look casual.

"Yeah?" asks Teemo, glancing to Tula. Rhonda nods.

"Yeah. Please?"

Rocky grunts with a smile and sets his mouthpiece before stepping up to a dummy, motioning for Rhonda to step up to another one.

"Why is she . . . ?" quietly asks Tula.

"Just watch. Trust me," Freddie answers.

Confused, she looks to Larrez, who nods and points as Rocky and Rhonda start. My Boxer summons an orb each of fire and ice before he starts punching the armor, going slow and not using too much force just yet. Tula gasps at the display, gasping again when Rhonda follows suit. She raises her staff and calls forth her own orbs, letting them float to either side as she hits the staff's head against the armor.

Rocky grunts and nods, keeping a steady rhythm even as he increases the force of his hits. Rhonda sounds frustrated as she tries to focus and hit harder with her staff. "I can't hit as hard as you!" she complains, much to the amusement of Rocky. He grunts again, getting Rhonda's focus as he starts hitting much harder.

She's the first to notice, but as Rocky continues, the others can see the ball of flame slowly growing with each hit. "It's . . ." Her eyes widen as she seems to understand, though she doesn't have the words to explain her epiphany. Rocky grins around his mouthguard as he merges the orbs, ending with a smaller ball of fire for a few moments before he consumes the energy and puts it into his punch, sending the armor smashing against the cave wall.

Rhonda doesn't have his mastery, but she's got the idea now. She lets the orb of ice fall to the ground as she focuses on the fire. "Like an explosion . . ." she mutters to herself before the fireball winks out of existence. A heartbeat later, her dummy crashes into the wall next to Rocky's, and the goblin slumps to the ground, spent.

Freddie quickly moves to help her while Tula stares at the scene.

"That's . . . It's . . ." she stammers as she points an accusing finger at Rocky. "First you . . . Then *she* . . . ?!" Her finger alternates between them for several cycles before she makes a decision and points it back to Rocky.

"How'd you *do* that?! Why fire *and* ice?" she demands, much less demure now.

"To show me," grunts Rhonda as she gets to her feet with Freddie's help. She smiles at him, resting a hand on his before he steps away. She leans on her staff slightly, distracted by its head for a moment. "Kinetic definitely needs a diamond . . ." she mutters to herself before turning her attention back to Tula.

"And probably show you, too. Don't let him fool you; his brain is anything but rotten. This is why I wanted you to come meet Rocky, Tula. Karn told me about your quest."

"*He's* an Ice Sage? It's a type of undead?"

Rhonda shakes her head. "It's a class. *My* class. Inspired by how Rocky fights and uses his affinities, and shaped by the trials Thedeim made for us. It's a class all about learning *and* teaching. Each new understanding gives a greater insight into not just magic but how *everything* works. I had Ice affinity innately, and gained Fire affinity through an epiphany . . . and now Kinetic, too."

She raises her staff and lets it go, making it float for a few moments as frost creeps along it. She doesn't keep it up for long, though, and soon grabs it to lean on again. "Whew, still not easy, but I've definitely got it. Anyway, Tula." She focuses back on the elf, who looks utterly dumbfounded at what she's seeing and hearing.

"I'd like to teach you, if you're interested. I think that's why Laermali sent you instead of a High Priest or something. My mentor tries to learn, but he's pretty set in his ways. I think we could help each other. I'm not sure that Sages should be common, if that's even what Laermali wants, but I'm willing to at least teach *you*, Tula. If you want to learn?"

She smiles and holds out her hand to the elf. Tula stares at her, eyes wide, before the elf faints.

Chapter 45

Thankfully, it doesn't take Tula too long to wake back up, but she still seems pretty overwhelmed. She doesn't give an answer yet, but I think once she gets a chance to calm down, she'll take Rhonda up on her offer. They escort her out, which thanks to a Teemo shortcut means it's only a couple minutes, and then they head for the lava labyrinth.

I shamelessly look over the map they have while they go. I've been wondering if there'll be people who speedrun the maze daily to try to get an accurate map of that day's layout, but it looks like most people are going with a more generic map, with the changing sections written in different colors and leaving it up to the adventurers to figure out the layout on their own.

I think it'd be a bit more difficult for those going really deep, but the melting pot area with the crucible ants isn't *that* far into the maze. They have to backtrack a couple times, but once you get the hang of reading the map, it's not hard to navigate. They fight a few encounters, and Rhonda practices her telekinesis as she can. For a lot of the denizens in the maze, she has a pretty good combo of stealing the heat from the different encounters, converting it to kinetic energy, and slamming the critters with a solid attack. The others need to keep up their guards and help, of course. One-on-one, Rhonda could probably handle anything in there, but I'm not going to send a single denizen against the group.

In the melting pot, the damanascus is getting pretty popular among my crucible ants. At first, it was just the one hill, but now there's a good half dozen to pick from. They go for a smaller one and don't hold back much in their attack. I smile when I see them work together to haul off the chunks Larrez breaks off, glad to see them plan ahead and not go for something they wouldn't have actually been able to carry off.

They're all pretty weighed down, but they have enough gas in the tank to fight through a couple more encounters and eventually head home. I hope they make some cool stuff out of the damanascus. It should work pretty well as armor, and should be easy to enchant for weapons. I just don't know how well it will hold an edge. It's been getting popular among the ants because it's popular among the delvers, but nobody has come back in with anything made from it, or at least, I haven't noticed. Armoring and enchanting take a while, so I'm not surprised nobody has anything yet. The crafters need to learn how to work it too, I'm sure.

Speaking of things that need work, I sit in with Teemo to hear what the nerd squad thinks of possible improvements for the composite armor. I'm surprised to see Poppy contributing, too, but Teemo's translations make it pretty obvious why. The resin is from trees, and they might be able to use a treated wooden core for the armor to help with rigidity. It also could give another surface for the easy layering of enchantments.

They still need something to fix the delamination problem, though. It'll be partially fixed by weaving the layers more properly. The first pass was barely more than taking two silk shirts and some mail then gluing them together with resin. I probably shouldn't be surprised they tend to come apart.

Coda points out the design issue without me needing to talk through Teemo, and they brainstorm ways to work around that. They really like the metal honeycomb, but I think it's just not going to be especially practical, at least on the scale of people. I'm pretty sure honeycomb is more for vehicle armor rather than personal. While it could work for breastplates, weaving the spidersilk through normal chainmail would be more practical, but I think there's an even better way.

If we use a thin wooden core, we should be able to perforate it and weave the silk through it without much issue. Metal wire should theoretically be an option, but we have an easier method than trying to get tension on metal without breaking the wood: the metal transmutation elixir. As far as I can tell, it makes ordinary steel, which should be a good way to add strength to the armor and hopefully keep the whole thing thin enough that it can be made into something wearable.

In the future, I'd love to weave orichalcum and mythril instead, but I think transmuting some of the silk will be the easier option. The nerds like the sound of the magical metals, but they also think we should try the easier method first. The transmuting process will give them time to apply enchantments, too, so it shouldn't make the process take too much longer.

Poppy commits to dedicating a small patch of her garden to a few trees for better resin and stronger wood, and also talks about the progress she's been able to make on the central tree with the help of Thing, Honey, and especially Queen. It sounds like a true hybrid is going to be off the table, which is a little sad, but her progress on plan B is very encouraging.

She had been trying to get the two separate trees to not interfere with each other too much, but Queen and Honey both suggested she try active symbiosis instead of simply the two tolerating each other.

Suddenly, the problem of roots for them both became a nonissue. If she gives the yew an overengineered root system, the willow vine can tap into it for soil nutrients and water. If she cuts back on yew leaves and encourages the willow, it can handle the photosynthesis for them both and share with the yew. Shore up the yew branches a bit to be able to handle the load of the willow vine, and have the willow really lean into the vine portion to have a good tensile strength, and the two separate plants should be able to survive while actively needing the help of and help*ing* the other.

I pat the bonds with them all, glad to see what looks like a very viable plan to me! It'll still take Poppy some time to get the trees into shape, but I think we have a workable goal to aim for now!

I keep with them through the night, troubleshooting potential issues with the tree and the armor, with Teemo translating. He even offers to lend his Spatial expertise in the construction of the armor, which could be really cool. No need to worry about clearance for tools when you have a smart-aleck rat who can bend the fabric of reality.

The sun rises as we look over a bunch of different thin planks of the wood I have available. I don't think it's technically ebony, but I have a very dense and dark wood that I like for the core; it might be a bit *too* dense to be easily worked, though. There are a couple oaks that are looking like good candidates, too. My scions are leaning toward oak. Teemo's in the middle of letting them know that's fine by me when I feel two familiar presences enter my domain.

Teemo pauses for a moment before quickly finishing. "So yeah, use whatever you guys think will be best. I gotta go!" He zips through a shortcut to catch up to my focus on the two familiar delvers strolling up to the house. My Voice hops up on the railing for the porch and waves as he raises his voice.

"Berdol! Olander! Time flies, eh? You two ready for the inspection, and the fight?"

Berdol nods, wearing his typical delving gear and looking eager, probably both for the fight and the inspection. "Definitely!"

Olander nods as well, wearing better gear than usual. His old stuff wasn't exactly bad, but his armor and glaive both have the look and feel of gear an experienced delver would wear. His armor is pretty heavy looking, though you wouldn't know it from how he moves. Before, he had basically been wearing chainmail, but now, he has heavier splint mail over the top, and a solid breastplate.

The mail reminds me of samurai armor with the armored drapes over the shoulders and thighs. He doesn't have a helmet, but he does have a thick circlet that makes me think of a metal sweatband; I can practically taste the enchantments on it. The rest is also enchanted, but I think he splurged on the circlet to be able to have maximum visibility.

His glaive is different from the simple steel one he'd been carrying around, too. This one is a black metal, or maybe a black finish? Either way, there's very little in the way of decoration on it, making it look and feel like the weapon of war it is.

In addition to his glaive, he has a large pack on his back, probably for whatever adventuring gear he likes to have. Potions, rations, and the like. Maybe to be able to carry back anything that catches his eye, too. I don't think it'll help him too much against Rocky, but I could be wrong. Or he's just wearing it as part of his full kit to show he's taking it seriously.

"I am. I'm looking forward to it, in fact. I've done what research I can on Rocky, and I think I'm as prepared as I can get."

"Awesome," replies Teemo, giving a thumbs-up. "Are you guys going to do the full inspection first?"

"I want to at least try," speaks up Berdol. "I don't think it should take too long, at least? Most of your sections are pretty stable. The lava labyrinth will take the longest, I expect."

"The forest might take a while, too, depending on how in-depth you want to look around. It's a lot of area."

"I'd like to get as close of a look as I can, please."

Teemo smiles. "That should be fine. It's still a work in progress, but the Boss doesn't have any problem with letting you see how things get made. We actually just finalized the plan for the big central tree, in fact."

"Oh?" asks Berdol, with Olander looking curious as well.

Teemo nods and slips through a shortcut to sit atop Olander's pack. "Yeah. I'll explain while you guys start. The manor is pretty much the same as it's always been: a good place for the newbies to start with. You should be able to examine while I chat about the tree, yeah?"

Olander chuckles and shifts his pack slightly to sit better. "I think so. If Berdol is too distracted, I'll at least be listening. I've heard rumors the new forest is supposed to be for very experienced delvers, so you definitely have my attention with it."

The elf chuckles as Berdol smacks him with his floating metal clipboard for insinuating he can't take notes and listen at the same time. Still, he smiles at the good-natured ribbing. "Then let's get this inspection underway. The sooner we get started, the sooner I can watch Rocky knock you around some!"

Chapter 46

I leave Teemo in charge of the inspection, trusting my denizens to know how these things go by now. I'll check back in on them when they get to the forest, but for now, I turn my attention to the arena. Rocky is doing a little last-minute practicing with his affinities, but nothing especially strenuous. No, what I'm here to watch is everyone else getting ready.

I've been treating this a lot like a big sporting event, and what's a sporting event without souvenirs and a concession stand or five? No bookies, though. I understand that angle is already covered by Karn of the adventurers' guild, and probably shadier people, too. My enclaves have enough to do without trying to figure out the odds for the outcome.

The spiderkin have been making a lot of hats and shirts. I'm not quite sure where they got the patterns for baseball hats and T-shirts, but I bet they're going to make a killing on them. They're mostly pretty simple solid colors. Yellow and blue seem to be the easiest with what we have available. I don't think they've figured out how to do silkscreen printing yet, but they still have Rocky and Olander's names clearly written on basically everything.

Not to be outdone, my ratkin have made noisemakers. Thankfully, a vuvuzela needs plastic, or Teemo kept that particular abomination under his hat. That didn't stop him from explaining the ratcheting clackers the ratkin are selling. They also have bells, chimes, and other metal noisemakers to sell, too.

Anyone not actually in the arena is still going to be able to hear when the fighting starts, if my ratkin have anything to say about it. Them and the spiderkin are both also selling all sorts of food. It looks like the bakery across the street even got ahold of a stall. The troll woman is incredibly round, but she moves around the kitchen like she was born in it. She doesn't look too impressed with the ovens available, but she's clearly a pro and starts adjusting them for some good bread making instead of a more general baking setup.

For my dwellers, griddlecakes are probably going to be a big hit, as well as cave lobster on a stick. It doesn't look like they've quite figured out how to batter and deep fry everything like at a fair, but I think the food on offer would make any carnie proud. It makes me wish I could have a taste, and makes me debate if I should unleash the true potential of oil frying things.

Maybe later, once someone shows a substitute for powdered sugar, or actual powdered sugar. It just wouldn't be fried anything without the option to bury it under powdered sugar.

The antkin are helping with the seating for now. They didn't really have a chance to prepare much, what with getting their leadership established. They also don't have their food sorted, so they can't really run any concessions, either. They're making up for lost time, though, with a bunch working on sculpting seats better than boring flat benches.

Nova is helping them out, too, ensuring they have plenty of magma to sculpt with and adding her own touches as they make more ergonomic seating like seen in a lot of modern sports complexes. Stone might be harder than plastic, but plastic isn't exactly known for its give, either. With a good shape, they should be comfortable.

They even make sure to put in that hole in the lower back like a lot of those seats have. I think they're usually for air flow, but the position and size are perfect for anyone with a tail. For the nonstandard body types, like my spiderkin and snakekin and others like that, they have to settle for a flat area of gravel to sit in. Nova and Slash work together to make sure there are no sharp pieces in there, and though I think it could be better, I don't think we planned far enough ahead to *get* better.

At least not yet. I'm pretty sure we can get some kind of fungus that grows like grass to help soften things for people who don't fit into normal seats. The gravel was actually the kobolds' idea. They're still adjusting and pretty wary around anyone not in an enclave, and even most in the enclaves, too.

Still, they saw the need for a solution and suggested the gravel. Apparently, it was a common thing for them back in the Maw. It's tempting to just ditch the idea for the inspiration, but I have to imagine it'll be more comfortable than regular rock. There are even a couple wyrms moving around under that section, keeping the gravel warm. The kobolds really like it, with more than a couple groups opting to get early seats in the gravel section rather than the molded chairs.

Townsfolk are starting to funnel in, too, and the flow only increases as the day continues. Rocky accepts a few challenges, giving the people a good chance to see what he can do, and to whet their appetites for the main event, too. The fights aren't especially strenuous, with the challengers forfeiting before Rocky needs to knock them out. I think they mostly want something to do, or to show off a bit.

Soon, Berdol and Olander get to the forest, where my newest scions are waiting for them. Poppy and Titania look excited to meet the two inspectors, while Zorro and Goldilocks are a bit more subdued. I think they're still under the impression that my scions are dignified, like the Stag. Tiny and Poe are probably the only ones who even come close. They'll learn, I'm sure.

Berdol takes notes as Olander and Teemo watch, the catkin noting each scion down before introducing himself. "So a pixie, a living vine, a fox, and a bear?" He points at each, and they nod in their ways before he offers a hand to each.

"I'm Berdol! The other scions have probably mentioned Tarl as the usual inspector, but he's busy with the new dungeon in Silvervein. Do any of you have any titles yet?" he asks as Titania shakes his finger and Poppy extends a few thin tendrils to shake his hand as well. Zorro looks uncertain, but raises his paw to shake also. Goldilocks offers hers, and it's Berdol's turn to struggle with the size difference as he does his best to shake hers, too.

"Nah, no titles yet," supplies Teemo. "I think Poppy is probably on the way to one. They're all working hard, but hers is a kind of work I don't think dungeons do a lot of. That seems to be a good way to get a title."

Berdol jots that down as Olander nods. "It's partially why so many scions don't gain additional titles. Even the different boss titles are usually only gained after killing a number of delvers."

Teemo snorts at that. "Hopefully, we'll continue not picking up any of those, then."

"Hopefully, yeah. With the danger of your new expansion, it'll only get harder to keep that streak going, you know," points out Olander.

"Yeah, but with everyone working on it, and my shortcuts, anything not instantly fatal should be able to be handled. What do you think of the spawners the Boss has planned so far, Olander? He thinks there's a lot of potential, but you're the one with experience in high-level fighting."

He takes his time to formulate his answer, following Berdol as he wanders the forest. While there's still a lot to be done to really solidify the seasons, there's a definite contrast to the different sections.

"The fighting bees are unusual, but should be a good baseline encounter, especially when combined with the later fey and plants. Rumblebees are good for midtier groups, but the armory bees that come next can be a real threat to delvers who don't know what they're doing. They are among the most tactically minded denizens I've met in dungeons, despite their relative individual weakness. When backed up with stronger denizens, I think you should be able to push even someone like me to keep on his toes."

"Cool. Any suggestions for the bears or foxes? I know the Boss likes the idea of magic for the foxes, but he's open to suggestions."

"Foxes almost always go with Illusion magic, which can be a real force multiplier for your denizens. In a fair fight, I could probably handle any encounter here without much problem. But with the armory bees and Illusion foxes, fair fights should be basically off the table, not to mention the vines and elementals.

"I'd suggest making the bears fighters. Most of the other denizens you're planning for aren't really made for the front line. The elementals can do it somewhat, but they're usually better for harrying attacks instead of wading in and trading blows." Olander shakes his head, chuckling. "It'll be like fighting a full party, or several full parties, depending on how many you send. That kind of coordination will push the delvers to their limits and force them to improve."

Teemo nods at that. "That's basically the Boss's plan, yeah. Let me show you guys the garden and the planned central tree, then we can head for the arena."

Berdol nods at that while Olander tries to hide his excitement at the prospect of finally getting to square off against Rocky. "What kind of tree are you going with? You've been having trouble getting one just right, right?" asks Berdol. Teemo nods as he leads them down a shortcut.

"Yeah, the Boss has a specific look and structure in mind, and we haven't been able to find a tree that matches all the needs."

"Until now," comments Olander, making Teemo smirk and shake his head.

"Not really. It'll technically be two trees, but they'll be so deep in symbiosis they might as well be one. Yew will be the base, with its twisting branches and reinforced roots. Willow will be changed to more of a vine, seeping water and soil nutrients from the yew, and giving back the fruits of photosynthesis."

Berdol notes it all down as Olander considers that. "It sounds workable to me, but I'm no druid. I bet you'll have more than a few want to come look, if it works," the elf eventually comments as they exit the shortcut to Poppy's garden. It doesn't take them too long to look around, and I pat the bond with my Vine Scion to make sure she doesn't feel dejected about them not seeming that impressed. I don't think either of them are really into plants. *Don't worry, Poppy. I'm plenty impressed to make up for it.*

They might also be distracted with wanting to finish up and head to the arena, which I don't blame them for. It feels like the entire town would be down here if I had room. There's even a rivalry building between people supporting Rocky and those supporting Olander. So far, it still seems to be healthy, and not one that will lead to a riot no matter who wins.

Berdol officially calls the inspection done, and he and Olander waste no time following Teemo through a shortcut and to the arena.

A guitar riff quiets the crowd once Slash spots them. He holds out a finger for Aranya to speak into, amplifying her voice for all to hear. "And here's the challenger, Olander! Let's give him a warm welcome and a few minutes to prepare! Because soon, he'll face Rocky, Lord Thedeim's fighting scion! Will the delver give Rocky his first defeat? Or will Rocky's streak only grow? We'll soon see!"

Chapter 47

Olander looks taken aback for a few moments before he smiles wide at the crowd and the reception. Noisemakers make it practically impossible for anyone to say or hear anything intelligible, but the energy of the arena is infectious. Teemo points Berdol to the ringside seats before he directs Olander into a small side room.

They have to pass a lot of spectators to get there, with everyone loudly cheering for the coming spectacle. Once inside the smaller room with the doors closed, they can finally hear themselves think.

"I hope you're ready to give them a good show!" Teemo speaks up first.

Olander nods with a smile. "Absolutely. I've seen a few adventurer tournaments, so I know vaguely what to expect. I didn't expect that much enthusiasm, though!"

Teemo laughs at that. "People have only gotten to see little peeks at what Rocky can do. With you here, not only will they get to see a lot more but they might even get to see him lose! Of course they're going to want to see, no matter the outcome!"

Olander shakes his head, chuckling. "I see that now, heh."

"And if you don't mind, the Boss has a suggestion to help pump up the crowd even more."

"Oh?" asks Olander, looking vaguely suspicious. "I hope he's not going to ask me to throw, or something like that."

Teemo laughs again. "Are you nuts? Rocky would never forgive him if he did that! He just says you should put on a bit of a show when you walk out there. Rocky will come out with his music and some fancy magic, and you should do the same. The Boss can cover the pyrotechnics if you want. And the music, too, come to think of it. Anything in particular you'd like?"

Olander mulls it over for a few seconds before shrugging. "No music comes to mind. I'm told your Slash is pretty good at picking, though."

My Voice nods at that. "Yeah, he's got good taste. So, when the music changes, that'll be your cue to come strutting to the arena. Then it'll be on you two. Just listen for the bell and stop when it rings."

Olander nods and opens the door to listen for his cue, doing some warm-ups as he waits. On the other side of the arena, Rocky is bouncing on his toes and keeping himself limber and ready. I can practically taste the excitement boiling off the bond with him, and soon, his music starts playing.

The crowd slowly quiets as a single note is strummed in a steady rhythm. What other song is *Rocky* supposed to walk out to, hmm? He grins wide, taking his first steps in time with the power chords as he enters the arena proper, his fists high as he encourages the crowd.

He handles his own pyrotechnics and cryotechnics and . . . whatever the word would be for his other affinities. An arc of flame follows a right hook, then an icy mirror from a left, followed by a thundercrack punctuating an uppercut. He grins and points across the arena at Olander before he climbs into the ring, folding his arms as he leans against the turnbuckle in his corner. The champ is here waiting, ready and eager for the challenger.

Slash's choice for Olander is an unusual one, but I agree with it. Good, bad, or ugly doesn't matter here, just skill. And it sounds really cool on an electric guitar, too. The tall elf exits the waiting room, marching without any rush, his head held high. Nova handles his special effects, slamming glaives of magma out of the ground as he passes in time with his steps and the beat of the song.

Olander's somber facade breaks as the tempo increases, and he rushes the stage, glaive held in a wide grip for a heavy slash. He smoothly shucks his pack as he nears the ring, dropping it just outside before he leaps in, landing steady and pointing his glaive across the way at Rocky. The two stand there, eyeing each other as the classic refrain plays.

Slash finishes with a flourish, and the two combatants take their stances, each more than eager to get started as Aranya's voice carries over the shouting crowd. "It's finally time! Olander versus Rocky! Shake hands, gentlemen! Just because this is a fight doesn't mean there will be any hard feelings!"

The two smirk and step forward, each offering their dominant hand to shake. A single pump before the two step back to their corners, each taking their own stance. "You both know the rules! May the best win! Fight!"

The two quickly step forward, though neither taps into their affinities just yet. Though Rocky is nimble, Olander has the advantage of reach, so my zombie has to weather the storm of slashes and stabs just to get in. Olander sets his feet wide, giving him plenty of leverage to slash, stab, and swing the wide blade of his glaive in whatever angle he needs to keep Rocky away.

My Boxer's feet are light as he dances, dodges, and weaves, avoiding the steel as he probes for an opening. Olander slowly steps forward, pressing Rocky back while he seeks an opportunity to get inside the elf's reach, which he eventually finds. He takes a half step back to avoid a wide swing, and bats at the blade as it passes, disrupting Olander's rhythm. It's only for a moment, but that's all Rocky needs to get in.

My zombie rains punches upon the elf, who steps back and adjusts his grip from one suited to a polearm to one more for a staff, letting him spin and block in close quarters. It's Olander's turn to slowly give ground as he avoids accepting any solid blows. Straights are parried to the side with the haft of his glaive, hooks blocked with the flat of his blade, uppercuts sidestepped, and jabs accepted and deflected with his armor and long practice of using it.

But he can only remain on the defensive for so long. He's slowly but surely being driven back to his corner. If he lets Rocky cut off his maneuverability, the fight will be all but over! Of course, he knows that, and he's not going to just let it happen.

He misses parrying a straight and gets a new dent in his armor for it, but it also gives him a chance to counter. Rocky gets his dukes back up just as the wide blade flashes toward his face, and he gets driven back several steps with a solid gash across both forearms.

He takes another step back to assess the damage, and Olander takes a moment to do the same. If his heart were still beating, Rocky would probably be bleeding pretty well right now. The cut isn't to the bone, or even through much of his muscle, but the crowd still cheers at the most damage they've seen him take before!

Olander is earning similar cheers as he rolls his shoulders, getting used to how differently his armor sits now with that dent in the middle of his chest. I think it might barely affect his breathing, but much like Rocky, it's not going to be something to slow him down too much.

The two grin and rush back at each other, the flow of the fight rapidly shifting back and forth now that they've gotten a feel for their foe. They still don't use their affinities, instead relying on their raw skill rather than on any special abilities. The glaive swipes at Rocky, who blocks, then blocks the follow-up from the other end of the weapon before he steps in and hammers Olander's stomach with several body blows.

A low sweep of Olander's weapon forces Rocky to jump to avoid it, only to line himself up for a heavy kick that sends him back several paces. Each foe leans out of the way of devastating attacks, letting them miss by millimeters; each leans in to give extra weight to a blow that can't be avoided. Their stances constantly shift as the battle goes on, light to move in, solid to defend, light to dodge, solid to hit.

Rocky brings a brutal left hook to bear as Olander spins the butt end of his weapon up, and each freezes as the bell rings, their attacks a hair's breadth from impacting the temple of the other. They hold for a few seconds, each grinning like madmen who have finally found a proper challenge, before they each straighten up and go back to their corners.

Aranya's voice is difficult to hear over the roaring crowd, but she doesn't let that stop her. "What a first round! Even without using their affinities, how many could stand up to that kind of attack? That was clearly just the warm-up, everyone! I think I need a couple minutes to recover more than they do! Soon, it'll be round two, and I don't think we've seen anything yet!"

Chapter 48

Rocky

The zombie fidgets in his corner as he looks across the ring at Olander. From the elf's own fidgeting, he might be more eager to get back out there than even Rocky! He smiles around his mouthguard as the first round replays in his mind, savoring and analyzing every moment of the fight.

Olander is at a disadvantage if Rocky can get inside his reach, but his experience with that glaive gives him very few chances to *do* that. He feels like he has a better handle on Olander's fighting style now, but he doesn't let that inflate his confidence. Not only will Olander have a better idea of the zombie's style, but adding in affinities will surely change a lot in how the next round will go.

If Olander's affinity usage is anything like how he fights, it'll be simple yet brutally effective and efficient. No movement was wasted in their first clash; every attack and counter, every block and parry, was done with precision. He'll eat his gloves if Olander doesn't wield his Kinetic affinity similarly.

He can't wait to see how the elf handles mixed affinities. He looks eager, not worried, so he has to have *some* way of dealing with them. Rocky sets his mouthguard as the bell rings, putting up his dukes to see just what Olander has in mind for this round.

The two circle for a few moments, channeling their affinities and looking for any weakness in their foe. Neither finds one, so Olander initiates with the advantage of his reach. Rocky can feel the kinetic energy in the blade rapidly spike as Olander does a deceptively simple swipe.

His first instinct is to steal the energy, but his gut says that'd be a fool's gambit. With that much experience and seemingly just the one affinity, there's no way Rocky is wrenching control away that easily from the elf.

But that doesn't mean he's without options.

His right hand moves in an uppercut as he channels his own Kinetic affinity, creating a blade of raw force to counteract the attack. He hardly hears the cheer of the crowd as the forces meet and send a shower of sparks up into the air. Most would take it as the energy being neutralized, but energy doesn't vanish.

It just changes form.

Kinetic loves to make heat, and that's exactly what Rocky wants. He seizes the energy with his Fire affinity, bolstering it as he forms ice around a fist, and brings the flaming attack down on Olander.

The elf subtly shifts his stance and smoothly transitions his horizontal slash into an upward one, slashing into the heat before he flexes his Kinetic affinity, scattering the energy to the sides. Rocky can't get a grip on it before it dissipates, but he still has his icy fist, and Olander is out of position with that defense!

He darts forward and slams the frozen fist into Olander's side, earning a grunt before he has to dance back to avoid the whirling glaive. The elf doesn't look discouraged by giving up the first hit, instead pressing forward, his glaive still held short and letting him present a dangerous whirling obstacle to anything Rocky might wish to do. The zombie is forced back, and additionally forced to move quickly as Olander pours on more kinetic control, increasing his speed and putting Rocky on the back foot.

He's forced into a circular retreat, taking cuts on his arms and stomach as he tries to find an opening. He can see the pattern of Olander's movement, but the elf is just too fast for him to take advantage of the momentary openings!

Perfect. This is the kind of fight Rocky's been wanting! Something to push him! He steps heavier as he continues to retreat, tapping into his Sonic affinity to keep him in the right rhythm. He can see the flaw in Olander's current strategy. Sure, he's fast, but he's going faster than he can react right now. It's difficult to imagine the kind of training to let him move himself so quickly, but his own retreat is the proof of how effective it is.

But at that kind of speed, even a little disruption can throw it all off-balance. Rocky stomps once more and steps forward this time, feeling the floor of the ring moving just how he needs it to now. Ordinarily, it wouldn't be too much for someone to adjust to, and ordinarily, the opening he's making wouldn't be enough to take much advantage of.

But this is no ordinary fight. Moments are eternities against a foe like Olander. The elf's eyes widen as he feels something is wrong, but by then, it's too late. Rocky doesn't go for anything too fancy, instead falling back on the tried-and-true fire hand/ice hand.

Left, right, jab, uppercut, haymaker! He slips past Olander's guard to land blow after blow on his armor, embracing four of his affinities to allow him to make each hit count the most. Fire and ice alternate, ruining the temper of the armor. Kinetic impacts seek to dent and rend, while Sonic affinity ensures he times his hit perfectly to resonate and reinforce the energy of each blow!

A blast of raw force sends Rocky stumbling back from his onslaught on the elf, who looks significantly worse for wear after just a few seconds of pummeling. While he may be bruised, he doesn't look upset about it. He stands tall, his armor bent and dented, and levels his glaive at Rocky.

"I haven't been this pressed in ages!" he exclaims, full of adrenaline and excitement. Rocky knows that feeling, and grins as he slams his gloved fists together, conjuring his favorite orbs of fire and ice. Olander once again initiates, darting forward with blinding speed once more.

And though Rocky can tell he's still going through some kind of kata, it's much more complex, and much more deadly. The kinetic force is no longer concentrated in the glaive. Crescents and spikes of force manifest for the briefest of moments—just long enough for an attack—before they're withdrawn back to Olander to lash out with again.

Rocky is forced on the defensive once again; this time, using his ice as armor. He learned long ago from sparring with Fluffles: telekinesis is hard to parry, so use armor. Ice is great for how well it absorbs energy, and though Olander is very efficient, he's not perfect. Rocky can slowly siphon energy from him, but does he have the time to wear the elf down before he gets sliced into an undead ice sculpture?

He doubts it, so he steps up his own offense. They trade blows, Olander's armor collecting more dents and scratches but still holding. Rocky's ice gets chipped away, but his fiery attacks let him siphon more heat away to make more. It's quickly apparent to Rocky that this is not a winning strategy. Olander's armor is not doing well, but the elf himself seems just as full of energy as ever! If Rocky is going to do something, he needs to do it soon.

He taps into his Mental affinity, still not very practiced with it, but he doesn't need it to attack. He needs to come up with something. And he gets an idea. He redoubles his efforts, subtly shifting his attacks. He still uses primarily Fire, but a bit of Kinetic gives him a bit more punch, just not where Olander seems to be expecting it.

Each time Rocky is blocked by the spinning haft of Olander's glaive is another step toward victory for the zombie. He has to go slowly, or the elf might notice. He listens to the hum of the glaive as he keeps attacking, the low sound slowly getting louder and louder with each hit, each small pulse of kinetic force vibrating along the entire weapon, raw Kinetic giving way to harmonious Sonic, singing the sound of victory.

Rocky drops his dukes just a hair, giving Olander an opening that the elf can't help but take advantage of. He's already shifted to a thrust empowered with kinetic force before he realizes his weapon doesn't feel quite right. But by then, it's too late.

One hand comes up from underneath the glaive, hitting it right behind the head and striking with the building resonance before the other hand comes down. He hits right at the middle of the haft, staying in tune to the beat of the weapon's vibration, and a snap rings across the arena just before the bell does.

He grins in triumph and holds out half of Olander's glaive to the elf, who looks shocked.

"Is that victory for Rocky?!" exclaims Aranya to the roar of the crowd.

The elf's confusion quickly gives way to a laugh as he accepts the rest of his weapon. "Not on your life!" he shouts as he turns to walk back to his corner and starts digging through his bag.

"Can I get a longer break between rounds this time? I need to put on my *best* for this! I didn't think I'd need to, but I'm glad to be wrong!"

Rocky grins at that and nods before strutting to his own corner to watch whatever Olander has cooking. If he's bringing out his best, maybe Rocky can, too.

Chapter 49

Olander

He hopes he can get his armor and glaive repaired after this. They were both what he used before he got promoted, and he never imagined anything less than a Conduit would be able to damage them like Rocky has. The armor damage is one thing; it's designed to break so he doesn't, but snapping the haft on his glaive was truly shocking.

He chuckles as he stows away the two pieces of his old weapon. He let himself underestimate the zombie *again.* After his show against Onyx, Olander knew he was strong, but he should have realized the undead Boxer has a lot going on upstairs, too. He might look like a zombie, but he needs to be treated like a dragon for how strong and clever he is.

The fight replays as he takes off his battered armor, tossing each piece into his travel bag and letting it sort and store each piece properly as he thinks. *Be wary of consecutive hits.* He's seen singers break glass with their voice, and their explanation feels a lot like how Rocky is using his Thunder affinity. He needs to remember his kinetic defenses, not just offense.

Fire and ice also play a role in the zombie's combination attacks. Even if his old armor wasn't covered in dents, he would bet the temper is ruined as well. It might be time to finally hang the old suit up as a memento.

He grunts as he gets his chest plate off, relieved to be able to breathe easily again, and looks at the damage for a moment before it joins its companions in his bag. It's definitely going to only be fit for decoration after this. Maybe he *won't* repair the glaive, come to think of it. It'd look pretty good hung on the wall, both pieces angled over the head of his old suit.

He shakes his head as he removes the last of his armor, pulling the chain undershirt over his head to toss into his bag. This is not the time to get distracted. He still has a fight to win.

And a cover to burn.

He hopes Tula won't be too mad with him once she realizes. He also hopes Berdol won't treat him too differently. Their reactions were pretty high on his list of reasons not to go all out. But now that he *truly* has a proper challenge before him, he has to just hope the dynamic with them won't be shattered along with the identity of ordinary retired Olander.

He pulls his glaive from the bag, glad to have dimensional storage for his really good stuff. Where his old glaive was a dark, dangerous thing with no frills, his Wideblade Glaive is covered from tip to tang and beyond in intricate engravings. The haft looks like solid gold, with the blade gleaming silver, but Olander knows it's all a single piece. Even his title as crown inspector couldn't get the mastersmith to reveal the details, just that it's an alloy of mythril and orichalcum with a few other interesting things, and that the coloration difference was because of a difference in treatment.

Scattered gasps come from the crowd, but Olander does his best to ignore them as he props his weapon against the turnbuckle. He needs to get his armor on. Said armor is of the same alloy with the golden treatment, and he doesn't rush putting it on. Murmurs travel through the crowd as those who recognize his armor tell those who don't.

He ignores them, instead focusing on his preparations. The defensive enchantments are second to none on this armor, but his personal favorite feature is the automatic fitting. He only has to slip his foot into the sabbaton for it to tighten itself. Then comes the greave, which he only needs to close around his calf before the enchantment takes over.

Each piece of armor goes on easily and connects seamlessly like a second skin. He always thought it made him look like a partial spiderkin, or other race with an exoskeleton; he wouldn't be surprised if the mastersmith took them as inspiration. He finishes with changing out his circlet for an intricate gold-colored one. He never could get used to full helmets, even with special sight enchantments. He trusts his eyes and ears more than anything he's seen enchanters manage.

He takes his glaive and stands, the crowd murmuring and trying to figure out what his true identity means for the fight. He levels his glaive at Rocky with one arm—the zombie looking eager—and speaks up.

"I am Olander Wideblade, inspector to the crown! I have been charged with bringing King Horlon himself information about this dungeon! Are you prepared?"

The crowd goes silent as Rocky shakes his head, and for a brief, terrible moment, Olander fears the zombie may forfeit. Instead, he starts embracing his titles.

Boxer is expected, and Olander only wonders how much better the zombie's form will get with that title embraced. *Affinity Savant* gets Olander's blood pumping. He's already seen the undead pull off insane elemental combinations; what will that title mean for the coming round? He can only try to imagine—and try to contain his eagerness.

Rocky's grin echoes his own as the Boxer starts unlacing his gloves, tossing one over his shoulder, then the other, before embracing his third title: *No Kid Gloves.* He meets Olander's eyes and hits a fist into his palm, nodding to show that *now* he's ready.

Olander laughs. "Are you sure you're not a Conduit, too? No?"

Rocky grunts and shakes his head as Aranya's voice carries over the crowd.

"Neither is holding back for this round! Olander the retired adventurer is none other than Olander Wideblade, crown inspector, and I'm told one of the strongest delvers in the land! It looks like they're both ready, too. Let the third round begin!"

The bell rings and energetic music fills the arena as Slash does his part to ensure both fighters are at the top of their games. If Rocky is going all out, how can Olander not do the same? He taps into his Fate affinity as Rocky's mana floods the ring.

The elf grips his glaive properly and takes a defensive stance as the attack bears down on him. Like a lot of the zombie's other attacks, it's a building combination, but Olander is watching carefully now. He can feel his armor trying to shake itself apart, cold creeping to try to embrittle it, and heat waiting just out of contact to obliterate anything that snaps off.

He doesn't let the vibrations build, dampening them with his Kinetic affinity like a hand might stop the ringing of a bell. After a few moments, the energy recedes, and he can see Rocky with a manic smile, elated that Olander could counter such an attack. The Boxer rushes in, and Olander eagerly follows suit.

The two clash in great gouts of mana, booms echoing through the arena, columns of flame and spears of ice flying to the ceiling, yet each combatant still in control enough that the crowd is in no danger. It may have not been explicitly stated in the rules, but even a speck of active mana landing among the crowd would be seen by either fighter as a loss.

Olander slashes, blocks, and stabs while Rocky weaves, counters, and adapts, each testing their own limits as well as those of their foe. Olander taps his Fate affinity deeper, moving through his fast technique of the spinning glaive. Without his second affinity, it was only half the technique it could be, and though he feels Rocky disrupting his footing like in the previous round, he lets his instinct guide him through all the attempted disruption.

He follows how he should move, subtly disrupting Rocky's own attempts to attack, ducking a crescent of flame, sidestepping a patch of ice, deflecting a hammer blow upward, and riding the flow of the fight. It takes longer than usual, but he finally feels the time to strike, channeling his affinity as he brings the blade of his glaive around.

He's not called Wideblade just for the odd shape of his weapon. Sure, it gives his attacks more force, but that's a bonus for his signature weapon. The glaive head almost appears to morph into a hammer, but even that is a trick of the eyes. He multiplies the cutting edge of his weapon more times than he can count, and what's worse for his foes, getting hit by a single one is the same as getting hit by all!

"Inescapable Demise!" he shouts as the blade swings up to slice into Rocky's side.

And then fate twists.

Defiance! pulses through the arena, the refusal carried by Rocky's mastery of Thunder affinity, and an explosion erupts from the Boxer's fist. Instead of overwhelming Olander, however, the force sends Rocky flying back and out of the reach of the attack that shouldn't be *able* to miss!

He doesn't get the time to declare that's not how that works as Rocky hits the ropes and rebounds toward him, the chill and weight of a glacier in one fist and an inferno in the other. He reinforces the haft of his weapon and blocks both fists, planting his feet and not letting the attack overwhelm him. His instinct whispers a plan, and he moves before he's even aware of it, knowing to trust in the quiet pull of his affinity. A swift, empowered kick sends Rocky up into the air and sets Olander up for another Wideblade technique to catch the undead as he plummets.

"Destined to Fall!"

Once again, destiny twists as Rocky shouts his refusal to accept fate. Olander feels the kinetic energy but for a moment, and he quickly shatters it, but it's still enough for Rocky to gain footing in the air and leap back.

The elf takes a moment to examine his foe; he can feel the diminished energies around the zombie now. Whatever he did to deny those two attacks, it took a lot out of him. Olander is also drained from those attacks, but still far from spent. Rocky rushes forward, the potency of his affinities concentrated into small points on his fists, and Olander knows he needs to avoid them.

He spins his glaive once more as he gives ground, parrying at the wrist instead of clashing directly against his attacks. His affinity whispers a plan, and for the first time in a long time, he doesn't immediately follow. It's reckless, even for him. But with Rocky putting his all into his onslaught, it's his best chance.

He drops his guard for just a moment, the blade of his glaive just a hair out of place. But just like he had to take Rocky's opening last round, the Boxer has to take this one. He can feel the scion's Fate affinity resonating with what's about to happen, and Olander tries to ignore the incoming fist as he brings the butt of his glaive up. He angles his head just slightly to accept the pulsating orb of kinetic energy, knowing it's his best bet to handle the incoming force.

He's not sure if it's his own move or Rocky's, or somehow a combination attack, but the words and concept solidify just before fist and haft make contact. "Cross Counter!"

Olander is driven to the mat by the impact of Rocky's technique, his mind reeling from the impact. The only coherent thought is that the zombie somehow adapted his own Wideblade technique to work over different affinities. All the other energies converted to Kinetic for that punch! Affinity Savant indeed! He shakes his head and stands, his balance still uneven, but a wide smile on his face.

Rocky hits the floor a few moments later, thrown out of the ring by the force of Olander's contribution. The crowd roars as Aranya's voice carries over it.

"Winner by ring out! Olander!"

Chapter 50

Rocky and I both need to pick our jaws up off the floor after that fight, though him more literally than me. I don't have mine anymore, and Rocky's landed just out of his reach. Once he gets it back on, it's in danger of falling off again for how wide he's smiling. He's a bit slow to get up after that rough landing. Olander definitely did a number on my Boxer for that W.

The elf is posing for the crowd as they go nuts, savoring the victory and praise as Rocky digs under the ring for the reward he's been wanting to give out for a while now. Instead of a chest, he pulls out a wide, flat wooden box. Olander looks on curiously as the former champion gets back into the ring. He tucks the box under his arm before approaching Olander and holding the elf's hand up high, making the victory official.

"And there it is!" comes Aranya's voice over the crowd, thanks to Slash. "Olander is officially the victor in this bout, and what a fight it was! He's not the crown inspector for nothing, clearly!"

Rocky takes a step back and holds the box out for Olander to open, which he does with curious eyes. I don't think anything I've had to offer has been powerful enough for him to be interested in as an adventurer, but maybe this particular trophy will stick with him, if only for how unique it is.

I've seen the awards Karn's guild has gotten, usually a plaque or a scroll, maybe a banner. I've got my own ostentatious wall hanger to offer. Or hip hanger, if you're feeling ambitious.

Olander looks confused at the huge belt while Teemo's voice echoes around the arena as he explains from Aranya's shoulder. "That's the Champion's Belt. Hold it up so everyone can get a look at it! Far away, there's a long tradition of belts like this being fought over by only the best fighters of their discipline. There's only one. The Boss won't be making another like it. Though you can bet Rocky will be challenging you to get the title back eventually!"

Olander picks up the belt and holds it high, letting everyone see the large orange circle representing my core. It sits square in the middle of the word *Champion*, the two halves continuing along the belt, with smaller lettering above and below the core declaring it to belong to the Champion of Rocky's Arena.

Eventually, he slings it over his shoulder, letting it rest there, before he notices a second, more ordinary belt still in the box. "That second belt is yours, too," explains Teemo. "Rocky says no champ should go down to a cheap shot, and that belt will help protect you. I doubt you'll recognize the enchant, though I see Old Staiven in attendance! You should come take a look, if Olander doesn't mind. And bring your apprentice, too!"

Old Staiven is indeed in the audience, as well as Rhonda, Freddie, and Tula. Rezlar is here, too, but he's not going incognito, so he's not able to sit next to his friends. Olander looks up to the announcer's section and nods, making Teemo and Aranya smile before my High Priestess continues.

"Then, if you don't mind, Rocky will show you to the waiting room, and we'll do a short interview before letting the master enchanter take a look at your prize."

As they all head for the side room, some people get up and leave, while others settle in to chat about the fight. The shop stalls certainly aren't going to complain about people taking their time in leaving. It just gives them more of a chance to sell them something!

Rocky and Olander get to the room first, and the two relax as they wait. "I can't believe how hard you hit, Rocky. No wonder people were confident in you. I need to ask Teemo how you do it. You throw around a *lot* of mana for a scion who's not a Conduit."

My Boxer grunts and nods as Olander examines the large belt, taking in the details and savoring the victory. Aranya, Teemo, and Slash arrive not too long after. "Staiven and the kids will be a few more minutes," explains Teemo. "They want to get some souvenirs before they sell out. Ready for that interview?"

Both Olander and Rocky nod, so Aranya begins. "We're in the recovery room with Olander and Rocky. That was an amazing fight, you two! Any initial thoughts you want to share about it?"

They both nod, with Olander expounding first. "In a real fight, don't make the mistakes I did. Even after that first round, I *still* underestimated Rocky in the second, and he broke my glaive for it. That's why you always have a backup weapon."

Aranya nods and turns to Rocky, who grunts as Teemo translates. "Rocky says it's a good example to not rest on your laurels. There's always someone stronger, and he met that someone today. He's looking forward to trying again someday, too."

Aranya smiles. "Do you expect you'll accept his challenge when he makes it, Olander?"

"Absolutely. Rocky isn't the only one who's feeling inspired after that fight. He'll need to step up his training, because I don't intend to slack off on mine!"

My Boxer grins at the challenge as Aranya continues. "So, you're the inspector for the king? I've seen inspectors from the guild, but I don't know what the difference is."

Olander shrugs. "The biggest difference is who I report to. Instead of the Dungeoneer's Guild, I report to the crown directly. It's not an easy position to earn or keep, so only the best of the best will hold it."

"As you proved here today! Why the subterfuge, though? Why act like an ordinary retired adventurer instead of in an official capacity? And why drop the charade now?"

Olander winces at that before answering. "I often go undercover for missions. It's easier for a retired adventurer to go look at a dungeon than someone with the weight and backing of the crown. People will try to put things in the best light for the crown inspector, but they won't care one way or the other about the opinion of a random retired adventurer, even if he's strong.

"As for why I dropped it now . . . I would have liked to keep my cover, but Rocky here is too good for me to be able to hold back like that. I already have the information I need for the king. I hope the friends I've made here can forgive me for keeping quiet about this, too," he admits.

"I'm sure they'll forgive you," reassures Aranya.

"I hope so."

Aranya gives him an encouraging smile before continuing. "If you don't mind me asking, what will you be telling the king about Lord Thedeim?"

"Well, the specifics are for him only, but I don't think it'd be a betrayal to say I've got a pretty positive opinion on not only Thedeim but Fourdock, too."

"I'm sure everyone is happy to hear that! I'll let you relax now. Congratulations on the victory, and I hope we'll see you in the arena again, Champion!" Slash lowers his finger and leans against the wall, relaxing as Teemo speaks up.

"Boss says Staiven should be here soon. Do you want to let in just him, or the others, too?"

"Which others?" replies Olander. It looks to me like he doesn't want to have a crowd, but he probably remembers Teemo telling Staiven to bring his apprentice.

"Rhonda and Freddie, and their friend Tula."

"Tula's with them?"

Teemo nods. "Yeah, them and Larrez brought her for a delve just the other day. You know her?"

Olander slowly nods. "She's one of the friends I mentioned."

"Berdol, too?"

"Yes."

"He's waiting outside as well. Do you want everyone, or just Staiven?"

Olander tries to hide his nervousness as he thinks it over before steeling himself and answering. "All of them are fine. If they forgive me, it'll be good to clear the air quickly. If they don't . . . I'd rather not delay knowing."

Teemo nods as Aranya goes and opens the door, letting the group into the small room. It's large enough for everyone to have a seat, but not many more people would fit.

They barely get inside before Berdol shouts at Olander.

"That was amazing! I've never seen Kinetic used like that before!"

Olander winces at the volume, but his professional countenance starts to melt as he processes what the catkin said.

"What kind of belt did you get?" asks Tula curiously, looking at the more ordinary one over Olander's shoulder.

"You . . . both don't care that I kept it from you? That I'm the crown inspector?"

Berdol shakes his head and speaks up first. "Not really? It feels even weirder now that I know who you are that you were supposed to listen to me on an inspection, but that's it. I might ask you more about dungeons later, though. Tarl has been teaching me a lot, but I bet you know even more!"

Tula shakes her head as well. "It makes a lot more sense why you're here. I just hope you won't forget about us when you head back to the capital. Can I write you?"

Olander sags in relief and smiles at the two. "I'm not heading back just yet. I'll write up my report and send it. The king doesn't need me there in person. If he does, he can send for me. And if he has anything else for me to do, he can send for that, too."

Tula smiles with just a hint of a blush, and Olander's cheeks get a tinge of pink before Old Staiven decides to interrupt. "With that out of the way, what say we answer the young lady's question about your new belt, hmm?"

"Oh! Uh, yes. Here." Olander hands over the belt and everyone watches as Staiven examines it. It's not long before he's thinking out loud about what he's seeing.

"What a strange enchantment. Scoot over, Freddie, I want to lay this on the bench to get a better look." The young orc quickly moves, and Staiven resumes examining, waving Rhonda closer to show her Thing's masterwork.

"The protection array is pretty standard for a reactionary defense. You usually see this for things that are either difficult to maintain or that just don't need to be up all the time. The trigger runes are very unusual . . ."

"How so?" asks Olander, earning a raised eyebrow from Staiven.

"Hmm . . . you probably know the basics, I'd imagine. The runes are Death and Life runes, so I'd ordinarily say it's a protection from Death magics, but the layout is all wrong. It's laid out more like Lightning or maybe Thunder runes. I can't make heads or tails of it."

Rhonda furrows her brow at the description, peering closer before she gasps in recognition. "I know what it is!"

"Well, don't keep us in suspense, my apprentice," remarks Staiven, looking a little grumpy, but I can see the proud glint in his eyes as she explains.

"I've seen this before, when I got my class! Thing was working on the axe, and I was trying to help. I don't remember what I said, but he froze for a second before practically throwing the axe runework off the table and starting another array. For *Lifedrinking*."

Olander looks concerned as Tula gasps, but Rhonda barrels on and continues. "Then he *countered* it! I remember at the time thinking that the formation was all wrong for the runes, but then, the Lifedrinking spell simply vanished! It's a protection-from-Lifedrinking belt!"

"Is that even possible?" asks Tula, looking at the object with suspicion.

"Yep," answers Teemo while Staiven continues to examine the enchantment. "Thing cracked it a while ago, but there hasn't been much demand for it. When Rocky started working on the rewards for the arena, the two belts were among the first things he wanted made."

"I think he's right," confirms Old Staiven, a finger tracing the runes. "I haven't seen this technique in counterspelling before, but I think it'll work. I'm not eager to test it out, though," he adds with a smirk before giving Olander the belt back.

"Protection from Lifedrinking . . ." mutters the elf, and I have to give Rocky a pat on the back through the bond. I think he finally managed to give the crown inspector a piece of loot he's actually impressed with.

Chapter 51

The way Olander holds the protection belt reminds me of a few little facts, and a few options I have, too. Teemo nods at the budding idea and speaks up for me.

"So, are you sending that belt off to the king, too? The Boss knows how nasty Lifedrinking can be, but he doesn't know how widespread it is. Is it a big concern when delving elsewhere?"

Olander takes a few seconds to weigh the answer, the others giving him time to think without their input, before he responds. "I probably *should* send the belt with my report. Not many dungeons make much use of it, but past a certain level, it does become a lot more common."

"Then how about, instead of giving up your hard-won loot, you send them a sample with some notes from Honey and Thing?"

Olander blinks a few times as he processes that. "Would that be alright?"

Teemo smirks and nods. "It's the Boss's idea to do just that. It's not for free, though."

Olander's look steels. "What do I need to do?"

"Tell the king's best nerds to come visit if they want a better explanation than the sample and notes. The Boss has a lecture hall room that he didn't think he'd ever have a reason to use, but he's getting enough scions with big brains who he figures might like to try their appendages at teaching."

Olander's resolve is stopped in its tracks at the offer, though most of the others around smile, more used to how I tend to do things. "That's it? And he'd use a lecture hall for that? It's usually for training denizens or imparting knowledge to dwellers."

Teemo nods. "He'd be happy to share. Just make sure the nerds know their tuition costs will involve them doing a bit of delving. No free rides here."

Olander snorts at that and nods. "I think the king might find his greatest minds fighting each other to come."

"I'll certainly be attending," speaks up Staiven, with Rhonda looking eager as well. Tula looks interested, too, but I don't think she's as eager to delve as the others just yet. She does seem to have something to say, though.

"Would followers of the Great Mother Laermali be allowed to attend, too?"

Teemo shrugs. "If they come to learn, sure. I hope we won't be stepping on your toes with that, Rhonda?" he asks the goblin with a wink, who is quick to shake her head.

"It's no problem! I want to learn as much as you have to offer, too, so I can't complain about Tula or anyone else trying to get the information from you instead!"

Old Staiven smirks at his young apprentice. "Maybe you'll be able to give a guest lecture or two of your own. You'll probably be easier to understand than most of the scions."

Teemo's look sours for a moment before a few ideas of mine make him brighten back up. "I'm not looking forward to trying to translate for everyone, but Boss has a couple ideas to fix that."

"How?" comes the obvious reply from most gathered.

"A modification of the axe and hat that Slash uses. He says it can produce more than just notes, like Slash showed with the voice amplification he was doing for Aranya in the match." All eyes turn to my Earth elemental, who simply nods before making his exit.

"Looks like he's gonna go tell the nerd brigade they have a new project. Honey and Thing will want to write the notes on Lifedrinking and make a simple array to send off, and he and Queen can go over how they made his stuff. I'll need to stop by later to explain what to do to make a voice without a mouth, but it hopefully won't be too hard to explain . . ." Teemo doesn't look too confident in that. Aranya pats his head with a finger to help encourage him.

"Speaking of explaining," pipes up Olander, "how does Rocky have so much mana to use? He puts so much behind each attack, but I don't understand how he has the mana to spend like that."

My Boxer grunts with a smile, and Teemo translates. "Moldybrain here isn't called a savant for nothing. He puts out about half his mana with his first attack, and uses the rest to redirect the energies. With his range of affinities, he can grab most of what would usually just be considered lost and repurpose it for his next attack."

"So that's what he did . . ." mutters Olander as he folds his arms, thinking over pieces of the fight.

"Can you do that, Rhonda?" asks Tula.

"I . . . Not yet? I know how to use fire to easily make more ice, but I haven't had a chance to practice with Kinetic too much. Seeing how Rocky fought, though . . . I really want to try."

"We should go see Larrez and try to get a time for us all to delve again. And give him a souvenir. He's gonna be so sad he missed the fight, but I guess they can't just leave the manor empty. *Someone* had to stay behind to make sure nobody could sneak in."

Teemo smirks at that but doesn't say anything about it, instead changing the subject. "Then it sounds like a good time for me to head to the forest and explain things to the nerds. Congrats again on the victory, Olander. Hopefully, you'll give Rocky a chance to get the belt back before too long."

The crown inspector grins wide. "I'm looking forward to it! But duty calls, and I really do need to finalize my report. When can I get the notes and sample?"

Teemo shrugs. "In a couple days, probably. Honey has pretty high standards when it comes to sharing information, and I'm sure Thing will want to share his breakthrough. Just come check in on us when you're done with your part," he suggests. Olander nods and stands.

"Then I'll go and meet with the lord mayor before I get to the paperwork. With my presence being public knowledge now, I wouldn't want to snub him."

My Voice sticks out his tongue. "Bleh, politics. Welp, I'm not gonna keep you any longer."

He dips into a shortcut as the others make small talk, nobody quite ready to fully part company just yet. I leave them to it and redirect Teemo to the Sanctum instead of the forest. Sure, the nerds are usually there, but no way was anyone going to miss this fight!

It only takes a couple nudges to get everyone else moving to the Sanctum, and I'm glad Coda has been working to continue slowly expanding it. Though I think much more, and it'll need Teemo to give it the old Tardis treatment. Or I could move shop once again.

My core is way bigger than it was the last time we moved, but between everyone, I'm sure we can figure out something if we need to. With all the space Tiny takes up, it's not a bad idea, but with how comfortable the smaller scions look just sitting on him, I don't think anyone is too concerned.

Anyway, time for a staff meeting!

"Alright, everyone good? Then, meeting started. Boss wants to try to do this more often than . . . just this one time, come to think of it. He doesn't have anything specific in mind to bring up, but he wants to take a sec to make sure everyone is on the same page and see if anyone has any suggestions. So I'll go first: the Sanctum is definitely getting a bit cramped, even without Tiny in here." He smiles at my largest scion before continuing.

"So, he was wondering about me making the space in here bigger than the outside. I can do it, but I think it'd be a temporary solution. With all the stuff he's working on, I think we should look into a real Sanctum Complex."

A complex? I chew on the idea as my scions do the same, with Coda seeming to be the first to ask a question. "He asks where we would put it," translates Teemo.

Hmm. Expanding is an option, but that'd probably bring another invader to deal with, and it doesn't guarantee the space would be good for something like that. If I use space we already have . . . it'd have to be in the forest of four seasons somewhere. Could the trunk of the tree handle being hollowed out enough for something like that?

Teemo relays my question, and I don't need a translation to see Coda and Poppy both look nervous about that idea. "They say it might work, but it'd take a lot of reinforcing."

Let's not, then. I really don't want the tree to crack in half with the first strong breeze. What about in the roots?

This time, my scions look thoughtful before answering. "It'd be difficult to get started, but it should be doable. Roots naturally like to coil around big rocks and stuff for stability. Poppy says the tree will probably bore into the bedrock, but she can't know exactly what it'll do before you use the expansion to grow it."

I nod to myself about that and consider the options. *We can't really start just yet, but if Poppy can help guide the roots to encourage it to leave large voids between the roots, we should be able to plan out modularly. Hopefully, the area under the forest won't be quite so dense with tunnels and such. In fact . . . we should get the rockslides to survey the area. I'd hate to learn the whole expansion is over a sinkhole, but I'd hate it even more to find out only when the tree falls in.*

Teemo nods at that and turns to Leo. "Leo, get the rockslides and wyrms to survey under the forest, especially where the tree will be going. If we *are* going to set up a complex down there, it'd be good to know there's nothing already sitting in the space."

Leo woofs in acknowledgement before Teemo continues. "Coda, draw up some preliminary designs, but nothing too detailed. We can't plan that surely until it's grown. Poppy, can you encourage the tree to have roots that spread out, giving us room to build between them?"

She nods with her frontmost flower, and Teemo nods as well. "Then I think that's a good enough plan for the moment. Anyone have anything to add?"

Most of the scions indicate no, but Zorro and Goldilocks look like they want to say something. "Go ahead, you two. If you have a need, or think you see a problem, speak up."

They share a glance before Zorro makes fox noises. Teemo waits for him to finish before smiling. "The cost won't be an issue. We can put in work to reduce it, and Boss still has a good wad of mana from the Maw to spend, too. Don't worry, he's not going to starve himself."

Zorro still looks worried, so I pat the bond with him—and with Goldilocks, for good measure. *I'm glad you're thinking about me, but you don't need to worry about this, bud.* I can still feel concern through the bond, but at least not as much. He'll just have to wait and see.

"Alright, anyone have any other business? Anything to ask for or make sure the Boss knows about?"

Thing, Honey, and Queen all vie for Teemo's attention, who chuckles as he listens. "They're talking over each other, but all three of them are looking forward to using the lecture hall once you designate it. For now, one of the rooms in the manor would probably be the easiest place to put it."

My three scholarly scions put on their best begging poses. I don't know how Honey and Queen manage to make puppy eyes with compound lenses, but they manage. Even Thing gets it across by plucking and doodling a finger through Tiny's fuzz like a kid sitting in the grass who wants something but doesn't want to actually ask.

Fine. Fine! I'll designate it! You three will have to share for now, though. I think the Sanctum will make a good lecture hall once we move. I spend the mana and turn a room that I think was a study into a lecture hall, though it looks more like a cramped classroom right now, with a handful of small desks and a new chipped chalkboard on the wall.

The three celebrate while Teemo laughs. "Now don't forget about the notes Olander needs, too!" They all three nod before they start communicating among themselves. Teemo leaves them to it.

"Alright, anything else?"

Chapter 52

Zorro

Being a scion is a lot to get used to. He's still trying to adjust, not only to the increase in intelligence but also to how differently Thedeim runs things. Take the meeting, for example.

The Southwood would never have a meeting like this of his scions . . . not that he had enough to even allow for a meeting until very recently. He would command it, and it'd be done as he commanded.

With Thedeim, things are suggested and prepared, but it's on the scions to follow through. The entire forest is a great example of that in action. He actually let Goldilocks and himself pick where their spawners go, and named the two on top of that! At least the other scions' reactions to his incredulity helped him not to feel insane.

But though his spawner is in the autumn section, he still doesn't feel like he has a *place.* That apprehension is why he spoke up about his concerns about the cost of the new areas. Even with the influx from the Maw and the arena match, can his new home afford to spend that much at once? Teemo reassured him, and he could even feel the warmth of the dungeon on his fur as he tried to comfort the vulpine, but he still worries.

The meeting soon adjourns with nobody else seeming to have too much to discuss, at least as one big group. The attention of Thedeim wanders, and Zorro watches as some of the scions chat amongst themselves, while others head off to do whatever it is they need to do. It's a surprise when one turns to him and speaks.

"Walk with me, pup," speaks Leo. Zorro is quick to heed him. They might both be scions and have similar status, but the wolf is not one Zorro intends to slight. Even if he wasn't more physically powerful than Zorro, he still remembers the strategic acumen displayed to protect the Southwood.

"What do you need, Warden Leo?" he asks as he hurries to his side, earning a chuckle from the wolf as he leads the way through a shortcut into the woods.

"Just Leo is fine, pup. I mostly wanted to talk. You and Goldilocks are still adjusting, and I wanted to make sure you're doing alright. I remember when I first joined and had to find my own place in this pack."

Zorro tries to minimize his discomfort as he answers. "It's . . . a lot to take in, but I'm sure I'll live up to Thedeim's expectations of me in time."

The large wolf smirks. "Ah, you really *are* having a bit of difficulty adjusting. Goldilocks seems to be settling in and starting to work with Titania and Poppy, but you're still following a meandering scent in circles, pup."

Zorro lowers his tail and whimpers before getting poked in the side by the Warden. "I'm not tearing you down, just pointing out the facts. A lot of his other scions took a lot longer than you are to find their place. Jello, for example, only recently found her passion with metalworking, and Coda tried a lot of different things before being inspired to build. If you want to try something, I have something you can try."

"You do?" Zorro quickly replies, not needing to think about the offer. He can't imagine anything around that actually needs doing. Despite the chaos and lack of orders, things really do seem to run smoothly in the dungeon.

Leo nods and sits down. "Let me call some of your potential coworkers, then I'll explain." Zorro watches in confusion as Leo throws his head back and howls, the sound carrying through the forest and probably beyond. Before Zorro can even ask what is going on, Poe wings through the trees and lands beside the two. He eyes Zorro for a moment before nodding to Leo.

"Warden. Have you explained it to him yet?" asks the raven, looking formal and intimidating to the Fox Scion.

"Not yet, but we can do that while the denizens gather." He turns his attention to the fox before continuing. "Poe and I are in charge of a lot of things outside the Alpha's borders. He handles reconnaissance from the air, while I coordinate with our ground forces. If the Alpha ever expands to the ocean, I'd bet he'll want one for under the waves, too."

Poe nods and picks up the thought. "However, most of our efforts are close to Lord Thedeim's borders. Patrols are one thing, but the Warden and I both have felt something has been missing for some time. Young Violet's scion Nose, however, was who finally showed us what we were missing."

Zorro tilts his head at that. "Nose? That's . . . That's the mole, right? I haven't had much of a chance to meet her scions yet . . ."

The two don't berate him for his lack of knowledge, instead nodding before Leo continues. "That's the one. He got a title that I think could be very useful to the Alpha: Explorer. It'll involve a lot of going on expeditions."

"It's not a request either of us makes lightly, Zorro. You've hardly found stability here, yet we would be tasking you with venturing beyond the borders to investigate and explore," adds Poe, looking apologetic at asking so much from the new scion. For Zorro, however, the idea has some appeal.

"I . . . wouldn't mind exploring, but I don't feel very prepared to go far beyond the borders just yet. I'm . . . not very strong," he admits, but the two experienced scions don't look bothered by that limitation at all.

"The best way to get stronger is to do," points out Leo. "And an explorer is supposed to look, not fight. With your illusions, you should be able to get into places and out of them without even being noticed, and easily give others the slip if you *are* discovered."

"And you will not be alone," follows up Poe, as a few smaller ravens and crows land nearby. A couple beats later, a wyrm pokes its head out of the earth, and a rockslide quietly breaches the surface, too. "Lord Thedeim has many denizens experienced in gathering information from outside. The Warden and I would ask that you work with them, join them on their patrols, and gain the knowledge and experience to advance. Once you have a firmer grip on yourself and your abilities, you can use them to seek whatever discoveries Lord Thedeim may require."

The denizens greet Zorro as he tries to process the opportunity being given to him. He'd have to go on expeditions a lot . . . but he'd be lying to himself if the idea of seeing more of the outside wasn't tempting to him. It was part of the reason he volunteered to even join Thedeim in the first place!

"I want to try," he answers, trying not to let his nerves show.

"Great!" Leo smiles at the smaller scion, his tail wagging. "I'll leave you to Poe for your first expedition, then. I need to organize the wyrms and rockslides to check the foundation of the forest. Be nice to him, Poe."

"I'm always polite and professional," replies the large corvid before turning his attention on Zorro. "Do you know the path to the war room?"

Zorro thinks, trying to recall the labyrinthine tangle of shortcuts Teemo has made, but he's apparently too slow for Poe's liking. Without a word, the large raven takes flight, grabbing Zorro up in his talons before smoothly entering a shortcut.

"It may be prudent to have you get more familiar with the shortcut system before sending you on expedition, but I really would appreciate a scion's eyes on this one."

Zorro can't even think to scream as he's carried through the strange space, and soon, he's deposited atop the table in the war room. He takes a few minutes to gather himself, wondering if he may have gotten in over his head, but Poe doesn't rush him now that he's here. Once he looks around, he sees the delay might not just be for his sake, as Poe is looking through the drawers for a specific map. He gives a small caw of triumph once he finds it, quickly spreading it over the table for Zorro to see, and taps a talon on it.

"This is the location Fourdock wishes to build their hold, in case something happens that requires the town to evacuate. As far as I'm aware, they have done their own surveys, but I don't know how detailed they are. The snows should have receded enough to make the trip possible, though it will likely still be arduous.

"I intend to send you along with a wyrm, several rockslides, and a flock of ravens as support. The rockslides should be able to ensure their namesake doesn't occur and injure anyone, while the wyrm can provide warmth and quicker reconnaissance of the underground area. The ravens will be able to see if anything else has happened in the area over the winter, while you will help direct them all in detail while there.

"Lord Thedeim supports the idea of this hold, and Coda especially is looking forward to aiding in its construction. I want you to make sure this location will be suitable, as far as you can ascertain. The mountain must be stable here, water must be available, and if the path leading to the site is unstable or unsuitable, I want you to chart a better one."

He stops speaking and looks at Zorro, finally noticing how overwhelmed he looks. Instead of frustration at the inexperienced scion, Poe's demeanor instead softens slightly.

"I know it's a lot, but please, just try your best. I don't expect perfection from you, especially not for your first expedition. There will be multiple follow-ups as plans progress, so don't think you'll need to spot every potential issue that could arise. Just focus on the obvious ones. Coda will likely accompany you on later expeditions, and *that* is when the two of you will focus on the details. For now, just try to learn. I can forgive mistakes, but I will not forgive refusing to learn from them."

"But . . . what if I make a lot of mistakes? A lot of *big* mistakes?"

Poe tilts his head in a smile, laying a wing over the smaller scion. "Then you simply have a lot to learn. We all started knowing nothing of our purpose, Zorro. Before you know it, you'll be helping a different new scion, wondering what you did to make it seem like you may have any answers, let alone *all* of them. You'll do fine, Zorro. And if this isn't your purpose, you'll simply have to keep looking. You'll find it eventually."

Zorro looks at the map, wondering. There's pressure to do well, of course, but Poe's encouragement strikes a chord in him. Exploring may or may not be his purpose, but sitting around doing nothing definitely is *not* it. He'll take those risks, make those mistakes, and learn those lessons.

"When do we start?"

Chapter 53

While there's a lot of prep to be done for the upward expansion in the forest, there's still a lot of other small things to do, and things for Thing to do, too. The anti-Lifedrinking enchantment is simple enough to make once you know what you're doing, so it's not a big deal for Thing to make two copies of it: one for Olander to give to the king, and one for the enchanter caste of my antkin.

I expect I'll have it be relatively common to find in the forest once it's up and running properly, but until then, I think the best way to start distribution will be with my antkin. And it'll give them a leg up on having a valuable export. Even if it eventually becomes more common, they'll still have the chance to establish themselves as quality craftsmen.

In fact, I should check how they're doing. Their progress to dwellership has been a bit longer than others', but they're also going for a lot more complex of a society than my other two enclaves. My ratkin remind me a lot of medieval monks with a pretty quiet life, while my spiderkin feel a lot like a tribal village. The antkin college is going to have a lot more structure, which isn't surprising considering how social ants are.

Their bars are about ninety percent full and holding, and I think the physical changes are basically done. There's only been small little additions since I last looked, basically everyone just filling in a bit and looking less like awkward teens. Now they just need to secure their food, and they should be golden.

It didn't take them long at all to expand their planned fields to grow food crops. Right now, I think they're going simple with the same mushrooms my ratkin use as their version of a staple grain. There are a few smaller plots with experimental patches of more exotic plants found in the volcanic zone, but I don't know if they want to use them for food or as ingredients for alchemy and enchanting.

The prep for hunting is also proceeding apace. Jello is even helping the engineer caste with their design and prototyping. They love the compound bows, and though the engineers don't have much to add, the enchanters are testing all sorts of different enchants while the alchemists toy with specialized heads. My original flexible spearhead is still too complex to really be usable, but the quick change allows for a lot of interesting options.

Alchemical arrowheads are the big thing the alchemists want to toy with. In an ordinary quiver, a syringe-style delivery system could easily leak, and a shattering one could break. But with a few headless arrows, alchemical options can be stored in a pouch or even bandolier and quickly attached before firing. I don't think it'll be a good option for in the middle of a fight, but on a hunt, the first arrow should be a surprise and give them all the time they need to pick and affix whatever the situation calls for.

Poisons are an obvious choice, but are also obviously not the best thing to use on something you intend to eat. Venom milked from my vipers can theoretically be neutralized by cooking, or simply be eaten and digested, but that's the kind of theoretical that doesn't have many people volunteering.

There is some interesting potential in the kind of things I'd consider a Control effect. Blinding is a big one, as are hallucinogens. Basically, any powder in the eyes can effectively blind something momentarily, and with all the mushrooms my dwellers have access to, I'm sure they have their pick of hallucinogenic spores to test. A couple were experimenting with something that was acting a lot like mustard gas is supposed to, but I'm glad that particular research was closed before too long without me needing to ask them to stop.

There may not be any conventions here to make it a war crime, but it's also just not a good weapon. A proper weapon destroys only when and what you want, but something like a corrosive gas is difficult to aim and to keep from going off early. The heads would have to be designed to break, and while a bit of blinding or hallucinating powder in a pouch would be annoying, a bit of mustard gas in a pouch would eat through it and probably whoever was wearing it.

Still, the other two are testing pretty well. The blinding is temporary, as are the hallucinations, and they lose potency pretty quickly if in open air. They're also experimenting with explosive heads, as well as impeding ones, but those are a lot harder to pull off.

Just like with a chemical, explosives also need to only explode when you want them to. C4 is used in practically every military thing because, despite how much boom it has, it's incredibly stable. I've heard of people setting the stuff on fire and hitting it with hammers to no ill effect. I dunno if that's true, but that's still the kind of standard to strive for in an explosive. It's hard to do, though, since stable things don't tend to explode.

The classic, and one I'm pretty sure even ancient Romans had access to, is what amounts to a little pot full of oil with a rag attached. Light the rag, fire, and whatever you hit bursts into flames. Not the most energetic, but I'm willing to call that the lowest level of explosion. It's also one that very few things my antkin are hunting would even notice. They are interested in the volcanic area, where "on fire" is practically the default.

So, much like Rhonda, they need to learn to translate the heat into actual blam. That project is going to take them a while, I imagine, but if they manage to make something stable and potent, I might get to introduce the glory of the Second Amendment to my dwellers. Magic makes it kinda moot, and I dunno if archery skills would translate, but it'd still be cool, even if I wouldn't hold my breath on that development.

For impeding arrows, they're looking into sticky things and various ways to tie things up at a distance. I doubt they'll have much luck with sticky, but alchemy doesn't seem to follow *all* the rules of chemistry, so maybe they can manage to make something that will make a big splash and harden to be strong enough to stop something before it can get away. My money is on the enchanters needing to tackle that one, once they get done with the anti-Lifedrinking.

Tying things up, however, has potential. Spidersilk opens up a lot of options with how strong and light it is. There's an experimental net arrow, which looks a lot like a cattail reed with fletching. The head is a carefully wrapped net around a spring-loaded core. The acceleration of being fired activates a mechanical fuse, causing it to expand while in flight, with small weights ringing the circular net. It looks really cool in action, but they're having trouble getting the fuse to be fully reliable, and even once they fix that, it'll have a very specific range that it'll be best used in.

The other leader in tying-things-up-at-a-distance technology is the lovechild of arrows and bolas. It's pretty simple: tie two weighted arrows together and you have some bolas you can probably shoot further than you could throw. Maybe. I don't know how far people can actually throw them. Ordinarily, nocking two arrows would be silly at best, as you'd have a hard time getting even one on target, let alone two, but that works in the bolas' favor. They *want* to fly away from each other, at least to an extent, so they can wrap around anything that is caught in the joining line of spidersilk.

Their prototypes still need some work, and I'm sure the hunters will need a lot of practice to make it function, but I think it'll be doable. The medics are very interested in the modified arrows, too, so I expect a lot of them will prefer to focus on that, disabling and hindering instead of actually taking lives themselves.

All three enclaves are working together to iterate on the composite armor, too. Each new version returns from testing utterly destroyed, but good data is being gathered. My spiderkin are experimenting with new weaves of silk, the ratkin test how well different thicknesses of metal work in the whole, while the antkin alchemists work to improve the resin used to hold everything together.

My scions are doing their part, too, with Jello working on a particularly clever bit of metalworking. She clearly was interested in the metal honeycomb that I thought would be impossible to recreate, and though she's not at true honeycomb, she's managed something very similar. She takes two thin sheets and puts long cuts about halfway down each, similar to how you can notch two pieces of paper to make an *x* and have it stand on its own. It's just that she has a lot more notches in these sheets.

Once she has them all slotted together, it looks like a complicated way to not accomplish much—but then, she bends it. It'll be *very* difficult for the smiths to mimic, since she does it inside herself, but she can crimp each long tab along the middle, leaving her with a long chain of hollow diamond shapes! She's playing around with trying to forge weld the notches back together or patching it with things like clay and then using the transmutation elixir, but I think she's managed a very good facsimile of honeycomb!

If she bent it twice, I think she'd be there, but I don't know if that'll help much, with them only being connected at the corner. It might need two more sheets connected along the edges like corrugated cardboard, but just this is a lot more than I expected to be possible to make!

I pat the bond with her as I watch her work, proud of her dedication. She even pulls another innovation as I watch, setting a sheet down for the crucible ants to swarm on and through. With their heat and propensity to carry around a bit of metal in their bellies, they can act like little welders, sealing up the seams under Jello's careful watch.

Looking good, Jello. Looking real good.

Chapter 54

Rezlar

The young lord mayor does his best not to fidget as he sits at his large dining table. The fight between Rocky and Olander was beyond his wildest expectations, even *with* Miller quietly making him aware of who Olander was well beforehand. It really makes him appreciate the fight he and his friends had with the Boxer and see just how much further they can all grow.

He's still not cut out for actually being an adventurer, but it's still fun to grow in strength together, and to just hang out. He gets precious little time to do either, and with all the happenings over winter and into spring, he doubts he'll have an excess of time to spend with them. This dinner is a prime example of that, in fact.

With Olander making his presence officially known, there's no avoiding an official meeting, complete with all the trappings of ceremony. At least Fourdock is remote enough that he doesn't have any other nobility nearby enough to get to the meeting in time. So he does his best to suck it up and put on a polite face as he nods to Miller, signaling for him to let Olander Wideblade into the dining hall for a shared dinner.

The ashen elf smoothly moves to the grand doors and opens them, speaking clearly as he does. "Announcing Crown Inspector Olander Wideblade, newly acclaimed Champion of Rocky's Arena."

Said champion is fully decked out in his attire of office, armor gleaming and glaive on his back. Rezlar notices the simpler enchanted belt around his hips, as well as the wooden box containing the official Champion's Belt under the tall elf's arm. He gives a nod that just technically reaches the threshold for a bow, acknowledging his host while also ensuring his own station is recognized, before his eyes dart around the room for a few moments. He smiles to himself as he strides forward.

"I hope I'm not being presumptuous in guessing you'd prefer not to stand on ceremony, Lord Mayor?"

Rezlar does his best to school his surprise, but he can tell Olander is fooled not at all. He sighs and slumps slightly, waving a hand at the seat to his right. "You would be correct, Crown Inspector."

"Just Olander, if we're going to forgo formalities," he replies as Miller pulls out the chair for him and he smoothly takes his seat.

"Then just Rezlar for me as well."

Miller exits to get the first course, leaving Rezlar to figure out how to talk to Olander. What can he even say? Thankfully, the adventurer kicks off the conversation.

"I hope the auditors aren't proving too onerous?"

Rezlar smiles at that and shakes his head. "They're no problem at all. I was honestly expecting some form of audit once they processed the tax report. Thedeim has been great for almost every industry in Fourdock, and once the ships are built, we'll be a bustling trade hub, I think."

Olander nods at that. "That's what it seems like to me, yeah. I'm better at hitting things than in trading, but even I know a thriving dungeon is more of a gold mine than a literal gold mine!" He chuckles at his own joke as Miller brings in a few flaky pastries filled with a vegetable and cheese mix.

"Indeed. I hope the crown will improve the roads to Fourdock soon, too. I think we'll have a lot of sea and land trading to do, especially with the shortcuts to the Southwood. I haven't had a chance to meet any of the orcish nomads yet, but the dungeon seems like it gets a lot of them as delvers. It could be a good way to get some of their more exotic goods, too."

Olander finishes a bite of pastry with an appreciative sound. "Oh, that's good. And trade with the orcs would be good, too. Most goods from the Wanderlands go through Meeting, and the city-state makes sure they get their share of whatever passes through." He smirks as he lifts another forkful of pastry. "Do you think you could manage something similar with the Dwarven Holds?"

Rezlar snickers at the idea around his own mouthful, swallowing before answering. "I doubt it, but you can never tell with Thedeim around. That kind of unpredictability is why we're looking to build a hold of our own in the mountains; in case anything happens, and the town needs to evacuate."

Olander quirks an eyebrow at that as Miller takes away their plates. "Are you worried about Thedeim?" he asks, clearly doubtful. Rezlar laughs and shakes his head before explaining.

"When he vassalized Hullbreak, the dungeon tried to send a scion to wipe out the town, threatening them both with starvation if Thedeim didn't back down. His Conduit dealt with both the storm and the scion, and Thedeim was successful in bringing Hullbreak to heel, but it was still a concerning time for the citizenry. It's going to be a joint project between Fourdock and Thedeim. I think there will be more than one breakthrough in the construction."

Olander nods at that. "Ah, that makes sense. I had heard a few scattered accounts of 'Fluffles the Stormeater,' but never got the chance to get details beyond a Dungeoneer report."

Rezlar nods as well. "It was also what spurred me to . . . well, take my lordship more seriously. I was basically absent, letting the local merchant guilds keep the town running smoothly. I didn't want to make a mistake and destroy everything. But I didn't have any contingencies for an emergency like that, and the townsfolk were rightfully wondering why not. So now we have a plan, and I'm taking a more direct role in the governance of Fourdock. Even if a lot of it is just approving the plans of the different guilds."

Olander chuckles at that. "It seems to be working, at least. And it beats forcing everyone to do things your way and making them hate you for it. When you have competent lieutenants, a competent *commander* just orders them to do what they were getting ready to do anyway."

They chat more as the meal progresses; about scandals and triumphs in the capital, about delving, and about life in general. Rezlar finds himself more and more at ease around the other elf, glad he's neither too pompous nor intimidating. He certainly has a presence, and some of his delving tales reinforce for Rezlar that it's not the career for him, but he's also easy to talk to.

As dessert is served, Rezlar wonders if he could ask him for some advice. Miller has given his own input, and though Rezlar trusts his butler fully, he's not going to pretend he's unbiased. But Olander doesn't have any attachment to cloud his judgement, and no reason to try to manipulate his decision.

He's quiet through the final course, trying to find a way to be subtle about it, and only after he sets his fork down does he realize Olander has been quietly waiting for him to say something.

If subtlety will be seen right through, be direct, then. "Olander."

"Yes?" he replies, leaning back in his chair, satisfied with the meal.

"How did . . . How did your friends take you revealing your position?"

Olander tilts his head in confusion before giving a warm smile. "Ah. They took it very well. A lot better than most others have before, if I'm honest."

Rezlar winces at that as Olander continues. "A lot of times, people will want to use your position for their own gain, though some are more direct about it than others. It takes a bit of experience to recognize when someone will put their ambitions ahead of a friendship, and those times . . . are painful, don't doubt that." The older elf pauses for a few seconds, a complex look on his face as he relives a few memories.

"But it's not a guarantee. I've made lasting friendships while undercover, just as I've had crushing disappointments. In the end, I think it's better to tell them the truth, if it's possible. It's good to have people you don't need to pretend around, and if they turn out to not be those kinds of people, it's better to know early than late."

Rezlar considers that as Miller clears the table of the dishes, leaving their drinks. His eyes follow the ashen elf as he thinks. Miller seems pretty confident Freddie and Rhonda will handle the truth well, but he's still worried about what might happen if they don't.

He's knocked from his thoughts as Olander speaks up. "Rezlar."

He shakes himself and looks at the older elf, who wears a serious face as he speaks now. "I know it's not easy. Sometimes, I'd rather fight a murderous dungeon on my own than face something like that. But just like facing down a monster will make you stronger, facing this with the truth will do the same. Even if the worst happens, there'll be others for you to learn to lean on and trust. Even if it's a disaster, don't let it cut you off from others. Because when it goes well, it's worth all the other pains."

"Well said, sir," replies Miller. Rezlar doesn't even jump at his sudden appearance. He's simply too used to the sudden comings and goings of his butler. "I've given the young master similar advice myself, but sometimes, one needs to hear from one not so invested."

Olander snorts at that. "And listen to your butler. I'm pretty sure giving good advice is one of the main subjects at butling school."

Miller dons a small smirk at that. "Ah, have you had a chance to listen to many of my colleagues? Perhaps you might enjoy the profession, once you're done being the crown inspector?"

Olander shakes his head. "I don't think I'm the type. I'm more the sort to make messes rather than clean them up."

"Ah, but sir, a proper butler keeps the messes from happening in the first place."

The two banter back and forth as Rezlar thinks over the advice. He really does want to tell them. It's mostly been the fear of them taking it poorly that has kept him from it. But the more he thinks about it, the more he thinks Olander is right about it making him stronger. He's had people he thought were friends betray him, before he came here. Sure, they were the treasons of children, and petty in scope, but it still sticks with him. He really *did* let them isolate him from people in general.

But . . . he doesn't *want* to be alone!

He nods to himself, resolve firm. He'll tell them. Now, he just needs to figure out how—and when.

Chapter 55

Parm

In the Ratkin Enclave, many of the displaced kobolds have come to settle. For some, it seemed the quietest place to call home. Others thought it would be a good place to try to be close to Aranya. To call her an inspiration would be an understatement, and though they've since learned she splits her time evenly among the enclaves, the initial assumption was that she would spend most of her time with the ratkin.

Parm considers himself mostly in the first group, hoping for some quiet peace to try to come to terms with everything. This morning, he lays in bed, still trying to do just that. It felt like, one day, he was tending to a pale elf and dwarf after a training incident, and the next he was suddenly free. He still sometimes reaches for the ornamental bands and chains he no longer has, reaching for something to keep his hands busy as he thinks.

He hates that he misses them sometimes. Most kobolds who had the chains were true believers in the Maw, but Parm simply never saw the point in trying to resist. You did what you were told the first time, or you did it the second time with a new bruise at best. Even his class was something he was told to take. He doesn't know why he was told to be an apothecary instead of a healer or even an alchemist, he just knew asking was a good way to earn attention, and earning attention never went well.

He doesn't hate being an apothecary, and he even understands the difference between his class and a lot of the other options. Healers are excellent for recovery in a battle, patching up wounds so the warriors can continue to fight. Alchemists serve a similar role, with the addition of buffing abilities. They need to plan ahead, but a proper plan and a few potions can turn the tide of a fight.

On the other hand, an apothecary focuses on keeping the more ordinary people healthy, mixing salves and balms for more mundane aches and pains, and medicines for illnesses. Very few healers can treat a disease, and though an alchemist could probably brew a potion to do it, they tend to focus on a much larger volume, enough that making a single potion simply isn't worth their time.

When Thedeim's forces attacked Silvervein, Parm didn't know what to do. He was supposed to go to the medical ward, so he went, even as soldiers and clergy ran to their posts to try to stop the invaders. He tended his patients, and when the foreign soldiers entered, he thought he'd die. He thought his *patients* would die.

Instead, the elf with the gleaming shield on his back removed his chains. He must have had Metal affinity, as he snapped the bands with a wave of his hand, gathered all the chains into a ball with a clenched fist, and let the scrap fall to the ground with a thud. Then he asked what Parm wanted to do.

"Do?" He still remembers the confusion he felt. He still feels it even today, whenever he needs to make a decision for all but the most basic things. The elf smiled at him and asked if he liked healing. Numbly, he had nodded, and the elf had offered to take him to the field hospital where he could help.

When he saw the hospital, he thought he understood. A foreign dungeon was taking over, and he would be its thrall now instead. Following orders there felt natural, though not being berated for his pace seemed odd. Still, he'd wrapped wounds and produced painkillers as needed, trying not to think about the fates of the people being swarmed over with ants. Noticing things was also a good way to gain unwanted attention.

After it was all over, he patiently waited to be dismissed or told where he could try to get some sleep. Instead, a ratkin had noticed him and asked what he was doing.

"Waiting to be dismissed or told where to go," he'd quietly answered, his gaze on the floor. A few seconds passed before the ratkin responded.

"How long have you been here?"

"Uh . . . all day?" he uncertainly answered. He really wasn't sure how long it had been. He was hungry at that point, but he had long learned not to try to use that as an excuse. It would usually work well with members of the Maw's clergy, but most of the others would only begrudgingly let him eat, and then pile on as much work as possible to make up for lost time. It was easier to just sometimes go hungry.

He'd had to suppress a flinch when the ratkin took his hand, but the voice only confused him more. No pity nor malice . . . just maybe a bit of annoyance at someone else. "They didn't make you take a break to eat something? Healers, I swear . . . Well, let's get you something to eat, then probably back home? I don't know what all the kobolds are doing, but last I heard, they were grouping up at their enclave."

"If I'm supposed to go there, I'll just go. You don't need to concern yourself with me," he tried, only to be waved off.

"I dunno about *supposed to*, but that's what I hear most of you guys are doing after being freed. Some just bolted. I guess they saw a chance at freedom and took it, without thinking ahead for things like food and water and protection."

Parm had nodded along, taking a few moments to process exactly what he was hearing. ". . . Freed?"

The ratkin stopped and gave him a confused look. "Yeah. Didn't anyone explain it to you?"

He subconsciously reached for his wrist chains to fiddle with, finding their absence oddly jarring as he slowly shook his head. "They . . . an elf removed my chains a-and asked what I wanted to do. I-I was working in the medical ward . . . he suggested I come here, so I let him bring me."

The ratkin had nodded at that. "Ah, yeah, a lot of the Shield guys were pretty busy, and we didn't have the enclave secured for a while. The hospital was probably the safest place for you, and you probably saved more than one life while there, too. Uh . . . you okay?"

Parm definitely was not, and sometimes, he's still not sure. The following hours passed in a daze, with only sparse details sticking in his mind. The rolled pancakes were a little overdone, and the tastes unfamiliar, if pleasant. The cool wall of the cave tunnel as he curled up against it, trying to process everything. Someone carrying him through a place of impossible geometry . . . then the familiar enclave, with signs of a fierce battle.

He wanted to help the injured, but was quietly reassured and told to relax. He couldn't relax, but being told to helped relieve him of the burden of needing to panic. Then he was brought to see Aranya.

The red kobold looked stunning in her white robe, and looked dangerous with that strange sword at her hip, even with her trying to look comforting. Her orange pendant stood out as well, seeming to radiate a gentle warmth and soothing power.

"Are you alright?"

He had wanted to say yes. All his life, the only acceptable answer to that question was yes. Sometimes, he could sidestep it by pointing out an injury, but even then came the implied answer that he could still do whatever they wanted him to do. But he couldn't bring himself to speak that lie again. He struggled, tried to force it, but he just couldn't.

". . . No . . ." he'd whispered, and soon felt arms around him. Not to harm him but to support him. He couldn't open his eyes as the tears flowed, not that he could have seen through them anyway. He still doesn't know how long she held him like that, and from what he's heard, he's not the only one to break down and need her support that day.

Ever since, he's been trying to cope with everything, and he's not alone. In a way, it's a comfort to know he's not the only one feeling lost, not the only one who sometimes locks up when asked what he wants for breakfast or other simple decisions. He's getting better, as are a lot of others, but he still feels fragile at times.

Like right now. He lies in his cot, feeling a building pressure. Not to get out of it, no. He'll get out eventually. That choice isn't the one weighing on him right now. He can feel a big decision looming behind him, or perhaps before him. Whichever direction it is, he can't ignore it much longer.

He needs to talk to one of the scions. At the time, he may have pretended not to notice what the ants were doing to people. There was a lot of blood, and so many ants . . . He was certain he didn't *want* to know. But after talking with some of the people who were operated on, the truth became clear. Now he wishes he had paid more attention. Whatever they were doing . . . he wants to learn. Seeing how the people recovered, it reminded him a lot of how his patients would recover with the help of his balms and salves, a slower healing that's no less appreciated than the quicker offered by healers and others.

He wants to learn. He doesn't know if he would have become an apothecary if he had been given the choice . . . but now, he has the choice to become something more. He's no fighter, but he can still make a difference in people's lives without lifting a weapon. There may be a little bloodshed involved still, but he can handle a bit of blood on his hands if it saves a patient.

His resolve shudders as he sits up, the fear of upsetting his delicate stability trying to remove what could upend everything once again, but he refuses to let it falter this time. He needs this, even if it terrifies him. He gets up and gets dressed, preferring a simple robe to the pants and shirts the ratkin are embracing, and heads for Larx's residence.

He doesn't know how to get in contact with Queen, but he bets the ratkin elder does.

Chapter 56

It's looking like I'll need to expand downward in the forest once everything is ready. I have a little bit of depth available in there right now; I've been able to dig a pretty shallow couple of caves, but my claims basically stop once we hit rock. I've been paying attention to Leo's scouting efforts, and it's looking like the area under the forest is pretty solid, so that'll be good, even if I'll need to spend more than expected to make room for roots.

Thankfully, the fight between Olander and Rocky has helped shore up my mana reserves. I've taken to trying to keep a decent surplus, even after keeping a steady flow into the ally emergency fund. Zorro didn't need to worry about my current income and mana usage, but it's never a bad idea to keep enough around to handle emergencies.

Interestingly enough, while the fight itself was a pretty good boon of mana, all the attendant stuff made even more. People selling things, buying things; I'm pretty sure even the wagering helped make me mana. We're going to need to do more exhibition matches in the future, definitely.

It looks like everyone else is doing well with their mana, too. Violet has a steady trickle going into the pool thanks to her sewer stuff. Who knew waste management could be so lucrative? She's slowly upgrading her spawners, and Onyx has been trying to get advice for what to do next from Teemo.

For now, all I can really suggest is to continue working through the backlog of sewer stuff, and maybe have Coda take a look around once things are as clean as they can reasonably get. I've heard most cities build their sewers with dungeons in mind, but I dunno how that actually works.

Hullbreak is also steadily contributing. People have been itching to delve him, and now that the weather's warming up, I think he actually has more mana than he knows what to do with. He's spending it on his seacave expansion, and Coda and I both have been resisting going to give him advice without him asking. The progress is slow, but I think that's more like normal pacing for most dungeons. He's definitely taking a lot of inspiration from the lighthouse for the sections above water, roughly carving the walls to look like brickwork. I think it'll be a great delving spot once he's finished with it.

Southwood, too, is thriving in spring and storing mana in the ally pool. He's experimenting with a few combat encounters using his current denizens. Most aren't really good for a fight, but I think he's aiming for a more casual combat than the steady ramping of training that I do. I can also see the uptick when the nomadic orcs come to visit him, which is cool. I bet they're going to enjoy having a more stable Southwood, as well as a new place to trade with in Silvervein.

Closer to home, Zorro is cutting his teeth on exploring. I don't know if it's quite what he wants to do, but he's giving it a solid try, which is all I can ask for. He's also started sneaking out into Fourdock, using his illusions to appear like a random stray as he wanders the city. Teemo says Leo and Poe are testing him to try being an Explorer like Nose, but I wonder if I could use an extra set of eyes and ears in and around Fourdock. Much as I try to ignore it, there's no denying that I'm getting a lot of attention from the kingdom and from several different gods.

I might actually need to dirty my nonexistent hands with . . . *politics.* If I'm going to deal with *that,* I'll need to know what the movers and shakers are actually up to. I swing my focus to Teemo to suggest he have a talk with Zorro, only to see he wants my attention, too.

"Oh hey, Boss. Good timing." He gives me a few seconds to parse what's going on, with Larx and a kobold waiting. It looks like they're in Larx's home in the enclave, and judging by the tea and little biscuits, the ratkin elder has been entertaining the kobold.

So, what's up?

"Parm here has something he wants to ask you," he answers, gesturing at the kobold who looks like he's going to have a nervous breakdown. He looks like he wants to bolt or curl up in his chair until I go away, but soon, words flow like he's afraid they'll never come out if he stops now.

"I need to talk to Queen, please! I saw the healing she was practicing when you . . . when you l-liberated us, and it was like nothing I'd ever seen before! Please, I'll do anything to learn!"

If I could, I'd raise an eyebrow at his outburst. He seems pretty timid and unsure of himself, like a lot of the kobolds. Most are adjusting pretty well, but some are having a bit of a crisis as they figure out how to do things without being told to. If I had to guess, I'd say he's in the group having trouble. *I don't want to rain on his parade, but . . .*

Teemo nods along to my thoughts before he speaks for me. "Alright, I've got good news and bad news for you, Parm. The bad news is: I'm not going to take you to Queen. Her style of healing is pretty revolutionary, as far as I can tell, but I refuse to sit and translate for her for the actual months or years it'd take for her to explain everything, not to mention doing the same for Thing and Honey. If you want to learn from her, you'll have to wait until the Boss's speaker project is finished . . . and I don't think we've even had a chance to *start* on it."

Parm looks devastated at that news, pulling his legs up and hugging them, prompting Teemo to quickly continue. "However! The *good* news is Queen isn't the only one who knows that kind of healing, and I think they'll be more than happy to teach you."

The pain of having his hope dashed is waylaid by confusion as he looks at my Voice. "What? But I thought . . . Who?"

Larx smiles as he realizes exactly who, and Teemo spells it out only a moment later. "The antkin. They have a lot of different castes, and one is a medic caste. Their method of healing is directly inspired by Queen and the Boss, focusing on knowing exactly what to fix and how, rather than just throwing mana at the problem. That's the kind of healing you're interested in, right?"

Parm leans forward in his chair, looking desperate once more. "Yes. Yes! I'm . . . I'm not cut out for the kind of situations where fast healing is needed. Back in . . . Back then, and I guess now . . . I'm an apothecary. I treat the more ordinary pains, illnesses, and problems people have in their lives. I want to be able to do that even better, and Queen's method just . . . felt *right*."

Teemo smiles at that. "Perfect. It's not going to be quick, just so you know. There's a *lot* to know about how the body works, and that's without getting into the differences between, say, an elf and a spiderkin."

Parm nods easily to that. "I know. Even pale elves and pale dwarves will have different reactions to different mixtures, and some will be allergic. I . . . I can learn," he insists, even as he rubs his wrists at some memory.

"Well, I think the antkin will be better teachers than what you used to have. Let's go get you introduced, then. Are you ready to go see Dean Tam?"

"Um . . . right now?"

Teemo nods and slips through a shortcut to land on Parm's shoulder. "No time like the present, right? Unless you had something else you needed to do?"

He looks over to Larx for advice, who simply smiles and starts cleaning up. "If you want more of the tea biscuits, you know where to find me, Parm."

With Larx refusing to be his excuse, Parm swallows heavily and nods. "Alright. How do we get there?"

"We'll just take a left through Larx's pantry, hang a Q through a shortcut, and then it's a hop, skip, and a jump to the medical college." I laugh as Parm tries to make sense of that. Teemo smiles. "I'll guide you, don't worry. See you later, Larx!"

"Do visit again, you two, and Lord Thedeim as well." He chuckles as the others head for the shortcut, and like Teemo promised, they soon are standing outside the medical college. It honestly looks a bit intimidating, despite how clean and peaceful it seems. It's probably because of that, honestly. Hospitals can try to hide it all they want, but nobody is there for happy reasons. Well, maybe the maternity ward, but everyone else is there because something is wrong.

Teemo continues to guide Parm through the complex, not giving him a chance to lose his nerve. Medical ants give them curious looks as they pass, but nobody tries to stop them. Teemo is pretty recognizable, and none of them want to mess with official business, even if I rarely think of it that way.

Oddly to me, Parm seems to relax more and more as they travel. If he's used to healing the sick and injured, he's probably pretty used to this kind of atmosphere, even if the medical college hasn't really seen any outside patients yet. He even has a peaceful smile by the time they find Dean Tam's office and Teemo announces them.

"Hey, Tam! Are you busy?"

Parm's nervousness returns in full force as Tam looks up from her slate. Her mandibles and antennae twitch in a smile as she sees her guests. "Ah, Voice Teemo and . . . a friend. To what do I owe the pleasure?"

"Are you accepting enrollment yet?" asks my Voice, earning a surprised stare from the dean.

"Enrollment?"

"You're a college; you need to teach, right? Hard to teach without enrolling students. Parm here wants to sign up."

Tam and Parm both look a bit lost, though the antkin recovers quickly enough. "I . . . suppose that's true. Parm, was it? You're interested in learning?"

"Ah . . . yes? I saw Queen's work in, uh, the field hospital, and I wanted to be able to do the same thing she did. T-Teemo said she's unavailable, though . . ."

Tam nods. "And he and Lord Thedeim suggested us. We *do* focus on similar methods of healing, though it's much slower and more involved than most magical methods."

"That's-That's fine. I'm an apothecary, so I'm used to the slow, steady pace that most people need to heal."

Tam's eyes brighten at that. "Ah, an apothecary? Then I think I know how you can pay your tuition, too. We have a lot of alchemical methods available, and though they're good for preventing any unwanted infections, we don't know much about treating diseases specifically. If you are willing to teach us, we will be more than happy to teach you what we know in turn."

Parm blinks at that. "T-Teach you? But . . ."

Tam laughs, bright and happy. "We don't know everything, Parm. We really do have a significant hole in our knowledge, and you could be a step in filling it, if you're willing?"

Lost, Parm looks to Teemo, who shrugs. "It's up to you, but if you want to learn, this is probably your best option."

The kobold still looks uncertain, but he turns his attention back to Tam and gives a small nod. "I guess? If you really want to listen to a sl—a *former* slave."

Tam nods and stands, moving around her desk to hold out her hand to shake. "Saving lives is too important to worry about pride, titles, and standing. As far as anyone here cares, your position as an apothecary makes you someone to listen to, no matter your past."

Parm stares at her for a few awkward seconds before Teemo flicks his ear. "Psst, shake her hand."

"Oh! Uh, yes!" He fumbles for her hand to shake. "Saving lives . . . just helping people be healthy again, is all I want to do."

Tam's mandibles pinch in a happy grin. "Then you'll fit right in! Let me introduce you to some people and let you get settled in, then I need to go over a curriculum. I don't think any of us were expecting anyone to want to come learn even before we finished officially becoming dwellers!"

Teemo quietly makes his exit through a shortcut as Tam leads Parm away, the kobold still looking nervous, but also growing more and more eager to start this chapter of his life. While I doubt it'll be easy, I don't doubt that it'll be satisfying.

Chapter 57

Right, what were you wanting to talk about before I told you about Parm?" asks Teemo as he heads back to the Sanctum to relax a bit. I dunno how much relaxing he's going to do once I tell him about the need for . . . *politics!*

Teemo shudders at that. "Is it too late to volunteer to interpret for everyone in the lecture hall, ever?"

Yes. Luckily for you, I don't intend to just jump into those uncharted waters without some prep. If we're lucky, you won't even have to get too much of it on you.

"That'd be a good trick. What's your idea?" he asks as he pops out of a short-cut and onto Yvonne's hammock, making himself comfortable while she's away doing ranger stuff.

The first part is to adjust where Poe and Leo send Zorro. If he's not a fan of the new assignment, we'll offload it to the other foxes . . . and we'll probably need to send some of them out, too, just to keep track of everything. I want him to scout Fourdock and possibly the other places around. I need eyes and ears to keep me informed on what the major powers are up to.

Teemo looks grumpy at the idea. "Better them than me, at least, but I still don't like the idea of spying on everyone."

I'm not exactly a fan of it either, but we're just drawing too much attention from powerful groups not to. So far, those groups have been the ones who are confident in their own position, so they don't need to do anything sneaky to get some of what we have. But the vultures will start circling, if they aren't already, and I need to know what they're up to if I'm going to head them off.

My Voice heaves a sigh, neither of us really happy with the situation, but both accepting that we can't just ignore it and hope it'll go away. "I'll bring it up to Leo, Poe, and Zorro, then. You'll probably want to upgrade the fox spawner if you're intending to send some out on expedition like that, too."

Yep. You might need to head out on expedition more than a few times as well. We probably don't need many shortcuts in and around Fourdock, but I'd like the spy network to eventually encompass the kingdom, if not further.

Teemo gives a low whistle at that. "You plan big, Boss."

It won't be all at once, but if we keep growing, we're going to keep attracting attention. At least we have a good method for extending our influence. We'll set up small outposts like we did on the way to the Southwood, and probably use bees and/ or bats to deliver messages down the line and back here.

"Do you want to try using the rockslides to listen in on things?"

Maybe once we have specific locations to keep an ear on? For now, I think the foxes will be plenty. They'll just use subtle illusions to make themselves look like stray cats or dogs, and hopefully be able to listen in on what we need to hear.

"Hmm . . . Do you want to try bees, or maybe fey? The living vines could be good to hide in gardens, too."

Maybe? We can certainly give them a test run around Fourdock to see if they pan out, though the vines will probably only work for some of the year.

"You should definitely buy gremlins from Violet at some point, too. They'd make great observers."

Yep, once the tree is in, that's one of the things I want to add. I also might try to splurge and get something with Spatial affinity, too.

Teemo gives an exaggerated gasp and points an accusatory finger at my core. "You're *replacing* me?!"

Yes. Heh, of course not. I just don't want to take up all your time with maintaining the shortcuts everywhere, especially once we get the network up and running.

Teemo snickers and drops the act before pointing something out. "It might not be a good idea to make a vast network of shortcuts outside. Remember how Kennith entered the ones to the Southwood? I wasn't too careful with hiding them, but it sounded to me like he probably would have spotted them even if I was."

Hmm . . . that could be a problem, yeah. He's probably a master of Spatial affinity, but he's also probably not the only one out there. It'd only take one for people to start investigating. In fact . . . we might be boned for using illusion foxes, too. What if illusionists can spot them at a glance, too?

Teemo sits up and folds his arms, considering. "Yeah, that'd give the whole game away. We could still make do with rockslides and a few flying denizens, but that'd take a lot longer to set up." He pauses and smirks at my core. "Unless you think the wyrms can sneak them into places without getting noticed."

I chuckle at the idea of my wyrms melting their way through the ground not being something any town would raise an alarm about. *Well, we have a master illusionist we can ask, at least.*

"Yeah?" asks Teemo, and I'm surprised he doesn't remember.

Torlon, the Head Priest of the local Church of the Crystal Shield. The illusions he used to run the maze and beat Tiny were top notch. I bet we could ask him.

My Voice smacks his forehead. "Ah, right! He'd definitely know if illusions are easy to spot. Do you think he'd be suspicious of why we're asking?"

Maybe? The Shield certainly has some kind of spy network of its own, even if it's just followers reporting through prayer or something.

"Why don't you try that, too?"

I . . . don't think I have enough followers for that. And it feels weird to try to send them out specifically for that purpose. Starting off on a bad foot, you know?

He nods. "Yeah, that's fair. You are starting to get a bit of a following here, though."

Why do you have to remind me of something else *I'm trying not to think too hard about?*

"Because ignoring it won't make it go away, and I'm supposed to keep you from letting things like that get out of hand."

I mentally sigh and rail against his logic for a few seconds, but I can only drag my feet for so long. I shift my attention to the little afterlife I've set up, and I can feel things there are going pretty smoothly; at least, it seems like it. A few people have finished with their projects by now, though time is pretty weird between there and here. The workshop is finished, as are more than a few chairs. Everyone who's finished has opted for reincarnation, eager to see what else there is to see, and I hope they'll be in a position to come back eventually.

The happy chatter and the sound of tools at work helps calm my nerves. I still don't think I'm cut out for this sort of thing, but at least I'm not making a hash of it. It helps encourage me to pay attention to the little motes of warmth that are my followers who are still breathing, even if their numbers feel overwhelming if I focus on them.

The glow from my enclaves isn't too surprising, and I'm more used to that, at least. I never asked it of them, but it's not too surprising . . . Not anymore, at least. I've had my panic attacks about it by now, and I'm mostly adjusted. Kinda.

"You alright, Boss?"

Yeah, sorry. Just . . . taking stock, I guess. You're right that I can't ignore the whole godhood angle either. I just . . . didn't expect to see so many outside the enclaves. I follow the little warm drafts of my followers, leading to someplace a bit diagonal from normal reality. It feels like I've fallen into the night sky, but the stars are more orange than anything else. It reminds me of when I first started looking around my dungeon domain, a floating viewpoint peering into dusty cabinets and abandoned rooms.

It feels like that, but I'm zoomed much further out, and the physical building is as ephemeral as mist. I can pick out the points of warmth that are my followers, but very little besides. I can see the groups, and at a glance, I recognize the enclaves. The antkin stick out a bit, as I feel a lot of potential, but they don't quite qualify just yet. That has to be because they haven't finished transitioning to dwellers yet.

And my enclaves are not my only followers. I can feel the people of Silvervein who are following me, and it's more than I expected. It's maybe a hundred people, but even that's surprising. I can also feel several hundred more who don't follow me, yet still acknowledge me. I don't get as much warmth from them as the others, but it's still noticeable. That's probably why deities tend to organize into pantheons, I suppose. Even if someone only really worships one at a time, they still accept the others. And there are probably at least a few who try to honor the whole lot.

I'm still happy with being officially on my own, even if I think the Shield and I are pretty closely aligned. It's even easier to see when I look at Fourdock as a whole. I have more followers here than in Silvervein, but practically everyone acknowledges me. It's the kind of thing that makes me want to panic again, but I do my best to stamp that down. Freaking out about it doesn't help and is probably an overreaction on top of that. If I still had a pulse, it'd be racing, but at least I don't feel like I'm metaphorically hyperventilating.

I cross my somethings behind my back before jumping at the realization that I have a form here, too. I know I have a form in my afterlife, but I didn't think I had one here. It's difficult to get a good look at myself, and it's not just because of the lack of mirrors. I can look at my extremities, but I hesitate to call them arms and legs.

Can a nebula have hands? Because that's the closest to what I can describe what I look like. I look like a nebula with a vaguely humanoid void inside it. What's more, the shape is constantly shifting, and it's difficult to tell if it's an illusion, like looking at a reflection in the water, or if the void is actually subtly flowing and changing the nebula.

Alright, stop staring at yourself and keep looking around. You need to get used to this stuff before you actually *make a mess of something.* I cross my limbs behind my back and resume looking around, careful not to touch anything as I look at the followers of the Shield. I can pretty easily spot the ones who acknowledge me, and see their devotion to the Shield, or the similar acknowledgement for the people who aren't too involved with that sort of thing.

It's interesting to see their faith in the Shield, and more than a bit humbling to see my own followers have no less confidence in me. It makes me want to make sure their faith isn't misplaced, even if there are certainly better targets for it. Still, if they're going to give it to me, I'm not going to squander it.

"Ah, I was hoping we could meet. We are, as the mortals would say, neighbors, correct?"

I whip my focus around and hold up my limbs defensively, wondering who could be talking to me here, of all places?! Looking at the answer, it seems obvious in hindsight. While I can feel a lot of acknowledgement for other deities among the populace of Fourdock, there's one who has the clear majority of followers.

Floating among the sea of mortals with me is a large crystalline heater shield. As far as I can tell, it has no eyes or mouth or face . . . but I guess I'm not one to talk. Its voice is clear and jovial, like someone used to making fast friendships that last a lifetime.

"I hope we can talk, Thedeim. There is much for us to talk about, after all."

Chapter 58

I'm at a bit of a loss as to what to do. It's like meeting a celebrity and them saying they've heard about *you*, not the other way around. The Shield's chiming laughter sounds, and I wonder how long I've just been staring at it.

"Sorry. I'm . . . still pretty new to all this," I admit. The Shield bobs in the air in understanding.

"It is no problem. I think most dungeon cores would have difficulty adjusting to divinity. Though I also think you are not like most dungeon cores."

I snort at that. "That's what I hear, heh. I know I run things a lot differently than others."

The Shield bobs in a nod. "Yes, I hear of your strangeness from many of my believers in Fourdock. I also hear it from Order and the Raven, on the occasions we get to meet. From them, I get the feeling that, as the mortals say, you are not from around here, yes?"

I give it a wary look, though I don't know if that actually translates with my weird void self. I'd like to keep my origins a secret, just because it's the kind of thing that could set off disastrous change if not done right. I probably shouldn't be surprised Order and the Raven know at least the basics. From what I can tell, the Raven is supposed to know where souls belong, so he's gotta know my belonging here is temporary. Order, too, is basically in charge of the system, and it has to have some kind of flag noting I'm an anomaly of *some* flavor.

After a few more moments' thought, I decide to trust the Shield. Even if we've only technically just met, we've basically been working together for a while now. "Yeah, pretty much. The details are more than what I wanna get into right now, though."

The Shield glows in excitement. "Yes, I knew it! Are you from Beyond?" it eagerly asks. I'm not sure how to answer that.

"I . . . Maybe? I have a few guesses for where the Beyond leads, and back home is one of them, but I don't know for certain. I wasn't exactly party to the secrets of reality there."

"Ah, but you are! Or at least somewhat. I have heard Freddie's prayers for Rhonda's safety with her class, so I know you are doing wondrous things with magic. I even suggested to Laermali that she send an acolyte instead of her High Priest!" The Shield glows in happiness as I chew on that fact.

"You sent her to me?" I ask, wondering why it would do something like that.

"She was coming, so I worked to protect the peace of your meeting. She heads a pantheon, if you did not know, so she is used to being heeded. Even Order and the Raven suggested she listen to my advice, and I am glad it has been working out!"

"What, did you guys have a meeting about me?"

"Meeting?" asks the Shield, dimming for a moment as it processes the term before the glow returns. "Yes! A meeting is accurate! Order wished to speak with the three of us about you after your ascension."

I sigh at that. "I really *have* been drawing the gaze of some big eyes . . ."

"And you will draw more, I am sure! *Change* is such a tantalizing domain; tempting and yet dangerous. And you are aware of it!" The Shield's bright glow softens as a quiet chime of happiness comes from it, tinged with bittersweet. "I was not very aware of what *protection* entailed when I ascended."

"How *did* you, if you don't mind me asking? I've heard a few snippets in passing, but the Shield followers . . . er, your followers are usually more concerned with training against my undead than in discussing theology where I can hear."

The Shield bobs again in a nod, conjuring a crystalline rack to rest on, even as we both float among the stars that are the people of Fourdock.

"I sometimes think the mortals know more of it than I do, even if they embellish. I think it is fitting; perhaps they get to protect some of my own beginnings. I don't remember much of my early time with Jayna. I am told mortals do not remember their birth and early years, either. I started as an artifact created by a long-forgotten dungeon. Some of my believers think I was forged from a dungeon core, but Order has repeatedly said that is not possible."

The Shield pauses, glowing warmly at some memory before it continues. "My earliest memory is of her face, quietly singing a hymn as she polished me. I think she knew I was intelligent even before I did, and she did her best to instill in me her beliefs as a paladin. She did not have a deity at the time, and simply devoted herself to protection, at least at first. Through many battles, I was her bulwark. I do not know when it happened, but her devotion slowly anchored to me. I knew so little at the time, and I did not understand what that meant. I still do not know why . . ."

It trails off, dimming for a few moments before shaking itself and continuing.

"From there, the legends detail what she did in my name. It took a long time to accept that . . ." It trails off again, and I get the distinct feeling it's giving me a knowing smirk before it continues. "When she got old, she told me her time was limited, and the Raven would come for her. I did not want that, so when I saw the Raven, I tried to protect her. I encased her in crystal, and accidentally transformed the gathered people's clothes to crystal, too. I saw the Raven fly in and perch on the encasement, then reach through like it was not there. And then he gave her to me."

Its glow dims for a while, and I wonder if it's done talking. I don't know what to say to something like that, even after my own experience with my fallen dwellers. We float there for a time before it finally resumes speaking.

"She is Beyond, now. She said she had done everything she could here, and she knew I would keep everyone protected." It snorts with a sound like breaking glass. "It took me a long time to realize how many people *everyone* is. I cannot get them all . . . but I try. And my believers do the same."

It shakes itself and absorbs the stand before resuming floating. "I did not think I would talk to you of that. I wanted to talk of the now and the future, not the past."

"Well, the past is a good foundation to build on. I'm still building mine here, and I don't know how much of before I should talk about. Or how much I even *can* talk about."

"Yes, you have a lot of mystery as well. I can see there is a you inside that glow, but even here, I cannot perceive it. I think it is something to do with the framework upon which Order's system is hung, but I do not know very much about it. He knows the most, but he says he knows almost nothing. Most of us simply accept when he says that is just how it works. Except, I think, you."

"Like the affinities," I offer. The Shield bobs in a nod.

"Like those, yes. Laermali herself says they should be more intertwined, but never could figure out how. But it seems that you have."

"More like Rocky has," I try to deflect before continuing. "Yeah, I know, he gets it from me. I know a lot of stuff from before. A lot of the rules of existence are understood there, but magic basically doesn't exist, so I guess I'm a fresh pair of eyes coming at it from a whole new perspective and seeing things that most people here . . . just haven't discovered, I suppose?"

The Shield chimes in happiness once more. "Like with the Legionnaire Paladin! I had been hoping to forge a class like that for some time now, but had been lacking some keystone concept for it. And then you were able to cultivate it in Freddie." The Shield beams in happiness, and I give a bashful smile.

"I'm glad it worked out like that. I just wanted to help him and Rhonda be the best they could be, give them the tools to craft their futures."

The Shield chimes louder. "A change to their best; a welcome one indeed! While I cannot speak for Rhonda, Freddie is thankful every night for how much his life has improved. A little change can prepare someone to protect themselves where they thought that to be impossible."

"Heh, yeah, I guess we work pretty well together like that," I admit.

"Perhaps we should work closer, then?"

"Like a pantheon? I think I should try to stay out of that, for a lot of reasons . . ."

The Shield bobs in understanding. "Yes. Not all of us join a pantheon. There are obligations involved." It tilts itself in what is *definitely* a smirk. "Including politics. I am told you try to avoid that as much as possible."

I nod at that, not even trying to deny it. "I try, but I think at this point, I've already stepped in it. I can either pretend otherwise and track it everywhere I go, or I can actually prepare and try to deal with it. I'm just getting a network off the ground to keep informed of whatever I need to be kept informed on."

"It is a good thing to get ahead of. Fewer inquisitions that way. Order and I had to learn that the hard way, as the mortals put it. It is good to learn from other's mistakes. Perhaps you can learn from another of ours, too."

"Oh? I'm always up to learning something, especially if it'll help me not to mess something up." I lean forward, interested to hear what advice it has to give.

"Order and I are not in a pantheon. It gives us more ability to deal with problems ourselves, but it also means we have to deal with them *ourselves*."

"I . . . don't think I'm going to be joining a pantheon anytime soon. I'm pretty good at dealing with problems, at least when I'm not pretending they don't exist. I'm happy to unofficially work together on things sometimes, but anything official is . . . dodgy."

"Dodgy?" asks the Shield, chewing on the word more than asking why working closer would be described as so. "Perhaps. But I had an idea, and Order was not opposed to it. Instead of you joining a pantheon, you should *form* one. Order and I would be interested in joining."

I stare at it for a while, trying to wrap my head around the words that came out of its not-mouth. "Is that . . . *What?!*"

It chimes in laughter, and I relax, thinking it's a joke. That's when it continues. "You do not have to do it right now! Consider it for a few centuries, or even millennia. Just know that the help you have given the two of us already is beyond what some pantheon mates would do for each other. The Legionnaire Paladin merges the camaraderie and protection that I have been striving to spread for a *long* time now, and your sending of the Harbinger to Order for investigation has made him aware of a weakness in his system to fix."

The Shield's warmth softens before it continues. "Just consider it, and consider your domain. It would be a very big change to how things are done. I think you would know best if it would be a positive or a negative one. Take all the time you need to think it over. Time is much less limited for you now."

It floats a bit sideways, kinda like how someone going through a shortcut looks. I can only assume it's headed to its own territory, maybe its afterlife to look over the people there? Maybe it's off to talk to its High Priest or something. Either way, I'm here, floating among the projections of the people of Fourdock, thinking about what the Shield had to say.

It was nice to get to know it a bit more, and I get the feeling we'll become friends, if we aren't already. The talk of *making* a pantheon sounds crazy, but there's a certain amount of sense to it, and makes me wonder the implications if the others are supposed to answer to me. I only intend to answer to Him, but what happens if others answer to me? I think I really will need those couple centuries to think it over, though that brings me to the last thing it said.

Actually having all the time in the world is another one of those things I was trying not to think too hard about.

Chapter 59

I come back to normal reality to see Teemo perched atop my core. *Was I out for long?*

He shakes his head at me. "Nah, not too long. I moved here because it felt like you were further away than you've ever been. Did you somehow pick up Spatial affinity, Boss? It felt like you were about a mile sideways."

I'm pretty sure it was a god thing. There's some kind of plane where I can sorta see people. It's difficult to explain. Did you hear any of the conversation I had with the Shield?

Teemo quirks an eyebrow. "That's what that was? I could feel something, but it felt like my Voice and Herald titles were fighting over it."

Heh, maybe we need to submit a bug report to Order.

Anomaly Logged

Oh. If only it was always so easy.

"What'd you two talk about? I know there was some kind of deal offered, but I don't know what."

The Shield and Order suggested I found a pantheon, saying they'd join if I did. I'm gonna take my time to think that one over.

Teemo laughs at that. "*They'd* join *yours?* If you run a pantheon like you do a dungeon, you'd probably accidentally absorb or overthrow all the others before long!"

Which is why I'm not going to do it for a while, if ever.

"Fair enough. Did you still want to talk to Torlon about illusions?" he asks, reminding me of what we were doing before I wandered off on a divine tangent.

That'd be great, yeah. Is Zorro around? If we're going to ask about illusions, he should probably be with us. Teemo and I both check the other scions and see that

Zorro is, in fact, home at the moment. He's currently down in the cavern layer, looking into a pool of water as he makes fine adjustments to his stray disguise. I give the bond a light tap with the request he come to the Sanctuary, and he drops his disguise in surprise at the attention.

I let some mirth seep through the bond as he navigates the shortcuts to get here, glad to see he's getting better at them. Soon, he's standing before my core, tail tucked between his legs.

"You're not in trouble, Zorro, so get that tail up," speaks Teemo, still sitting on my core. The vulpine scion forces his tail out from between his legs, but it's still not held at a confident angle. My Voice shrugs before continuing.

"Close enough. Anyway, Zorro, the Boss has something he'd like you to do. He knows you've been slipping out into Fourdock, and he'd like you to do that more. Leo and Poe aren't wrong in that an Explorer wouldn't be bad to have, but what the Boss really feels like he needs is someone to keep an eye on the delvers when they're outside. He's getting a lot of important attention, so he wants to have some kind of forewarning about what that attention could entail. Are you willing to not only go keep your ear to the ground but also teach the other foxes to do the same?"

I feel an immediate acceptance from him, but I push that aside, causing him to tuck his tail once more before Teemo explains.

"You don't have to; you know that, right? He's not ordering—he's offering. There's a difference."

Zorro makes adorable fox sounds as he explains himself, his tail even wagging a little by the time he's done and Teemo relays what he had to say.

"He says he would really like that. He likes the delvers, thinks they're interesting, and thinks he could keep us informed on Fourdock, though he thinks he'll need better foxes to really accomplish it."

I pat the bond with pride, glad Zorro is genuinely interested instead of just doing what I tell him. I upgrade the fox spawner until just before it spits out a new fox type as Teemo keeps talking.

"Alrighty, Boss'll upgrade that more once we get back from the Shield church. He wants us to ask Torlon about how easily illusions can be spotted, and see if he has any advice to offer, too."

Zorro's emotions are a bit jumbled at the news and the rapid pace now that he's accepted the new job, but I can feel his resolve building and attempting to organize the mess that is his mental state. Teemo slides down my core until he has to hop off at the equator, and lands right beside Zorro.

"Right, let's get going." He leads the fox through a shortcut and through the maze of connections, the two chatting along the way. Teemo encourages and thanks him for me, but I lose track of the conversation as I get distracted when they officially get marked as being on a sojourn. Teemo's shortcuts are definitely using at least one extra dimension, but there's apparently a demarcation of my territory even there.

It seems strange to me, so I start tracing the boundaries as they go, like I'm trying to wrangle some terrible wiring inside a PC. I swear I've seen some lack of cable management somehow use an extra dimension, too . . .

I don't get to map it out too much before Teemo and Zorro are standing outside the church with a bemused and aged wolfkin looking down at the pair. "Thedeim's Herald? And . . . the Fox Scion, I think?" he says, one hand resting atop his broom while the other strokes his chin as he probes his memories.

"That's us! I'm here as his Voice, not his Herald, though. He wants to ask Torlon about illusions and stuff."

The wolfkin gives a kindly smile at that. "Ah, then welcome! I don't think I'm prepared to accept a divine delegation, but friends are much easier! Much less ceremony; fewer choirs to organize and all that," he jokes as he opens the door for my two scions. "I think he's at the martial hall, helping Freddie train."

Teemo and Zorro peer into the church as my Voice speaks up. "Where's that? I haven't gone around poking shortcuts here, so I'm not very familiar."

The wolfkin holds the door open as he points out a boring door about halfway down the interior. "Just head through that door and down the hallway. The door at the end will open out into the courtyard, and you should be able to spot the training hall from there."

"Cool. Thanks!"

Teemo and Zorro head off as the old wolfkin chuckles at the unique experience of giving my scions directions. They have to ask someone to open the door for them to get into the hallway, and get the attention of someone else actually *in* the hallway to open the way outside, but it all goes pretty smoothly. I wonder if the people are used to the kind of weirdness that tends to happen around me, or if they're so used to guiding people through the temple that it barely registers that they're doing the same for a pair of scions.

Whatever the reason, it's a lot easier to get into the training hall, as the door is propped open to help with air flow. It looks to me like today is a cardio day. Freddie and Fiona run laps, with Torlon keeping track with a simple floating number display. I can see Zorro's interest through the bond as Teemo shouts.

"Hey, Torlon! You busy?"

The gnome looks up and smiles as he shakes his head. "Freddie is just helping me count to twenty, and demonstrating what it looks like, too."

"Eight," says the orc as he passes Torlon, and the counter ticks up by one.

"Good lad, helping out his senile teacher like that," snarks Teemo. Torlon smirks.

"That he is. So, what are you and . . . the Fox Scion doing here? I don't think you're looking to help me count, too?"

"Nope. The Boss wanted to pick your brain about illusions."

"Then he's come to the right brain. I might be losing my numbers, but I daresay there are few in Fourdock who know more about illusions than I do."

"Yeah, the Boss and Tiny both still remember the things you pulled out when you ran Tiny's maze."

The gnome smiles at the memory. "I really should challenge Tiny again someday. I hear he's refined his Fate affinity significantly since then. It's always a challenge to avoid tipping off people with that affinity."

"Yeah?" asks Teemo, Zorro taking a seat and looking up at the gnome as he explains.

"It's always the little things that give away an illusion, and fate has a way of magnifying the little inconsistencies even without the user consciously doing it. Anyway, what did you want to know about illusions?"

"Things like that, for starters. The Boss is making waves, and big people are starting to notice, so he wants to make sure he can catch wind of what they might do before they show up to do it. He could lean on Fate to divine it, but Tiny always says that sort of thing is unreliable at best, so he wants to disguise Zorro and the other foxes to have eyes and ears on the streets."

"Nine," comments Freddie as he passes, Torlon looking thoughtful as he processes Teemo's words.

"And he can't use his believers for that because they're concentrated in his enclaves?"

"Not as much as you might think, but he also doesn't want to have a core tenet to be snitching."

Torlon laughs at that. "A fair point! Spy foxes, hmm . . ." He turns his attention from Teemo to Zorro. "Can you turn invisible?"

In answer, he does just that, though Torlon immediately waves him off. "No, don't. Invisibility is very difficult. Staying still is easier, but moving is *incredibly* difficult."

Zorro reappears—looking dejected—as Teemo speaks up. "But we saw you—"

"Ten," interrupts Freddie, trying to hide his enjoyment at getting to mess with Teemo and having a good excuse. My Voice glares at his back before continuing. "We *didn't* see you when you did it. Even with his fancy dungeon senses, the Boss couldn't keep track of you when you were facing off against Tiny."

Torlon smiles. "That's because I'm not boasting when I say I'm very good with illusions. Especially when infiltrating a place, being invisible can make it harder for you. What if there's a door? What if someone bumps into you? Now you need to start layering more illusions to cover it up. It's much simpler to make something that shouldn't be there appear as something that does."

Zorro yips and dons his stray dog illusion, and Torlon kneels down to inspect it. "Ah, that's *much* better. When you cloak yourself like that, you only need to know yourself, not what your surroundings should look like from every angle and perspective." He reaches down and pets Zorro, and it looks almost like a graphical Z-fighting error as he does so. He nods as he stands.

"It's more difficult to maintain an illusion when someone is touching you, rustling your clothes or hair . . . or fur," he comments with a smile, then chuckles at a memory. "I had to learn that when I started disguising myself as an elven child for a while, before joining the Shield. People love ruffling the hair of urchins, and I'd expect stray dogs to be the same."

"So how—"

"Eleven."

"Don't make me make the laps longer, Freddie! I'll do it!" threatens my Voice as he gets interrupted by Freddie once more, who is the picture of innocence as he continues to jog.

"Take a rest, Freddie," manages Torlon with a straight face. I bet he has a lot of experience with not giving away the gag like that. "As for how to fix it, practice is the best method I've found. Or shorter, rougher hair. You'd need to actually trim it short and do something to make it more rough, but it'll be a lot easier to convincingly conceal and discourage all but the friendliest of people from touching too much."

Zorro looks down at himself, and I can feel him weighing his desire to do this against his desire to have soft, floofy fur. Teemo gives him an understanding look, and even Torlon nods at his dilemma.

"Think of it as motivation. If you're going to try to look like a stray, the closer you look, feel, and *smell*, the easier it will be to convince people. If you're going to do this, you'll have to get good if you want to have your luxurious pelt back."

Zorro gives a long, forlorn foxy squeak, hanging his head and tail low in defeat. I pat the bond with him, trying to encourage him. Floof is the toll to pay for sneakiness.

Chapter 60

While I'm pretty sure Zorro will need a trim if he's going to pass as a hungry stray, I don't rush him into getting it. He's practicing his illusions a lot, so I think it's only right if I upgrade the spawner and give him not only a bit of a boost from that but also some more foxes to practice with.

I still only have the basic ones, though they did at least come with Illusion affinity. It costs a bit extra to set a specific affinity for a spawner, but it wasn't much to worry about at the time. Upgrading later gets pretty spendy, though. If I were to upgrade either of the rat spawners to have Spatial affinity now that they're maxed out, it'd take a big bite out of the tree fund. I think I'll need to wait before getting anything with Spatial affinity.

Back to the foxes, though, the normal model looks like a normal fox, and they mostly deal with either luring illusions or flashes and pops to distract. They are definitely not set up for a real fight, and if I specialize them as casters like I expect I will, they'll still be a mostly support role.

Anyhow, let's spend some mana and get the next tier before I keep getting distracted with the options.

Out of the spawner comes a fox with two tails, labeled as a mischief fox. While the normal ones are probably more suited to be ordinary encounters, maybe around the manor, the mischiefs look like they try to avoid direct fighting at all. They have a lot more magic at their disposal, and I watch as the first one explores the forest until it finds a small pile of coins under a large leaf in the spring section.

It notes the location before darting off to grab a living vine, dragging it back in its mouth. The vine seems confused, but picks up on the idea as the mischief puts it by the coins and casts an illusion. The coins seem to double in number as the living vine burrows itself down, leaving just a flower above the ground. The mischief works on that, too, making it seem a bit bigger and like it's trying to hide the coins. Once satisfied, it hides, sticking around to ensure the illusion doesn't drop.

I chuckle at the trick, and hope it'll encourage more mana generation in the area. It seems pretty likely as I watch another mischief put its own spin on the trick, making the coins appear fewer instead. It looks like delvers here will need to either learn to spot illusions or take a gamble when they spot the bright flowers. The point isn't in hiding the potential treasure but rather in making delvers decide if it's worth rolling the dice.

I further upgrade the fox spawner a couple times to get a few more mischiefs, but I don't get near the next variety yet. I want to let them get a bit more used to things before I add more of them. I do nudge Zorro to guide some of the basic foxes to the manor house, where they should make a great addition to the encounters there.

I'm not done upgrading yet, however. I eye the other spawners in the forest, deciding which one to do next. The Earth elemental spawner might not be in there, but it doesn't escape my consideration. The Soil elementals are really cool, and I bet they'll synergize well with my vines as I keep upgrading them, but I think I'll leave them alone for now.

The elementals, that is. The living vines are square in my sights for upgrading, and I get them going up to the next spawn.

For a brief moment, I think the spawner itself is wandering off, but that's just what the new creature looks like. It's a living bramble, and seems to more or less be a bigger, gnarlier version of the vines. I even watch one merge with one of the elementals, making it look a lot meaner. They're still two different denizens, and I watch as they get used to coordinating so closely together, but they look like they'll be a massive pain to fight. Not only does the bramble have some pretty nasty thorns, but when backed up with the mass of the elemental, people are going to need to have a good bit of armor between them and any hits.

And since neither denizen really has a set shape, they can weave out of the way of a lot of attacks. I even spot a few vines investigating if there's enough room for them, too. I think the elemental is full with a single bramble, but I also wouldn't be surprised if the next spawn has more room.

I eye giving them an affinity, and even look at the specialization options, but don't set anything yet. Spatial vines could be cool, but I don't know if they're the right choice for helping maintain the shortcuts just yet. The idea is growing on me, though.

Especially if I specialize them for resources. They have a lot of herbalism synergy—not a surprise—but there's also a few more esoteric options. I could actually have some grow full-on potion fruits, or have buds made of precious metals or gems.

One particularly interesting one is mana flowers. If I understand this right, they are basically a passive mana income for me, drawing in stagnant and turbulent mana and smoothing it out directly. Individually, they don't do much, but if I had a bunch of them, it'd add up quick. And if I give them Spatial affinity before they get expensive enough to require a kidney or two, I might be able to have them siphon mana even outside my borders.

Definitely something to keep in mind, but I think that'll be a project for later. Maybe when I get to working on the whole spy network thing. Why set up just one network when I can set up two at once? Three if the Spatial stuff is an option and counts separately.

Much like with the foxes, I give the vine spawner another level or two to boost the spawn rate, and let the denizens go find good places to hang out.

Or get told where to hang out. Looks like Titania is taking it upon herself to make sure the forest is running smoothly, and I see Goldilocks watching as she directs the new denizens. I pat the bond with both of them before getting back to work, appreciating their efforts even as I work on putting even more on their plates.

I think I have two more spawners to upgrade before I let things settle again, and the first is going to be the bears. Olander said they'd be great as heavies, and now that I'm getting a better feel for the encounters in the forest, I agree with him even more than when he said it. Before I go upgrading it, I spend the mana to give the bears Kinetic affinity, too.

Ordinarily, I'd expect the fighting specialization to give that to them, but I can see an option for that path that will give them *Life* affinity, too. Not only should they be able to give themselves some regeneration or heal other denizens, but they should also be able to keep anyone they hurt too bad alive until a more specialized denizen can get there and help. It'll probably be weird for the delvers to be saved by the same thing that put them in that sort of state in the first place, but that's just the kind of dungeon I am.

The basic bears are just black bears, and they've been mostly wandering around and occasionally attacking the delvers who come through. The bears tend not to last too long, what with the more experienced adventurers being the ones to come check the area out. But with the new affinity and the upgrades, the spawner skips straight to coughing up grizzlies! That ought to get the delvers' attention.

I'm not quite sure what to do with the black bears, though. Maybe I'll ask Goldilocks to point them toward the cavern layer? They're a bit weak for the forest, but I think, especially with the added Kinetic affinity, they should fit right in with the difficulty curve there.

I'll poke her later. For now, I let the different bears explore and look for their niche in the changing forest.

Lastly but certainly not leastly, I'm going to upgrade the bee spawner. Olander mentioned armory bees when he came through with Berdol, and those sound really cool! It looks like they're the last spawn before I get the semi-intelligent denizen: Royals. The spawner isn't giving me much information besides the name yet, but it's not difficult to guess they're going to be leading all the other bees in the area. With something like that coordinating them, the armory bees could be a serious threat.

It also gives me an idea for some more aranea quests, but that'll be a long ways off. I think I want to max out the snake spawner next. For now, I upgrade the bees enough to get the armory variant; they spawn in squads, looks like.

While the rumblebees have specialized limbs, it seems that armory bees have simple graspers and come with their own variety of equipment. This particular squad is infantry, and they all have polearms. I think they're too short to technically be halberds, but the heads look right to me. They also have black-and-yellow armor which seems to be some variety of steel. I dunno how well normal steel will fare against adventurers like Olander, but it'll probably be better than chitin . . . and having both is *definitely* better.

They stand about four feet tall, though they hover an extra foot off the ground as they organize themselves before flying off in formation. I don't know what they're looking for, until they spot one of the living brambles and make a beeline for it. I expect them to just swoop in and relax, but they instead coordinate to pick it up and fly it to a cluster of trees that have grown closer together than most. Then they start using the bramble to make their hive.

The bramble isn't hurt, and in fact starts to grow little metallic tips on its thorns as the armory bees work. More squads spawn and start gathering brambles, and it looks to me like *armory* is a good name for them. They make their own honey, but it seems to work similarly to the metal transmutation elixir, turning whatever they dunk into it into steel. Interestingly, it doesn't affect the bees themselves. If I had to guess, it doesn't work on anything alive, with the possible exception of the brambles? Maybe they just feed the honey to it, and it works from there?

However it works, I can already feel Queen wanting to come take a look, and I'm not going to stop her. Honey is coming to investigate, too, so I imagine the two will have the secrets of the armory honey solved before too long. They're welcome to it.

As for myself, I sit back and watch the bees work, as well as the other new denizens. I never expected there to be so much interaction between denizens, though I probably should have. Most things in a forest interact at least a little over a year. With me having all four seasons at once, is it any surprise they're getting to it immediately?

Chapter 61

The next week or so goes by in the blink of an eye as I watch things settle from all the upgrades and the delvers get used to having someone like Olander around. He doesn't get a chance to delve in that time, probably dealing with all the political stuff he was trying to avoid, or maybe stealing time to just hang out with his friends.

The forest is seeing a lot more adventurers now, even if it's still a work in progress. The basic format is settled, and the denizens are adjusting to their roles quickly, though there are some growing pains. The first couple days, I had to keep extra healing slimes in the area, and I think Grim was spending more time there than in the cemetery. Goldilocks and Titania have been diligently sticking close to him, learning all they can about making the encounters just right, and ironing out the details with some of the other denizens.

A lot more delvers are getting injured in the forest than I was expecting, but I think that only reinforces the need for a more traditional crawl at a higher level. The manor fills that niche for the new delvers, but I really have wandered away from a combat focus for most of my other sections. Sure, they're not *free* from a fight anywhere, but the tunnels are more like a highway than a place to fight, the caverns are more for mining than fighting, the gauntlet is a challenge of skill, not martial prowess, and the labyrinth is a puzzle rather than something to hit really hard.

I'm glad that, even battered and bruised, the delvers are generally in good spirits about the whole thing. They're enjoying pushing their limits, finding out where they actually are in an environment where they won't have to die or lose a friend to do so. It's more than a bit reckless, but most are learning pretty quickly. A broken bone can be recovered at a good healer, but the loot tax for "defeat" isn't so easily fixed. A few groups have to learn a couple times that they aren't ready yet, but they're the exception, not the rule.

Zorro has finally admitted defeat with his fluff, and though I'm sad to see him have to trim it down a lot, it's plain to see how much easier it is for him to maintain his disguise with shorter fur. He's started going out on sojourns, wandering Fourdock and getting to know people and how the town itself is faring. It's more than a bit embarrassing to learn how often people talk about me, but at least, it's easy to rationalize why.

Most aren't really talking about *me* so much as the dungeon. Sure, *I'm* the dungeon, but there's a big difference. They talk about the challenges, rumors about certain sections, gossip about what the delvers are doing, or sometimes their own plans for delves. Those are actually fun to listen to, and informative, too. Delving is becoming more and more of a hobby for a lot of people, and it's relieving to hear them talk about the little details that the more experienced delvers don't even notice anymore.

Like the aranea quests. Sure, the guild people will just grab one on their way to whatever their actual quest is, but the more casual delvers really appreciate the guidance of the small quests. For them, the little plaques *are* their quests, not just a little bonus. The rewards are also a big draw for the newer adventurers, too.

While the aranea still refuse to give out more than a single item, like the infamous lone sock, they are starting to diversify their rewards beyond silkcraft. The ratlings and magmyrm have been slowly refilling the warehouses I have with miscellaneous things, and the aranea finally seem to feel there's enough for them to start giving out as rewards.

Now they sometimes give out a single mail gauntlet instead of a single silk sock. Gems are a pretty common alternative reward, along with the occasional potion. I still don't know what criteria they use to determine what they give out, but the only disappointment I've noticed so far is when a delver is rewarded with only one of an item that's usually paired.

There's another project that's growing, though I haven't had to do much myself to help, aside from upgrading the limestone quarry again. I might need to upgrade the iron ore vein soon, too, but I'll see how things go before I do. Rezlar is serious about the hold in the nearby mountains, and word is finally getting out that miners of all varieties will be needed, as well as more masons to learn the new ways of concrete.

Coda and Slash have been working to slowly expand the access shaft to the caverns. Every day, the miners work to bring up even more limestone, and my Civil Artificer is determined to ensure the traffic flows smoothly to and from the quarry, random encounters aside. I've seen him sketch out a few highway intersections, a wing claw tracing the flows as he figures things out. I've only done a few intersections in some games, so I don't know the details of why certain ones work better than others. All I know is that having traffic cross is bad.

Coda understands a lot more than that, so I'm happy to leave it to him after appreciating the geometry of his intersections. It's enough to tempt me more into buying Spatial affinity for something again, but I resist the siren song for now.

The price tag is a big deterrent, that's for sure. I could afford it for the plant spawner, but it won't be cheap. Still, there are a lot of potential benefits for not only having Spatial affinity but having it specifically for the plants. They certainly won't get bored from maintaining shortcuts, for example. Honestly, I'm holding off because I really like the idea of Spatial-affinity gremlins, after trading with Violet to get them. I just think it sounds cool, even if there's probably a better spawner to use for it.

The more I think about it, though, the more I think that idea will probably go the way of my folding spearheads or Zorro's floof. I doubt I could make my gremlins have both Shadow *and* Spatial affinities, at least not without breaking the bank. The initial spawner and affinity addition wouldn't be too bad, but I think the upgrades to the spawner will compete with the dragons if I do that. The stronger things are usually more expensive. I haven't felt the pinch too bad with the forest spawners just yet, but I bet once I get the tree in and upgrade them even further, they'll get more expensive than the dragons.

Speaking of, I check in on them and am happy to see most of them in and around the labyrinth, eating the Fire elemental invaders and challenging the delvers. I even spot a couple basilisks not far from the Antkin Enclave. It looks like an ambitious rancher ant is trying to tempt them, but they're staying at a distance for now. Nova is helping out with scouting the foundations of the forest, and it seems like things are going to be stable there for roots, thankfully. I'm still waiting for the full survey report, but so far, it's looking very promising.

Also looking promising are the antkin. I think they're just about ready to go hunt. They could probably prepare forever, but they're smart enough to recognize the diminishing returns. They'll have a lot of things to redesign as they get more action while out hunting, but right now, they're about as good as they're going to get.

The ranchers are still figuring out exactly what they want to use to hunt, with the current front-runner being what amounts to a boar spear for the burly antkin. The head looks closer to a glaive than a spearhead, but it should still stab easily.

The workers look like they favor the classic shield and shortspear combo, and are drilling in small formations. It looks like the enchanters even managed to make the shields able to link up somewhat, letting the protection magic shift to where it's needed. The links are a bit tenuous, so we'll see if it holds up in an actual fight, but the sparring tests look promising.

The medics are enjoying the compound bows, now that the engineering caste knows how to make them. It looks like the alchemists actually were able to make an effective glue arrow, too. Considering I haven't seen any delvers use something similar, I think they'll have a good product to put onto the market once they finish up with their progress bars.

All of them are wearing wyrm-hide armor, with the ranchers having the heaviest versions and the medics the lightest. I'm still not sure how they even manage to make the stuff, but it seems like a decent midpoint between something like boiled leather and actual steel. There are still the faint lines of magmalike coloring running through the hide, and while it stands out in my territory and on the surface, the antkin seem pretty confident in it helping them stay unnoticed in the volcanic section they intend to hunt in.

If nothing else, I doubt they have anything available that would give them better protection from the heat and fiery attacks of whatever's in there. Right now, they're making their final preparations for their first hunt. As I understand it, they're not expecting to go especially deep. This will be as much a scouting trip as a hunting trip, though the antkin intend to give them all a hero's send-off.

Aranya, Larx, and Folarn are coming to see them off in the morning, and I get the feeling Queen wants to make her presence known, too. It'll be a big deal for the antkin to make this work. The hunters look nervous but determined, which I take as a good sign. If they were strutting around and boasting, I'd worry for their safety. But there's a healthy amount of caution in their movements as they prepare their kits, making sure they'll be ready come morning.

It's tempting to ask Nova to go and keep an eye on them, but I think that'd be doing them a disservice. They've worked hard for this. I can't helicopter around them and fuss the whole time. They can do this, and I need to trust them enough to let them.

Chapter 62

Bem

The worker antkin tries to keep his cool as he walks with his fellow hunters. The others have dug an easier access tunnel to the volcanic area, where the deans and the High Priestess are waiting to send them off. He glances at his fellow workers, Gim and Tob, and hopes they're dealing with nerves better than he is. At first glance, it'd be easy to think they are, but Bem can see the rigidity in their posture and the tension in their mandibles.

Looking to the other castes, it's actually a relief to see them both looking nervous as well. Ran, the large rancher caste, has her spear in her hands and is trying to look confident, but her strong hand is gripping the haft hard enough that Bem swears he can see it compressing, while her weak hand is twitching, trying to fiddle away her nervous energy.

Jin's apprehension is easier to spot, with her constantly patting her pouches and pockets, ensuring she has everything she needs. Her compound bow rests on her back next to the quiver, a selection of alchemical heads strung across her thorax in a bandolier. Her hands glide over each piece of equipment, her mandibles twitching as she confirms them in her head for the tenth time or more.

Bem tries not to worry about going out into the wild volcanic region, remembering the assurances of the crafters about all their gear. "The armor will protect from the heat," "don't forget to link the shields if needed," "keep your eyes peeled," and more advice all seem to merge into a half-remembered sludge. He just hopes he'll remember things clearly if anything goes wrong.

Before he can start imagining the ways things *could* go wrong, his group rounds the bend and sees the deans and the High Priestess, as well as Elder Larx and Warmistress Folarn. The deans are better at hiding their nervousness than

Bem and his companions, but the way they stand makes him think they're relying heavily on High Priestess Aranya and the leaders from the other enclaves to keep their semblance of confidence.

The High Priestess looks completely at ease, smiling easily as she spots the hunters. Elder Larx smiles as well, his eyes seeming to take in every detail in a few moments before shining with pride in his soon-to-be fellow dwellers. The warmistress of the spiderkin looks more scrutinizing in her appraisal of the party, and when she gives a small nod of acceptance, Bem feels much more confident in their ability to not just die out there. Huntsmistress Vernew would probably better know if they'd be able to actually bring something back, but the large tarantula woman's approval speaks well of their ability to come back in the first place.

There's no grand speech as the hunters reach the leaders, but rather a simple prayer invoked by the High Priestess. "May Lord Thedeim bless this hunt to be fruitful and see you all return safely. If He sees fit to only grant one blessing, let it be safety," she finishes with a smile as a comforting blanket of orange descends over the antkin.

The little joke at the end doesn't lift Bem's spirits much, but it does at least help him remember what should be their highest priority out there: don't die. He's not certain if he or the others would go to Lord Thedeim's afterlife or return to their spawner, but nobody is eager to find out. Either way, there's no reason to take wild risks. The crafters have been working to reduce the risk in their own way, while their training has been to reduce it further.

He and the others stand straight, antennae crossed in a salute, before Bem replies. "We'll be careful, High Priestess, Deans. We'll bring back meat or knowledge; either will help the enclave."

The gathered leaders nod and step aside to let them pass, nobody standing on ceremony. If all goes well, they'll have ceremony enough when they officially become dwellers. They march with purpose and dignity until they round a bend in the tunnel, finally letting them relax a little and release the tension they've been holding.

As a group, they all sag, each exhaling a long sigh.

"No pressure . . ." mutters Tob, earning a snort of amusement from Gim.

"Just the future of the enclave; no big deal, right?" The nervous laughter helps ease the tension further, and soon, they all collect themselves. They don't need to talk as they continue down the tunnel, the temperature rising even as their armor keeps them comfortable.

"Feels like the armor's working," comments Jin as she takes her bow in hand. The others nod, with Ran speaking the thought on everyone's mind.

"Hopefully, it works as well against the beasts as the heat."

Soon, the tunnel opens up into a large cavern, a large magma flow winding through it and providing light. Tall mushrooms dot the subterranean landscape, with smaller varieties much more common. Lichen covers the floor like grass, with some acting like vines and clinging to the walls and ceiling, as well as draping over the tall mushrooms. Fiery bats flit about, too high to make tempting targets to hunt, at least not yet.

"How good do you think a bat is?" asks Gim, earning shrugs all around before Bem answers.

"I think we'd need a lot to feed the enclave. Lord Thedeim's bats don't seem to have too much meat on them." That earns nods as the group spreads out some, still keeping everyone easily in sight, but letting them all get a closer look at the growing things.

Bem is interested in a vine hanging over a shorter mushroom, bearing little black things which might be some kind of fruit. He tosses a rock to make sure it won't explode or something, and is glad when the vine continues to act as a normal boring plant, even if it's ashen gray with black teardrops on it.

He manages to pluck one but doesn't try to bite into it yet. He doesn't know if it's ripe, or if it's even edible! Better to bring a piece back for someone to take a closer look at. His nearest friend is Ran, who seems to be looking at something on the ground but not bending down to get a closer look.

"What'd you find, Ran?" he asks as he nears her. She holds up her strong hand to get him to stop.

"A big patty. Watch your step. I want to ask Jin if it would be worth hunting." Bem looks down and sees the large splat, and is glad there doesn't seem to be any other ones around for him to step in.

"I'll gather everyone up." Ran nods at that and starts looking around, probably to see if there are any signs of something eating the lichen or mushrooms. It doesn't take Bem long to gather the others. Gim found what looks like an edible mushroom to bring back, Tob found what looks like some kind of nut but he thinks is a weird type of spore from the tall mushrooms, and Jin has a handful of bright yellow fern shoots that might be edible. Bem is inclined to think the ferns will be better for medicine or alchemy than eating, but it's still an interesting thing to bring back.

"Ran found a big poop patty and wants Jin's opinion on it." The other two workers look disgusted at the idea, but Jin nods as she follows.

"I think Ran would be better able to tell what kind of thing would leave scat like that, but sure, I'll look." Soon, everyone is around the final product of something's meal, with Ran and Jin poking it with a stick and the workers keeping an eye out.

"It looked pretty grassy to me, but I wanted you to take a look."

"It does have a smell, doesn't it? I think it might have been eating the ferns I found. They probably have sulfur in them. I wonder if it's for nutrition or as some way to encourage predators to leave, thinking there's another predator already in the area."

They poke the patty apart, looking for any other information, but it seems like it's pretty boring, as far as poop goes. "I think it's some kind of bovine, maybe?" proclaims Jin, though that makes Ran frown.

"It looks like, but there are no other patties. They usually run in herds."

"Maybe it got kicked out?" suggests Tob, still keeping an eye out.

"Or is solitary in the first place," offers Gim.

"Either way, it seems like a good target to track first. Any objections?" asks Bem. Nobody raises any.

Unfortunately, deciding to track it is easier than actually doing it. The lichen-covered floor is springy enough that tracks vanish quickly. They manage to find a scattered trail by following patches of nibbled lichen and eaten ferns. They spot a lot of other wildlife as they go, and even carefully detour around a Fire elemental. As a group, they could probably take it, but nobody is going to eat a Fire elemental, so why take the risk, especially if the commotion could spook the actual target away.

They hear their quarry before they see it, the loud crunching of plants and possibly even rocks as it chews without a care in the world. Once they *do* spot it, it's no surprise it doesn't feel the need to eat quietly. It's a massive bison with obsidian horns that stick out to the sides, as tall at the shoulder as Ran, with a shaggy coat as black as coal. The tip of its tail glows brightly, but the rest of it seems to be flesh. If it sees them, it doesn't pay them any attention, so the group backs up out of its line of sight to discuss what to do.

"That's a *lot* of meat," points out Tob.

"And a lot of critter to fight," counters Ran.

"Do you think we can handle it?" asks Bem, while Ran considers.

"If it's on its own and doesn't seem bothered, it's probably meaner than most things around. The sides will have a thick hide, but that'll probably be easier to get through than that thick skull. Definitely watch for the horns, even from the side."

"Do you think the glue will work?" asks Jin.

"Hmm . . ." Ran and Bem peek out of cover to take a better look at the bison and the surroundings before ducking back.

"I think I'd try the sleeping spores instead," suggests Bem, with a nod from the rancher.

"I think that thing'll be stronger than the glue, yeah."

Jin nods and affixes several sleeping heads to her arrow shafts. "I'll pepper it as long as it stays at range, then switch to hunting heads."

"Ran will take the left if it gets close, and we'll take the right," says Bem, and that's all the planning that's needed. They learned during training that trying to plan something fancy was just a good way to tangle everyone up. It's better to have a basic plan and adjust on the fly as needed.

As a group, they move back out, and Jin lets the first sleeping arrow fly. She hits it right on the side of its head, causing it to sneeze as it breathes in the spores. It shakes its head a few times before resuming eating. "I hope it's not immune to these kinds of spores . . ." laments Jin as she fires again.

This time, it lifts its head and looks around, wondering what's going on. It eyes the group for a long minute, who all stay still, before it resumes eating. "One more, and if that doesn't work, we'll have to do this the hard way."

Jin lets loose a third arrow, which hits it right in the snout, triggering a violent sneezing fit from the bison before it looks around once more. Its gaze settles on the party again, and stays there longer than before while they wait for it to either go back to eating or fall asleep.

Thankfully, its lids start to droop as the spores finally do their job. It staggers away, but is easy enough to follow by sound alone, so they let it think it got away from them as they follow it. Soon enough, the noises quiet, and they sneak closer to find it asleep, legs tucked underneath itself. They quickly coordinate then surround the sleeping bison, each one taking their own target.

The crossbar for the boar spear is set too close to the head for Ran to really have a shot at reaching anything important from the side, but a good stab to the throat should work well enough. Bem, Gim, and Tob each prepare to go for the legs, looking to sever the tendons and minimize the potential thrashing. Jin stands at the head, ready to fire a hunting arrow into its eye and hopefully into the brain.

They all prepare carefully, with Ran slowly maneuvering her spear closer and closer. They all tense as she touches its hide, but it doesn't wake. This lets the others place their weapons exactly where they want, and the four melee hunters strike as one.

They're forced back as heat blooms from the bison, its blood looking like magma as it flows from the beast. Luckily, the triple dose of sleeping spores keeps it asleep until it's asleep forever. They all sigh in relief once it no longer draws breath, and keep giving it space to let the fiery blood continue to drain.

"I think that's a successful hunt, everyone. We'll let it drain as much as we can, gut it, then carry it home," congratulates Bem. They all give a cheer at that. Sure, they need to make sure nothing comes by to steal their hunt, but after the success of downing the bison, they feel confident in handling any scavengers who think they can get an easy meal.

Happily, nothing shows up to try to contest it, and after an hour, they heft the bison to carry home.

Chapter 63

The atmosphere in the Antkin Enclave is tense while they wait for the hunters to return. Aranya, Larx, and Folarn stick around and try to ease everyone's nerves, but they can only do so much. It's a big risk they're taking, and vital for them to succeed if they're going to finally fill those bars and become dwellers.

The castes all try to keep themselves busy, trying to kill time with tasks that aren't too important, lest they cause a mess by working while so distracted. Even the deans are nervous, each trying to distract themselves in their own ways. When the hunting party finally returns, relief washes over the entire enclave before a cheer follows behind.

They have some kind of weird buffalo thing with a coat a lot shaggier than I would have expected from something living in a volcanic region. They eventually drop it off with other workers for them to start butchering before the hunters are called to the deans to tell the tale of their hunt.

They seem a bit embarrassed about how simple the hunt was, but I at least am glad things went smoothly. Their explanation of the incredible body heat of the beast makes me wonder if the coat is actually a thermal conductor, letting the bison draw in the ambient heat and store it for later, probably to be used by the tail in some way.

The gear did well, but there's a lot of room for improvement. It sounds like the sleeping spores could be a lot more potent, though that's going to be a fine line to ride between making them more effective and not making them so effective that friendly fire becomes a big problem. The boar spear needs the guard lowered another foot or so, though Nik, the engineering dean, suggests utilizing the quick-swap heads to be able to put on a longer blade for larger foes. They'll probably test both options more in the future.

More pouches are requested, too. There's apparently a lot of potential things to gather, yet everyone was only able to bring back one sample each. They all look interesting, though a quick scan of my warehouse shows my bats have already brought back those samples and more from their own expeditions. I should add a couple molten gardens or something to the labyrinth, see if I can get the herbalists as obsessed as the miners and smiths with the area.

It takes them a couple hours to go over everything, and a couple hours for the workers to butcher the big bison for food. The butchery manages to finish first, and the bars tick up again, causing another cheer to echo through the enclave. The bar isn't full just yet, but they're making progress once more! Emboldened, the other hunting groups are sent out, with either Aranya or Larx blessing each one. I give a drop of power to each just as I did with the first. I'm not sure exactly how it'll help them, but I seriously doubt it'll hinder them, so I'm more than fine with helping out like that.

The hunters who aren't sent out redouble their training, while the crafting castes work on improving their equipment. As the hunting groups start returning, none have another big bison to show, but there's plenty of forage to bring back. One group even has a large serpent of some kind that they somehow fished out of a lava flow! Apparently, they spotted something in the lava and decided to test how well the suits insulate against heat. They weren't crazy enough to try to dive in, but they were able to get close enough to get a better look, though they can't look into the lava like they can with water.

Still, they could see fins occasionally breaching the surface, so it then became a matter of finding what a lava fish might like to eat, and how to actually reel something like that in. They found a good candidate for bait in the black teardrop fruit, noticing several mushrooms with the vines dangling over the pool. They tossed one in to check, and were happy to not only see it didn't immediately burst into flames but also to see it sucked under the surface by something.

A bit more testing showed that, though the vines quickly burned in the lava, the mushrooms seemed much more resistant. They took some time to carve a long, thick pole out of one, even managing to attach a few hunting arrowheads to the end as a kind of hook. It sounds like the pole was about as rigid as a pool noodle, but they didn't have much else to use.

With the hook baited, they tapped the surface a few times before the serpent came to take the bait, and it became a tug of war. Even with how big the serpent is, it wasn't a match for the hunters, especially not after they glued one of the workers to the floor and to the pole, giving them an anchor the thing couldn't beat. Once it tired itself out, they hauled it to shore and quickly dispatched it before freeing the worker and coming home with one heck of a fish tale.

After that, some of the crafters start focusing on trying to make better fishing gear, and the ranchers even start drawing up plans to create some kind of habitat to try to raise lava fish. I have no idea if it'll be easier or harder than the cave lobsters the spiderkin domesticated, but judging by how steadily the bars are progressing now, it seems to be just as viable an option.

Within just a few days, the bars are nearly full, which gives Teemo just enough time to explain to the spiderkin about a style of hat for the antkin and get enough made for everyone. Because if my college of ants are going to graduate to antkin, they should get to wear the traditional mortarboards.

They still prefer what are effectively togas to traditional robes, but I think they all look great as they gather before city hall, with the deans standing at the doors along with Aranya and Larx, as well as Folarn, Norloke, and Vernew. My High Priestess steps forward, and the murmuring of the crowd quiets as she starts to speak.

"I'm so happy to have been able to help a third of Lord Thedeim's enclaves along their path, and to see the new and unique challenges you faced and overcame. As your castes show, you all have a wide range of talents and skills, but the thirst for knowledge is one of many things you all share. Please never lose that thirst. As Lord Thedeim has shown, there is always something new to discover, some mystery to uncover, some new path to explore. I and the other enclaves are eager to have more friends to do all that and more with."

Polite applause follows as she steps back, letting Headmaster Ed come forward. "The details of our time as Lord Thedeim's magmyrm have faded, but the lessons we learned are ingrained in our souls. Cooperation. Curiosity. Compassion. We could not have achieved this without working together, and I think our points of stagnation showed this. We struggled to find a way to organize our cooperation at the start, and at the end, we had to all work together, playing to our strengths, to be able to find a way to sustain ourselves and not starve.

"Our college is testament to our curiosity, our drive to figure out how things work and apply that knowledge to the betterment of all. Ranching, engineering, enchanting, medicine, alchemy; each to discover new wonders, and the workers to apply it. Once again, we wouldn't accomplish any of this without each other.

"And we must never forget our compassion. Many would use vile methods to discover some secret, some new morsel of knowledge, excusing to themselves that they would help so many more with just that one sacrifice. A single ant may not matter to the colony, but we are *not* mere ants any longer." He looks to the deans to see if they have anything to add, but they each smile and shake their head in turn, letting the headmaster attend the entire college, as is his duty.

He reaches up to the tassel hanging from the scholarly hat, swapping it from one side to the other, with all the antkin doing the same. The bars wink out once they finish, and the headmaster smiles with his mandibles wide as he proclaims: "We are antkin! We are dwellers! We will ever seek out the new and use it to improve for all!"

Every new antkin cheers and throws their hats into the air. I couldn't be prouder of their well-earned graduation. Some antkin pick up their hats, while others leave them be, more interested in mingling than in a souvenir. The other two enclaves soon join them and see about having a party fit for a college, too. There's also a smattering of kobolds in the crowd, enjoying the atmosphere of triumph, and I even spot Parm as he picks up one of the hats.

I'm looking forward to the day he can toss his own into the air to celebrate his graduation, too.

Chapter 64

Gerlfi

The goblin summoner eyes the cemetery gates, his friends and party members at his side. He had been hoping for an opportunity like this, but once it actually became an option, he found himself scrambling to prepare! He's formed pacts with dungeon fey before. It's his specialty, in fact, so he knows he has to have something to offer that the fey actually want.

But what could a scion want?

It's a question that's been at the forefront of his mind ever since he learned Thedeim got a fey spawner. The odd dungeon has its quirks, but he had no doubt that a fey spawner would mean a Fey Scion, even if it took almost a week for the Dungeoneer's Guild to officially announce her: Titania.

Something about the name has *weight* to it. Bargaining with her will be no easy task. Luckily for him, Wold and Vieds both understand how significant it could be for him to form a pact with her. Wold, the large bearkin, knew without being told that a scion would need far more than milk and honey to agree to be summoned. Vieds, the changeling pyromancer, was even willing to check his mysterious contacts to see if they had any advice.

What he could give is easy enough to guess the generals of, but the specifics will be daunting: a scion wants something to help their dungeon. But what could he offer a dungeon like Thedeim? A year-old dungeon should be glad to get maybe some piece of enchanted gear to examine, maybe a seed to grow, a potion to learn. But by all accounts, Thedeim is the one making new enchantments, new potions—even new *seeds*, if he understands the rumors about a great tree correctly.

The next obvious thing would be to offer him a new variety of denizen. Thedeim has quite a number of spawners and seems to have no qualms about making even more. His latest expansion has him with fey, plants, bears, *and* foxes! And that doesn't even take into account the other spawners getting upgrades!

The difficult thing with getting a new denizen, however, is nobody in his party is a tamer of any sort. He's heard that some denizens can be tamed with little or no training, but to get one from a dungeon Thedeim doesn't already have close ties to would probably take a month to travel, delve, capture, and travel back.

Then Vieds had a simple suggestion; something that Gerlfi still isn't sure if it's genius or idiocy. With any other dungeon, he'd never even entertain the idea. But with Thedeim, it might just be crazy enough to work.

Ask Titania what she wants.

Sure, it ruins the mystery, but it's difficult to solve one with so few clues! So now, here he stands, at the gates to the cemetery, his friends at his side, preparing to enter and go through to the forest of four seasons beyond it.

Wold moves first, ever willing to take the fore and guard his friends from the dangers lurking ahead. Gerlfi chuckles and shakes his head as he follows, quietly laughing at himself for being so dramatic. He blames the fey, though not anywhere they might hear.

Vieds brings up the rear, closing the gate behind the group before speaking softly, so as not to spoil the atmosphere of the cemetery. "Do you think it'll work?"

"Ordinarily: no. But Thedeim isn't very ordinary."

Wold snorts at that and waves at Grim, the intimidating scion peacefully trimming the grass over the graves. The scion nods in reply, most of his attention on his duty. "That's an understatement. I'm looking forward to the encounters in the forest. I hear they're tough but rewarding."

Vieds eagerly nods, somehow managing to keep his voice down as he replies. "I'm definitely looking forward to it, even if Gerlfi can't form a pact! It's been a while since I had to worry about burning anything other than you two. It'll be good practice, if nothing else."

Wold rumbles a low chuckle as Gerlfi replies. "You've been doing well with that lately, too. Wold and I may actually need to see a barber soon, instead of simply letting you singe our hair to a more manageable length."

"I'm glad you appreciate my efforts for the good of the party. If you two would like me to give you a trim, I'd be happy to oblige."

"I prefer to let my winter coat shed naturally, thanks."

The three quietly banter and rib each other as they take the main path through the cemetery, soon finding themselves at the gates to the forest of four seasons.

They head through with little comment. Once inside, the three keep their eyes peeled as they ponder which way to go. After a few seconds to consider and consult his mental map, Gerlfi takes the lead.

"This way, I think. The scion's name feels linked to summer, and I think it's in this direction."

Wold moves back into the lead as Vieds pulls out his tome, the changeling going over what kind of fire expertise to bring to bear in the woods. "You guys heard about there being new denizens, yeah?"

Gerlfi nods, a hand grazing over his linked crystals, trying to decide which would be best for this situation. "The Dungeoneer's Guild hasn't updated the packet officially yet, but brambles and armory bees are all the other adventurers want to talk about."

"And grizzlies," adds Wold, earning a nod from both the others.

"I think I'll focus on area attacks, Gerlfi, if you want to summon something to help Wold in melee?" Vieds snaps his book closed and stows it, his plan now set, as the goblin turns to the large bearkin.

"Do you want something defensive or offensive?"

"Offense. Forming a shield wall with Freddie and Fiona is all well and good, but sometimes, I just want to tear foes apart with an ally looking for the same."

Gerlfi nods and pulls out a crystal. "Then I think Vieds will need to take extra care with his fire today. It's been a while since I summoned Kelpie. It should be wet enough that she'll accept, but she definitely doesn't like fire."

Vieds shudders and nods. "That horse terrifies me, but this does seem like a good place for it, yeah. I'll be extra careful, so keep an eye out for things on the edges escaping."

Gerlfi nods and speaks into the crystal. "Kelpie, I ask for your aid. I offer you a new battleground that can give the variety of a year in only a day. I offer you untested foes to learn your fury. And I offer you a bottle of brandy once we get back to the guild."

Moments later, water gushes from the ground, and a pale blue horse steps out onto the land. Seaweed replaces the hair of the mane and tail, and the eyes have a distinct predatory gleam to them. It looks around for a few moments before snorting, briefly revealing sharp teeth that don't belong in the mouth of any ordinary horse.

Gerlfi does his best to hide his relief that Kelpie seems to approve of the forest. Kelpies are notoriously difficult to pact with, as their violent nature makes them difficult to tempt. But offer one a new battleground and new foes, sweeten the deal with some potent booze, and even the quintessential wild horse will deign to listen for at least a while.

Calling Kelpie soon proves to be a good decision, as a pair of grizzly bears spot the group through the dense woodland of spring. Their challenging roar is echoed by Wold and Kelpie, leaving Gerlfi and Vieds to hurry to keep up with their charge.

"Lancing Orb!" cries Vieds as he weaves a sphere of fire to float over the battle. Wold and one grizzly clash, the denizen's paws slamming against the bearkin's club while a swift kick from Kelpie momentarily dazes the other grizzly. Vieds's orb shows its name as lines of fire dart down to sear the bear Wold is fighting, the party mostly letting Kelpie have her fun with the other one.

"Impact," casts Gerlfi, improving the strength of Kelpie's blows as she continues to kick and buck at the bear, pummeling the thing with the kind of viciousness her kind is known for. Wold's bear tries to disengage to somehow deal with the floating orb, but he shoves it as it tries, knocking it to the ground before slamming down his club to finish it off. Kelpie gets the hint and looks disappointed as her bear rears back to slash, only for her to dart forward and take a bite out of its neck.

She happily trots in a circle, chewing as the bear quickly bleeds out, while Gerlfi keeps repeating to himself that this was the most reasonable Kelpie he could find.

They have several more encounters—one against a bramble fused with a Soil elemental, and another with a group of armory bees. The first is handled by Kelpie washing out the elemental, and Vieds burning the bramble, while the second is more of a classic melee brawl.

After the bees, they take a break to catch their breaths.

"The guild wasn't joking about this area being tougher. It looks like even Kelpie is putting in effort," comments Vieds. Gerlfi nods at the sheen of sweat on the fey.

"Ordinarily, I'd offer to give her a dirt rub down, but I think she'd bite my hand off if I tried." Kelpie nickers and nods at that, looking in high spirits despite being so sweaty. At least she won't have any arrows in her quiver to argue Gerlfi didn't deliver on his offerings.

"Any idea where Titania is?" asks Wold, looking around the warm woodland.

Gerlfi shrugs. "I think we're in summer, but aside from that, I don't know. She might be around the garden in the center of the woods? I think the plant scion calls that area home, and a lot of Thedeim's scions group up."

Vieds nods at that. "We don't have any other . . . Kelpie's spotted something." The other two look and see the watery horse staring off into the woods, teeth bared at something they can't see. But now that they're paying attention, they can hear something . . . A buzzing sound that's only growing louder.

Though Kelpie is focused in one specific direction, bumblebees descend *all* around them, each ridden by a bark pixie. The numbers actually dim the area slightly, the flying denizens blotting out the sun with their numbers. Suddenly, the buzzing goes silent as every branch, twig, and leaf nearby is landed on, the fey staring intently at the adventurers. Only one bee stays in the air, and it's not difficult to tell it must be Titania on her own steed, staring down Kelpie as she continues to buzz forward at a steady, regal pace.

"Please be gentle, Kelpie. I need to pact with her."

The summoned fey snorts and paws the ground, clearly looking for a fight. Gerlfi just hopes the dungeon understands it's *her* who wants a fight, not him.

Chapter 65

Gerlfi

The goblin summoner nervously watches as Kelpie and Titania square off. With Kelpie, Gerlfi is well aware of what she's capable of. She's fast, strong, and devious, and only the promise of new and interesting foes was able to convince her to deal with him.

Titania, however . . . he doesn't have much to go on. He's pretty sure she's Life affinity, but he has no idea how she might wield it, or if she has any other affinities besides Fate to worry about. It seems Kelpie is determined to figure all that out and more.

The watery horse growls, sounding more like a wolf, and earns herself a glare from the small bark pixie atop the bee. It looks like Kelpie is trying to force Titania to surrender, which the smaller fey isn't going to entertain. Kelpie won't take such an insult lying down.

She leaps into the air in a flash, determined to swallow the diminutive scion. She lands and starts stomping in rage, and it takes Gerlfi a few seconds to understand why. Not only does it look like Titania and the bee easily dodged the attack, but the pixie has produced a small sword that looks like it may have been plucked from a bramble and dipped in armory honey. And the tip is green with Kelpie's blood.

Shocked, he focuses back on his summon and sees a thin line along her cheek. ". . . We should give them some room," he cautions not only his friends but the other pixies and nearby bees, too. He and his friends take several steps back, moving to the edge of the clearing as Kelpie turns her rage upon the scion who would dare injure her like that.

Water gushes from the ground, roaring like a stormy sea as Kelpie directs a white-capped wave to crash upon the pixie. In response, she points her tiny sword like a baton, and the gathered pixies and bees spring into action. Each bark pixie takes a large leaf as a shield, and in a staggering display of coordination, overlap and work together to stymie the rogue wave. Titania locks eyes with Kelpie as the wave crashes against her loyal denizens, daring the Kelpie to do better.

Enraged, the summon charges forward, only to skid to a halt. It seems Titania is done playing and has embraced a title that Gerlfi didn't even know existed. The Fey Queen glares down her nose at the upstart who is only just now beginning to understand her place.

Kelpie snarls and shapes the water into needles, but balks as Titania continues to glare at her, the other pixies forming a defensive perimeter around her. The scion and the summon keep eye contact for several long seconds before Kelpie finally looks away, letting the watery needles splash to the ground.

Titania is magnanimous in victory, and shoos her away with a wave of her hand. Kelpie doesn't look happy about it, but she lies by a tree, where the other bark pixies swarm her. Some tend to her wound, but most are simply curious about the rare water fey.

"She stared down Kelpie?" asks Vieds in awe. Gerlfi is right there with him. Kelpies *love* fighting things, especially stronger things. For her to yield like that . . .

"Good luck forming a pact," rumbles Wold, and the goblin has to glare at his large friend.

"Yeah, thanks." Much as it's cathartic to give his friend the stink eye, he probably shouldn't keep Titania waiting. She seems to be more relaxed and has let her title fade for now, but the commanding presence of that title is difficult to forget. He takes a few moments to gather himself before turning and giving her a deep bow.

"Queen Titania. I had been hoping to ask an audience?"

The scion urges her bee forward, looking amused at the turn of events, and motions for him to continue.

"As you may have surmised, I am a summoner, and I specialize in fey. I offer them pacts, and when I call on them through my crystals, I can bring forth a portion of them to work on my behalf. And of course, work implies payment. Other bark pixies, I might offer bread, milk, and honey to do something. Kelpie, for example, wanted new and interesting foes . . . and a bottle of brandy."

Tinkling chimes fill the air as Titania laughs at the mundane bribe for such a powerful fey, even as her cohorts lick their lips at the idea of rich food and strong drink. Her eyes shine with amusement as she motions for him to continue. So far, so good.

"I would like to pact with you as well . . . though I admit I don't know what you would ask in return. I'm an adventurer, so most of your summons would involve combat or dealing with traps, whichever you prefer, or even both, if you so wish. If you are not interested in either, I thank you for listening."

Titania taps her chin as she considers. Gerlfi would expect she is not opposed to fighting. That bramble thorn at her hip shows her willingness, and the way she was able to draw first blood against Kelpie shows her ability with it as well. But what would she want in return?

No queen would be satisfied with mere milk and honey. Even a bottle of brandy was laughable to her. Maybe there isn't even anything she wants? That might be the most disappointing conclusion to trying to form a pact that he can imagine.

Before he gets a chance to try to imagine worse, he feels his affinity sing with a pact offer.

Communication affinity is surprisingly common, just not among adventurers. It takes a vast network of them to quickly and efficiently carry messages across the kingdom and beyond, while others often find themselves writing laws, writing news . . . writing almost anything, really. The ability to clearly and concisely convey ideas is a much more useful thing than many first consider.

The incoming pact offer is unusual. He's never heard a pact demand a tithe of any other pact payments. If her time summoned overlaps with the summon of any other fey, she demands her queenly right to a portion. A tenth isn't much, but the symbolic fealty of the other fey will not go unnoticed. Still . . . if Kelpie is willing to let the bark pixies start braiding her mane and tail, such a demand will probably not be a deal-breaker.

The other price is one he needs to carefully consider. She wants time for time. An hour of her time will be an hour of Gerlfi's, doing as she directs just as she would do what he directed. She looks pretty satisfied with herself for the offer, and Gerlfi finds himself very tempted.

To have not only a scion but a *titled* one would be no small increase in his power, especially since he gets the feeling her title significantly enhances friendly fey in her presence. Numerous as the pixies may have been, they should *not* have been able to stop that wave from Kelpie.

"A tithe from other summoned fey and an equal payment of time from me, correct?" he asks to confirm, and she nods, the binding powers of the crystals starting to flow between the two.

"A tithe from other fey and equal payment of time is the deal," he repeats, Titania's confirmation strengthening the enchantment from the crystals.

"Then a tithe and time is the bargain struck and the pact forged," he finalizes as she nods, the crystal's magic taking firm root in them both as the pact is agreed in triplicate and understood by all. Gerlfi can't help but pull out the crystal that now holds their pact, and Titania flies her mount closer for both to inspect it.

Neither takes too long, and soon, Titania hovers back a few feet to give Gerlfi room to bow to her once more. "Thank you for the pact, Titania. May it prove fruitful for the both of us."

Her tinkling laughter sounds once more before she motions for the other pixies to leave Kelpie alone, though the damage is done. Her mane and tail are both freshly brushed and braided, with ribbons woven through. They've even painted a heart formed from two crashing waves on what he would call her upper thighs, though he doesn't remember offhand what it's called on a horse. Kelpie herself, despite her makeover, looks absolutely miserable, and doesn't even nip at Gerlfi as he pats her withers.

"Let's get out of here and get you that brandy, hmm? Looks like you need it."

"And something for us, too," insists Vieds as they make their way out of the forest. "We need to toast your success! I'm pretty sure there aren't a lot of summoners who can claim a *scion* in their arsenal!"

"And hopefully you haven't bitten off more than you can chew," warns Wold, earning a sideways look from Gerlfi.

"You think I can't keep my end of the pact?"

Wold smirks at him before replying. "Ordinarily, I wouldn't doubt you. But you've agreed to give your time to a scion of *Thedeim*. What kind of crazy things will she ask you to do?"

Gerlfi's eyes widen at that as Vieds laughs. "Good luck with that!"

Kelpie nuzzles the top of Gerlfi's head as they continue to make their exit, commiserating with him and his mistake. Maybe he'll need a bottle of brandy, too.

Chapter 66

I'm impressed with Gerlfi and Titania both. I knew he summons fey; I just never connected the dots that he might like to summon *my* fey. I'm also proud of Titania for her deal. She's going to be double-dipping to make a ton of mana whenever she gets summoned, which is great for me, and she'll get to see more of the world; at least if Gerlfi and his party ever wander on to a new dungeon, heh.

I'm also glad she didn't go for some of the nastier stuff out of fairy tales. No stealing someone's day of birth or dooming them to die by pricking their finger on a spinning wheel, or things like that. I mean, Gerlfi wouldn't take a deal like that, but I'm still glad she didn't even try.

Fey fun aside, the forest is coming together nicely. Titania and Goldilocks are working incredibly well together. The Fey Queen is great at keeping the denizens operating smoothly behind the scenes, and Goldilocks is developing a great eye for detail when it comes to what delvers can handle. It's great that she's been stepping up in that role, too, giving Poppy more time to focus on the tree and her garden.

I think she's putting the finishing touches on the one I'll use to expand. She's been carefully trimming and adjusting it like I'd imagine someone with a bonsai tree. The roots are looking good and strong, the symbiosis between the yew and willow seems stable, and I can feel Poppy's pride in her accomplishment, even as she worries something might go wrong when I do the expansion.

I make sure to encourage her through the bond. I'm feeling pretty confident in the design and in the smaller tree that's going to be the centerpiece of the forest soon.

Right now, I'm more waiting on the last results of the surveys, and to build up a bit more mana before I pull the trigger. If I was just expanding up, I'd probably have enough to get some things going, but with the plans to go down, too, I'm going to need more mana than what I have now. I could dip into the emergency fund, but no matter how much I want the tree up and running, it doesn't qualify as an emergency.

Even if I *really* want it.

I can be patient, though. Even with the forest running at basic capacity, the mana income is pretty significant. With Titania and Goldilocks making adjustments, things are only getting more efficient, and it'll probably only get better as we go.

The Antkin Enclave is only getting better, too. With them now their own people, they're diving into working with my other enclaves and trading with Fourdock. As I understand it, merchants are technically supposed to wait until an official treaty to trade, but there are loopholes to be abused. There are still taxes getting paid, so I'm not worried about causing a stink.

The enchanters have Thing's anti-Lifedrinking enchantment, and basically every armor-creating crafter is begging them to enchant this or that with it. A lot of delvers are interested, too, but the ones planning to stick around probably don't see too much need to have it now. I bet the crafters are looking to make a mint selling the gear to someone elsewhere. I don't mind, especially since it should help the antkin build a reputation and the wealth to do even more.

The alchemists seem like they're on the verge of a breakthrough with the go-juice, too. When Queen's is used on a denizen, it just flat-out gives them a new affinity and a bit more speed. The version the antkin are trying to adapt for non-denizens looks like it adds electric damage to their attacks and gives a good amount of lightning resist, too. The only problem with it right now is the duration.

In their testing, they barely get enough time to deal or receive a single attack. I think their goal is for it to last similarly as long as the Aqua Affinity potions that Staiven makes. They have the formulation for it on a board while they talk shop, and though most of it goes over my head, that'd be the obvious connection.

The engineering caste is working closely with my ratkin as they do a joint venture to produce what people are starting to call dweller bows—the compound bows. The metalworking required is well within the ratkin's ability to do, while the engineers constantly work on improvements to the design. The worker caste helps as well, putting everything together and letting everyone focus on their specialty.

It makes me worry a little about overspecializing and people thinking their particular part is the most important one, but they all seem to be getting along well and enjoying the camaraderie. The engineers are also working closely with the alchemists and the spiderkin to continue to refine the composite armor. They've seen how Jello makes the metal honeycomb, so now they're trying to replicate it in their own way.

Working together, they've even had limited success with recreating it. While a lot of the antkin lost their Magma affinity for a variety of others after the bars winked out, there are still a lot with it. That, combined with the number of ratkin with Metal affinity, lets them smoothly weld the sheets together. It's still quite a bit of work to cut and especially to shape, but I'm confident they'll streamline the process as they get more used to it.

I watch them all work together for a little bit before I feel Aranya and Teemo both wanting my attention. They're sitting in the public war room, and it takes me a moment to recognize the figure sitting with them as Rezlar. Where his Larrez persona is pretty plainly a fencer, this outfit makes him look like a rogue of some variety. Instead of Larrez's tan, he's sporting a skin tone more like the ash gray of Miller, who I am certain is around here somewhere.

Before I can get distracted trying to find him, Teemo speaks up. "Ah, the Boss's here."

Aranya nods with a happy smile. "I feel Him too. Would you please repeat your question, young . . . sir," Aranya says to Rezlar with a knowing smile, playing along with his disguise despite nobody else being around.

Rezlar inhales to build his courage, then explains. "I need to tell Freddie and Rhonda who I am, but I don't know how to do it."

"Just tell them," suggests Teemo before I can give an answer. *Usually, I think that'd be the best way, but something like this isn't so simple, I think. Just sitting down at a table and blurting it out is awkward and forced at best.*

Teemo shakes his head but speaks up for me. "That's not the Boss's advice, though, just mine. He says it'd usually be what he'd suggest, too, but it's not the sort of revelation to just drop on someone out of nowhere."

Aranya nods before adding her own opinion. "Perhaps you should invite them over and ease them into it?"

Rezlar sighs. "Have the lord mayor call them to a dinner? That feels like trying to impress them with status, or imply they'll have to acknowledge it."

Teemo winces at that idea, though it does give me one of my own, which Teemo relays. "Why not have Larrez invite them to a guided tour or something? You could hang out, show them a couple cool things, and have lunch or something at a normal table instead of the big one. Make an excuse to go help get the food from the kitchen, take off the disguise, and come back in with the food."

Aranya smiles at that idea. "They're clever enough to probably realize, though if they don't, it'd be reasonable enough to explain at that point."

Rezlar chews that over. "No airs, just showing them around . . . and bring in the food like a friend instead of sitting at the table and having it brought to me like a lord. That . . . I think that could work?"

"Definitely," encourages Teemo. "Especially with your butler around to make sure everything goes smoothly. There are probably a lot of moving parts in an idea like that, but he seems pretty good at making sure things mesh."

Rezlar looks more and more confident as he considers the idea, and soon gives my Voice and my High Priestess a thankful smile. "Thank you, Teemo, Aranya, and . . . and Lord Thedeim."

Teemo quirks an eyebrow at him for me, even as Aranya beams with a bright smile.

"You're going to follow Him?" she asks, and Rezlar gives a nervous nod.

"Yes. I'm not sure what all it entails, but . . . He's changed so much of my life for the better."

Teemo blows a raspberry, making Rezlar look worried while Aranya titters with controlled laughter. "That's fine; the Boss doesn't really know what following him entails, either. Just don't go bowing and scraping, please? It's embarrassing for him."

Rezlar's worry turns to confusion as Aranya speaks up, still trying to contain her mirth. "Leave the bowing and scraping to the priests and priestesses. It's our job to embarrass Him at least a little. Just act with love and kindness, and be vigilant for things to improve, and think through what improving them would entail. Knocking down a wall might seem like a path to freedom, but don't let the roof above collapse on your head."

Rezlar looks relieved to hear that, and I feel a burst of energy from him as he dedicates himself to that sort of philosophy. I take a peek at his status, worried he might have changed class to a cleric or something, but I'm relieved to see he's still a kind of fencer.

"Though speaking of big changes, is He ready to commit His denizens to helping with the hold? The snows are melting, and the trails are clearing. I believe the surveyors are still narrowing down the best sites, but we can get started on the road out of town, at least."

I poke Coda to come, and even though he's relaxing right now, the idea of planning a road has him grabbing his blueprinting stuff and flying for the war room.

I leave them to it, still feeling a bit awkward about gaining another convert. It's nice to help take a bit of weight off his shoulders, but I worry about his faith being misplaced. I think all I can really do is try to live up to his expectations, as well as my other followers'. It's a bit of weight on my own shoulders, but I have my own faith to keep me strong and hopefully help me walk this tightrope without falling.

Chapter 67

Rezlar

He feels . . . good. He would even go so far as to say he feels great! Thoughts of the future still make him nervous, but not the kind of paralyzing fear he used to feel. He thinks it might be because he actually feels like he can affect what will happen now.

For a long time, it seemed like the entire course of his life was plotted out by his father. It had seemed inevitable that he would effectively just be a puppet, enacting whatever laws his father wished. Once he had learned the basics with Fourdock, he'd be placed in charge of some other part of the land governed by the Earl if'Gofnar.

And then Thedeim . . . *Lord* Thedeim appeared and started inadvertently knocking plans askew. He smiles at that thought as he waits at the entrance to his estate, his mind wandering as he awaits the arrival of his friends. It's the little changes that lead to the largest shifts, and though he's not dedicated enough to become any sort of divine class, he still feels a warm comfort in the knowledge that if you prepare for it, change can be steered instead of resisted. If resisted, it *will* eventually break through, but riding the change is like riding the tide, and things become much easier once you learn how to manage the ebb and flow.

He even toys with the idea of advancing his class in the divine direction, trying not to laugh at the idea of himself as a paladin of Change. It's easy to imagine Freddie in shining armor, leading the charge against evil, but Rezlar just can't see himself in that kind of position. He expects he'll have his hands more than full with directing Fourdock toward prosperity, even with the help of Lord Thedeim and the other powerful individuals of the town.

His battlefield is more likely to be in courts of nobility, wielding bureaucracy with the same deftness he does his rapier. It's a much less glamorous battle than most, but still a necessary one. He may, one day, even need to do battle with his father, and though he dreads facing a foe as powerful as he is, Rezlar still has a spark of confidence that victory could be possible. Eventually.

Before that niggling doubt can worm further into him, he smiles as he spots Freddie and Rhonda, along with their spiders. All four wave at him, and he resists the urge to wave back. He's Larrez right now, and even if he's stationed at the gate with one of the veterans who knows who he is, he still needs to maintain the proper procedures.

That doesn't mean he can't smile widely at his friends as they near. "Rhonda! Freddie! And Fiona and Lucas, of course! I'm glad you all could make it!"

"I'm glad we could make it, too!" replies Rhonda, looking eager to explore.

"I'm surprised the mayor approved of something like this. It seems like a security risk to me," comments Freddie, though he looks very curious to get a good look around as well.

"Miller says having a fresh set of eyes can reveal problems even someone like him could have overlooked," excuses Rezlar, hoping they're not too suspicious.

The guardsman at the gate chuckles at that. "If you kids find something he managed to overlook, I'll eat my boots." His subtle laughter hitches for a moment as he glances around before lowering his voice. "Though if he did leave something for you to spot, could you pretend not to notice it? He's the sort to leave something like that just to challenge me to be true to my word."

Rezlar and the others laugh as they promise to try to not make him eat his footwear, and he soon smiles and straightens. "Guardsman Larrez!"

Rezlar stands at attention, and the veteran eyes his form before giving a nod of approval.

"You are relieved to guide this group about the manor at your discretion. Enjoy the tour," he finishes, winking at Freddie and Rhonda before turning his attention back to keeping an eye out at the entrance.

Rezlar leads his friends out to the gardens first. Even though they've been there before, he still likes them, and they're a good place to decide where to go next. "So . . . these are the gardens. The groundskeeper does amazing work. The hardest part of patrolling here is not getting distracted by all the interesting plants."

"You're telling me," comments Rhonda, her hands drifting over the various plants as the group walks. "Master Staiven never has much luck growing herbs himself, but the groundskeeper's gotta be really high level to be able to grow all this. Have they delved Thedeim to get any of the plants here?"

Rezlar pauses at that. "I . . . don't know, actually. I'm not really familiar with herbalism to know how difficult these were to get."

They wander around for a few more minutes, enjoying the sights, before Rezlar decides it's probably time to move on. "So, what do you two want to see next?"

"I could probably spend all day just in the garden," admits Rhonda.

"How about the library?" asks Freddie. "I bet the mayor has all sorts of history books. The church mostly has records of church stuff, but it could be interesting to read about Fourdock itself, or the kingdom at large."

Rezlar nods and leads the way, though the group takes their time to look at the paintings and other bits of art displayed along the walls. "I think most of what the mayor has is boring political treatises, trade records, and accounting books. Oh, there are some records of the Gofnar War and the treaty with the orcs, though."

Freddie looks interested in that. "I've heard diplomacy with the orcs is pretty difficult, thanks to how loose their government is."

Rezlar snorts at the understatement as they reach the library. "I've heard people argue they don't really have a government at all. It seems to work pretty well for them, though."

Rhonda nods as she looks over a few maps on display in the library, the tip of her staff tracing the Gofnar River back to Lake Gofnar, and the Also-Gofnar River that feeds it from the mountains. "I can't believe they called it the Also-Gofnar River. Or that the orcs actually decided to honor it as part of the border!"

Freddie chuckles as he looks over the map as well. "The Wanderlands seem pretty lackadaisical, but the orcs have their honor. They were kinda playing with the wording of the agreement when they started crossing the river there for raids. I've read a couple accounts of Shield paladins protecting small settlements, and they said the spirit of the agreement was that the elves wouldn't have to worry about orcish incursions.

"At the time, they didn't have much of an idea of where the feeding river went. As they and the elves kept exploring, they found a lot more land than expected. The elves called it the North Horlon River for a time before some say the king, in annoyance, declared it to be the Also-Gofnar River."

Rezlar and Rhonda both snicker at the idea, doubly humorous for the simple fact that it seems a very plausible way for it to get the name. Even Freddie smiles at the silliness before he continues. "So the orcs honored the agreement and haven't done any raiding since. I've heard the Beastkin Principalities tried to establish the Gofnar Plains to give them the same protection, but the orcs only made that agreement with the elves, so the beastkin still get raided."

Rezlar nods at that. "That's my understanding, too. I hear they don't get raided as often anymore, with the orcs finding it easier to trade the resources of their Wanderlands for whatever they might want from the beastkin. Still, they sometimes still raid them, either in desperation from a harsh winter, or just to keep them on their toes."

"Do you know much about the Principalities?" asks Freddie. Rezlar shakes his head.

"Not really. I just know their government has a pretty chaotic reputation, with the best way to unite them being to try to actually attack. A quick raid is one thing, but trying to annex territory sees them put aside their differences and repel armies with gusto. The sheer variety of their people makes it almost impossible to defend against, and once a single avenue is opened, the rest can rush in and obliterate any hostile forces."

Freddie nods at his analysis. "That's what the Shield histories indicate, too. I'm pretty sure there are more detailed histories of Shield followers protecting the settlements of the Principalities, just not in the archives here."

They poke around the library for a little more, Rhonda and Freddie pulling out a book to glance into. What books might be interesting are simply too long to dig into on this kind of tour, though, and soon, they head back out into the manor at large.

"Are you two hungry yet?"

"I can always eat," answers Freddie with a smile while Rhonda echoes him.

"Same! Magic takes just as much energy as holding up a shield!"

Rezlar smiles at that, both glad and nervous about the upcoming part of the plan to reveal himself. "There's a smaller staff dining room just off the kitchen, so we don't have to try to eat at the big table in the dining hall."

The group follows as Freddie speaks up. "It'd be kinda cool to eat at a fancy table like nobles," he says with amusement, though Rezlar disagrees.

"I've had to stand guard in there before at a dinner. *Everything* at a dinner like that is a political ploy, from the seating to the serving order . . . even the menu! Serving some noble's hated dish is a common way of trying to leverage something."

Freddie's amusement sours at that, and Rhonda sticks out her tongue at the thought. "Eating fancy would be nice, but without the side of intrigue, thanks."

Rezlar snorts in laughter at that. "I think the mayor would agree. Much better to have a meal with friends than something like that."

"So, what's for lunch?" asks Freddie as they enter the kitchen, where a stout halfling is pulling something from the oven.

"Ah, perfect timing! These lamb rolls are just finished."

Even Fiona and Lucas look interested in the rolls, and Rezlar makes a mental note to make sure to bring plates for them as well. "Those look great! I'll get them seated and come get them."

The head chef nods, giving Rezlar a thumbs-up where the young noble's friends can't see. "I'll take mine in the garden. You guys enjoy; there's plenty!"

He makes his exit, and they wave him farewell before Rezlar ushers them to the staff dining area.

To Rezlar, it feels a lot like the tavern area in the adventurers' guild, just not as big, nor as crowded. It just feels . . . friendly. He can't hide his nerves as he gets his friends seated and gets them some water, and he hopes they just take it as him trying to be hospitable, because that's partially what it is.

He hurries back to the kitchen and tries to calm himself, running his mana in a fencing kata to help focus. He also needs the water to wash off his disguise, and he's glad for the practice at quickly swapping clothing that Miller put him through. His water washes the disguise off quickly, and he channels it down the sink before he changes into his most casual "normal" clothes.

He still feels overdressed to meet his friends, but it's too late now to change his mind. He grabs a large tray and enough plates for everyone, including the spiders, and plenty of the lamb rolls, too, before he makes his way for the door.

"I hope you guys are hungry! These rolls taste even better than they smell!"

He sees their eager looks for the food quickly change to confusion, but he does his best to act like nothing is out of the ordinary as he sets the tray on the table and sets out the plates. He's relieved that Lucas and Fiona, at least, don't react at all to his change in attire and lack of disguise. They probably don't really understand the difference between Larrez and Rezlar.

Silence reigns as he sets out the plates and takes a pair of rolls for himself before he sits down. He tries to play it cool, but he's starting to get nervous at their reaction so far.

"Larrez?" asks Rhonda, peering at him in confusion. Freddie, however, seems to understand as he shakes his head.

"Rezlar," he corrects her before turning his look to the elf. Rezlar swallows heavily before Freddie finally smiles.

"I *thought* I saw you meet with Torlon a while ago, but everyone said the only meeting he had was with the mayor that day!"

"The mayor?" echoes Rhonda, until it finally clicks. Rezlar can see her mind racing as she clearly comes up with questions and tries to organize which to ask first. Freddie beats her to it.

"Why us?" he asks, looking genuinely curious, which is better than accusatory.

"Well . . . at the time, I wanted to try to get more used to people, and to try to train myself some, so Miller suggested I join the adventurers' guild. Karn wasn't too happy, but I think that was more the paperwork he'd have to do rather than in accepting me. And he really did want me to invite you two because he wanted you in the guild."

"Huh," comments Freddie before he takes a couple rolls himself and sets an extra on Fiona's plate. Rhonda hurries to give Lucas one as he finishes his first, and gets one for herself, too, before she speaks up.

“So we’ve been adventuring with the lord mayor? No wonder you’re always weird when it comes to money!”

Rezlar gives them a bashful nod at that. “Yeah, I . . . It always felt wrong to let you two pay for anything for me.”

Freddie shrugs and swallows before answering. “That’s what friends do. Maybe now we can split the bill for food at the guild without needing to add it all up separately.”

Rezlar smiles at them in relief. He was confident they’d accept him, and he’s glad to see they’re even more understanding than he would have dared hope.

The rest of the meal feels like they’re at the guild, just talking about everything and nothing at all, the conversation and companionship lasting longer than the food. They probably could have kept hanging out together until dinner if not for Miller entering the room with a fresh jug of water, and a tray with a letter on it.

“Please pardon me, Young Master. I know you wished to not be interrupted, but you’ve received a missive that should probably be perused with haste.”

Rezlar fights down the annoyance at being interrupted, but if Miller himself is doing it, it’s not going to be for anything trivial. He sighs, accepting that the kingdom doesn’t stop for the king’s leisure, so why should it for his?

“Thank you, Miller,” he says, taking the letter from the tray, only to freeze as he recognizes the seal.

“Is something wrong?” asks Freddie in the same tone he’d use to warn of danger while delving.

“Yes and no . . .” reluctantly answers Rezlar, starting to glare at the seal like he could somehow change it. “It’s from my father, the Earl if’Gofnar.”

Chapter 68

Spring is one of those seasons I often forget actually exists, probably because of where I used to live. North enough and high enough that winter would often muscle into the territory of the other seasons, and though I think Fourdock is definitely north enough, being close to the ocean makes it difficult for winter to really try to dig in its fingers and hang on.

I also wasn't really involved in farming, so it's not like I had to pay attention to when crops were planted. But as I look over the expedition reports, I'd say spring is solidly, unquestionably here. Winter has been beaten back and made to sit in the corner, and summer is still a ways off. Which means that birds are singing, bees are buzzing, and delving is booming.

I'm not kidding, either. I thought the delvers over winter were just sticking with their normal schedules, but that really was them taking it easy. I think most groups were doing a delve or two a week; now, they're doing long delves, day after day, as long as they don't break anything or get some other serious injury.

They still happen, and though I'd like to be able to stop it, I don't think it'd help the delvers. Even the most brutal bootcamp doesn't *actually* shoot at you, so there's always a lot in a fight that can only be theoretical knowledge. But by letting them fight enough to get seriously hurt, they learn how to deal with that kind of situation, no matter how unpleasant it is.

I really do want to make sure my delvers are ready to take on mean dungeons and be able to not only survive but thrive. I would be concerned about how many seem to be specializing in dealing with me, if it weren't for the fact that so many of them probably wouldn't be delving me at all if it weren't for the effort my scions and I take to make sure people survive.

There's a lot of casual delvers, and as I read the reports coming in from the foxes, it's not surprising to see why. Even here, people dream of what they think is impossible. Everyone wants to be that cool swordsman or wizard, the stealthy rogue, the valiant paladin, but most people have classes that definitely aren't made for fighting.

That doesn't make them helpless, though. A hammer strike designed to drive nails works just as well against monsters. It's just that nails don't often fight back. But with the safety of my territory, a lot of civilian classes like to come and test themselves. It makes me think of people who like to go paintballing or skydiving or things like that. A way to get a bit of excitement in a mostly safe way, and to keep in shape.

Some professions are pretty simple to see applied to a delve. A carpenter knows a hammer, a lumberjack knows an axe, a tailor knows scissors. They might not sound like a weapon, but they're just two specialized blades. Two short swords are apparently enough for at least a couple skills to translate, or maybe that one guy is just weird.

Either way, watching the more casual delvers is probably even more fun than the pros. The experienced delvers are confident and look a lot cooler, but the casuals just have so much more to learn, and it's fun seeing them do it. That group didn't leave enough room in their packs, so now they can't carry what they want; this group over here has no idea if they can handle the gauntlet, but trying sounds fun. This other group might be getting sent out in defeat after getting lost in the tunnels and being low on healing supplies.

I wonder how many more professionals there would be if they were able to cut their teeth on a dungeon like me? I don't know if *all* of the pros have lost people in their parties, but I'd bet they all had at least an acquaintance who didn't make it out of a different dungeon. That actually makes it easy to spot the new arrivals.

With spring solidly in control, the roads are open, and delvers seem to be flocking to me and to Fourdock. The ones freshly here all move carefully, suspiciously, even around the manor. Oddly, they seem to get even more on edge when the denizens avoid them. Maybe in other dungeons, the meaner things tend to keep the easier denizens away. I guess it'd make sense. Sure, I still get mana from them killing the weaker denizens, but if I wanted to maximize the mana the delvers give me, their time would be better spent fighting the big things rather than the small fry.

I keep them away because there's no shortage of lower-level delvers to challenge the easy denizens instead. And it'll encourage the stronger adventurers to go to the stronger areas. Even with the forest only at . . . I dunno, forty percent? Even with it clearly unfinished, delvers are already crawling all over it. The armory bees are a hit, with the delvers almost always taking their weapons and looking joyous whenever they get some of the honey.

From what Honey and Queen have been able to tell, it's a lot safer to handle than the metal elixir, and I've seen a few adventurers use it to patch up armor and sometimes weapons. Just smear a bit of mud or clay on it, apply some armory honey, and you have an instant patch! I doubt it's as good as a professional job, but certainly better than just leaving damaged gear as it is.

As far as defeating the stronger delvers, the most dangerous combo in the forest right now seems to actually be mischief foxes and dreamblooms. My delvers definitely are having trouble discerning illusions from reality, and when that kind of deception is combined with loot from the packrats and ravens, a lot of delvers are learning the hard way that, if it looks like free loot, it probably isn't.

Which the mischiefs take advantage of, actually leaving a few piles of free loot in areas suspiciously free of denizens. The mind games are great, and I'm definitely going to need to spend some to put a few chests around the forest. Sure, their locations will eventually be mapped out, but the delvers will never know which is free for the taking and which is a clever trap to knock them out and defeat them.

I giggle to myself as I watch a group eye a pile of jewelry lying in the middle of a little glade packed full of dreamblooms. There's no illusion here, just a simple pile of bait and the implied question: Do you dare?

They bicker at the edge of the field of flowers, the three elves arguing about if any of it is real, if they should take an antidote and just charge out there, send just one, splitting up is bad and you are stupid—no, *you're* stupid, your *face* is stupid, and so on. Before they make a decision, I feel Aranya trying to get my attention, so I shift my focus over to her.

While all three enclaves have their own places to . . . worship me, I guess, the Ratkin Enclave is working on a larger place. A cathedral, compared to the shrines of the others. I'd try to discourage them, but more and more people are showing up to get service, and I don't just mean attend a sermon . . . though there's more who show up for that than I would have expected, too. Healing is very popular, and it looks like a couple of my clerics even offer rental services as support to parties who need it out in my territory.

But that's not what Aranya is trying to get my attention for. Instead, she has another kobold next to her, her scales seafoam green compared to Aranya's red, and she has an elf and a changeling standing nearby, looking nervous and hopeful as they wait. But her companions and even her scales can't keep my attention away from the bow she has. It looks a lot like the ones my delvers make, but looking closer, it has a *much* stronger draw than any of them, and the pulleys aren't quite optimized to leverage the mechanical advantage. Still, I wouldn't want to get shot by someone who can manage to draw it.

"Ah, Lord Thedeim is watching. Would you please repeat your request?" Aranya says with a smile, though the three gathered look even more nervous, especially the lady kobold. Seeing as she's almost certainly from the Maw, I can't blame her. Still, she steels her resolve and speaks.

"O-Oh Great Lord Thedeim," she begins, only to be interrupted by Aranya with an understanding smile.

"You can just call Him Thedeim if you wish. He tries to get me to do it all the time, in fact. Just be honest with Him, and I'm sure He'll do what He can to help."

The pale-green kobold nervously nods and starts again. "Th-Thedeim . . . ?" she starts, pausing to see if she gets smote. As she continues to be perfectly fine, she slowly continues. "I . . . I'm a hauler, but I don't want to be. I . . . The Maw, it . . ." she stutters, trying to find the words. Aranya pats her shoulders, encouraging the woman. After a few seconds, she gathers herself and continues. "I want to advance my class, but as far as I know, there *isn't* an advancement for a hauler. Can . . . Can you help me?"

I consider her for a few moments before carefully touching her status. While I think I can take a peek without people noticing, it still feels a bit invasive to do so, but if she wants my help, I think I need to get a closer look at what I'd be working with. I don't know if I can do anything, but I'm certainly willing to try.

Her eyes widen when she feels me, and I can feel her flinch away for a moment before she deliberately and slowly leans into my request.

Looking over her status, the first thing I notice is she has a *ton* of strength, and that doesn't even count her abilities to enhance her lifting and hauling ability. She also has a ton of endurance, which isn't a surprise either. What *is* a surprise is that I can feel two potential ways to nudge her.

One is a concept I can feel is a pretty solid one that exists here already. It's a type of heavy archer that feels like it usually comes from being a siege archer or similar who would stay mostly in towers or atop walls and guard whatever's inside. The closest translation for what comes after would be a sniper, which often advances further into a variety of assassin. I don't think she'd want to go that far, but slow rate of fire, heavy hits, and some camouflage ability would probably be a great thing if she wants to be an adventurer of some variety.

The other one feels a lot more ephemeral, but I think I know what to solidify it into. Teamsters always make me think of the mafia, but they're not about breaking kneecaps and making offers people can't refuse. They're all about getting things from point A to point B. If you want it moved, a teamster should know how to move it. And though there are merchants and other people, I'm sure, who move things around, I can feel a difference that I can't quite describe. Maybe if I knew more about the logistics of moving things, I would, but all I really need to know is there *is* a difference.

I pull back from the kobold's status and see she looks shaken, though Aranya helps steady her. "Easy there, Marle. His touch can be intense, but not harmful." I feel a bit bad as she nods, tears in her eyes. I hope she's just trying to deal with emotions rather than pain from anything I did.

"I can feel He has found two paths for you as well."

Marle turns hope-filled eyes on my High Priestess as she talks. "The first is a siege archer, a ranged combat class specializing in distance and devastating ranged attacks." Marle looks uncertain at that, so Aranya continues. "The other is an advancement for the hauler class. No one would dare *demand* you move something. Rather, they would ask or even beg, knowing you can get it where they need it quickly and safely. Those are the paths before you."

Marle looks back at her friends, looking for guidance. Without peeking at their status, it's still pretty easy to identify them as some kind of woodworkers. "It's . . . up to you, Marle. You could be a real adventurer, if you want," encourages the elf, though it's pretty clear he'd be sad to see her go. A siege archer is a pretty advanced adventuring class, and she'd probably want to take on delves a lot tougher than they could handle.

She closes her eyes and takes a shuddering breath before opening them. "I want to advance my current class. I don't *hate* hauling . . . I just hated being *stuck*."

Aranya smiles and draws on her mana, and I give her a drop of my power to help this along. I hope I won't be stepping on Order's toes with this, but Marle really does need some help.

I watch her status, seeing that the archer path is already gone. It probably vanished as soon as she made her decision; it makes me wonder if this is how Order actually decides what class to give people in the first place. I back out as I feel the change start to work, not wanting to intrude on her privacy more than I already have.

From the outside, it feels incredibly anticlimactic. Just a slow wave of orange sweeping across her, and it's done. Aranya catches her as she falls, her legs giving out as she comes to terms with the fact that things really *have* changed for her.

"I'm a teamster . . ." she mutters, repeating herself as if she can't believe it. My High Priestess motions Marle's friends forward, letting them support the stunned kobold.

"Get her to a seat over there and just give her some time. She'll need friends to help her on her new path." The two nod with determination and focus on Marle, gently guiding her to a seat as I get a pop-up.

Class Change. Interesting. I Should Have Known.

Order doesn't elaborate with the message, but I get the feeling he's more shaking his head and chuckling than frowning and grumbling. I feel like, instead of stepping on his toes, I've accidentally solved an issue he's been having. Either way, I don't get any other pop-ups, and Aranya seems to have the situation under control here, so I let my attention wander back to the group at the dreambloom field.

Looks like they decided the field was an illusion, and they're all taking a nice nap right now. I nudge Goldilocks to get a few denizens to deliver them to the gates, and resume watching the delvers do their thing, feeling nicely satisfied at how things are going. There'll be something on the horizon to try to shake things up some more eventually, but for now, I'm happy to watch the delvers work to improve themselves, seeking challenge and the rewards that come with it.

Chapter 69

It looks like Coda's planning session with Rezlar went really well. As the surveying efforts under the forest wind down, Coda is more than happy to snatch up the denizens and point them at surveying and preparing the path for the road, as well as getting a better look inside the mountain Rezlar wants to build in. From what I can tell from the initial reports, the mountain itself seems pretty boring, as far as mountains go.

There's enough soil for trees and bushes and stuff to grow in, but it's not especially deep. The top third or so is pretty barren, though I can't tell if it's because of the thick snowcap or if the winds at that kind of altitude keep anything from finding purchase to grow. Either way, nature is pretty stable without anything really exceptional. Deeper into the mountain, it also seems pretty lackluster.

With it so close to what used to be a major trading hub before the disaster with Hullbreak, the mountain has already been pretty thoroughly prospected for ores and the like. Rezlar says the thing is basically just a solid chunk of granite, and so far, the expeditions are saying the same thing. There's the usual cracks and such, but the cave systems are pretty cramped and damp. I don't think there's much risk of anything nasty hiding in there. Collapses while digging out the hold are a potential problem, but that's what these deep surveys are for.

To me, it looks like trying to build something in a pile of gravel, but Coda and Rezlar don't seem too worried. Mountains are usually a lot less solid than people expect, and there are ways to help support everything even without using Earth-affinity people to help fuse things back into whatever shape is needed for stability. A lot like mountains, big construction projects need to be a lot less solid than most people think, too.

Where a mechanical engineer can either overengineer something to basically never break or just decide to *let* something break if the user is determined to use it so wrong, a civil project deals in forces that can't really be stopped. If that earthquake decides to move these two pieces of land a centimeter apart, good luck trying to stop it.

There's a shocking amount of flex built into even simple civil projects, with the seams between blocks helping provide the buffer to let things move just a little without compromising the whole structure. It still feels like a house of cards to me, but with how the masons are drooling over the preliminary designs, I'm going to trust Coda on this one.

Roads are a different matter, and I'm not even going to try to pretend I understand how to keep them from turning into gravel over the course of a year. The slower speed of wagons and horses probably helps, but with the temperature difference over the year, it's probably still going to need a lot of maintenance. I wish I knew what asphalt was made of so I could try to explain it, but I honestly have no idea. I think tar is a major component, maybe?

It's probably less of a bother here, though. On Earth, fixing a road takes a crew and a bunch of huge machinery. Here, an Earth-affinity person just needs to check every so often and patch things up. There's still going to be a big crew involved with this road; people grinding, mixing, moving, pouring, smoothing, and that's just the concrete itself. It doesn't count the people clearing the way, smoothing the terrain, putting gravel or something beneath for drainage, and whatever other little details I'm forgetting that all contribute to a true and proper road.

And with Coda's lead, my denizens contribute as well. It's interesting to watch through his eyes as he works with Rezlar and his civil planners. The more martial of Fourdock's people might be spending a lot of their time with me, but a lot of the civilian populace is involved in this project. Between the road and the reinvigorated docks, Rezlar is really stepping up and showing he has the know-how to not only keep Fourdock running but to see it grow, too.

I even catch glimpses of Rhonda and Freddie as they help out in their own ways. Rhonda's herbalism expertise helps the people clearing the way know the difference between things to either use as fuel or mulch, and things that alchemists and other crafters will be interested in. I might have the lion's share of cool plants in the area, but why waste what they find?

Freddie is helping with processing the concrete; not only with physically helping crush and mix but also to help encourage people and not let them get too tired. I don't know if he can do proper healing with laying his hands, but he sure seems like he can help alleviate fatigue. He's also not a terrible singer, and a few catchy hymns make the work feel a lot less like drudgery than it could.

While they work on the road, I feel a familiar set of feet cross the threshold to the manor grounds, and I'm glad to see not only Olander but Tula as well! The crown inspector is wearing his more subdued gear, the stuff he was wearing when still undercover, which makes me suspect this is more of a casual visit than an official one. Still, Teemo makes his way to meet them at the porch.

"Hey, you two! The Boss and I were starting to wonder if you didn't like us anymore!"

Olander laughs at that, shaking his head. "After everything I had to put in the report, I'd be right to! But now that it's finally done, and Tula and I have a chance to relax a bit, I thought it'd be a good idea to come chat. The king has a response."

Teemo quirks an eyebrow at that. "Is it one we should go somewhere more private to talk about?"

The tall elf shakes his head. "Nothing to be worried about. With Fourdock firmly on the rise, his majesty wants to ensure nothing will hinder that, so he's going to be moving some of the regional garrison to be stationed here. I need to tell Rezlar, too, but for you, it should mean that quite a few of the kingdom's finest will be wanting to delve you."

"The Boss isn't going to cry about new delvers, so long as they play nice. They don't get to claim any area just for themselves. Even the Shield's people in the crypts know they can't discourage other people from exploring in there," my Voice points out, which Olander nods along with.

"That shouldn't be a problem, especially with the vast area of your forest. An individual soldier would be no match for what you're working on in there, but squads should be able to find victory through their training and teamwork. I don't expect there'll be enough of them to even attempt to muscle out the ordinary delvers, and I'd hope there are none foolish enough to consider it. Even without the usual power differential between experienced delvers and normal soldiers, they'd run the risk of upsetting a *dungeon*."

Teemo snorts at that. "Well, we can hope. And if there's a few who don't get the memo, the denizens will be happy to relieve them of their stuff and dump them at the gate. I'd imagine their superiors would be pretty unhappy with them for losing kingdom property."

Olander laughs at that and nods. "Indeed! I'll probably be here for a while longer, too, so if you have any troubles, don't think twice about asking me about anything. His Highness seemed to be looking forward to a good working relationship between you and the kingdom."

Before Teemo can reply, Tula elbows Olander and gives him a significant look. "Ah, I almost forgot." He glances around before leaning forward and lowering his voice. "Rezlar will probably know more than I do, but the Earl if'Gofnar is expected to try to pull Fourdock tighter into his grasp. It's part of his territory under the crown, but one he's been happy to let be quiet for some time now. With its burgeoning prosperity, he's probably going to want to take a more direct hand in its administration at some point."

Teemo frowns at that for me. "Is he Rezlar's uncle?"

Tula shakes her head and answers for Olander. "His father."

Teemo's frown deepens as I chew on that. It's not difficult to guess that Rezlar's distaste for nobility and politics comes from his upbringing, which would certainly involve his father. Even if he was an absentee, an earl doesn't let his son get bullied without knowing. "I'll see what Rezlar wants to do about that, then."

Olander gives a toothy smile. "Do let him know I'll help as I can. With me being here officially, I'm limited in what I can do, but I'll still contribute. The Earl if'Gofnar is . . . not the most favored by the crown, even with his skill at deflecting potential scandals."

My Voice gives him an appreciative smile. "The Boss and I appreciate that, and I'm sure Rezlar will, too. Thedeim's working on figuring out how to politic, so he'll probably need all the help he can get, especially if this guy is as skilled as you're implying."

Olander nods at that and straightens up. "Still, we're not here just to deliver news."

"Yeah?"

"Yeah!" answers Tula, looking excited. "I heard your antkin are officially dwellers now! I want to see if they'll teach me how the anti-Lifedrinking enchantment works!"

Teemo chuckles at her enthusiasm. "I think they'll make you join their college if you want a trade secret like that. Still, no harm in asking."

Olander nods. "That's what I told her, but it's still an interesting enclave to visit. I hear they're hunting in the volcanic region deep below? I want to see if they'd be willing to pay for a few recipes I know for cooking volcanic creatures. The Holds have a volcanic dungeon that's quite the maze, so I've picked up a few recipes that might be useful to the antkin. Good food is a good way to stay motivated on a long delve, you know."

"Oh yeah? Well, if you know anything especially good, maybe you'll be able to trade it for some magic theory lessons. You two want a shortcut, or to head down on your own?"

Olander looks to Tula, who shrugs in return. "Well, since Tula doesn't seem to have an opinion, I'd like to make our own way down. After all the time writing that report, I'm looking forward to stretching my legs and knocking the rust off my glaive."

"Then you two have fun! If you're feeling rusty, you'll probably have just enough time to get back up to speed before the Boss triggers the tree expansion. It's looking like a week, maybe two, to build up enough mana to expand and upgrade more spawners."

Olander's eyes sparkle at that. "I'm looking forward to it! With an expansion like that, he'll have the eyes of the whole kingdom on him!"

"Yeah, but he's going to do it anyway," jokes Teemo. "That's why he's dipping his toes into politics now, before he jumps in the deep end with the expansion."

"Then I wish him luck! Now, if you'll excuse us, I think Tula and I should grab a quest before we get going."

"Yep, don't let me keep you two. Have fun!" He waves before slipping down a shortcut to go chat with some of the antkin about the composite armor. As for me, I keep an eye on Olander and Tula, trying to keep from being too intrusive. I wouldn't want to spoil their date.

Chapter 70

Olander and Tula have a nice little delve together; I mostly let them do it without me constantly hovering. Tarl can sense when I'm focused on him, so I don't doubt Olander can, too. They visit the antkin, where Tula talks nerd with the enchanter caste, while Olander gets to see the progress being made on the composite armor. He's deeply interested in it, of course, but even offering his advice doesn't keep him distracted from Tula for too long.

In the end, he trades a few recipes to get Tula a slate with the theory behind the enchantment, though it's general enough that I don't think she could reproduce it on her own. Honestly, I think the theory might be over her head, but with how happy she is to get it, she's probably looking forward to learning enough to understand it.

Once they head home, I ask Teemo to pen an invitation to Rezlar to talk tomorrow. Ordinarily, he'd just pop over and ask directly, but it's fun sometimes to break out the fancy parchment and deliver a letter via raven. Poe gives the birb directions to wait for a reply, which comes around sunset.

Teemo and I look over the letter together. "Looks like he'll be here late in the morning, and he wants to bring Freddie, Rhonda, and the spiders. Looks like the reveal went off without a hitch." My Voice smiles at the letter, and I agree.

Good for them. They're all good friends, and with how important Freddie is to the Shield, and how Rhonda's class is making waves, I don't think even his dad can raise a stink about any perceived difference in social class. Or maybe he can. I've never dealt with nobles—Rezlar doesn't count—but they can apparently be absolutely obsessed with status.

"You think the earl is like that?"

Hmm . . . I don't have a lot to go on just yet, but I get the feeling he doesn't really see anyone *as being on his level. Noble scion or orphan, all he cares about is what they can do for him.*

Teemo considers that before shrugging. "From what little bits we know of Rezlar's upbringing and how the crown apparently doesn't really like him, he's probably power hungry and smart about it, yeah. Tensions about blood can be real easy to play on for some people."

Yerp. Can you ask Leo, Poe, and Zorro to get me a better map of the roads nearby? I don't exactly expect the earl to try to siege the town, but if I wanted to be sneaky about messing with things, I'd do it out on the roads, not within sight of Fourdock.

Teemo nods at that. "I'll see if Hullbreak can do the same with the sea. I'm sure he's keeping an eye on things out there, but probably more for invaders than delver issues. I'll also check if Violet's heard anything. The earl probably hasn't done much, if anything, yet, but there's no harm in checking."

Sounds good. I want to be at least a little prepared for the meeting with Rezlar tomorrow. In fact, invite at least Onyx to come attend. We might be able to figure out something to let First Mate come, too. Violet has an outlet to the sea, and with a bit of your Spatial fun, Hullbreak's Voice should fit just about anywhere. We might need to flood a couple passages . . . Ask Coda if it's viable, yeah?

Teemo laughs and gives me a mocking salute. "You're the boss, Boss. With the First Mate's Water affinity, it'll probably be a lot less messy, at least. We'll see if we can improvise something."

The night is pretty busy with prep, but it looks like we'll be able to let First Mate attend, too. We have to dig out a pretty large pool underneath the public war room, but that plus a hatch means Hullbreak can finally participate in affairs on land. He still seems a bit reluctant to do so, but he's not required to say anything. I mostly just want to include him and not let him be a sea hermit.

Violet and Onyx, on the other hand, are incredibly excited, even if my protégée can't really understand everything that's going on. That's what a good Voice is for. The room is all set, and it looks like my enclaves intend to have a presence for this meeting, too. Aranya doesn't even pretend that she didn't tell them, and honestly, I can't be mad. Someone potentially making a power play on Fourdock will definitely impact them, so my enclaves *should* have a say in what's happening.

Thankfully, not every single leader for the enclaves is here. Just Larx, Folarn, and Ed. The antkin headmaster looks a bit out of his league, but Larx and Folarn encourage him by telling him that they felt the same way for their first diplomatic meeting, too.

Right around the time I think fancier people would be having brunch, Rezlar steps into my territory with his usual entourage, with the addition of Freddie, Rhonda, Fiona, and Lucas. He and Miller bid his guards to delve while they go to the meeting, and Teemo personally escorts them all to the public war room so we can get this party started.

"Alright, quick introductions to make sure everyone's on the same page. We have Rezlar, Miller, Freddie, Rhonda, Lucas, Fiona, Ed, Larx, Folarn, Aranya,

Onyx, and The First Mate. If you don't know I'm Teemo, you might want to talk to a healer," he jokes as everyone gets settled, taking his own spot at the table before continuing. "I think it's on you to start us off, Rezlar. All we know so far is that an earl is coming, and that he's probably not going to be as cooperative as most of our other visitors."

Rezlar chuckles ruefully at that, nodding. "That's an understatement. Earl Paulte Heindarl Bulifinor Magnamtir if'Gofnar wants to become a duke, maybe even marry his way into the line of succession somewhere, so he's been working on a lot of plans. I don't know them specifically, but he'll practically be forced to monopolize Your output if he wants to keep those dreams alive."

All gathered frown as he explains. "He's been slowly monopolizing certain herbal imports from the orcish nomads, and positioning himself to be a prime investor in an upstart mythril mine in the Dwarven Holds. Between Your herbalism and mining nodes, you could topple his plans without even meaning to. He's going to come here and try to flex his power as earl to levy significant taxes and probably found or sponsor his own gathering and mining parties to get as much as he can, trying to muscle out any competition along the way."

"I think he's going to have a rude awakening," snorts Onyx. Rezlar smirks at that.

"Probably, but he's also used to getting his way. He's probably monopolized more than a few dungeons, so he knows what he's doing. Unfortunately for him, Lord Thedeim isn't like other dungeons."

"How do we discourage him?" asks Folarn, looking thoughtful. "Your kingdom probably wouldn't appreciate it if we just remove him, so what do we do?"

Rezlar nods. "Attacking him directly would be a bad idea, at least at the start. Doing something like that unprovoked would force the crown to lean on the Dungeoneer's Guild to classify Lord Thedeim as belligerent, possibly even murderous. You'll probably be forced to be reactive instead of proactive when dealing with him."

"What about you?" asks Ed. "You are his underling. Won't you be forced to do as he says?"

Rezlar sighs, though he perks up from the encouraging looks from his friends. "I'll have to play politics with him for as long as I can. Even if we were at the same status, I don't think I could *stop* him, but I should be able to delay and hinder him by citing chain of command and throwing every last regulation I can in his way. Ordinarily, an earl would just plow through that kind of tactic, but with Olander here, he'll have to play by the rules or risk the attention of the crown."

"Why isn't he *here*, then?" asks Aranya, noting the inspector's distinct absence.

"Politics again," answers Larx, who lets Rezlar explain.

"He has the right of it. If he were here, my father would learn about it and could claim bias or even a conspiracy to harm him from the crown itself. Olander staying away from any meetings gives him deniability and makes it a lot harder for the earl to raise any sort of fuss."

"When's he supposed to get here?" asks Teemo.

"In about a week and a half."

Teemo smiles at that news. "Sounds like good timing to maybe put him on the back foot."

Rezlar looks interested at that. "Oh?"

"Yeah. That's just about when the Boss expects to be able to grow the tree. I don't care how confident your dad is, he's going to second-guess his plans at that kind of show of power, especially if the townsfolk don't seem all that worried or surprised about it."

Rezlar chews that over as Onyx speaks up. "Does he have the mana for it?"

"He should. He technically could do it now, but he'll need a lot more to be able to place and upgrade the spawners for it, too."

"I think the Admiral might be underestimating how much those spawners will cost," speaks up the First Mate, with Onyx looking worried. Teemo doesn't look too concerned, though.

"He's been pretty good with his pricing so far," he points out, but the First Mate is insistent.

"He's used to dealing with flat areas. That kind of volume is going to cost a *lot* to populate, even for the Admiral. Trust me, watching the Captain fill even the shallow harbor with enough denizens to make it not feel lifeless was a great teacher for how much it'll take. Even if he could blanket the current forest with enough denizens for the delvers to walk across, it'll still feel sparse once the tree is up and they all spread out."

I frown at that as I go over my numbers, starting to worry she knows what she's talking about. Even in a place like the labyrinth or the tunnels, places with a lot of verticality, I can still work with simple square footage and plan the density from there. With the forest, it feels about right for density right now, and I had been planning to roughly double the spawns once the tree goes up. But . . . the more I look at it, the more I think I'm vastly underestimating how much mana I'll need to fill the place in, or to even make it not feel like a ghost town.

"But he has an easy solution to get things started," comments the First Mate, looking satisfied now that I'm getting a better understanding for just how much the upward expansion is going to increase the delvable area.

"What's that?" asks Teemo for me, because I don't see much. Maybe run some more expedition matches? A rematch between Olander and Rocky would certainly bring in the delvers, but it hasn't been long enough for much to change the expected outcome.

"The ally pool," points out Onyx. "This sounds like a different kind of emergency than usual, but putting this earl on the defensive sounds pretty important."

"Let's not get too hasty," interjects Teemo. "We can still do the tree and add what we can with what the Boss has available at the time. It doesn't need to be running full tilt immediately."

"You've gotta raise your flag proud and high, Admiral. He'll soon see an empty display for what it is. If you want to make him think twice, he needs to think you can drop a proper expansion like that whenever you want."

Miller nods and speaks up. "She's quite right. Were he only a passing threat, he might be cowed and move on, but the earl cannot let Fourdock go. Any displays will need to be genuine, not a farce."

Teemo sighs for me. "Alright, fine. Do you think getting the tree up and properly populated would force him to rethink his plans for the Boss, Rezlar?"

The elf nods. "I do. He's not the most experienced delver, but he should know what dungeons are usually capable of. With Your age and an expansion like that, he'll be forced to change his plans, and hopefully give me more time to delay."

"Alright, then we'll dip into the ally fund to pay for the spawners. If he *does* bring along delvers to try to implement his plan, they'll just be more mana to be able to pay it off. Do you need any help with the political side of things, Rezlar?"

He starts to shake his head, but then pauses and looks at the enclave leaders. "Actually . . . can I impose on the enclaves? Relations with enclaves are notoriously tenuous yet lucrative. If you string him along while still being rather direct with me, it will give me a lot more leverage to remain in power, especially if you can delay him."

Larx smiles at that. "I think we can manage that. Especially the antkin. Feign some bureaucratic bloat and force his people to spend more time walking around than talking, and I think you could cost him a lot of time."

Ed's mandibles twitch in a smile at that idea. "I'll talk it over with the deans, but I think they'll be happy to give them plenty of exercise."

Folarn nods. "The spiderkin can do similar, though we don't have as many leaders for them to juggle."

"Then I think we have a plan," declares Teemo, to the nods of everyone. "Now we just have to hope he gets the hint and leaves on his own, instead of forcing us to make him."

Rezlar nods, looking optimistic. "He won't back down easily, and if he does, he'll hold a grudge for the rest of his life, but I think we can weather that storm. With any luck, I'll be able to convince him that leaving Fourdock to prosper in its own way will only help his ambitions. There are worse ways to angle for a dukedom than to have someplace like Fourdock to point at as one of his example townships."

Freddie and Rhonda look a little sour at the idea of the earl getting to take any credit for Fourdock, but the older people in the room nod in understanding. Sometimes, the best way to make someone take the L is to let them think they have a W.

Chapter 71

Earl Paulte Heindarl Bulifinor Magnamtir if'Gofnar

What had at first seemed like it was going to practically be a vacation is quickly spiraling into a challenge. He hasn't even laid eyes on Fourdock in decades, and yet news of the town has him sailing in an emotional hurricane, his vessel riding waves high, only to sink low and threaten to capsize, often in the course of a single update!

While he had been keeping half an ear to the doings of Fourdock, he admits to only himself that he could have paid more attention. He sent little Rezlar there precisely *because* it's such a quiet, unimportant, out of the-way place. The lad simply doesn't have the stomach nor will for proper politics, despite his head for numbers. Sending him to a place like this, practically an exile, would be seen as a punishment by many, but Rezlar was more than happy to get away from the games of the nobility.

How was he supposed to know something like this dungeon Thedeim would hit the town? Some people insist the town is cursed when it comes to dungeons, and sometimes, the earl wonders. A strong belligerent shuts down the harbor, and a true murderous dungeon springs up in the cemetery. He sometimes wonders if the disaster in the harbor was done deliberately by a rival, but they would have had to be exceptionally subtle and patient if that was the case. None of his other trade ventures ever had a setback like that, and he would say they were *far* more fragile than the shipping through Fourdock.

All that is to say Fourdock has a tradition of dungeons that make a greater impact than average. When his sources told him the murderous dungeon had been subsumed, it barely qualified as trivia in his mind. A young dungeon had gotten lucky; perhaps the town would become even more quiet and boring.

Then the harbor was vassalized and reopened. Even more, the young dungeon protected the town. Others might be glad to see an altruistic dungeon, especially for Fourdock, but Paulte is no fool. He's hardly an expert, but a young upstart does *not* overcome an established power without someone pulling the strings. He refuses to believe a dungeon could get that lucky twice in such quick succession.

Combined with how its choices of nodes perfectly undermine his own efforts in herbalism and mining, he doesn't like how these winds are blowing. Could someone have figured out a way to groom the dungeon to do exactly what they want, grow the nodes and the town exactly in a way to undermine him? It seems outrageous, but there are simply too many coincidences for him to accept. Even the dungeon supposedly having Fate affinity feels just a little too convenient to him.

Someone is trying to cripple his ascension to duke, but who? While his fellow earls would of course love to slash his sails, he doubts any of them have the resources for something like this. He questions if even the *crown* would have the resources for something like this! Or, to be more precise, the crown would likely attack his more tenuous deals and topple them without needing to invest the kind of energy it would take to set up something like this dungeon Thedeim.

The only group he can think of who even *might* try something like this would be the Dungeoneers, but they don't stand to gain much by snubbing him. Perhaps he personally insulted someone high up in the organization? While not impossible, he has very few dealings with them. He can't recall anything that would have given them cause to personally attack his interests.

And even if they *were* attacking his interests, they're doing a poor job of it. He might not have any shell companies to claim ownership of the goods extracted from that dungeon, but Fourdock is prospering because of it, and in turn, so is he. It doesn't hold a candle to his Port Gofnar right now, but the glory days of Fourdock were lucrative indeed. And if he wants to get even more money, he needs to get his fingers into the pie that is Thedeim.

Sponsoring an adventurers' guild is a common thing for the nobility to do. Dungeons can be *very* lucrative, and some adventurers are more mercenary than actual mercenaries! Give them a bit of coin and point them at a dungeon, and they'll bring you back ten percent, and thank you for the privilege! And though it may be a bit uncouth to muscle in on the territory of an established guild, competition is a vital part of adventuring. If a few rival parties vanish inside the dungeon, that's just the cost of delving, sometimes.

He doesn't doubt a tactic like that will work with Thedeim, either. The ridiculous claim that nobody has died inside is such blatant propaganda that he doesn't know how they get away with spreading it. It just means those who die get quietly vanished, which suits his goals just fine. That party clearly didn't die; they just left for greener pastures in some other dungeon. He wonders how many times he'll have to give that excuse before the local guild gets the hint and agrees to merge.

He idly looks out the window to his carriage, spotting a few of the adventurers playing guardsmen for him as he travels. The Calm Seas Guild has a good ring to it, and though Jondar Helmsplitter is the official guild leader, that didn't stop the stout elf from letting Earl Paulte pay for the charter. Still, it keeps the power balance between them clear: the earl is in charge. Jondar is shrewd enough to understand who he gets his gold from; otherwise, Paulte wouldn't have chosen him for this.

It will take some time to overtake the dungeon, but Paulte doesn't see that being much of an issue. Miners and herbalists don't care who they sell to, though the smiths and alchemists who gather their own materials will certainly complain about having to sell instead of using what they've gathered. Such heavy-handed regulation would usually be frowned upon by the local mayor, but little Rezlar won't dare to resist him.

Just a few words, maybe a disappointed glance or two, and he'll cave, letting his father do what's best. He probably won't even put up a fight if he uses the lad as a target for the displeasure of the commoners. The lad's butler is skilled enough to keep him out of any harm.

He frowns at that thought. He still doesn't know how his late wife managed to secure a contract with someone like Miller. Even with all his contacts, he can't find anything concrete indicating he's anything more than a simple butler. But he's not foolish enough to believe that for a moment. Even his own head maid refuses to meddle in his affairs, which is all the confirmation he needs. He doesn't need to know Miller's exact skill to know he doesn't wish to upset the elf. Could *he* be the one behind the dungeon's actions?

He could easily have the motivation. There is no love lost between the two of them, but would he dare to do something like this? The more he thinks, the more he suspects. If Miller somehow has the ear of the dungeon, he could prop up Rezlar while also thwarting the earl's own plans. Ridiculous as it sounds . . . if there's anyone who *could* accomplish something like that, it'd be someone like Miller.

That will be a difficult obstacle to overcome. Removing someone as strong as he suspects Miller is . . . will cost more than money. The assassin's guild will demand a favor if they even accept at all. He suppresses a shudder at the idea. Working with assassins is simple enough, but he's abused the promise of a favor enough to not want to give anyone that kind of power over him.

Still, it's hardly more than a guess on his part that Miller is behind the dungeon somehow. He can wait to get more information before deciding how to act.

He looks out of his carriage once more, enjoying the view as he relaxes. Fourdock has plenty of room to expand into, both along and away from the coast. He idly imagines a sprawling city until Fourdock finally comes into view.

He should commission a painting of this vista as a memento of Fourdock before it flourishes.

Such idle thoughts are brought to a halt along with his carriage, the sudden stop earning a frown before he speaks up. "Why have we stopped?" he demands before he feels it. He doesn't have the raw power of an adventurer of his level, but he can still sense the ebb and flow of mana. And right now, there is a swirling whirlpool over Fourdock!

He leans out of his carriage as he peers at the immense energy, his guards looking nervous. He can't fathom what's happening, wondering if the town is somehow under attack, before he finally understands why it feels familiar.

When a dungeon expands its borders, mana is used to transform the area into whatever it is that lets dungeons exist. He's seen a few expansions before . . . but nothing like this. Even at this distance, he feels he should be holding his hat so it doesn't fly off, even though an expansion rarely has that sort of physical effect. Expansions are usually rather subtle in their changes.

Usually.

This one, it seems, is not going to be so. Beyond Fourdock, he can see a tree sprouting from the forest, the mana forcing it to grow far beyond what is natural or even *possible!* And yet it grows—thick twisting branches, long hanging leaves, and a distant rumble as roots force their way through the ground. He has the composure to keep his mouth shut, though many of his guards do not, as the tree grows and grows until finally stopping at close to a mile in height!

His mind races to explain what he just saw before a thump from atop his carriage draws his attention. A raven is sitting there—not exactly an auspicious omen—and sets down a small scroll. It caws at him before taking off, leaving the scroll behind. He takes it, forcing his hand to be steady, and examines it for any magic or potential traps.

"Resume moving," he orders before he sits down, pondering the message. He could throw it out, but that would probably be a very bad idea. He's pretty sure it's not from *The* Raven, but it's still a big risk to ignore something delivered by the deity's lesser kin. The scroll has a small seal of orange wax on it, depicting a circle with intricate swirls, which makes him even more suspicious of who the owner could be. He's never seen that seal before. What rabble is trying to claim to have a *seal* to make themselves feel more important?

Well, there's a simple way to find out.

A small dagger breaks the seal, and he reads the message. Though short and friendly, it makes his blood run cold. There is much more going on than he could have suspected.

Welcome to Fourdock.
—Thedeim

About the Author

Khenal is the author of the Dungeon Life series. Born and raised in a small town in Northern California, he studied mechanical engineering but graduated from college in the middle of the Great Recession. Unable to find an engineering job, Khenal turned to content creation, streaming videos on Twitch and posting stories to Reddit and Royal Road.

